classics

# *Rudyard Kipling*

## 2 Books in 1

# The Second Jungle Book

# &

# Selected Short Stories

A Wilco Book

Outstanding works of universal interest

This Omnibus edition printed in 2007

ISBN NO.: 81-8252-298-6

# Rudyard Kipling

## The Second Jungle Book & Selected Short Stories

Complete and Unabridged

*Published by*
Wilco
PUBLISHING HOUSE
ITTS House, 33, Sri Saibaba Marg,
Kalaghoda, Mumbai – 400 023. INDIA
Tel: (91-22) 22041420 / 22842574
Fax: (91-22) 22041429
E mail: wilcos@vsnl.com
Website: www.wilcobooks.com

About The Author

# RUDYARD KIPLING

(1865-1936)

Rudyard Kipling was born in India where his father was a teacher at Mumbai's J.J. School of Arts. In his early childhood young Kipling was exposed to the fascinating sounds and sights of India. This was to have a deep impression on his writings which he began when he was just 13.

His famous novels *Jungle Books* and *Captains Courageous* were written while he was in America. *The Jungle Book* became so popular that this sequel: *The Second Jungle Book* was published within a year (1895). Apart from these, Kipling's balladic poems are equally acclaimed; from among them, the 'Absentminded Beggar' brought-in huge sums of money to the author. The philanthropist Kipling however donated the entire proceeds to the benefit of British soldiers engaged in the Boer War.

Fate dealt a cruel blow to him when he lost his own son John, at the tender age of 18, in World War I. In 1907, Kipling became the first British author to get the Nobel Prize for literature. His autobiography *Something of Myself* was published posthumously.

About the Author

# RUDYARD KIPLING

(1865-1936)

Rudyard Kipling was born in India. His father was a teacher at Mumbai's J.J. School of Arts. In his early childhood young Kipling was exposed to the fascinating sounds and sights of India. This was to have a deep impression on his writings which he began when he was just 13.

His famous novels [illegible] and *Captains Courageous* were written while he was in America. *The Jungle Book* became so popular that its sequel *The Second Jungle Book* was published within a year (1895). Apart from these, Kipling's ballads and poems are equally acclaimed. Among them, the 'Absent-Minded Beggar' brought in huge sums of money to the author. The philanthropist Kipling, however, donated the entire proceeds to the benefit of British soldiers engaged in the Boer War.

Fate dealt a cruel blow to him when he lost his own son John, in the battle field of the First World War. In 1907, Kipling became the first British author to get the Nobel Prize for literature. His autobiography *Something of Myself* was published posthumously.

# THE SECOND JUNGLE BOOK

# CONTENTS

# HOW FEAR CAME

The stream is shrunk – the pool is dry,
And we be comrades, thou and I;
With fevered jowl and dusty flank
Each jostling each along the bank;
And by one drouthy fear made still,
Forgoing thought of quest or kill.
Now 'neath his dam the fawn may see,
The lean Pack-wolf as cowed as he,
And the tall buck, unflinching, note
The fangs that tore his father's throat.
*The pools are shrunk – the streams are dry,*
And we be playmates, thou and I,
*Till yonder cloud – Good Hunting! – loose*
*The rain that breaks our Water Truce.*

THE LAW of the Jungle – which is by far the oldest law in the world – has arranged for almost every kind of accident that may befall the Jungle People, till now its code is as perfect as time and custom can make it. You will remember that Mowgli spent a great part of his life in the Seeonee Wolf-Pack,* learning the Law from Baloo, the Brown Bear; and it was Baloo who told him, when the boy grew impatient at the constant orders, that the Law was like the Giant Creeper, because it dropped across every one's back and no one could escape. "When thou hast lived as long as I have, Little Brother, thou wilt see how all the Jungle obeys at least one Law. And that will be no pleasant sight," said Baloo.

This talk went in at one ear and out at the other, for a boy who spends his life eating and sleeping does not worry about anything till it actually stares him in the face. But, one year, Baloo's words came true, and Mowgli saw all the Jungle working under one Law.

* Refers to the Classic Library Best-Seller: Kipling's *The Jungle Book.*

It began when the winter Rains failed almost entirely, and Ikki, the Porcupine, meeting Mowgli in a bamboo-thicket, told him that the wild yams were drying up. Now everybody knows that Ikki is ridiculously fastidious in his choice of food, and will eat nothing but the very best and ripest. So Mowgli laughed and said, "What is that to me?"

"Not much *now*," said Ikki, rattling his quills in a stiff, uncomfortable way, "but later we shall see. Is there any more diving into the deep rock-pool below the Bee-Rocks, Little Brother?"

"No. The foolish water is going all away, and I do not wish to break my head," said Mowgli, who, in those days, was quite sure that he knew as much as any five of the Jungle People put together.

"That is thy loss. A small crack might let in some wisdom." Ikki ducked quickly to prevent Mowgli from pulling his nose-bristles, and Mowgli told Baloo what Ikki had said. Baloo looked very grave, and mumbled half to himself: "If I were alone I would change my hunting-grounds now, before the others began to think. And yet – hunting among strangers ends in fighting; and they might hurt the Man-cub. We must wait and see how the *mohwa* blooms."

That spring the *mohwa-tree*, that Baloo was so fond of, never flowered. The greeny, cream-coloured, waxy blossoms were heat-killed before they were born, and only a few bad-smelling petals came down when he stood on his hind legs and shook the tree. Then, inch-by-inch, the untempered heat crept into the heart of the Jungle, turning it yellow, brown, and at last black. The green growths in the sides of the ravines burned up to broken wires and curled films of dead stuff; the hidden pools sank down and caked over, keeping the last least footmark on their edges as if it had been cast in iron; the juicy-stemmed creepers fell away from the trees they clung to and died at their feet; the bamboos withered, clanking when the hot winds blew, and the moss peeled off the rocks deep in the Jungle, till they were as bare and as hot as the quivering blue boulders in the bed of the stream.

The birds and the monkey-people went north early in the year, for they knew what was coming; and the deer and the wild pig broke far away to the perished fields of the villages, dying sometimes before the eyes of men too weak to kill them. Chil, the Kite, stayed and grew fat, for there was a great deal of carrion, and evening after evening he brought the news to the beasts, too weak to force their way to fresh hunting-grounds, that the sun was killing the Jungle for three days' flight in every direction.

Mowgli, who had never known what real hunger meant, fell back on stale honey, three years old, scraped out of deserted rock-hives – honey black as a sloe, and dusty with dried sugar. He hunted, too, for deep-boring grubs under the bark of the trees, and robbed the wasps of their new broods. All the game in the jungle was no more than skin and bone, and Bagheera could kill thrice in a night, and hardly get a full meal. But the want of water was the worst, for though the Jungle People drink seldom they must drink deep.

And the heat went on and on, and sucked up all the moisture, till at last the main channel of the Waingunga was the only stream that carried a trickle of water between its dead banks; and when Hathi, the wild elephant, who lives for a hundred years and more, saw a long, lean blue ridge of rock show dry in the very centre of the stream, he knew that he was looking at the Peace Rock, and then and there he lifted up his trunk and proclaimed the Water Truce, as his father before him had proclaimed it fifty years ago. The deer, wild pig, and buffalo took up the cry hoarsely; and Chil, the Kite, flew in great circles far and wide, whistling and shrieking the warning.

By the Law of the Jungle it is death to kill at the drinking-places when once the Water Truce has been declared. The reason of this is that drinking comes before eating. Every one in the Jungle can scramble along somehow when only game is scarce; but water is water, and when there is but one source of supply, all hunting stops while the Jungle People go there for their needs. In good seasons, when water was plentiful, those who came down to drink at the Waingunga – or anywhere else, for that matter – did so at the risk of their lives, and that risk made no small part of the fascination of the night's doings. To move down so cunningly that never a leaf stirred; to wade knee-deep in the roaring shallows that drown all noise from behind; to drink, looking backward over one shoulder, every muscle ready for the first desperate bound of keen terror; to roll on the sandy margin, and return, wet-muzzled and well plumped out, to the admiring herd, was a thing that all tall-antlered young bucks took a delight in, precisely because they knew that at any moment Bagheera or Shere Khan might leap upon them and bear them down. But now all that life-and-death fun was ended, and the Jungle People came up, starved and weary, to the shrunken river – tiger, bear, deer, buffalo, and pig, all together – drank the fouled waters, and hung above them, too exhausted to move off.

The deer and the pig had tramped all day in search of something better than dried bark and withered leaves. The buffaloes had found no wallows to be cool in, and no green crops to steal. The snakes had left the Jungle and come down to the river in the hope of finding a stray frog. They curled round wet stones, and never offered to strike when the nose of a rooting pig dislodged them. The river-turtles had long ago been killed by Bagheera, cleverest of hunters, and the fish had buried themselves deep in the dry mud. Only the Peace Rock lay across the shallows like a long snake, and the little tired ripples hissed as they dried on its hot side.

It was here that Mowgli came nightly for the cool and the companionship. The most hungry of his enemies would hardly have cared for the boy then, His naked hide made him seem more lean and wretched than any of his fellows. His hair was bleached to tow colour by the sun; his ribs stood out like the ribs of a basket, and the lumps on his knees and elbows, where he was used to track on all fours, gave his shrunken limbs the look of knotted grass-stems. But his eye, under his matted forelock, was cool and quiet, for Bagheera was his adviser in this time of trouble, and told him to go quietly, hunt slowly, and never, on any account, to lose his temper.

"It is an evil time," said the Black Panther, one furnace-hot evening, "but it will go if we can live till the end. Is thy stomach full, Man-cub?"

"There is stuff in my stomach, but I get no good of it. Think you, Bagheera, the Rains have forgotten us and will never come again?"

"Not I! We shall see the *mohwa* in blossom yet, and the little fawns all fat with new grass. Come down to the Peace Rock and hear the news. On my back, Little Brother."

"This is no time to carry weight. I can still stand alone, but – indeed we be no fatted bullocks, we two."

Bagheera looked along his ragged, dusty flank and whispered. "Last night I killed a bullock under the yoke. So low was I brought that I think I should not have dared to spring if he had been loose. *Wou*!"

Mowgli laughed. "Yes, we be great hunters now," said he. "I am very bold – to eat grubs," and the two came down together through the crackling undergrowth to the river-bank and the lace-work of shoals that ran out from it in every direction.

"The water cannot live long," said Baloo, joining them. "Look across. Yonder are trails like the roads of Man."

On the level plain of the farther bank the stiff jungle-grass had died standing, and, dying, had mummied. The beaten tracks of the deer and the pig, all heading toward the river, had striped that colourless plain with dusty gullies driven through the ten-foot grass, and, early as it was, each long avenue was full of first-comers hastening to the water. You could hear the does and fawns coughing in the snuff-like dust.

Up-stream, at the bend of the sluggish pool round the Peace Rock, and Warden of the Water Truce, stood Hathi, the wild elephant, with his sons, gaunt and gray in the moonlight, rocking to and fro – always rocking. Below him a little were the vanguard of the deer; below these, again, the pig and the wild buffalo; and on the opposite bank, where the tall trees came down to the water's edge, was the place set apart for the Eaters of Flesh – the tiger, the wolves, the panther, the bear, and the others.

"We are under one Law, indeed," said Bagheera, wading into the water and looking across at the lines of clicking horns and starting eyes where the deer and the pig pushed each other to and fro. "Good hunting, all you of my blood," he added, lying own at full length, one flank thrust out of the shallows; and then, between his teeth, "But for that which is the Law it would be *very* good hunting."

The quick-spread ears of the deer caught the last sentence, and a frightened whisper ran along the ranks. "The Truce! Remember the Truce!"

"Peace there, peace!" gurgled Hathi, the wild elephant. "The Truce holds, Bagheera. This is no time to talk of hunting."

"Who should know better than I?" Bagheera answered, rolling his yellow eyes up-stream. "I am an eater of turtles – a fisher of frogs. *Ngaayah*! Would I could get good from chewing branches!"

"*We* wish so, very greatly," bleated a young fawn, who had only been born that spring, and did not at all like it. Wretched as the Jungle People were, even Hathi could not help chuckling; while Mowgli, lying on his elbows in the warm water, laughed aloud, and beat up the scum with his feet.

"Well spoken, little bud-horn," Bagheera purred. "When the Truce ends that shall be remembered in thy favour," and he looked keenly through the darkness to make sure of recognising the fawn again.

Gradually the talking spread up and down the drinking-places. One could hear the scuffling, snorting pig asking for more room; the buffaloes grunting among themselves as they lurched out across the sandbars, and the deer telling pitiful stories of their long foot-sore wanderings in quest of food. Now and again they asked some question of the Eaters of Flesh across the river, but all the news was bad, and the roaring hot wind of the Jungle came and went between the rocks and the rattling branches, and scattered twigs, and dust on the water.

"The men-folk, too, they die beside their ploughs," said a young sambhur. "I passed three between sunset and night. They lay still, and their Bullocks with them. We also shall lie still in a little."

"The river has fallen since last night," said Baloo. "O Hathi, hast thou ever seen the like of this drought?"

"It will pass, it will pass," said Hathi, squirting water along his back and sides.

"We have one here that cannot endure long," said Baloo; and he looked toward the boy he loved.

"I?" said Mowgli indignantly, sitting up in the water. "I have no long fur to cover my bones, but – but if *thy* hide were taken off, Baloo — "

Hathi shook all over at the idea, and Baloo said severely:

"Man-cub, that is not seemly to tell a Teacher of the Law. *Never* have I been seen without my hide."

"Nay, I meant no harm, Baloo; but only that thou art, as it were, like the cocoanut in the husk, and I am the same cocoanut all naked. Now that brown husk of thine -- " Mowgli was sitting cross-legged, and explaining things with his forefinger in his usual way, when Bagheera put out a paddy paw and pulled him over backward into the water.

"Worse and worse," said the Black Panther, as the boy rose spluttering. "First Baloo is to be skinned, and now he is a cocoanut. Be careful that he does not do what the ripe cocoanuts do."

"And what is that?" said Mowgli, off his guard for the minute, though that is one of the oldest catches in the Jungle.

"Break thy head," said Bagheera quietly, pulling him under again.

"It is not good to make a jest of thy teacher," said the bear, when Mowgli had been ducked for the third time.

"Not good! What would ye have? That naked thing running to and fro makes a monkey-jest of those who have once been good hunters, and pulls the best of us by the whiskers for sport." This was Shere Khan, the Lame Tiger, limping down to the water. He waited a little to enjoy the sensation he made among the deer on the opposite to lap, growling: "The jungle has become a whelping-ground for naked cubs now. Look at me, Man-cub!"

Mowgli looked – stared, rather – as insolently as he knew how, and in a minute Shere Khan turned away uneasily. "Man-cub this, and Man-cub that," he rumbled, going on with his drink, "the cub is neither man nor cub, or he would have been afraid. Next season I shall have to beg his leave for a drink. *Aurgh*!"

"That may come, too," said Bagheera, looking him steadily between the eyes. "That may come, too – *Faugh*, Shere Khan! – what new shame hast thou brought here?"

The Lame Tiger had dipped his chin and jowl in the water, and dark, oily streaks were floating from it down-stream.

"Man!" said Shere Khan coolly, "I killed an hour since." He went on purring and growling to himself.

The line of beasts shook and wavered to and fro, and a whisper went up that grew to a cry. "Man! Man! He has killed Man!" Then all looked towards Hathi, the wild elephant, but he seemed not to hear. Hathi never does anything till the time comes, and that is one of the reasons why he lives so long.

"At such a season as this to kill Man! Was no other game afoot?" said Bagheera scornfully, drawing himself out of the tainted water, and shaking each paw, cat-fashion, as he did so.

"I killed for choice – not for food." The horrified whisper began again, and Hathi's watchful little white eye cocked itself in Shere Khan's direction. "For choice," Shere Khan drawled. "Now come I to drink and make me clean again. Is there any to forbid?"

Bagheera's back began to curve like a bamboo in a high wind, but Hathi lifted up his trunk and spoke quietly.

"Thy kill was from choice?" he asked; and when Hathi asks a question it is best to answer.

"Even so. It was my right and my Night. Thou knowest, O Hathi." Shere Khan spoke almost courteously.

"Yea, I know," Hathi answered; and, after a little silence, "Hast thou drunk thy fill?"

"For to-night, yes."

"Go, then. The river is to drink, and not to defile. None but the Lame Tiger would so have boasted of his right at this season when – when we suffer together – Man and Jungle – and People alike. Clean or unclean, get to thy lair, Shere Khan!"

The last words rang out like silver trumpets, and Hathi's three sons rolled forward half a pace, though there was no need.

Shere Khan slunk away, not daring to growl, for he knew – what every one else knows – that when the last comes to the last, Hathi is the Master of the Jungle.

"What is this right Shere Khan speaks of?" Mowgli whispered in Bagheera's ear. "To kill Man is *always*, shameful. The Law says so. And yet Hathi says — "

"Ask him. I do not know, Little Brother. Right or no right, if Hathi had not spoken I would have taught that lame butcher his lesson. To come to the Peace Rock fresh from a kill of Man – and to boast of it – is a jackal's trick. Besides, he tainted the good water."

Mowgli waited for a minute to pick up his courage, because no one cared to address Hathi directly, and then he cried: "What is Shere Khan's right, O Hathi?" Both banks echoed his words, for all the People of the Jungle are intensely curious, and they had just seen something that none except Baloo, who looked very thoughtful, seemed to understand.

"It is an old tale," said Hathi; "a tale older than the Jungle. Keep silence along the banks and I will tell that tale."

There was a minute or two of pushing a shouldering among the pigs and the buffalo, and then the leaders of the herds grunted, one after another, "We wait," and Hathi strode forward, till he was nearly knee-deep in the pool by the Peace Rock. Lean and wrinkled and yellow-tusked though he was, he looked what the Jungle knew him to be – their master.

"Ye know, children," he began, "that of all things ye most fear Man"; and there was a mutter of agreement.

"This tale touches thee, Little Brother," said Bagheera to Mowgli.

"I? I am of the Pack – a hunter of the Free People," Mowgli answered. "What have I to do with Man?"

"And ye do not know why ye fear Man?" Hathi went on. "This is the reason. In the beginning of the Jungle, and none know when that was, we of the Jungle walked together, having no fear of one another. In those days there was no drought, and leaves and flowers and fruit grew on the same tree, and we ate nothing at all except leaves and flowers and grass and fruit and bark."

"I am glad I was not born in those days," said Bagheera. "Bark is only good to sharpen claws."

"And the Lord of the Jungle was Tha, the First of the Elephants. He drew the Jungle out of deep waters with his trunk; and where he made furrows in the ground with his tusks, there the rivers ran; and where he struck with his foot, there rose ponds of good water; and when he blew through his trunk, – thus, – the trees fell. That was the manner in which the Jungle was made by Tha; and so the tale was told to me."

"It has not lost fat in the telling," Bagheera whispered, and Mowgli laughed behind his hand.

"In those days there was no corn or melons or pepper or sugar-cane, nor were there any little huts such as ye have all seen; and the Jungle People knew nothing of Man, but lived in the Jungle together, making one people. But presently they began to dispute over their food, though there was grazing enough for all. They were lazy. Each wished to eat where he lay, as sometimes we can do now when the spring rains are good. Tha, the First of the Elephants, was busy making new jungles and leading the rivers in their beds. He could not walk in all places; therefore he made the First of the Tigers the master and the judge of the Jungle, to whom the Jungle People should bring their disputes. In those days the First of the Tigers ate fruit and grass with the others. He was as large as I am, and he was very beautiful, in colour all over like the blossom of the yellow creeper. There was never stripe nor bar upon his hide in those good days when the Jungle was new. All the Jungle People came before him without fear, and his word was the Law of all the Jungle. We were then, remember ye, one people. Yet upon a night there was a dispute between two bucks – a grazing-quarrel such as ye now settle with the horns and the fore-feet – and it is said that as the two spoke together before the First of the Tigers lying among the flowers, a buck pushed him with his horns, and the First of the Tigers forgot that he was the master and judge of the Jungle, and, leaping upon that buck, broke his neck.

"Till that night never one of us had died, and the First of the Tigers, seeing what he had done, and being made foolish by the scent of the blood, ran away into the marshes of the North, and we of the Jungle, left without a judge, fell to fighting among ourselves; and Tha heard the noise of it and came back. Then some of us said this and some of us said that, but he saw the dead buck among the flowers, and asked who had killed, and we of the Jungle would not tell because the smell of the blood made us foolish. We ran to and fro in circles, capering and crying out and shaking our heads. Then Tha gave an order to the trees that hang low, and to the trailing creepers of the Jungle, that they should mark the killer of the buck so that he should know him again, and he said, "Who will now be master of the Jungle People?" Then up leaped the Gray Ape who lives in the branches, and said, "I will now be master of the Jungle." At this Tha laughed, and said, "So be it," and went away very angry.

"Children, ye know the Gray Ape. He was then as he is now. At the first he made a wise face for himself, but in a little while he began to scratch and to leap up and down, and when Tha came back he found the Gray Ape hanging, head down, from a bough, mocking those who stood below; and they mocked him again. And so there was no Law in the Jungle – only foolish talk and senseless words.

"Then Tha called us all together and said: 'The first of your masters has brought Death into the Jungle, and the second Shame. Now it is time there was a Law, and a Law that ye must not break. Now ye shall know Fear, and when ye have found him ye shall know that he is your master, and the rest shall follow.' Then we of the jungle said, 'What is Fear?' And Tha said, 'Seek till ye find.' So we went up and down the Jungle seeking for Fear, and presently the buffaloes — "

"Ugh!" said Mysah, the leader of the buffaloes, from their sand-bank.

"Yes, Mysah, it was the buffaloes. They came back with the news that in a cave in the Jungle sat Fear, and that he had no hair, and went upon his hind legs. Then we of the Jungle followed the herd till we came to that cave, and Fear stood at the mouth of it, and he was, as the buffaloes had said, hairless, and he walked upon his hinder legs. When he saw us he cried out, and his voice filled us with the fear that we have now of that voice when we hear it, and we ran away, tramping upon and tearing each other because we were afraid. That night, so it was told to me, we of the Jungle did not lie down together as used to be our custom, but each tribe drew off by itself – the pig with the pig, the deer with the deer; horn to horn, hoof to hoof, – like keeping to like, and so lay shaking in the Jungle.

"Only the First of the Tigers was not with us, for he was still hidden in the marshes of the North, and when word was brought to him of the Thing we had seen in the cave, he said. 'I will go to this Thing and break his neck.' So he ran all the night till he came to the cave; but the trees and the creepers on his path, remembering the order that Tha had given, let down their branches and marked him as he ran, drawing their fingers across his back, his flank, his forehead, and his jowl. Wherever they touched him there was a mark and a stripe upon his yellow hide. *And those stripes do his children wear to this day!* When he came to the cave, Fear, the Hairless One, put out his hand and called him 'The Striped One that comes by night,' and the First of the Tigers was afraid of the Hairless One, and ran back to the swamps howling."

Mowgli chuckled quietly here, his chin in the water.

"So loud did he howl that Tha heard him and said, 'What is the sorrow?' And the First of the Tigers, lifting up his muzzle to the new-made sky, which is now so old, said: 'Give me back my power, O Tha. I am made ashamed before all the Jungle, and I have run away from a Hairless One, and he has called me a shameful name.' 'And why?' said Tha. 'Because I am smeared with the mud of the marshes,' said the First of the Tigers. 'Swim, then, and roll on the wet grass, and if it be mud it will wash away,' said Tha; and the First of the Tigers swam, and rolled and rolled upon the grass, till the Jungle ran round and round before his eyes, but not one little bar upon all his hide was changed, and Tha, watching him, laughed. Then the First of the Tigers said: 'What have I done that this comes to me?' Tha said, 'Thou hast killed the buck, and thou hast let Death loose in the Jungle, and with Death has come Fear, so that the people of the Jungle are afraid one of the other, as thou art afraid of the Hairless One.' The First of the Tigers said, 'They will never fear me, for I knew them since the beginning.' Tha said, 'Go and see.' And the First of the Tigers ran to and fro, calling aloud to the deer and the pig and the sambhur and the porcupine and all the Jungle Peoples, and they all ran away from him who had been their judge, because they were afraid.

"Then the First of the Tigers came back, and his pride was broken in him, and, beating his head upon the ground, he tore up the earth with all his feet and said: 'Remember that I was once the Master of the Jungle. Do not forget me, O Tha! Let my children remember that I was once without shame or fear!' And Tha said: 'This much I will do, because thou and I together saw the Jungle made. For one night in each year it shall be as it was before the buck was killed – for thee and for thy children. In that one night, if ye meet the Hairless One – and his name is Man – ye shall not be afraid of him, but he shall be afraid of you, as though ye were judges of the Jungle and masters of all things. Show him mercy in that night of his fear, for thou hast known what Fear is.'

"Then the First of the Tigers answered, 'I am content'; but when next he drank he saw the black stripes upon his flank and his side, and he remembered the name that the Hairless One had given him, and he was angry. For a year he lived in the marshes waiting till Tha should keep his promise. And upon a night when the jackal of the Moon [the Evening Star] stood clear of the Jungle, he felt that his Night was upon him, and he went to that cave to meet the Hairless One. Then it happened as Tha promised, for the Hairless One fell down before him and lay along the ground, and the First of the Tigers struck him and broke his back, for he thought that there was but one such Thing in the Jungle, and that he had killed Fear. Then, nosing above the kill, he heard Tha coming down from the woods of the North, and presently the voice of the First of the Elephants, which is the voice that we hear now — "

The thunder was rolling up and down the dry, scarred hills, but it brought no rain – only heat – lightning that flickered along the ridges – and Hathi went on:

"*That* was the voice he heard, and it said: 'Is this thy mercy?' The First of the Tigers licked his lips and said: 'What matter? I have killed Fear.' And Tha said: 'O blind and foolish! Thou hast untied the feet of Death, and he will follow thy trail till thou diest. Thou hast taught Man to kill!'

"The First of the Tigers, standing stiffly to his kill, said. 'He is as the buck was. There is no Fear. Now I will judge the Jungle Peoples once more.'

"And Tha said: 'Never again shall the Jungle Peoples come to thee. They shall never cross thy trail, nor sleep near thee, nor follow after thee, nor browse by thy lair. Only Fear shall follow thee, and with a blow that thou canst not see he shall bid thee wait his pleasure. He shall make the ground to open under thy feet, and the creeper to twist about thy neck, and the tree-trunks to grow together about thee higher than thou canst leap, and at the last he shall take thy hide to wrap his cubs when they are cold. Thou hast shown him no mercy, and none will he show thee.'

"The First of the Tigers was very bold, for his Night was still on him, and he said: 'The Promise of Tha is the Promise of Tha. He will not take away my Night?' And Tha said: 'This one Night is thine, as I have said, but there is a price to pay. Thou hast taught Man to kill, and he is no slow learner.'

"The First of the Tigers said: 'He is here under my foot, and his back is broken. Let the Jungle know I have killed Fear.'

"Then Tha laughed, and said: 'Thou hast killed one of many, but thou thyself shalt tell the Jungle – for thy Night is ended.'

"So the day came; and from the mouth of the cave went out another Hairless One, and he saw the kill in the path, and the First of the Tigers above it, and he took a pointed stick — "

"They throw a thing that cuts now," said Ikki, rustling down the bank; for Ikki was considered uncommonly good eating by the Gonds* – they called him Ho-Igoo – and he knew something of the wicked little Gondee axe that whirls across a clearing like a dragon-fly.

"It was a pointed stick, such as they put in the foot of a pit-trap," said Hathi, "and throwing it, he struck the First of the Tigers deep in the flank. Thus it happened as Tha said, for the First of the Tigers ran howling up and down the Jungle till he tore out the stick, and all the Jungle knew that the Hairless One could strike from far off, and they feared more than before. So it came about that the First of the Tigers taught the Hairless One to kill – and ye know what harm that has since done to all our peoples – through the noose, and the pitfall, and the hidden trap, and the flying stick and the stinging fly

* Jungle tribesmen of central India.

that comes out of white smoke [Hathi meant the rifle], and the Red Flower [fire] that drives us into the open. Yet for one night in the year the Hairless One fears the Tiger, as Tha promised, and never has the Tiger given him cause to be less afraid. Where he finds him, there he kills him, remembering how the First of the Tigers was made ashamed. For the rest, Fear walks up and down the Jungle by day and by night."

"*Ahi! Aoo!*" said the deer, thinking of what it all meant to them.

"And only when there is one great Fear over all, as there is now, can we of the Jungle lay aside our little fears, and meet together in one place as we do now."

"For one night only does Man fear the Tiger?" said Mowgli.

"For one night only," said Hathi.

"But I – but we – but all the Jungle knows that Shere Khan kills Man twice and thrice in a moon."

"Even so. *Then* he springs from behind and turns his head aside as he strikes, for he is full of fear. If Man looked at him he would run. But on his one Night he goes openly down to the village. He walks between the houses and thrusts his head into the doorway, and the men fall on their faces, and there he does his kill. One kill in that Night."

"Oh!" said Mowgli to himself, rolling over in the water. "*Now* I see why it was Shere Khan bade me look at him! He got no good of it, for he could not hold his eyes steady, and – and I certainly did not fall down at his feet. But then I am not a man, being of the Free People."

"*Umm!*" said Bagheera deep in his furry throat. "Does the Tiger know his Night?"

"Never till the Jackal of the Moon stands clear of the evening mist. Sometimes it falls in the dry summer and sometimes in the wet rains – this one Night of the Tiger. But for the First of the Tigers, this would never have been, nor would any of us have known fear."

The deer grunted sorrowfully and Bagheera's lips curled in a wicked smile. "Do men know this – tale?" said he.

"None know it except the tigers, and we, the elephants – the children of Tha. Now ye by the pools have heard it, and I have spoken."

Hathi dipped his trunk into the water as a sign that he did not wish to talk.

"But – but – but," said Mowgli, turning to Baloo, "why did not the First of the Tigers continue to eat grass and leaves and trees? He did but break the buck's neck. He did not *eat*. What led him to the hot meat?"

"The trees and the creepers marked him, Little Brother, and made him the striped thing that we see. Never again would he eat their fruit; but from that day he revenged himself upon the deer, and the others, the Eaters of Grass," said Baloo.

"Then *thou* knowest the tale. *Heh*? Why have I never heard?"

"Because the Jungle is full of such tales. If I made a beginning there would never be an end to them. Let go my ear, Little Brother."

# THE LAW OF THE JUNGLE

JUST TO give you an idea of the immense variety of the Jungle Law, I have translated into verse (Baloo always recited them in a sort of sing-song) a few of the laws that apply to the wolves. There are, of course, hundreds and hundreds more, but these will do for specimens of the simpler rulings.

Now this is the Law of the Jungle – as old and as true as the *sky;*

And the Wolf that shall keep it may prosper, but the Wolf that *shall break it must die.*

As the creeper that girdles the tree-trunk the Law runneth *forward and back –*

For the strength of the Pack is the Wolf, and the strength *of the Wolf is the Pack.*

Wash daily from nose-tip to tail-tip; drink deeply, but never *too deep;*

And remember the night is for hunting, and forget not the *day is for sleep.*

The jackal may follow the Tiger, but, Cub, when thy whiskers *are grown,*

Remember the Wolf is a hunter – go forth and get food of *thine own.*

Keep peace with the Lords of the Jungle – the Tiger, the Panther, *the Bear;*

And trouble not Hathi the Silent, and mock not the Boar in *his lair.*

When Pack meets with Pack in the Jungle, and neither will *go from the trail,*

Lie down till the leaders have spoken – it may be fair words *shall prevail.*

When ye fight with a Wolf of the Pack, ye must fight him
*alone and afar,*

Lest others take part in the quarrel, and the Pack be diminished
*by war.*

The Lair of the Wolf is his refuge, and where he has made him
*his home,*

Not even the Head Wolf may enter, not even the Council may
*come.*

The Lair of the Wolf is his refuge, but where he has digged it
*too plain,*

The Council shall send him a message, and so he shall change
*it again.*

If ye kill before midnight, be silent, and wake not the woods
*with your bay,*

Lest ye frighten the deer from the crops, and the brothers go
*empty away.*

Ye may kill for yourselves, and your mates, and your cubs as
*they need, and ye can;*

But kill not for pleasure of killing, and seven times never kill
*man.*

If ye plunder his Kill from a weaker, devour not all in thy
*pride;*

Pack-Right is the right of the meanest; so leave him the head
*and the hide.*

The Kill of the Pack is the meat of the Pack. Ye must eat where
*it lies;*

And no one may carry away of that meat to his lair, or he
*dies.*

The Kill of the Wolf is the meat of the Wolf. He may do what
*he will,*

But, till he has given permission, the Pack may not eat of that
*Kill.*

Cub-Right is the right of the Yearling. From all of his Pack he
*may claim,*

Full-gorge when the killer has eaten; and none may refuse
*him the same.*

Lair-Right is the right of the Mother. From all of her year she
*may claim,*

One haunch of each kill for her litter, and none may deny her
*the same.*

Cave-Right is the right of the Father – to hunt by himself for
*his own.*

He is freed of all calls to the Pack; he is judged by the Council
*alone.*

Because of his age and his cunning, because of his gripe and
*his paw,*

In all that the Law leaveth open, the word of the Head Wolf
*is Law.*

Now these are the Laws of the Jungle, and many and mighty
*are they;*

But the head and the hoof of the Law and the haunch and the
*hump is – Obey!*

# THE MIRACLE OF PURUN BHAGAT

The night we felt the earth would move
    We stole and plucked him by the hand,
Because we loved him with the love
    That knows but cannot understand.

And when the roaring hillside broke,
    And all our world fell down in rain,
We saved him, we the Little Folk;
    But lo! he does not come again!

Mourn now, we saved him for the sake
    Of such poor love as wild ones may.
Mourn ye! Our brother will not wake,
    And his own kind drive us away!

*Dirge* of the Langurs.*

THERE WAS once a man in India who was Prime Minister of one of the semi-independent native States in the north-western part of the country. He was a Brahmin, so high-caste that caste ceased to have any particular meaning for him; and his father had been an important official in the gay-coloured tag-rag and bobtail of an old-fashioned Hindu Court. But as Purun Dass grew up he felt that the old order of things was changing, and that if any one wished to get on in the world he must stand well with the English, and imitate all that the English believed to be good. At the same time a native official must keep his own master's favour. This was a difficult game, but the quiet, close-mouthed young Brahmin, helped by a good English education at a Bombay University, played it coolly, and rose, step-by-step, to be Prime Minister of the kingdom. That is to say, he held more real power than his master the Maharajah.

*A mourning song.

When the old king – who was suspicious of the English, their railways and telegraphs – died, Purun Dass stood high with his young successor, who had been tutored by an Englishman; and between them, though he always took care that his master should have the credit, they established schools for little girls, made roads, and started State dispensaries and shows of agricultural implements, and published a yearly blue-book on the "Moral and Material Progress of the State," and the Foreign Office and the Government of India were delighted. Very few native States take up English progress altogether, for they will not believe, as Purun Dass showed he did, that what was good for the Englishman must be twice as good for the Asiatic. The Prime Minister became the honoured friend of Viceroys, and Governors, and Lieutenant-Governors, and medical missionaries, and common missionaries, and hard-riding English officers who came to shoot in the State preserves, as well as of whole hosts of tourists who travelled up and down India in the cold weather, showing how things ought to be managed. In his spare time he would endow scholarships for the study of medicine and manufactures on strictly English lines, and write letters to the "Pioneer", the greatest Indian daily paper, explaining his master's aims and objects.

At last he went to England on a visit, and had to pay enormous sums to the priests when he came back; for even so high-caste a Brahmin as Purun Dass lost caste by crossing the black sea. In London he met and talked with every one worth knowing – men whose names go all over the world – and saw a great deal more than he said. He was given honorary degrees by learned universities, and he made speeches and talked of Hindu social reform to English ladies in evening dress, till all London cried, "This is the most fascinating man we have ever met at dinner since cloths were first laid."

When he returned to India there was a blaze of glory, for the Viceroy himself made a special visit to confer upon the Maharajah the Grand Cross of the Star of India – all diamonds and ribbons and enamel; and at the same ceremony, while the cannon boomed, Purun Dass was made a Knight Commander of the Order of the Indian Empire; so that his name stood Sir Purun Dass, K.C.I.E.

At a grand dinner that evening in the spacious Viceregal tent, he stood up with the badge and the collar of the Order on his breast, and responding to the toast of his master's health, made a speech few Englishmen could have bettered.

Next month, when the city had returned to its sun-baked quiet, he did a thing no Englishman would have dreamed of doing; for, so far as the world's affairs went, he died. The jewelled order of his knighthood went back to the Indian Government, and a new Prime Minister was appointed to the charge of affairs, and a great game of General Post began in all the subordinate appointments. The priests knew what had happened, and the people guessed; but India is the one place in the world where a man can do as he pleases and nobody asks why; and the fact that Dewan Sir Purun Dass, K.C.I.E., had resigned position, palace, and power, and taken up the begging-bowl and ochre-coloured dress of a Sannyasi, or holy man, was considered nothing extraordinary. He had been, as the Old Law recommends, twenty years a youth, twenty years a fighter, – though he had never carried a weapon in his life, – and twenty years head of a household. He had used his wealth and his power for what he knew both to be worth; he had taken honour when it came his way; he had seen men and cities far and near, and men and cities had stood up and honoured him. Now he would let those things go, as a man drops the cloak he needs no longer.

Behind him, as he walked through the city gates, an antelope skin and brass-handled crutch under his arm, and a begging-bowl of polished brown *coco-de-mer* in his hand, barefoot, alone, with eyes cast on the ground – behind him they were firing salutes from the bastions in honour of his happy successor. Purun Dass nodded. All that life was ended; and he bore it no more ill-will or good-will than a man bears to a colourless dream of the night. He was a Sannyasi – a houseless, wandering mendicant, depending on his neighbours for his daily bread; and so long as there is a morsel to divide in India, neither priest nor beggar starves. He had never in his life tasted meat, and very seldom eaten even fish. A five-pound note would have covered his personal expenses for food through any one of the many years in which he had been absolute master of millions of money. Even when he was being lionised in London he had held before him his dream of peace and quiet – the long, white, dusty Indian road, printed all over with bare feet, the incessant, slow-moving traffic, and the sharp-smelling wood smoke curling up under the fig-trees in the twilight, where the wayfarers sit at their evening meal.

When the time came to make that dream true the Prime Minister took the proper steps, and in three days you might more easily have found a bubble in the trough of the long Atlantic seas, than Purun Dass among the roving, gathering, separating millions of India.

At night his antelope skin was spread where the darkness overtook him – sometimes in a Sannyasi monastery by the roadside; sometimes by a mud-pillar shrine of Kala Pir, where the *Jogis*, who are another misty division of holy men, would receive him as they do those who know what castes and divisions are worth; sometimes on the outskirts of a little Hindu village, where the children would steal up with the food their parents had prepared; and sometimes on the pitch of the bare grazing-grounds, where the flame of his stick fire waked the drowsy camels. It was all one to Purun Dass – or Purun Bhagat, as he called himself now. Earth, people, and food were all one. But unconsciously his feet drew him away northward and eastward; from the south to Rohtak; from Rohtak to Kurnool; from Kurnool to ruined Samanah, and then up-stream along the dried bed of the Gugger river that fills only when the rain falls in the hills, till one day he saw the far line of the great Himalayas.

Then Purun Bhagat smiled, for he remembered that his mother was of Rajput Brahmin birth, from Kulu way – a Hill-woman, always home-sick for the snows – and that the least touch of Hill blood draws a man in the end back to where he belongs.

"Yonder," said Purun Bhagat, breasting the lower slopes of the Shiwaliks, where the cacti stand up like seven-branched candlesticks – "yonder I shall sit down and get knowledge"; and the cool wind of the Himalayas whistled about his ears as he trod the road that led to Simla.

The last time he had come that way it had been in state, with a clattering cavalry escort, to visit the gentlest and most affable of Viceroys; and the two had talked for an hour together about mutual friends in London, and what the Indian common folk really thought of things. This time Purun Bhagat paid no calls, but leaned on the rail of the Mall, watching that glorious view of the Plains spread out forty miles below, till a native Mohammedan policeman told him he was obstructing traffic; and Purun Bhagat salaamed reverently to the Law, because he knew the value of it, and was seeking for a Law of his own. Then he moved on, and slept that night in an empty hut at Chota Simla, which looks like the very last end of the earth, but it was only the beginning of his journey. He followed the Himalaya-Thibet road, the little ten-foot track that is blasted out of solid rock, or strutted out on timbers over gulfs a thousand feet deep; that dips into warm, wet, shut-in valleys, and climbs out across bare, grassy hill-shoulders where the sun strikes like a burning-glass; or turns through dripping, dark forests where the tree-ferns dress the trunks from head to heel, and the pheasant calls to his mate. And he met Thibetan herdsmen with their dogs and flocks of sheep, each sheep with a little bag of borax on his back, and wandering wood-cutters, and cloaked and blanketed Lamas from Thibet, coming into India on pilgrimage, and envoys of little solitary Hill-states, posting furiously on ring-streaked and piebald ponies, or the cavalcade of a Rajah paying a visit; or else for a long, clear day he would see nothing more than a black bear grunting and rooting below in the valley. When he first started, the roar of the world he had left still rang in his ears, as the roar of a tunnel rings long after the train has passed through; but when he had put the Mutteeanee Pass behind him that was all done, and Purun Bhagat was alone with himself, walking, wondering, and thinking, his eyes on the ground, and his thoughts with the clouds.

One evening he crossed the highest pass he had met till then – it had been a two-day's climb – and came out on a line of snow-peaks that banded all the horizon – mountains from fifteen to twenty thousand feet high, looking almost near enough to hit with a stone, though they were fifty or sixty miles away. The pass was crowned with dense, dark forest – deodar, walnut, wild cherry, wild olive, and wild pear, but mostly deodar, which is the Himalayan cedar; and under the shadow of the deodars stood a deserted shrine to Kali – who is Durga, who is Sitala, who is sometimes worshipped against the smallpox.

Purun Dass swept the stone floor clean, smiled at the grinning statue, made himself a little mud fireplace at the back of the shrine, spread his antelope skin on a bed of fresh pine-needles, tucked his bairagi – his brass-handled crutch – under his armpit, and sat down to rest.

Immediately below him the hillside fell away, clean and cleared for fifteen hundred feet, where a little village of stone-walled houses, with roofs of beaten earth, clung to the steep tilt. All round it the tiny terraced fields lay out like aprons of patchwork on the knees of the mountain, and cows no bigger than beetles grazed between the smooth stone circles of the threshing-floors. Looking across the valley, the eye was deceived by the size of things, and could not at first realise that what seemed to be low scrub, on the opposite mountain-flank, was in truth a forest of hundred-foot pines. Purun Bhagat saw an eagle swoop across the gigantic hollow, but the great bird dwindled to a dot ere it was half-way over. A few bands of scattered clouds strung up and down the valley, catching on a shoulder of the hills, or rising up and dying out when they were level with the head of the pass. And "Here shall I find peace," said Purun Bhagat.

Now, a Hill-man makes nothing of a few hundred feet up or down, and as soon as the villagers saw the smoke in the deserted shrine, the village priest climbed up the terraced hillside to welcome the stranger.

When he met Purun Bhagat's eyes – the eyes of a man used to control thousands – he bowed to the earth, took the begging-bowl without a word, and returned to the village, saying, "We have at last a holy man. Never have I seen such a man. He is of the Plains – but pale-coloured – a Brahmin of the Brahmins." Then all the housewives of the village said, "Think you he will stay with us?" and each did her best to cook the most savoury meal for the Bhagat. Hill-food is very simple, but with buckwheat and Indian corn, and rice and red pepper, and little fish out of the stream in the valley, and honey from the flue-like hives built in the stone walls, and dried apricots, and turmeric, and wild ginger, and bannocks of flour, a devout woman can make good things, and it was a full bowl that the priest carried to the Bhagat. Was he going to stay? asked the priest. Would he need a 'chela' – a disciple – to beg for him? Had he a blanket against the cold weather? Was the food good?

Purun Bhagat ate, and thanked the giver. It was in his mind to stay. That was sufficient, said the priest. Let the begging-bowl be placed outside the shrine, in the hollow made by those two twisted roots, and daily should the Bhagat be fed; for the village felt honoured that such a man – he looked timidly into the Bhagat's face – should tarry among them.

That day saw the end of Purun Bhagat's wanderings. He had come to the place appointed for him – the silence and the space. After this, time stopped, and he, sitting at the mouth of the shrine, could not tell whether he were alive or dead; a man with control of his limbs, or a part of the hills, and the clouds, and the shifting rain and sunlight. He would repeat a Name softly to himself a hundred hundred times, till, at each repetition, he seemed to move more and more out of his body, sweeping up to the doors of some tremendous discovery; but, just as the door was opening, his body would drag him back, and, with grief, he felt he was locked up again in the flesh and bones of Purun Bhagat.

Every morning the filled begging-bowl was laid silently in the crutch of the roots outside the shrine. Sometimes the priest brought it; sometimes a Ladakhi trader, lodging in the village, and anxious to get merit, trudged up the path; but, more often, it was the woman who had cooked the meal overnight; and she would murmur, hardly above her breath. "Speak for me before the gods, Bhagat. Speak for such a one, the wife of so-and-so!" Now and then some bold child would be allowed the honour, and Purun Bhagat would hear him drop the bowl and run as fast as his little legs could carry him, but the Bhagat never came down to the village. It was laid out like a map at his feet. He could see the evening gatherings, held on the circle of the threshing-floors, because that was the only level ground; could see the wonderful unnamed green of the young rice, the indigo blues of the Indian corn, the dock-like patches of buckwheat, and, in its season, the red bloom of the amaranth, whose tiny seeds, being neither grain nor pulse, make a food that can be lawfully eaten by Hindus in time of fasts.

When the year turned, the roofs of the huts were all little squares of purest gold, for it was on the roofs that they laid out their cobs of the corn to dry. Hiving and harvest, rice-sowing and husking, passed before his eyes, all embroidered down there on the many-sided plots of fields, and he thought of them all, and wondered what they all led to at the long last.

Even in populated India a man cannot a day sit still before the wild things run over him as though he were a rock; and in that wilderness very soon the wild things, who knew Kali's Shrine well, came back to look at the intruder. The langurs, the big gray-whiskered monkeys of the Himalayas, were, naturally, the first, for they are alive with curiosity; and when they had upset the begging-bowl, and rolled it round the floor, and tried their teeth on the brass-handled crutch, and made faces at the antelope skin, they decided that the human being who sat so still was harmless. At evening, they would leap down from the pines, and beg with their hands for things to eat, and then swing off in graceful curves. They liked the warmth of the fire, too, and huddled round it till Purun Bhagat had to push them aside to throw on more fuel; and in the morning, as often as not, he would find a furry ape sharing his blanket. All day long, one or other of the tribe would sit by his side, staring out at the snows, crooning and looking unspeakably wise and sorrowful.

After the monkeys came the barasingha, that big deer which is like our red deer, but stronger. He wished to rub off the velvet of his horns against the cold stones of Kali's statue, and stamped his feet when he saw the man at the shrine. But Purun Bhagat never moved, and, little by little, the royal stag edged up and nuzzled his shoulder. Purun Bhagat slid one cool hand along the hot antlers, and the touch soothed the fretted beast, who bowed his head, and Purun Bhagat very softly rubbed and ravelled off the velvet. Afterward, the barasingha brought his doe and fawn – gentle things that mumbled on the holy man's blanket – or would come alone at night, his eyes green in the fire-flicker, to take his share of fresh walnuts. At last, the musk-deer, the shyest and almost the smallest of the deerlets, came, too, her big rabbity ears erect; even brindled, silent *mushick-nabha* must needs find out what the light in the shrine meant, and drop out her moose-like nose into Purun Bhagat's lap, coming and going with the shadows of the fire. Purun Bhagat called them all "my brothers," and his low call of "*Bhai! Bhai*!" would draw them from the forest at noon if they were within earshot. The Himalayan black bear, moody and suspicious – Sona, who has the V-shaped white mark under his chin – passed that way more than once; and since the Bhagat showed no fear, Sona showed no anger, but watched him, and came closer, and begged a share of the caresses, and a dole of bread or wild berries. Often, in the still dawns, when the Bhagat would climb to the very crest of the pass to watch the red day walking along the peaks of the snows, he would find Sona shuffling and grunting at his heels, thrusting, a curious fore-paw under fallen trunks, and bringing it away with a *whoof* of impatience; or his early steps would wake Sona where he lay curled up, and the great brute, rising erect, would think to fight, till he heard the Bhagat's voice and knew his best friend.

Nearly all hermits and holy men who live apart from the big cities have the reputation of being able to work miracles with the wild things, but all the miracle lies in keeping still, in never making a hasty movement, and, for a long time, at least, in never looking directly at a visitor. The villagers saw the outline of the barasingha stalking like a shadow through the dark forest behind the shrine; saw the minaul, the Himalayan pheasant, blazing in her best colours before Kali's statue; and the langurs on their haunches, inside, playing with the walnut shells. Some of the children, too, had heard Sona singing to himself, bear-fashion, behind the fallen rocks, and the Bhagat's reputation as miracle-worker stood firm.

Yet nothing was farther from his mind than miracles. He believed that all things were one big Miracle, and when a man knows that much he knows something to go upon. He knew for a certainty that there was nothing great and nothing little in this world: and day and night he strove to think out his way into the heart of things, back to the place whence his soul had come.

So thinking, his untrimmed hair fell down about his shoulders, the stone slab at the side of the antelope skin was dented into a little hole by the foot of his brass-handled crutch, and the place between the tree-trunks, where the begging-bowl rested day after day, sunk and wore into a hollow almost as smooth as the brown shell itself; and each beast knew his exact place at the fire. The fields changed their colours with the seasons; the threshing-floors filled and emptied, and filled again and again; and again and again, when winter came, the langurs frisked among the branches feathered with light snow, till the mother-monkeys brought their sad-eyed little babies up from the warmer valleys with the spring. There were few changes in the village. The priest was older, and many of the little children who used to come with the begging-dish sent their own children now; and when you asked of the villagers how long their holy man had lived in Kali's Shrine at the head of the pass, they answered, "Always."

Then came such summer rains as had not been known in the Hills for many seasons. Through three good months the valley was wrapped in cloud and soaking mist – steady, unrelenting downfall, breaking off into thunder-shower after thunder-shower. Kali's Shrine stood above the clouds, for the most part, and there was a whole month in which the Bhagat never caught a glimpse of his village. It was packed away under a white floor of cloud that swayed and shifted and rolled on itself and bulged upward, but never broke from its piers – the streaming flanks of the valley.

All that time he heard nothing but the sound of a million little waters, overhead from the trees, and underfoot along the ground, soaking through the pine-needles, dripping from the tongues of draggled fern, and spouting in newly-torn muddy channels down the slopes. Then the sun came out, and drew forth the good incense of the deodars and the rhododendrons, and that far-off, clean smell which the Hill people call "the smell of the snows." The hot sunshine lasted for a week, and then the rains gathered together for their last downpour, and the water fell in sheets that flayed off the skin of the ground and leaped back in mud. Purun Bhagat heaped his fire high that night, for he was sure his brothers would need warmth; but never a beast came to the shrine, though he called and called till he dropped asleep, wondering what had happened in the woods.

It was in the black heart of the night, the rain drumming like a thousand drums, that he was roused by a plucking at his blanket, and, stretching out, felt the little hand of a langur. "It is better here than in the trees," he said sleepily, loosening a fold of blanket; "take it and be warm." The monkey caught his hand and pulled hard. "Is it food, then?" said Purun Bhagat. "Wait awhile, and I will prepare some." As he kneeled to throw fuel on the fire the langur ran to the door of the shrine, crooned and ran back again, plucking at the man's knee.

"What is it? What is thy trouble, Brother?" said Purun Bhagat, for the langur's eyes were full of things that he could not tell. "Unless one of thy caste be in a trap – and none set traps here – I will not go into that weather. Look, Brother, even the barasingha comes for shelter!"

The deer's antlers clashed as he strode into the shrine, clashed against the grinning statue of Kali. He lowered them in Purun Bhagat's direction and stamped uneasily, hissing through his half-shut nostrils.

"*Hai! Hai! Hai*!" said the Bhagat, snapping his fingers, "Is *this* payment for a night's lodging?" But the deer pushed him toward the door, and as he did so Purun Bhagat heard the sound of something opening with a sigh, and saw two slabs of the floor draw away from each other, while the sticky earth below smacked its lips.

"Now I see," said Purun Bhagat. "No blame to my brothers that they did not sit by the fire to-night. The mountain is falling. And yet – why should I go?" His eye fell on the empty begging-bowl, and his face changed. "They have given me good food daily since – since I came, and, if I am not swift, to-morrow there will not be one mouth in the valley. Indeed, I must go and warn them below. Back there, Brother! Let me get to the fire."

The barasingha backed unwillingly as Purun Bhagat drove a pine torch deep into the flame, twirling it till it was well lit. "Ah! ye came to warn me," he said, rising. "Better than that we shall do; better than that. Out, now, and lend me thy neck, Brother, for I have but two feet."

He clutched the bristling withers of the barasingha with his right hand, held the torch away with his left, and stepped out of the shrine into the desperate night. There was no breath of wind, but the rain nearly drowned the flare as the great deer hurried down the slope, sliding on his haunches. As soon as they were clear of the forest more of the Bhagat's brothers joined them. He heard, though he could not see, the langurs pressing about him, and behind them the *uhh! uhh!* of Sona. The rain matted his long white hair into ropes; the water splashed beneath his bare feet, and his yellow robe clung to his frail old body, but he stepped down steadily, leaning against the barasingha. He was no longer a holy man, but Sir Purun Dass, K.C.I.E., Prime Minister of no small State, a man accustomed to command, going out to save life. Down the steep, plashy path they poured all together, the Bhagat and his brothers, down and down till the deer's feet clicked and stumbled on the wall of a threshing-floor, and he snorted because he smelt Man. Now they were at the head of the one crooked village street, and the Bhagat beat with his crutch on the barred windows of the blacksmith's house, as his torch blazed up in the shelter of the eaves. "Up and out!" cried Purun Bhagat; and he did not know his own voice, for it was years since he had spoken aloud to a man. "The hill falls! The hill is falling! Up and out, oh, you within!"

"It is our Bhagat," said the blacksmith's wife. He stands among his beasts. Gather the little ones and give the call."

It ran from house to house, while the beasts, cramped in the narrow way, surged and huddled round the Bhagat, and Sona puffed impatiently.

The people hurried into the street – they were no more than seventy souls all told – and in the glare of the torches they saw their Bhagat holding back the terrified barasingha, while the monkeys plucked piteously at his skirts, and Sona sat on his haunches and roared.

"Across the valley and up the next hill!" shouted Purun Bhagat. "Leave none behind! We follow!"

Then the people ran as only Hill folk can run, for they knew that in a landslip you must climb for the highest ground across the valley. They fled, splashing through the little river at the bottom, and panted up the terraced fields on the far side, while the Bhagat and his brethren followed. Up and up the opposite mountain they climbed, calling to each other by name – the roll-call of the village – and at their heels toiled the big barasingha, weighted by the failing strength of Purun Bhagat. At last the deer stopped in the shadow of a deep pinewood, five hundred feet up the hillside. His instinct, that had warned him of the coming slide, told him he would he safe here.

Purun Bhagat dropped fainting by his side, for the chill of the rain and that fierce climb were killing him; but first he called to the scattered torches ahead, "Stay and count your numbers"; then, whispering to the deer as he saw the lights gather in a cluster: "Stay with me, Brother. Stay – till – I – go!"

There was a sigh in the air that grew to a mutter, and a mutter that grew to a roar, and a roar that passed all sense of hearing, and the hillside on which the villagers stood was hit in the darkness, and rocked to the blow. Then a note as steady, deep, and true as the deep 'C' of the organ drowned everything for perhaps five minutes, while the very roots of the pines quivered to it. It died away, and the sound of the rain falling on miles of hard ground and grass changed to the muffled drum of water on soft earth. That told its own tale.

Never a villager – not even the priest – was bold enough to speak to the Bhagat who had saved their lives. They crouched under the pines and waited till the day. When it came they looked across the valley and saw that what had been forest, and terraced field, and track-threaded grazing-ground was one raw, red, fan-shaped smear, with a few trees flung head-down on the scarp. That red ran high up the hill of their refuge, damming back the little river, which had begun to spread into a brick-coloured lake. Of the village, of the road to the shrine, of the shrine itself, and the forest behind, there was no trace. For one mile in width and two thousand feet in sheer depth the mountain-side had come away bodily, planed clean from head to heel.

And the villagers, one by one, crept through the wood to pray before their Bhagat. They saw the barasingha standing over him, who fled when they came near, and they heard the langurs wailing in the branches, and Sona moaning up the hill; but their Bhagat was dead, sitting cross-legged, his back against a tree, his crutch under his armpit, and his face turned to the north-east.

The priest said: "Behold a miracle after a miracle, for in this very attitude must all Sannyasis be buried! Therefore where he now is we will build the temple to our holy man."

They built the temple before a year was ended – a little stone-and-earth shrine – and they called the hill the Bhagat's hill, and they worship there with lights and flowers and offerings to this day. But they do not know that the saint of their worship is the late Sir Purun Dass, K.C.I.E., D.C.L., Ph.D., etc., once Prime Minister of the progressive and enlightened State of Mohiniwala, and honorary or corresponding member of more learned and scientific societies than will ever do any good in this world or the next.

## A SONG OF KABIR[1]

Oh, light was the world that he weighed in his hands!
    Oh, heavy the tale of his fiefs and his lands!
He has gone from the guddee and put on the shroud,
    And departed in guise of *bairagi*[2] avowed!

Now the white road to Delhi is mat for his feet,
    The sal and the kikar must guard him from heat;
His home is the camp, and the waste, and the crowd –
    He is seeking the Way as *bairagi* avowed!

He has looked upon Man, and his eyeballs are clear
    (There was One; there is One, and but One, *saith* Kabir);
The Red Mist of Doing has thinned to a cloud –
    He has taken the Path for *bairagi* avowed!

To learn and discern of his brother the clod,
    Of his brother the brute, and his brother the God.
He has gone from the council and put on the shroud
    ("Can ye hear?" saith Kabir), a *bairagi* avowed!

1. The revered Indian mystic and saint (1440-1518).
2. A fakir.

# LETTING IN THE JUNGLE

Veil them, cover them, wall them round –
    Blossom, and creeper, and weed –
Let us forget the sight and the sound,
    The smell and the touch of the breed!

Fat black ash by the altar-stone,
    Here is the white-foot rain,
And the does bring forth in the fields unsown,
    And none shall affright them again;
And the blind walls crumble, unknown, o'erthrown.....
    And none shall inhabit again!

YOU WILL REMEMBER that after Mowgli had pinned Shere Khan's hide to the Council Rock, he told as many as were left of the Seeonee Pack that henceforward he would hunt in the Jungle alone; and the four children of Mother and Father Wolf said that they would hunt with him. But it is not easy to change one's life all in a minute – particularly in the Jungle. The first thing Mowgli did, when the disorderly Pack had slunk off, was to go to the home-cave, and sleep for a day and a night. Then he told Mother Wolf and Father Wolf as much as they could understand of his adventures among men; and when he made the morning sun flicker up and down the blade of his skinning-knife, – the same he had skinned Shere Khan with, – they said he had learned something. Then Akela and Gray Brother had to explain their share of the great buffalo-drive in the ravine, and Baloo toiled up the hill to hear all about it, and Bagheera scratched himself all over with pure delight at the way in which Mowgli had managed his war.

It was long after sunrise, but no one dreamed of going to sleep, and from time to time, during the talk, Mother Wolf would throw up her head, and sniff a deep snuff of satisfaction as the wind brought her the smell of the tiger-skin on the Council Rock.

"But for Akela and Gray Brother here," Mowgli said, at the end, "I could have done nothing. Oh, mother, mother! if thou hadst seen the black herd-bulls pour down the ravine, or hurry through the gates when the Man-Pack flung stones at me!"

"I am glad I did not see that last," said Mother Wolf stiffly. "It is not *my* custom to suffer my cubs to be driven to and fro like jackals. *I* would have taken a price from the Man-Pack; but I would have spared the woman who gave thee the milk. Yes, I would have spared her alone."

"Peace, peace, Raksha!" said Father Wolf, lazily. "Our Frog has come back again – so wise that his own father must lick his feet; and what is a cut, more or less, on the head? Leave Men alone. "Baloo and Bagheera both echoed: "Leave Men alone."

Mowgli, his head on Mother Wolf's side, smiled contentedly, and said that, for his own part, he never wished to see, or hear, or smell Man again.

"But what," said Akela, cocking one ear – "but what if men do not leave thee alone, Little Brother?"

"We be *five*," said Gray Brother, looking round at the company, and snapping his jaws on the last word.

"We also might attend to that hunting," said Bagheera, with a little *switch-switch* of his tail, looking at Baloo. "But why think of men now, Akela?"

"For this reason," the Lone Wolf answered: "when that yellow chief's hide was hung up on the rock, I went back along our trail to the village, stepping in my tracks, turning aside, and lying down, to make a mixed trail in case one should follow us. But when I had fouled the trail so that I myself hardly knew it again, Mang, the Bat, came hawking between the trees, and hung up above me. Said Mang, "The village of the Man-Pack, where they cast out the Man-cub, hums like a hornet's nest."

"It was a big stone that I threw," chuckled Mowgli, who had often amused himself by throwing ripe paw-paws into a hornet's nest, and racing off to the nearest pool before the hornets caught him.

"I asked of Mang what he had seen. He said that the Red Flower blossomed at the gate of the village, and men sat about it carrying guns. Now I know, for I have good cause," – Akela looked down at the old dry scars on his flank and side, – "that men do not carry guns for pleasure. Presently, Little Brother, a man with a gun follows our trail – if, indeed, he be not already on it."

"But why should he? Men have cast me out. What more do they need?" said Mowgli angrily.

"Thou art a man, Little Brother," Akela returned. "It is not for *us*, the Free Hunters, to tell thee what thy brethren do, or why."

He had just time to snatch up his paw as the skinning-knife cut deep into the ground below. Mowgli struck quicker than an average human eye could follow but Akela was a wolf; and even a dog, who is very far removed from the wild wolf, his ancestor, can be waked out of deep sleep by a cart-wheel touching his flank, and can spring away unharmed before that wheel comes on.

"Another time," Mowgli said quietly, returning the knife to its sheath, "speak of the Man-Pack and of Mowgli in *two* breaths – not one."

"*Phff*! That is a sharp tooth," said Akela, snuffing at the blade's cut in the earth, "but living with the Man-Pack has spoiled thine eye, Little Brother. I could have killed a buck while thou wast striking."

Bagheera sprang to his feet, thrust up his head as far as he could, sniffed, and stiffened through every curve in his body. Gray Brother followed his example quickly, keeping a little to his left to get the wind that was blowing from the right, while Akela bounded fifty yards up wind, and, half-crouching, stiffened too. Mowgli looked on enviously. He could smell things as very few human beings could, but he had never reached the hair-trigger-like sensitiveness of a Jungle nose; and his three months in the smoky village had set him back sadly. However, he dampened his finger, rubbed it on his nose, and stood erect to catch the upper scent, which, though it is the faintest, is the truest.

"Man!" Akela growled, dropping on his haunches.

"Buldeo!" said Mowgli, sitting down. "He follows our trail, and yonder is the sunlight on his gun. Look!"

It was no more than a splash of sunlight, for a fraction of a second, on the brass clamps of the old Tower musket, but nothing in the Jungle winks with just that flash, except when the clouds race over the sky. Then a piece of mica, or a little pool, or even a highly-polished leaf will flash like a heliograph. But that day was cloudless and still.

"I knew men would follow," said Akela triumphantly. "Not for nothing have I led the Pack."

The four cubs said nothing, but crept down hill on their bellies, vanishing into the thorn and under-brush as a mole melts into grass.

"Whither go ye, and without word?" Mowgli called.

"*H'sh*! We roll his skull here before mid-day!" Gray Brother answered.

"Back! Back and wait! Man does not eat Man!" Mowgli shrieked.

"Who was a wolf but now? Who drove the knife at me for thinking he might be Man?" said Akela, as the four wolves turned back sullenly and dropped to heel.

"Am I to give reason for all I choose to, do?" said Mowgli furiously.

"That is Man! There speaks Man!" Bagheera muttered under his whiskers. "Even so did men talk round the King's cages at Oodeypore. We of the Jungle know that Man is wisest of all. If we trusted our ears we should know that of all things he is most foolish." Raising his voice, he added, "The Man-cub is right in this. Men hunt in packs. To kill one, unless we know what the others will do, is bad hunting. Come, let us see what this Man means toward us."

"We will not come," Gray Brother growled. "Hunt alone, Little Brother. *We* know our own minds. The skull would have been ready to bring by now."

Mowgli had been looking from one to the other of his friends, his chest heaving and his eyes full of tears. He strode forward to the wolves, and, dropping on one knee, said: "Do I not know my mind? Look at me!"

They looked uneasily, and when their eyes wandered, he called them back again and again, till their hair stood up all over their bodies, and they trembled in every limb, while Mowgli stared and stared.

"Now," said he, "of us five, which is leader?"

"Thou art leader, Little Brother," said Gray Brother, and he licked Mowgli's foot.

"Follow, then," said Mowgli, and the four followed at his heels with their tails between their legs.

"This comes of living with the Man-Pack," said Bagheera, slipping down after them. "There is more in the Jungle now than Jungle Law, Baloo."

The old bear said nothing, but he thought many things.

Mowgli cut across noiselessly through the Jungle, at right angles to Buldeo's path, till, parting the undergrowth, he saw the old man, his musket on his shoulder, running up the trail of overnight at a dog-trot.

You will remember that Mowgli had left the village with the heavy weight of Shere Khan's raw hide on his shoulders, while Akela and Gray Brother trotted behind, so that the triple trail was very clearly marked. Presently Buldeo came to where Akela, as you know, had gone back and mixed it all up. Then he sat down, and coughed and grunted, and made little casts round and about into the Jungle to pick it up again, and, all the time he could have thrown a stone over those who were watching him. No one can be so silent as a wolf when he does not care to be heard; and Mowgli, though the wolves thought he moved very clumsily, could come and go like a shadow. They ringed the old man as a school of porpoises ring a steamer at full speed, and as they ringed him they talked unconcernedly, for their speech began below the lowest end of the scale that untrained human beings can hear. [The other end is bounded by the high squeak of Mang, the Bat, which very many people cannot catch at all. From that note all the bird and bat and insect talk takes on.]

"This is better than any kill," said Gray Brother, as Buldeo stooped and peered and puffed. "He looks like a lost pig in the Jungles by the river. What does he say?" Buldeo was muttering savagely.

Mowgli translated. "He says that packs of wolves must have danced round me. He says that he never saw such a trail in his life. He says he is tired."

"He will be rested before he picks it up again," said Bagheera coolly, as he slipped round a tree-trunk, in the game of blindman's-buff that they were playing. "*Now*, what does the lean thing do?"

"Eat or blow smoke out of his mouth. Men always play with their mouths," said Mowgli; and the silent trailers saw the old man fill and light and puff at a water-pipe, and they took good note of the smell of the tobacco, so as to be sure of Buldeo in the darkest night, if necessary.

Then a little knot of charcoal-burners came down the path, and naturally halted to speak to Buldeo, whose fame as a hunter reached for at least twenty miles round. They all sat down and smoked, and Bagheera and the others came up and watched while Buldeo began to tell the story of Mowgli, the Devil-child, from one end to another, with additions and inventions. How he himself had really killed Shere Khan; and how Mowgli had turned himself into a wolf, and fought with him all the afternoon, and changed into a boy again and bewitched Buldeo's rifle, so that the bullet turned the corner, when he pointed it at Mowgli, and killed one of Buldeo's own buffaloes; and how the village, knowing him to be the bravest hunter in Seeonee, had sent him out to kill this Devil-child. But meantime the village had got hold of Messua and her husband, who were undoubtedly the father and mother of this Devil-child, and had barricaded them in their own hut, and presently would torture them to make them confess they were witch and wizard, and then they would be burned to death.

"When?" said the charcoal-burners, because they would very much like to be present at the ceremony.

Buldeo said that nothing would be done till he returned, because the village wished him to kill the Jungle Boy first. After that they would dispose of Messua and her husband, and divide their lands and buffaloes among the village. Messua's husband had some remarkably fine buffaloes, too.

It was an excellent thing to destroy wizards, Buldeo thought; and people who entertained Wolf-children out of the Jungle were clearly the worst kind of witches.

But, said the charcoal-burners, what would happen if the English heard of it? The English, they had heard, were a perfectly mad people, who would not let honest farmers kill witches in peace.

Why, said Buldeo, the head-man of the village would report that Messua and her husband had died of snake-bite. *That* was all arranged, and the only thing now was to kill the Wolf-child. They did not happen to have seen anything of such a creature?

The charcoal-burners looked round cautiously, and thanked their stars they had not; but they had no doubt that so brave a man as Buldeo would find him if any one could. The sun was getting rather low, and they had an idea that they would push on to Buldeo's village and see that wicked witch. Buldeo said that, though it was his duty to kill the Devil-child, he could not think of letting a party of unarmed men go through the Jungle, which might produce the Wolf-demon at any minute, without his escort. He, therefore, would accompany them, and if the sorcerer's child appeared – well, he would show them how the best hunter in Seeonee dealt with such things. The Brahmin, he said, had given him a charm against the creature that made everything perfectly safe.

"What says he? What says he? What says he?" the wolves repeated every few minutes; and Mowgli translated until he came to the witch part of the story, which was a little beyond him, and then he said that the man and woman who had been so kind to him were trapped.

" Man trapping Man!" exclaimed Bagheera.

"So he says. I cannot understand the talk. They are all mad together. What have Messua and her man to do with me that they should be put in a trap; and what is all this talk about the Red Flower? I must look to this. Whatever they would do to Messua they will not do till Buldeo returns. And so — " Mowgli thought hard, with his fingers playing round the haft of the skinning-knife, while Buldeo and the charcoal-burners went off very valiantly in single file.

"I go hot-foot back to the Man-Pack," Mowgli said at last.

"And those?" said Gray Brother, looking hungrily after the brown backs of the charcoal-burners.

"Sing them home," said Mowgli, with a grin; I do not wish them to be at the village gates till it is dark. Can ye hold them?"

Gray Brother bared his white teeth in contempt. We can head them round and round in circles like tethered goats – if I know Man."

"That I do not need. Sing to them a little, lest they be lonely on the road, and, Gray Brother, the song need not be of the sweetest. Go with them, Bagheera, and help make that song. When night is shut down, meet me by the village – Gray Brother knows the place."

"It is no light hunting to work for a Man-cub. When shall I sleep?" said Bagheera, yawning, though his eyes showed that he was delighted with the amusement. "Me to sing to naked men! But let us try."

He lowered his head so that the sound would travel, and cried a long, long, "Good hunting" – a midnight call in the afternoon, which was quite awful enough to begin with. Mowgli heard it rumble, and rise, and fall, and die off in a creepy sort of whine behind him, and laughed to himself as he ran through the Jungle. He could see the charcoal-burners huddled in a knot; old Buldeo's gun-barrel waving, like a banana-leaf, to every point of the compass at once. Then Gray Brother gave the *Ya-la-hi! Yalaha!* call for the buck-driving, when the Pack drives the nilgai, the big blue cow, before them, and it seemed to come from the very ends of the earth, nearer, and nearer, and nearer, till it ended in a shriek snapped off short. The other three answered, till even Mowgli could have vowed that the full Pack was in full cry, and then they all broke into the magnificent Morning-song in the Jungle, with every turn, and flourish, and grace-note that a deep-mouthed wolf of the Pack knows. This is a rough rendering of the song, but you must imagine what it sounds like when it breaks the afternoon hush of the Jungle: –

One moment past our bodies cast
No shadow on the plain;
Now clear and black they stride our track,
And we run home again.
In morning hush, each rock and bush
Stands hard, and high, and raw:
Then give the Call: "Good rest to all
*That keep The Jungle Law!"*

Now horn and pelt our peoples melt
In covert to abide;
Now, crouched and still, to cave and hill
Our Jungle Barons glide.
Now, stark and plain, Man's oxen strain,
That draw the new-yoked plough;
Now, stripped and dread, the dawn is red
*Above the lit talao**.

Ho! Get to lair! The sun's aflare
Behind the breathing grass:
And cracking through the young bamboo
The warning whispers pass.
By day made strange, the woods we range
With blinking eyes we scan;
While down the skies the wild duck cries
*"The Day – the Day to Man!"*

* A lake

The dew is dried that drenched our hide
Or washed about our way;
And where we drank, the puddled bank
Is crisping into clay.
The traitor Dark gives up each mark
Of stretched or hooded claw;
Then hear the Call: "Good rest to all
*That keep the Jungle Law!*"

But no translation can give the effect of it, or the yelping scorn the Four threw into every word of it, as they heard the trees crash when the men hastily climbed up into the branches, and Buldeo began repeating incantations and charms. Then they lay down and slept, for, like all who live by their own exertions, they were of a methodical cast of mind; and no one can work well without sleep.

Meantime, Mowgli was putting the miles behind him, nine to the hour, swinging on, delighted to find himself so fit after all his cramped months among men. The one idea in his head was to get Messua and her husband out of the trap, whatever it was; for he had a natural mistrust of traps. Later on, he promised himself, he would pay his debts to the village at large.

It was at twilight when he saw the well-remembered grazing-grounds, and the *dhâk-tree* where Gray Brother had waited for him on the morning that he killed Shere Khan. Angry as he was at the whole breed and community of Man, something jumped up in his throat and made him catch his breath when he looked at the village roofs. He noticed that every one had come in from the fields unusually early, and that, instead of getting to their evening cooking, they gathered in a crowd under the village tree, and chattered, and shouted.

"Men must always he making traps for men, or they are not content," said Mowgli. "Last night it was Mowgli – but that night seems many Rains ago. To-night it is Messua and her man. To-morrow, and for very many nights after, it will be Mowgli's turn again."

He crept along outside the wall till he came to Messua's hut, and looked through the window into the room. There lay Messua, gagged, and bound hand and foot, breathing hard, and groaning: her husband was tied to the gaily-painted bedstead. The door of the hut that opened into the street was shut fast, and three or four people were sitting with their backs to it.

Mowgli knew the manners and customs of the villagers very fairly. He argued that so long as they could eat, and talk, and smoke, they would not do anything else; but as soon as they had fed they would begin to be dangerous. Buldeo would be coming in before long, and if his escort had done its duty, Buldeo would have a very interesting tale to tell. So he went in through the window, and, stooping over the man and the woman, cut their thongs, pulling out the gags, and looked round the hut for some milk.

Messua was half wild with pain and fear (she had been beaten and stoned all the morning), and Mowgli put his hand over her mouth just in time to stop a scream. Her husband was only bewildered and angry, and sat picking dust and things out of his torn beard.

"I knew – I knew he would come," Messua sobbed at last. "Now do I *know* that he is my son!" and she hugged Mowgli to her heart. Up to that time Mowgli had been perfectly steady, but now he began to tremble all over, and that surprised him immensely.

"Why are these thongs? Why have they tied thee?" he asked, after a pause.

"To be put to the death for making a son of thee – what else?" said the man sullenly. "Look! I bleed."

Messua said nothing, but it was at her wounds that Mowgli looked, and they heard him grit his teeth when he saw the blood.

"Whose work is this?" said he. "There is a price to pay."

"The work of all the village. I was too rich. I had too many cattle. *Therefore* she and I are witches, because we gave thee shelter."

"I do not understand. Let Messua tell the tale."

"I gave thee milk, Nathoo; dost thou remember?" Messua said timidly. "Because thou wast my son, whom the tiger took, and because I loved thee very dearly. They said that I was thy mother, the mother of a devil, and therefore worthy of death."

"And what is a devil?" said Mowgli. "Death I have seen."

The man looked up gloomily, but Messua laughed. "See!" she said to her husband, "I knew – I said that he was no sorcerer. He is my son – my son!"

"Son or sorcerer, what good will that do us?" the man answered. "We be as dead already."

"Yonder is the road to the Jungle" – Mowgli pointed through the window. "Your hands and feet are free. Go now."
"We do not know the Jungle, my son, as – as thou knowest," Messua began. "I do not think that I could walk far."

"And the men and women would he upon our backs and drag us here again," said the husband.

"*H'm*!" said Mowgli, and he tickled the palm of his hand with the tip of his skinning-knife; "I have no wish to do harm to any one of this village – *yet*. But I do not think they will stay thee. In a little while they will have much else to think upon. Ah!" he lifted his head and listened to shouting and trampling outside. "So they have let Buldeo come home at last?"

"He was sent out this morning to kill thee," Messua cried. "Didst thou meet him?"

"Yes – we – I met him. He has a tale to tell and while he is telling it there is time to do much. But first I will learn what they mean. Think where ye would go, and tell me when I come back."

He bounded through the window and ran along again outside the wall of the village till he came within ear-shot of the crowd round the peepul-tree. Buldeo was lying on the ground, coughing and groaning, and every one was asking him questions. His hair had fallen about his shoulders; his hands and legs were skinned from climbing up trees, and he could hardly speak, but he felt the importance of his position keenly. From time to time he said something about devils and singing devils, and magic enchantment, just to give the crowd a taste of what was coming. Then he called for water.

"*Bah*!" said Mowgli. "Chatter – chatter! Talk, talk! Men are blood-brothers of the *Bandar-log*. Now he must wash his mouth with water; now he must blow smoke; and when all that is done he has still his story to tell. They are very wise people – men. They will leave no one to guard Messua till their ears are stuffed with Buldeo's tales. And – I grow as lazy as they!"

He shook himself and glided back to the hut. Just as he was at the window he felt a touch on his foot.

"Mother," said he, for he knew that tongue well, what dost *thou* here?"

"I heard my children singing through the woods, and I followed the one I loved best. Little Frog, I have a desire to see that woman who gave thee milk," said Mother Wolf, all wet with the dew.

"They have bound and mean to kill her. I have cut those ties, and she goes with her man through the Jungle."

"I also will follow. I am old, but not yet toothless." Mother Wolf reared herself up on end, and looked through the window into the dark of the hut.

In a minute she dropped noiselessly, and all she said was: "I gave thee thy first milk; but Bagheera speaks truth: Man goes to Man at the last."

"Maybe," said Mowgli, with a very unpleasant look on his face; "but to-night I am very far from that trail. Wait here, but do not let her see."

"*Thou* wast never afraid of *me*, Little Frog," said Mother Wolf, backing into the high grass, and blotting herself out, as she knew how.

"And now," said Mowgli cheerfully, as he swung into the hut again, "they are all sitting round Buldeo, who is saying that which did not happen. When his talk is finished, they say they will assuredly come here with the Red – with fire and burn you both. And then?"

"I have spoken to my man," said Messua. Khanhiwara is thirty miles from here, but at Khanhiwara we may find the English – "

"And what Pack are they?" said Mowgli.

"I do not know. They be white, and it is said that they govern all the land, and do not suffer people to burn or beat each other without witnesses. If we can get thither to-night, we live. Otherwise we die."

"Live, then. No man passes the gates to-night. But what does *he* do?" Messua's husband was on his hands and knees digging up the earth in one corner of the hut.

"It is his little money," said Messua. "We can take nothing else."

"Ah, yes. The stuff that passes from hand to hand and never grows warmer. Do they need it outside this place also?" said Mowgli.

The man stared angrily. "He is a fool, and no devil," he muttered. With the money I can buy a horse. We are too bruised to walk far, and the village will follow us in an hour."

"I say they will *not* follow till I choose; but a horse is well thought of, for Messua is tired." Her husband stood up and knotted the last of the rupees into his waist-cloth. Mowgli helped Messua through the window, and the cool night air revived her, but the Jungle in the starlight looked very dark and terrible.

"Ye know the trail to Khanhiwara?" Mowgli whispered.

They nodded.

'Good. Remember, now, not to be afraid. And there is no need to go quickly. Only – only there may be some small singing in the Jungle behind you and before."

"Think you we would have risked a night in the Jungle through anything less than the fear of burning? It is better to be killed by beasts than by men," said Messua's husband; but Messua looked at Mowgli and smiled.

"I say," Mowgli went on, just as though he were Baloo repeating an old Jungle Law for the hundredth time to a foolish cub – "I say that not a tooth in the Jungle is bared against you; not a foot in the Jungle is lifted against you. Neither man nor beast shall stay you till you come within eye-shot of Khanhiwara. There will be a watch about you." He turned quickly to Messua, saying, "*He* does not believe, but thou wilt believe?"

"Ay, surely, my son. Man, ghost, or wolf of the Jungle, I believe."

"*He* will be afraid when he hears my people singing. Thou wilt know and understand. Go now, and slowly, for there is no need of any haste. The gates are shut."

Messua flung herself sobbing at Mowgli's feet, but he lifted her very quickly with a shiver. Then she hung about his neck and called him every name of blessing she could think of, but her husband looked enviously across his fields, and said: "*If* we reach Khanhiwara, and I get the ear of the

English, I will bring such a lawsuit against the Brahmin and old Buldeo and the others as shall eat the village to the bone. They shall pay me twice over for my crops untilled and my buffaloes unfed. I will have a great justice."

Mowgli laughed. "I do not know what justice is, but – come next rains and see what is left." They went off toward the Jungle, and Mother Wolf leaped from her place of hiding. "Follow!" said Mowgli; "and look to it that all the Jungle knows these two are safe. Give tongue a little. I would call Bagheera." The long, low howl rose and fell, and Mowgli saw Messua's husband flinch and turn, half minded to run back to the hut.

"Go on," Mowgli called cheerfully. "I said there might be singing. That call will follow up to Khanhiwara. It is *Favour of the Jungle*."

Messua urged her husband forward, and the darkness shut down on them and Mother Wolf as Bagheera rose up almost under Mowgli's feet, trembling with delight of the night that drives the Jungle People wild.

"I am ashamed of thy brethren," he said, purring. "What? Did they not sing sweetly to Buldeo?" said Mowgli.

"Too well! Too well! They made even ME forget my pride, and, by the Broken Lock that freed me, I went singing through the Jungle as though I were out wooing in the spring! Didst thou not hear us?"

"I had other game afoot. Ask Buldeo if he liked the song. But where are the Four? I do not wish one of the Man-Pack to leave the gates to-night."

"What need of the Four, then?" said Bagheera, shifting from foot to foot, his eyes ablaze, and purring louder than ever. "I can hold them, Little Brother. Is it killing at last? The singing and the sight of the men climbing up the trees have made me very ready. Who is Man that we should care for him – the naked brown digger, the hairless and toothless, the eater of earth? I have followed him all day – at noon – in the white sunlight. I herded him as the wolves herd buck. I am Bagheera! Bagheera! Bagheera! As I dance with my shadow, so danced I with those men. Look!" The great panther leaped as a kitten leaps at a dead leaf whirling overhead, struck left and right into the empty air, that sang under the strokes, landed noiselessly, and leaped again and again, while the half purr, half growl gathered head as steam rumbles in a boiler. "I am Bagheera – in the jungle – in the night, and my strength is in me. Who shall stay my stroke? Man-cub, with one blow of my paw I could beat thy head flat as a dead frog in the summer!"

"Strike, then!" said Mowgli, in the dialect of the village, *not* the talk of the Jungle, and the human words brought Bagheera to a full stop, flung back on haunches that quivered under him, his head just at the level of Mowgli's. Once more Mowgli stared, as he had stared at the rebellious cubs, full into the beryl-green eyes till the red glare behind their green went out like the light of a lighthouse shut off twenty miles across the sea; till the eyes dropped, and the big head with them – dropped lower and lower, and the red rasp of a tongue grated on Mowgli's instep.

"Brother – Brother – Brother!" the boy whispered, stroking steadily and lightly from the neck along the heaving back. "Be still, be still! It is the fault of the night, and no fault of thine."

"It was the smells of the night," said Bagheera penitently.

"This air cries aloud to me. But how dost *thou* know?"

Of course the air round an Indian village is full of all kinds of smells, and to any creature who does nearly all his thinking through his nose, smells are as maddening as music and drugs are to human beings. Mowgli gentled the panther for a few minutes longer, and he lay down like a cat before a fire, his paws tucked under his breast, and his eyes half shut.

"Thou art of the Jungle and *not* of the Jungle," he said at last. "And I am only a black panther. But I love thee, Little Brother."

"They are very long at their talk under the tree," Mowgli said, without noticing the last sentence. "Buldeo must have told many tales. They should come soon to drag the woman and her man out of the trap and put them into the Red Flower. They will find that trap sprung. Ho! ho!"

"Nay, listen," said Bagheera. "The fever is out of my blood now. Let them find *me* there! Few would leave their houses after meeting me. It is not the first time I have been in a cage; and I do not think they will tie *me* with cords."

"Be wise, then," said Mowgli, laughing; for he was beginning to feel as reckless as the panther, who had glided into the hut.

"*Pah*!" Bagheera grunted. "This place is rank with Man, but here is just such a bed as they gave me to lie upon in the King's cages at Oodeypore. Now I lie down." Mowgli heard the strings of the cot crack under the great brute's weight. "By the Broken Lock that freed me, they will think they have caught big game! Come and sit beside me, Little Brother; we will give them 'good hunting' together!"

"No; I have another thought in my stomach. The Man-Pack shall not know what share I have in the sport. Make thine own hunt. I do not wish to see them."

"Be it so," said Bagheera. "Ah, now they come!"

The conference under the peepul-tree had been growing noisier and noisier, at the far end of the village. It broke in wild yells, and a rush up the street of men and women, waving clubs and bamboos and sickles and knives. Buldeo and the Brahmin were at the head of it, but the mob was close at their heels, and they cried, "The witch and the wizard! Let us see if hot coins will make them confess! Burn the hut over their heads! We will teach them to shelter wolf-devils! Nay, beat them first! Torches! More torches! Buldeo, heat the gun-barrels!"

Now here was some little difficulty with the latch of the door. It had been very firmly fastened, but the crowd tore it away bodily, and the light of the torches streamed into the room where, stretched at full length on the bed, his paws crossed and lightly hung down over one end, black as the Pit, and terrible as a demon, was Bagheera. There was one half-minute of desperate silence, as the front ranks of the crowd clawed and tore their way back from the threshold, and in that minute Bagheera raised his head and yawned – elaborately, carefully, and ostentatiously – as he would yawn when he wished to insult an equal. The fringed lips drew back and up; the red tongue curled; the lower jaw dropped and dropped till you could see half-way down the hot gullet; and the gigantic dog-teeth stood clear to the pit of the gums till they rang together, upper and under, with the snick of steel-faced wards shooting home round the edges of a safe. Next instant the street was empty; Bagheera had leaped back through the window, and stood at Mowgli's side, while a yelling, screaming torrent scrambled and tumbled one over another in their panic haste to get to their own huts.

"They will not stir till day comes," said Bagheera quietly.

"And now?"

The silence of the afternoon sleep seemed to have overtaken the village; but, as they listened, they could hear the sound of heavy grain-boxes being dragged over earthen floors and set down against doors. Bagheera was quite right; the village would not stir till daylight. Mowgli sat still, and thought, and his face grew darker and darker.

"What have I done?" said Bagheera, at last coming to his feet, fawning.

"Nothing but great good. Watch them now till the day. I sleep." Mowgli ran off into the Jungle, and dropped like a dead man across a rock, and slept and slept the day round, and the night back again.

When he waked, Bagheera was at his side, and there was a newly-killed buck at his feet. Bagheera watched curiously while Mowgli went to work with his skinning-knife, ate and drank, and turned over with his chin in his hands.

"The man and the woman are come safe within eye-shot of Khanhiwara," Bagheera said. "Thy lair mother sent the word back by Chil, the Kite. They found a horse before midnight of the night they were freed, and went very quickly. Is not that well?"

"That is well," said Mowgli.

"And thy Man-Pack in the village did not stir till the sun was high this morning. Then they ate their food and ran back quickly to their houses."

"Did they, by chance, see thee?"

"It may have been. I was rolling in the dust before the gate at dawn, and I may have made also some small song to myself. Now, Little Brother, there is nothing more to do. Come hunting with me and Baloo. He has new hives that he wishes to show, and we all desire thee back again as of old. Take off that look which makes even me afraid! The man and woman will not be put into the Red Flower, and all goes well in the Jungle. Is it not true? Let us forget the Man-Pack."

"They shall be forgotten in a little while. Where does Hathi feed to-night?"

"Where he chooses. Who can answer for the Silent One? But why? What is there Hathi can do which we cannot?"

"Bid him and his three sons come here to me."

"But, indeed, and truly, Little Brother, it is not – it is not seemly to say 'Come,' and 'Go,' to Hathi. Remember, he is the

Master of the Jungle, and before the Man-Pack changed the look on thy face, he taught thee the Master-words of the Jungle."

"That is all one. I have a Master-word for him now. Bid him come to Mowgli, the Frog: and if he does not hear at first, bid him come because of the Sack of the Fields of Bhuratpore."

"The Sack of the Fields of Bhuratpore," Bagheera repeated two or three times to make sure. "I go. Hathi can but be angry at the worst, and I would give a moon's hunting to hear a Master-word that compels the Silent One."

He went away, leaving Mowgli stabbing furiously with his skinning-knife into the earth. Mowgli had never seen human blood in his life before till he had seen, and – what meant much more to him – smelled Messua's blood on the thongs that bound her. And Messua had been kind to him, and, so far as he knew anything about love, he loved Messua as completely as he hated the rest of mankind. But deeply as he loathed them, their talk, their cruelty, and their cowardice, not for anything the Jungle had to offer could he bring himself to take a human life, and have that terrible scent of blood back again in his nostrils. His plan was simpler, but much more thorough; and he laughed to himself when he thought that it was one of old Buldeo's tales told under the peepul-tree in the evening that had put the idea into his head. "It *was* a Master-word," Bagheera whispered in his ear. "They were feeding by the river, and they obeyed as though they were bullocks. Look where they come now!"

Hathi and his three sons had arrived, in their usual way, without a sound. The mud of the river was still fresh on their flanks, and Hathi was thoughtfully chewing the green stem of a young plantain-tree that he had gouged up with his tusks. But every line in his vast body showed to Bagheera, who could see things when he came across them, that it was not the

Master of the Jungle speaking to a Man-cub, but one who was afraid coming before one who was not. His three sons rolled side by side, behind their father.

Mowgli hardly lifted his head as Hathi gave him "Good hunting." He kept him swinging and rocking, and shifting from one foot to another, for a long time before he spoke; and when he opened his mouth it was to Bagheera, not to the elephants.

"I will tell a tale that was told to me by the hunter ye hunted to-day," said Mowgli. "It concerns an elephant, old and wise, who fell into a trap, and the sharpened stake in the pit scarred him from a little above his heel to the crest of his shoulder, leaving a white mark." Mowgli threw out his hand, and as Hathi wheeled the moonlight showed a long white scar on his slaty side, as though he had been struck with a red-hot whip. "Men came to take him from the trap," Mowgli continued, "but he broke his ropes, for he was strong, and went away till his wound was healed. Then came he, angry, by night to the fields of those hunters. And I remember now that he had three sons. These things happened many, many Rains ago, and very far away – among the fields of Bhuratpore. What came to those fields at the next reaping, Hathi?"

"They were reaped by me and by my three sons," said Hathi.

"And to the ploughing that follows the reaping?" said Mowgli.

"There was no ploughing," said Hathi.

"And to the men that live by the green crops on the ground?" said Mowgli.

"They went away."

"And to the huts in which the men slept?" said Mowgli.

"We tore the roofs to pieces, and the Jungle swallowed up the walls," said Hathi.

"And what more?" said Mowgli.

"As much good ground as I can walk over in two nights from the east to the west, and from the north to the south as much as I can walk over in three nights, the Jungle took. We let in the Jungle upon five villages; and in those villages, and in their lands, the grazing-ground and the soft crop-grounds, there is not one man to-day who takes his food from the ground. That was the Sack of the Fields of Bhuratpore, which I and my three sons did; and now I ask, Man-cub, how the news of it came to thee?" said Hathi.

"A man told me, and now I see even Buldeo can speak truth. It was well done, Hathi with the white mark; but the second time it shall be done better, for the reason that there is a man to direct. Thou knowest the village of the Man-Pack that cast me out? They are idle, senseless, and cruel; they play with their mouths, and they do not kill the weaker for food, but for sport. When they are full-fed they would throw their own breed into the Red Flower. This I have seen. It is not well that they should live here any more. I hate them!"

"Kill, then," said the youngest of Hathi's three sons, picking up a tuft of grass, dusting it against his fore-legs, and throwing it away, while his little red eyes glanced furtively from side to side.

"What good are white bones to me?" Mowgli answered angrily. "Am I the cub of a wolf to play in the sun with a raw head? I have killed Shere Khan, and his hide rots on the Council Rock; but – but I do not know whither Shere Khan is gone, and my stomach is still empty. Now I will take that which I can see and touch. Let in the Jungle upon that village, Hathi!"

Bagheera shivered, and cowered down. He could understand, if the worst came to the worst, a quick rush down the village street, and a right and left blow into a crowd, or a crafty killing of men as they ploughed in the twilight; but this scheme for deliberately blotting out an entire village from the eyes of man and beast frightened him. Now he saw why

Mowgli had sent for Hathi. No one but the long-lived elephant could plan and carry through such a war.

"Let them run as the men ran from the fields of Bhuratpore, till we have the rain-water for the only plough, and the noise of the rain on the thick leaves for the pattering of their spindles – till Bagheera and I lair in the house of the Brahmin, and the buck drink at the tank behind the temple! Let in the Jungle, Hathi!"

"But I – but we have no quarrel with them, and it needs the red rage of great pain ere we tear down the places where men sleep," said Hathi swaying doubtfully.

"Are ye the only eaters of grass in the Jungle? Drive in your peoples. Let the deer and the pig and the nilgai look to it. Ye need never show a hand's-breadth of hide till the fields are naked. Let in the Jungle, Hathi!"

"There will be no killing? My tusks were red at the Sack of the Fields of Bhuratpore, and I would not wake that smell again."

"Nor I. I do not wish even their bones to lie on the clean earth. Let them go and find a fresh lair. They cannot stay here. I have seen and smelled the blood of the woman that gave me food – the woman whom they would have killed but for me. Only the smell of the new grass on their door-steps can take away that smell. It burns in my mouth. Let in the Jungle, Hathi!"

"Ah!" said Hathi. "So did the scar of the stake burn on my hide till we watched the villages die under in the spring growth. Now I see. Thy war shall be our war. We will let in the jungle!"

Mowgli had hardly time to catch his breath – he was shaking all over with rage and hate before the place where the elephants had stood was empty, and Bagheera was looking at him with terror.

"By the Broken Lock that freed me!" said the Black Panther at last. "Art *thou* the naked thing I spoke for in the Pack when all was young? Master of the Jungle, when my strength goes, speak for me – speak for Baloo – speak for us all! We are cubs before thee! Snapped twigs under foot! Fawns that have lost their doe!"

The idea of Bagheera being a stray fawn upset Mowgli altogether, and he laughed and caught his breath, and sobbed and laughed again, till he had to jump into a pool to make himself stop. Then he swam round and round, ducking in and out of the bars of the moonlight like the frog, his namesake.

By this time Hathi and his three sons had turned, each to one point of the compass, and were striding silently down the valleys a mile away. They went on and on for two days' march – that is to say, a long sixty miles – through the Jungle; and every step they took, and every wave of their trunks, was known and noted and talked over by Mang and Chil and the Monkey People and all the birds. Then they began to feed, and fed quietly for a week or so. Hathi and his sons are like Kaa, the Rock Python. They never hurry till they have to.

At the end of that time – and none knew who had started it – a rumour went through the Jungle that there was better food and water to be found in such and such a valley. The pig – who, of course, will go to the ends of the earth for a full meal – moved first by companies, scuffling over the rocks, and the deer followed, with the small wild foxes that live on the dead and dying of the herds; and the heavy-shouldered nilgai moved parallel with the deer, and the wild buffaloes of the swamps came after the nilgai. The least little thing would have turned the scattered, straggling droves that grazed and sauntered and drank and grazed again; but whenever there was an alarm some one would rise up and soothe them. At one time it would be Ikki the Porcupine, full of news of good feed just a little farther on; at another Mang would cry cheerily and flap down a glade to show it was all empty; or Baloo, his mouth full of roots, would shamble alongside a wavering line and half frighten, half romp it clumsily back to the proper road. Very many creatures broke back or ran away or lost interest, but very many were left to go forward. At the end of another ten days or so the situation was this. The deer and the pig and the nilgai were milling round and round in a circle of eight or ten miles radius, while the Eaters of Flesh skirmished round its edge. And the centre of that circle was the village, and round the village the crops were ripening, and in the crops sat men on what they call *machans* – platforms like pigeon-perches, made of sticks at the top of four poles – to scare away birds and other stealers. Then the deer were coaxed no more. The Eaters of Flesh were close behind them, and forced them forward and inward.

It was a dark night when Hathi and his three sons slipped down from the Jungle, and broke off the poles of the *machans* with their trunks; they fell as a snapped stalk of hemlock in bloom falls, and the men that tumbled from them heard the deep gurgling of the elephants in their ears. Then the vanguard of the bewildered armies of the deer broke down and flooded into the village grazing-grounds and the ploughed fields; and the sharp-hoofed, rooting wild pig came with them, and what the deer left the pig spoiled, and from time to time an alarm of wolves would shake the herds, and they would rush to and fro desperately, treading down the young barley, and cutting flat the banks of the irrigating channels. Before the dawn broke the pressure on the outside of the circle gave way at one point. The Eaters of Flesh had fallen back and left an open path to the south, and drove upon drove of buck fled along it. Others, who were bolder, lay up in the thickets to finish their meal next night.

But the work was practically done. When the villagers looked in the morning they saw their crops were lost. And that meant death if they did not get away, for they lived year in and year out as near to starvation as the Jungle was near to them. When the buffaloes were sent to graze the hungry brutes found that the deer had cleared the grazing-grounds, and so wandered into the Jungle and drifted off with their wild mates; and when twilight fell the three or four ponies that belonged to the village lay in their stables with their heads beaten in. Only Bagheera could have given those strokes, and only Bagheera would have thought of insolently dragging the last carcass to the open street.

The villagers had no heart to make fires in the fields that night, so Hathi and his three sons went gleaning among what was left; and where Hathi gleans there is no need to follow. The men decided to live on their stored seed-corn until the rains had fallen, and then to take work as servants till they could catch up with the lost year; but as the grain-dealer was thinking of his well-filled crates of corn, and the prices he would levy at the sale of it, Hathi's sharp tusks were picking out the corner of his mud-house, and smashing open the big wicker chest, *leeped** with cow-dung, where the precious stuff lay.

When that last loss was discovered, it was the Brahmin's turn to speak. He had prayed to his own Gods without answer. It might be, he said, that, unconsciously, the village had offended some one of the Gods of the Jungle, for, beyond doubt, the Jungle was against them. So they sent for the head-man of the nearest tribe of wandering Gonds – little, wise, and very black hunters, living in the deep Jungle, whose fathers came of the oldest race in India – the aboriginal owners of the land. They made the Gond welcome with what they had, and he stood on one leg, his bow in his hand, and two or three poisoned arrows stuck through his top-knot, looking half afraid and half contemptuously at the anxious villagers and their ruined fields. They wished to know whether

* Spread evenly with a palm.

his Gods – the Old Gods – were angry with them and what sacrifices should be offered. The Gond said nothing, but picked up a trail of the Karela, the vine that bears the bitter wild gourd, and laced it to and fro across the temple door in the face of the staring red Hindu image. Then he pushed with his hand in the open air along the road to Khanhiwara, and went back to his Jungle, and watched the Jungle People drifting through it. He knew that when the Jungle moves only white men can hope to turn it aside.

There was no need to ask his meaning. The wild gourd would grow where they had worshipped their God, and the sooner they saved themselves the better.

But it is hard to tear a village from its moorings. They stayed on as long as any summer food was left to them, and they tried to gather nuts in the Jungle, but shadows with glaring eyes watched them, and rolled before them even at mid-day; and when they ran back afraid to their walls, on the tree-trunks they had passed not five minutes before the bark would be stripped and chiselled with the stroke of some great taloned paw. The more they kept to their village, the bolder grew the wild things that gambolled and bellowed on the grazing-grounds by the Waingunga. They had no time to patch and plaster the rear walls of the empty byres that backed on to the Jungle; the wild pig trampled them down, and the knotty-rooted vines hurried after and threw their elbows over the new-won ground, and the coarse grass bristled behind the vines like the lances of a goblin army following a retreat. The unmarried men ran away first, and carried the news far and near that the village was doomed. Who could fight, they said, against the Jungle, or the Gods of the Jungle, when the very village cobra had left his hole in the platform under the peepul-tree? So their little commerce with the outside world shrunk as the trodden paths across the open grew fewer and fainter. At last the nightly trumpetings of Hathi and his three sons ceased to trouble them; for they had no more to be robbed of. The crop on the ground and the seed in the ground had been taken. The outlying fields were already losing their shape, and it was time to throw themselves on the charity of the English at Khanhiwara.

Native fashion, they delayed their departure from one day to another till the first Rains caught them and the unmended roofs let in a flood, and the grazing-ground stood ankle deep, and all life came on with a rush after the heat of the summer. Then they waded out – men, women, and children – through the blinding hot rain of the morning, but turned naturally for one farewell look at their homes.

They heard, as the last burdened family filed through the gate, a crash of falling beams and thatch behind the walls. They saw a shiny, snaky black trunk lifted for an instant, scattering sodden thatch. It disappeared, and there was another crash, followed by a squeal. Hathi had been plucking off the roofs of the huts as you pluck water-lilies, and a rebounding beam had pricked him. He needed only this to unchain his full strength, for of all things in the Jungle the wild elephant enraged is the most wantonly destructive. He kicked backward at a mud wall that crumbled at the stroke, and, crumbling, melted to yellow mud under the torrent of rain. Then he wheeled and squealed, and tore through the narrow streets, leaning against the huts right and left, shivering the crazy doors, and crumpling up the caves; while his three sons raged behind as they had raged at the Sack of the Fields of Bhuratpore.

"The Jungle will swallow these shells," said a quiet voice in the wreckage. "It is the outer wall that must lie down," and Mowgli, with the rain sluicing over his bare shoulders and arms, leaped back from a wall that was settling like a tired buffalo.

"All in good time," panted Hathi. "Oh, but my tusks were red at Bhuratpore; To the outer wall, children! With the head! Together! Now!"

The four pushed side by side; the outer wall bulged, split, and fell, and the villagers, dumb with horror, saw the savage, clay-streaked heads of the wreckers in the ragged gap. Then they fled, houseless and foodless, down the valley, as their village, shredded and tossed and trampled, melted behind them.

A month later the place was a dimpled mound, covered with soft, green young stuff; and by the end of the Rains there was the roaring jungle in full blast on the spot that had been under plough not six months before.

# MOWGLI'S SONG AGAINST PEOPLE

I will let loose against you the fleet-footed vines –
I will call in the Jungle to stamp out your lines!
The roofs shall fade before it,
The house-beams shall fall,
And the Karela, the bitter Karela,
Shall cover it all!

In the gates of these your councils my people shall sing,
In the doors of these your garners the Bat-folk shall cling;
And the snake shall be your watchman,
By a hearthstone unswept;
For the Karela, the bitter Karela,
Shall fruit where ye slept!

Ye shall not see my strikers; ye shall hear them and guess;
By night, before the moon-rise, I will send for my cess,
And the wolf shall be your herdsman
By a landmark removed,
For the Karela, the bitter Karela,
Shall seed where ye loved!

I will reap your fields before you at the hands of a host;
Ye shall glean behind my reapers, for the bread that is lost,
And the deer shall be your oxen
By a headland untilled,
For the Karela, the bitter Karela,
Shall leaf where ye build!

I have untied against you the club-footed vines,
I have sent in the Jungle to swamp out your lines.
The trees – the trees are on you!
The house-beams shall fall,
And the Karela, the bitter Karela,
Shall cover you all!

# THE UNDERTAKERS

When ye say to Tabaqui, "My Brother!" when ye call the
Hyena to meat,
Ye may cry the Full Truce with Jacala – the Belly that runs on
four feet.

*– Jungle Law*

*"Respect the aged!"*

"It was a thick voice – a muddy voice that would have made you shudder – a voice like something soft breaking in two. There was a quaver in it, a croak and a whine.

*"Respect the aged! O Companions of the River – respect the aged!"*

Nothing could be seen on the broad reach of the river except a little fleet of square-sailed, wooden-pinned barges, loaded with building-stone, that had just come under the railway bridge, and were driving down-stream. They put their clumsy helms over to avoid the sand-bar made by the scour of the bridge-piers, and as they passed, three abreast, the horrible voice began again:

*"O Brahmins of the River – respect the aged and infirm!"*

A boatman turned where he sat on the gunwale, lifted up his hand, said something that was not a blessing, and the boats creaked on through the twilight. The broad Indian river, that looked more like a chain of little lakes than a stream, was as smooth as glass, reflecting the sandy-red sky in mid-channel, but splashed with patches of yellow and dusky purple near and under the low banks. Little creeks ran into the river in the wet season, but now their dry mouths hung clear above water-line. On the left shore, and almost under the railway bridge, stood a mud-and-brick and thatch-and-stick village, whose main street, full of cattle going back to their byres, ran straight to the river, and ended in a sort of rude brick pier-head, where people who wanted to wash could wade in step by step. That was the Ghaut[1] of the village of Mugger[2]-Ghaut.

Night was falling fast over the fields of lentils and rice and cotton in the low-lying ground yearly flooded by the river; over the reeds that fringed the elbow of the bend, and the tangled jungle of the grazing-grounds behind the still reeds. The parrots and crows, who had been chattering and shouting over their evening drink, had flown inland to roost, crossing the out-going battalions of the flying-foxes; and cloud upon cloud of water-birds came whistling and "honking" to the cover of the reed-beds. There were geese, barrel-headed and black-backed, teal, widgeon, mallard, and sheldrake, with curlews, and here and there a flamingo. A lumbering Adjutant-crane brought up the rear, flying as though each slow stroke would be his last.

*"Respect the aged! Brahmins of the River – respect the aged!"*

The Adjutant half turned his head, sheered a little in the direction of the voice, and landed stiffly on the sand-bar below the bridge. Then you saw what a ruffianly brute he really was. His back view was immensely respectable, for he stood nearly six feet high, and looked rather like a very proper bald-headed parson. In front it was different, for his Ally Sloper-like head and neck had not a feather to them, and there was a horrible raw-skin pouch on his neck under his chin – a hold-all for the things his pick-axe beak might steal. His legs were long and thin and skinny, but he moved them delicately, and looked at them with pride as he preened down his ashy-gray tail-feathers, glanced over the smooth of his shoulder, and stiffened into "Stand at attention."

A mangy little Jackal, who had been yapping hungrily on a low bluff, cocked up his ears and tail, and scattered across the shallows to join the Adjutant.

1. River or a lake embankment.
2. A crocodile.

He was the lowest of his caste – not that the best of jackals are good for much, but this one was peculiarly low, being half a beggar, half a criminal – a cleaner-up of village rubbish-heaps, desperately timid or wildly bold, everlastingly hungry, and full of cunning that never did him any good.

"*Ugh*!" he said, shaking himself dolefully as he landed. "May the red mange destroy the dogs of this village! I have three bites for each flea upon me, and all because I looked – only looked, mark you – at an old shoe in a cow-byre. Can I eat mud?" He scratched himself under his left ear.

"I heard," said the Adjutant, in a voice like a blunt saw going through a thick board – "I *heard* there was a new-born puppy in that same shoe."

"To hear is one thing; to know is another," said the Jackal, who had a very fair knowledge of proverbs, picked up by listening to men round the village fires of an evening.

"Quite true. So, to make sure, I took care of that puppy while the dogs were busy elsewhere."

"They were *very* busy," said the Jackal. "Well, I must not go to the village hunting for scraps yet awhile. And so there truly was a blind puppy in that shoe?"

"It is here," said the Adjutant, squinting over his beak at his full pouch. "A small thing, but acceptable now that charity is dead in the world."

"*Ahai*! The world is iron in these days," wailed the Jackal. Then his restless eye caught the least possible ripple on the water, and he went on quickly: "Life is hard for us all, and I doubt not that even our excellent master, the Pride of the Ghaut and the Envy of the River —— "

"A liar, a flatterer, and a Jackal were all hatched out of the same egg," said the Adjutant to nobody in particular; for he was rather a fine sort of a liar on his own account when he took the trouble.

"Yes, the Envy of the River," the Jackal repeated, raising his voice. "Even he, I doubt not, finds that since the bridge has been built good food is more scarce. But on the other hand, though I would by no means say this to his noble face, he is so wise and so virtuous – as I, alas I am not — "

"When the Jackal says he is gray, how black must the Jackal be!" muttered the Adjutant. He could not see what was coming.

"That *his* food never fails, and in consequence — "

There was a soft grating sound, as though a boat had just touched in shoal water. The Jackal spun round quickly and faced (it is always best to face) the creature he had been talking about. It was a twenty-four-foot crocodile, cased in what looked like treble-riveted boiler-plate, studded and keeled and crested; the yellow points of his upper teeth just overhanging his beautifully fluted lower jaw. It was the blunt-nosed Mugger of Mugger-Ghaut, older than any man in the village, who had given his name to the village; the demon of the ford before the railway bridge, came – murderer, man-eater, and local fetish in one. He lay with his chin in the shallows, keeping his place by an almost invisible rippling of his tail, and well the Jackal knew that one stroke of that same tail in the water would carry the Mugger up the bank with the rush of a steam-engine.

"Auspiciously met, Protector of the Poor!" he fawned, backing at every word. "A delectable voice was heard, and we came in the hopes of sweet conversation. My tailless presumption, while waiting here, led me, indeed, to speak of thee. It is my hope that nothing was overheard."

Now the Jackal had spoken just to be listened to, for he knew flattery was the best way of getting things to eat, and the Mugger knew that the Jackal had spoken for this end, and the Jackal knew that the Mugger knew, and the Mugger knew that the Jackal knew that the Mugger knew, and so they were all very contented together.

The old brute pushed and panted and grunted up the bank, mumbling, "Respect the aged and infirm!" and all the time his little eyes burned like coals under the heavy, horny eyelids on the top of his triangular head, as he shoved his bloated barrel-body along between his crutched legs. Then he settled down, and, accustomed as the Jackal was to his ways, he could not help starting, for the hundredth time, when he saw how exactly the Mugger imitated a log adrift on the bar. He had even taken pains to lie at the exact angle a naturally stranded log would make with the water, having regard to the current of he season at the time and place. All this was only a matter of habit, of course, because the Mugger had come ashore for pleasure; but a crocodile is never quite full, and if the Jackal had been deceived by the likeness he would not have lived to philosophise over it.

"My child, I heard nothing," said the Mugger, shutting one eye. "The water was in my ears, and also I was faint with hunger. Since the railway bridge was built my people at my village have ceased to love me; and that is breaking my heart."

"Ah, shame!" said the Jackal. "So noble a heart, too! But men are all alike, to my mind."

"Nay, there are very great differences indeed," the Mugger answered gently. "Some are as lean as boat-poles. Others again are fat as young ja – dogs. Never would I causelessly revile men. They are of all fashions, but the long years have shown me that, one with another, they are very good. Men, women, and children – I have no fault to find with them. And remember, child, he who rebukes the World is rebuked by the World."

"Flattery is worse than an empty tin can in the belly. But that which we have just heard is wisdom," said the Adjutant, bringing down one foot.

"Consider, though, their ingratitude to this excellent one," began the Jackal tenderly.

"Nay, nay, not ingratitude!" the Mugger said. They do not think for others; that is all. But I have noticed, lying at my station below the ford, that the stairs of the new bridge are cruelly hard to climb, both for old people and young children. The old, indeed, are not so worthy of consideration, but I am grieved – I am truly grieved – on account of the fat children. Still, I think, in a little while, when the newness of the bridge has worn away, we shall see my people's bare brown legs bravely splashing through the ford as before. Then the old Mugger will be honoured again."

"But surely I saw Marigold wreaths floating off the edge of the Ghaut only this noon," said the Adjutant. Marigold wreaths are a sign of reverence all India over.

"An error – an error. It was the wife of the sweetmeat-seller. She loses her eyesight year by year, and cannot tell a log from me – the Mugger of the Ghaut. I saw the mistake when she threw the garland, for I was lying at the very foot of the Ghaut, and had she taken another step I might have shown her some little difference. Yet she meant well, and we must consider the spirit of the offering."

"What good are marigold wreaths when one is on the rubbish-heap?" said the Jackal, hunting for fleas, but keeping one wary eye on his Protector of the Poor.

"True, but they have not yet begun to make the rubbish-heap that shall carry *me*. Five times have I seen the river draw back from the village and make new land at the foot of the street. Five times have I seen the village rebuilt on the banks, and I shall see it built yet five times more. I am no faithless, fish-hunting Garial, I, at Kasi to-day and Prayag to-morrow, as the saying is, but the true and constant watcher of the ford. It is not for nothing, child, that the village bears my name, and "he who watches long," as the saying is, "shall at last have his reward."

"*I* have watched long – very long – nearly all my life, and my reward has been bites and blows," said the Jackal.

"Ho! ho! ho!" roared the Adjutant.

"In August was the Jackal born;
The Rains fell in September;
"Now such a fearful flood as this,"
Says he, "I can't remember!"

There is one very unpleasant peculiarity about the Adjutant. At uncertain times he suffers from acute attacks of the fidgets or cramp in his legs, and though he is more virtuous to behold than any of the cranes, who are all immensely respectable, he flies off into wild, cripple-stilt war-dances, half opening his wings and bobbing his bald head up and down; while for reasons best known to himself he is very careful to time his worst attacks with his nastiest remarks. At the last word of his song he came to attention again, ten times adjutaunter than before.

The Jackal winced, though he was full three seasons old, but you cannot resent an insult from a person with a beak a yard long, and the power of driving it like a javelin. The Adjutant was a most notorious coward, but the Jackal was worse.

"We must live before we can learn," said the Mugger, "and there is this to say: Little jackals are very common, child, but such a mugger as I am is not common. For all that, I am not proud, since pride is destruction; but take notice, it is Fate, and against his Fate no one who swims or walks or runs should say anything at all. I am well contented with Fate. With good luck, a keen eye, and the custom of considering whether a creek or a backwater has an outlet to it ere you ascend, much may be done."

"Once I heard that even the Protector of the Poor made a mistake," said the Jackal viciously.

"True; but there my Fate helped me. It was before I had come to my full growth – before the last famine but three (by the Right and Left of Gunga, how full used the streams to be in those days!). Yes, I was young and unthinking, and when the flood came, who so pleased as I? A little made me very happy then. The village was deep in flood, and I swam above the Ghaut and went far inland, up to the rice-fields, and they were deep in good mud. I remember also a pair of bracelets (glass they were, and troubled me not a little) that I found that evening. Yes, glass bracelets; and, if my memory serves me well, a shoe. I should have shaken off both shoes, but I was hungry. I learned better later. Yes. And so I fed and rested me; but when I was ready to go to the river again the flood had fallen, and I walked through the mud of the main street. Who but I? Came out all my people, priests and women and children, and I looked upon them with benevolence. The mud is not a good place to fight in. Said a boatman, "Get axes and kill him, for he is the Mugger of the ford." "Not so," said the Brahmin. "Look, he is driving the flood before him! He is the godling of the village." Then they threw many flowers at me, and by happy thought one led a goat across the road."

"How good – how very good is goat!" said the Jackal.

"Hairy – too hairy, and when found in the water more than likely to hide a cross-shaped hook. But that goat I accepted, and went down to the Ghaut in great honour. Later, my Fate sent me the boatman who had desired to cut off my tail with an axe. His boat grounded upon an old shoal which you would not remember."

"We are not *all* jackals here," said the Adjutant. Was it the shoal made where the stone-boats sank in the year of the great drouth – a long shoal that lasted three floods?"

"There were two," said the Mugger; "an upper and a lower shoal."

"Ay, I forgot. A channel divided them, and later dried up again," said the Adjutant, who prided himself on his memory.

"On the lower shoal my well-wisher's craft grounded. He was sleeping in the bows, and, half awake, leaped over to his waist – no, it was no more than to his knees – to push off. His empty boat went on and touched again below the next reach, as the river ran then. I followed, because I knew men would come out to drag it ashore."

"And did they do so?" said the Jackal, a little awe-stricken. This was hunting on a scale that impressed him.

"There and lower down they did. I went no farther, but that gave me three in one day – well-fed *manjhis* (boatmen) all, and, except in the case of the last (then I was careless), never a cry to warn those on the bank."

"Ah, noble sport! But what cleverness and great judgment it requires!" said the Jackal.

"Not cleverness, child, but only thought. A little thought in life is like salt upon rice, as the boatmen say, and I have thought deeply always. The Garial, my cousin, the fish-eater, has told me how hard it is for him to follow his fish, and how one fish differs from the other, and how he must know them all, both together and apart. I say that is wisdom; but, on the other hand, my cousin, the Garial, lives among his people. *my* people do not swim in companies, with their mouths out of the water, as Rewa does; nor do they constantly rise to the surface of the water, and turn over on their sides, like Mohoo and little Chapta; nor do they gather in shoals after flood, like Batchua and Chilwa."

"All are very good eating," said the Adjutant, clattering his beak.

"So my cousin says, and makes a great to-do over hunting them, but they do not climb the banks to escape his sharp nose. *my* people are otherwise. Their life is on the land, in the houses, among the cattle. I must know what they do, and what they are about to do; and adding the tail to the trunk, as the saying is, I make up the whole elephant. Is there a green branch and an iron ring hanging over a doorway? The old Mugger knows that a boy has been born in that house, and must some day come down to the Ghaut to play. Is a maiden to be married? The old Mugger knows, for he sees the men carry gifts back and forth; and she, too, comes down to the Ghaut to bathe before her wedding, and – he is there. Has the river changed its channel, and made new land where there was only sand before? The Mugger knows."

"Now, of what use is that knowledge?" said the Jackal. "The river has shifted even in my little life." Indian rivers are nearly always moving about in their beds, and will shift, sometimes, as much as two or three miles in a season, drowning the fields on one bank, and spreading good silt on the other.

"There is no knowledge so useful," said the Mugger, "for new land means new quarrels. The Mugger knows. Oho! the Mugger knows. As soon as the water has drained off, he creeps up the little creeks that men think would not hide a dog, and there he waits. Presently comes a farmer saying he will plant cucumbers here, and melons there, in the new land that the river has given him. He feels the good mud with his bare toes. Anon comes another, saying he will put onions, and carrots, and sugar-cane in such and such places. They meet as boats adrift meet, and each rolls his eye at the other under the big blue turban. The old Mugger sees and hears. Each calls the other "Brother," and they go to mark out the boundaries of the new land. The Mugger hurries with them from point to point, shuffling very low through the mud. Now they begin to quarrel! Now they say hot words! Now they pull turbans! Now they lift up their lathis (clubs), and, at last, one falls backward into the mud, and the other runs away.

When he comes back the dispute is settled, as the iron-bound bamboo of the loser witnesses. Yet they are not grateful to the Mugger. No, they cry "Murder!" and their families fight with sticks, twenty a-side. My people are good people – upland Jats – Malwais of the Bet. They do not give blows for sport, and, when the fight is done, the old Mugger waits far down the river, out of sight of the village, behind the kikar-scrub yonder. Then come they down, my broad-shouldered Jats – eight or nine together under the stars, bearing the dead man upon a bed. They are old men with gray beards, and voices as deep as mine. They light a little fire – ah! how well I know that fire! – and they drink tobacco, and they nod their heads together forward in a ring, or sideways toward the dead man upon the bank. They say the English Law will come with a rope for this matter, and that such a man's family will be ashamed, because such a man must be hanged in the great square of the Jail. Then say the friends of the dead, "Let him hang!" and the talk is all to do over again – once, twice, twenty times in the long night. Then says one, at last, "The fight was a fair fight. Let us take blood-money, a little more than is offered by the slayer, and we will say no more about it." Then do they haggle over the blood-money, for the dead was a strong man, leaving many sons. Yet before amratvela (Nectar-time, the sunrise) they put the fire to him a little, as the custom is, and the dead man comes to me, and *he* says no more about it. Aha! my children, the Mugger knows – the Mugger knows – and my Malwah Jats are a good people!"

"They are too close – too narrow in the hand for my crop," croaked the Adjutant. "They waste not the polish on the cow's horn, as the saying is; and, again, who can glean after a Malwai?"

"Ah, I – glean – *them*," said the Mugger.

"Now, in Calcutta of the South, in the old days," the Adjutant went on, "everything was thrown into the streets, and we picked and chose. Those wore dainty seasons. But to-day they keep their streets as clean as the outside of an egg, and my people fly away. To be clean is one thing; to dust, sweep, and sprinkle seven times a day wearies the very Gods themselves."

"There was a down-country jackal had it from a brother, who told me, that in Calcutta of the South all the jackals were as fat as otters in the Rains," said the Jackal, his mouth watering at the bare thought of it.

"Ah, but the white-faces are there – the English, and they bring dogs from somewhere down the river in boats – big fat dogs – to keep those same jackals lean," said the Adjutant.

"They are, then, as hard-hearted as these people? I might have known. Neither earth, sky, nor water shows charity to a jackal. I saw the tents of a white-face last season, after the Rains, and I also took a new yellow bridle to eat. The white-faces do not dress their leather in the proper way. It made me very sick."

"That was better than my case," said the Adjutant. "When I was in my third season, a young and a bold bird, I went down to the river where the big boats come in. The boats of the English are thrice as big as this village."

"He has been as far as Delhi, and says all the people there walk on their heads," muttered the Jackal. The Mugger opened his left eye, and looked keenly at the Adjutant.

"It is true," the big bird insisted. "A liar only lies when he hopes to be believed. No one who had not seen those boats *could* believe this truth."

"*That* is more reasonable," said the Mugger. "And then?"

"From the insides of this boat they were taking out great pieces of white stuff, which, in a little while, turned to water. Much split off, and fell about on the shore, and the rest they swiftly put into a house with thick walls. But a boatman, who laughed, took a piece no larger than a small dog, and threw it to me. I – all my people – swallow without reflection, and that piece I swallowed as is our custom. Immediately I was afflicted with an excessive cold which, beginning in my crop, ran down to the extreme end of my toes, and deprived me even of speech, while the boatmen laughed at me. Never have I felt such cold. I danced in my grief and amazement till I could recover my breath and then I danced and cried out against the falseness of this world; and the boatmen derided me till they fell down. The chief wonder of the matter, setting aside that marvellous coldness, was that there was nothing at all in my crop when I had finished my lamentings!"

The Adjutant had done his very best to describe his feelings after swallowing a seven-pound lump of Wenham Lake ice, off an American ice-ship, in the days before Calcutta made her ice by machinery; but as he did not know what ice was, and as the Mugger and the Jackal knew rather less, the tale missed fire.

"Anything," said the Mugger, shutting his left eye again – "*anything* is possible that comes out of a boat thrice the size of Mugger-Ghaut. My village is not a small one."

There was a whistle overhead on the bridge, and the Delhi Mail slid across, all the carriages gleaming with light, and the shadows faithfully following along the river. It clanked away into the dark again; but the Mugger and the Jackal were so well used to it that they never turned their heads.

"Is that anything less wonderful than a boat thrice the size of Mugger-Ghaut?" said the bird, looking up.

"I saw that built, child. Stone by stone I saw the bridge-piers rise, and when the men fell off (they were wondrous sure-footed for the most part – but *when* they fell) I was ready. After the first pier was made they never thought to look down the stream for the body to burn. There, again, I saved much trouble. There was nothing strange in the building of the bridge," said the Mugger.

"But that which goes across, pulling the roofed carts! That is strange," the Adjutant repeated.

It is, past any doubt, a new breed of bullock. Some day it will not be able to keep its foothold up yonder, and will fall as the men did. The old Mugger will then be ready."

The Jackal looked at the Adjutant and the Adjutant looked at the Jackal. If there was one thing they were more certain of than another, it was that the engine was everything in the wide world except a bullock. The Jackal had watched it time and again from the aloe hedges by the side of the line, and the Adjutant had seen engines since the first locomotive ran in India. But the Mugger had only looked up at the thing from below, where the brass dome seemed rather like a bullock's hump.

"M – yes, a new kind of bullock," the Mugger repeated ponderously, to make himself quite sure in his own mind; and "Certainly it is a bullock," said the Jackal.

"And again it might be – " began the Mugger pettishly.

"Certainly – most certainly," said the Jackal, without waiting for the other to finish.

"What?" said the Mugger angrily, for he could feel that the others knew more than he did. "What might it be? I never finished my words. You said it was a bullock."

"It is anything the Protector of the Poor pleases. I am *his* servant – not the servant of the thing that crosses the river."

"Whatever it is, it is white-face work," said the Adjutant; "and for my own part, I would not lie out upon a place so near to it as this bar."

"You do not know the English as I do," said the Mugger. "There was a white-face here when the bridge was built, and he would take a boat in the evenings and shuffle with his feet on the bottom-boards, and whisper: "Is he here? Is he there? Bring me my gun." I could hear him before I could see him – each sound that he made – creaking and puffing and rattling his gun, up and down the river. As surely as I had picked up one of his workmen, and thus saved great expense in wood for the burning, so surely would he come down to the Ghaut, and shout in a loud voice that he would hunt me, and rid the river of me – the Mugger of Mugger-Ghaut! *me*! Children, I have swum under the bottom of his boat for hour after hour, and heard him fire his gun at logs; and when I was well sure he was wearied, I have risen by his side and snapped my jaws in his face. When the bridge was finished he went away. All the English hunt in that fashion, except when they are hunted."

"Who hunts the white-faces?" yapped the Jackal excitedly.

"No one now, but I have hunted them in my time."

"I remember a little of that Hunting. I was young then," said the Adjutant, clattering his beak significantly.

"I was well established here. My village was being builded for the third time, as I remember, when my cousin, the Garial, brought me word of rich waters above Benares. At first I would not go, for my cousin, who is a fish-eater, does not always know the good from the bad; but I heard my people talking in the evenings, and what they said made me certain."

"And what did they say?" the Jackal asked.

"They said enough to make me, the Mugger of Mugger-Ghaut, leave water and take to my feet. I went by night, using the littlest streams as they served me; but it was the beginning of the hot weather, and all streams were low. I crossed dusty roads; I went through tall grass; I climbed hills in the moonlight. Even rocks did I climb, children – consider this well. I crossed the tail of Sirhind, the waterless, before I could find the set of the little rivers that flow Gunga-ward. I was a month's journey from my own people and the river that I knew. That was very marvellous!"

"What food on the way?" said the Jackal, who kept his soul in his little stomach, and was not a bit impressed by the Mugger's land travels.

"That which I could find – *cousin*," said the Mugger slowly, dragging each word.

Now you do not call a man a cousin in India unless you think you can establish some kind of blood-relationship, and as it is only in old fairy-tales that the Mugger ever marries a jackal, the Jackal knew for what reason he had been suddenly lifted into the Mugger's family circle. If they had been alone he would not have cared, but the Adjutant's eyes twinkled with mirth at the ugly jest.

"Assuredly, Father, I might have known," said the Jackal. A mugger does not care to be called a father of jackals, and the Mugger of Mugger-Ghaut said as much – and a great deal more which there is no use in repeating here.

"The Protector of the Poor has claimed kinship. How can I remember the precise degree? Moreover, we eat the same food. He has said it," was the Jackal's reply.

That made matters rather worse, for what the Jackal hinted at was that the Mugger must have eaten his food on that land-march fresh and fresh every day, instead of keeping it by him till it was in a fit and proper condition, as every self-respecting mugger and most wild beasts do when they can. Indeed, one of the worst terms of contempt along the River-bed is "eater of fresh meat." It is nearly as bad as calling a man a cannibal.

"That food was eaten thirty seasons ago," said the Adjutant quietly. "If we talk for thirty seasons more it will never come back. Tell us, now, what happened when the good waters were reached after thy most wonderful land journey. If we listened to the howling of every jackal the business of the town would stop, as the saying is.

The Mugger must have been grateful for the interruption, because he went on, with a rush:

"By the Right and Left of Gunga! When I came there never did I see such waters!"

"Were they better, then, than the big flood of last season?" said the Jackal.

"Better! That flood was no more than comes every five years – a handful of drowned strangers, some chickens, and a dead bullock in muddy water with cross-currents. But the season I think of, the river was low, smooth, and even, and, as the Garial had warned me, the dead English came down, touching each other. I got my girth in that season – my girth and my depth. From Agra, by Etawah and the broad waters by Allahabad — "

"Oh, the eddy that set under the walls of the fort at Allahabad!" said the Adjutant. "They came in there like widgeon to the reeds, and round and round they swung – thus!"

He went off into his horrible dance again, while the Jackal looked on enviously. He naturally could not remember the terrible year of the Mutiny they were talking about. The Mugger continued:

"Yes; by Allahabad one lay still in the slack-water and let twenty go by to pick one; and, above all, the English were not cumbered with jewellery and nose-rings and anklets as my women are nowadays. To delight in ornaments is to end with a rope for a necklace, as the saying is. All the muggers of all the rivers grew fat then, but it was my Fate to be fatter than them all. The news was that the English were being hunted into the rivers, and by the Right and Left of Gunga! We believed it was true. So far as I went south I believed it to he true; and I went down-stream beyond Monghyr and the tombs that look over the river."

"I know that place," said the Adjutant. "Since those days Monghyr is a lost city. Very few live there now."

"Thereafter I worked up-stream very slowly and lazily, and a little above Monghyr there came down a boatful of white-faces – alive! They were, as I remember, women, lying under a cloth spread over sticks, and crying aloud. There was never a gun fired at us, the watchers of the fords in those days. All the guns were busy elsewhere. We could hear them day and night inland, coming and going as the wind shifted. I rose up full before the boat, because I had never seen white-faces alive, though I knew them well – otherwise. A naked white child kneeled by the side of the boat, and, stooping over, must needs try to trail his hands in the river. It is a pretty thing to see how a child loves running water. I had fed that day, but there was yet a little unfilled space within me. Still, it was for sport and not for food that I rose at the child's hands. They were so clear a mark that I did not even look when I closed; but they were so small that though my jaws rang true – I am sure of that – the child drew them up swiftly, unhurt. They must have passed between tooth and tooth – those small white hands. I should have caught him cross-wise at the elbows; but, as I said, it was only for sport and desire to see new things that I rose at all. They cried out one after another in the boat, and presently I rose again to watch them. The boat was too heavy to push over. They were only women, but he who trusts a woman will walk on duckweed in a pool, as the saying is: and by the Right and Left of Gunga, that is truth!"

"Once a woman gave me some dried skin from a fish," said the Jackal. "I had hoped to get her baby, but horse-food is better than the kick of a horse, as the saying is. What did thy woman do?"

"She fired at me with a short gun of a kind I have never seen before or since. Five times, one after another" (the Mugger must have met with an old-fashioned revolver); "and

I stayed open-mouthed and gaping, my head in the smoke. Never did I see such a thing. Five times, as swiftly as I wave my tail – thus!"

The Jackal, who had been growing more and more interested in the story, had just time to leap back as the huge tail swung by like a scythe.

"Not before the fifth shot," said the Mugger, as though he had never dreamed of stunning one of his listeners – "not before the fifth shot did I sink, and I rose in time to hear a boatman telling all those white women that I was most certainly dead. One bullet had gone under a neck-plate of mine. I know not if it is there still, for the reason I cannot turn my head. Look and see, child. It will show that my tale is true."

"I?" said the Jackal. "Shall an eater of old shoes, a bone-cracker, presume, to doubt the word of the Envy of the River? May my tail be bitten off by blind puppies if the shadow of such a thought has crossed my humble mind! The Protector of the Poor has condescended to inform me, his slave, that once in his life he has been wounded by a woman. That is sufficient, and I will tell the tale to all my children, asking for no proof."

"Over-much civility is sometimes no better than over-much discourtesy, for, as the saying is, one can choke a guest with curds. I do *not* desire that any children of thine should know that the Mugger of Mugger-Ghaut took his only wound from a woman. They will have much else to think of if they get their meat as miserably as does their father."

"It is forgotten long ago! It was never said! There never was a white woman! There was no boat! Nothing whatever happened at all."

The Jackal waved his brush to show how completely everything was wiped out of his memory, and sat down with an air.

"Indeed, very many things happened," said the Mugger, beaten in his second attempt that night to get the better of his friend. (Neither bore malice, however. Eat and be eaten was fair law along the river, and the Jackal came in for his share of plunder when the Mugger had finished a meal.) "I left that boat and went up-stream, and, when I had reached Arrah and the back-waters behind it, there were no more dead English. The river was empty for a while. Then came one or two dead, in red coats, not English, but of one kind all – Hindus and Purbeeahs – then five and six abreast, and at last, from Arrah to the North beyond Agra, it was as though whole villages had walked into the water. They came out of little creeks one after another, as the logs come down in the Rains. When the river rose they rose also in companies from the shoals they had rested upon; and the falling flood dragged them with it across the fields and through the Jungle by the long hair. All night, too, going North, I heard the guns, and by day the shod feet of men crossing fords, and that noise which a heavy cart-wheel makes on sand under water; and every ripple brought more dead. At last even I was afraid, for I said: "If this thing happen to men, how shall the Mugger of Mugger-Ghaut escape?" There were boats, too, that came up behind me without sails, burning continually, as the cotton-boats sometimes burn, but never sinking."

"Ah!" said the Adjutant. "Boats like those come to Calcutta of the South. They are tall and black, they beat up the water behind them with a tail, and they — "

"Are thrice as big as my village. *My* boats were low and white; they beat up the water on either side of them" and were no larger than the boats of one who speaks truth should be. They made me very afraid, and I left water and went back to this my river, hiding by day and walking by night, when I could not find little streams to help me. I came to my village again, but I did not hope to see any of my people there. Yet they were ploughing and sowing and reaping, and going to and fro in their fields, as quietly as their own cattle."

"Was there still good food in the river?" said the Jackal.

"More than I had any desire for. Even I – and I do not eat mud – even I was tired, and, as I remember, a little frightened of this constant coming down of the silent ones. I heard my people say in my village that all the English were dead; but those that came, face down, with the current were *not* English, as my people saw. Then my people said that it was best to say nothing at all, but to pay the tax and plough the land. After a long time the river cleared, and those that came down it had been clearly drowned by the floods, as I could well see; and though it was not so easy then to get food, I was heartily glad of it. A little killing here and there is no bad thing – but even the Mugger is sometimes satisfied, as the saying is."

"Marvellous! Most truly marvellous!" said the Jackal. "I am become fat through merely hearing about so much good eating. And afterward what, if it be permitted to ask, did the Protector of the Poor do?"

"I said to myself – and by the Right and Left of Gunga! I locked my jaws on that vow – I said I would never go roving any more. So I lived by the Ghaut, very close to my own people, and I watched over them year after year; and they loved me so much that they threw marigold wreaths at my head whenever they saw it lift. Yes, and my Fate has been very kind to me, and the river is good enough to respect my poor and infirm presence; only — "

"No one is all happy from his beak to his tail," said the Adjutant sympathetically. "What does the Mugger of Mugger-Ghaut need more?"

"That little white child which I did not get," said the Mugger, with a deep sigh. "He was very small, but I have not forgotten. I am old now, but before I die it is my desire to try one new thing. It is true they are a heavy-footed, noisy, and foolish people, and the sport would be small, but I remember the old days above Benares, and, if the child lives, he will remember still. It may be he goes up and down the bank of some river, telling how he once passed his hands between the teeth of the Mugger of Mugger-Ghaut, and lived to make a tale of it. My Fate has been very kind, but that plagues me sometimes in my dreams – the thought of the little white child in the bows of that boat." He yawned, and closed his jaws. "And now I will rest and think. Keep silent, my children, and respect the aged."

He turned stiffly, and shuffled to the top of the sand-bar, while the Jackal drew back with the Adjutant to the shelter of a tree stranded on the end nearest the railway bridge.

"That was a pleasant and profitable life," he grinned, looking up inquiringly at the bird who towered above him. "And not once, mark you, did he think fit to tell me where a morsel might have been left along the banks. Yet I have told *him* a hundred times of good things wallowing down-stream. How true is the saying, "All the world forgets the Jackal and the Barber when the news has been told!" Now he is going to sleep! Arrh!"

"How can a jackal hunt with a Mugger?" said the Adjutant coolly. "Big thief and little thief; it is easy to say who gets the pickings."

The Jackal turned, whining impatiently, and was going to curl himself up under the tree-trunk, when suddenly he cowered, and looked up through the draggled branches at the bridge almost above his head.

"What now?" said the Adjutant, opening his wings uneasily.

"Wait till we see. The wind blows from us to them, but they are not looking for us – those two men."

"Men, is it? My office protects me. All India knows I am holy." The Adjutant, being a first-class scavenger, is allowed to go where he pleases, and so this one never flinched.

"I am not worth a blow from anything better than an old shoe," said the Jackal, and listened again. "Hark to that footfall!" he went on. "That was no country leather, but the shod foot of a white-face. Listen again! Iron hits iron up there! It is a gun! Friend, those heavy-footed, foolish English are coming to speak with the Mugger."

"Warn him, then. He was called Protector of the Poor by some one not unlike a starving Jackal but a little time ago."

"Let my cousin protect his own hide. He has told me again and again there is nothing to fear from the white-faces. They must be white-faces. Not a villager of Mugger-Ghaut would dare to come after him. See, I said it was a gun! Now, with good luck, we shall feed before daylight. He cannot hear well out of water, and – this time it is not a woman!"

A shiny barrel glittered for a minute in the moonlight on the girders. The Mugger was lying on the sand-bar as still as his own shadow, his fore-feet spread out a little, his head dropped between them, snoring like a – mugger.

A voice on the bridge whispered: "It's an odd shot – straight down almost – but as safe as houses. Better try behind the neck. Golly! what a brute! The villagers will be wild if he's shot, though. He's the deota [godling] of these parts."

"Don't care a rap," another voice answered; he took about fifteen of my best coolies while the bridge was building, and it's time he was put a stop to. I've been after him in a boat for weeks. Stand by with the Martini as soon as I've given him both barrels of this."

"Mind the kick, then. A double four-bore's no joke."

"That's for him to decide. Here goes!"

There was a roar like the sound of a small cannon (the biggest sort of elephant-rifle is not very different from some artillery), and a double streak of flame, followed by the stinging crack of a Martini, whose long bullet makes nothing of a crocodile's plates. But the explosive bullets did the work. One of them struck just behind the Mugger's neck, a hand's-breadth to the left of the backbone, while the other burst a little lower down, at the beginning of the tail. In ninety-nine cases out of a hundred a mortally-wounded crocodile can scramble to deep water and get away; but the Mugger of Mugger-Ghaut was literally broken into three pieces. He hardly moved his head before the life went out of him, and he lay as flat as the Jackal.

"Thunder and lightning! Lightning and thunder!" said that miserable little beast. "Has the thing that pulls the covered carts over the bridge tumbled at last?"

"It is no more than a gun," said the Adjutant, though his very tail-feathers quivered. "Nothing more than a gun. He is certainly dead. Here come the white-faces."

The two Englishmen had hurried down from the bridge and across to the sand-bar, where they stood admiring the length of the Mugger. Then a native with an axe cut off the big head, and four men dragged it across the spit.

"The last time that I had my hand in a Mugger's mouth," said one of the Englishmen, stooping down (he was the man who had built the bridge), "it was when I was about five years old – coming down the river by boat to Monghyr. I was a Mutiny baby, as they call it. Poor mother was in the boat, too, and she often told me how she fired dad's old pistol at the beast's head." "Well, you've certainly had your revenge on the chief of the clan – even if the gun has made your nose bleed. Hi, you boatmen! Haul that head up the bank, and we'll boil it for the skull. The skin's too knocked about to keep. Come along to bed now. This was worth sitting up all night for, wasn't it?"

Curiously enough, the Jackal and the Adjutant made the very same remark not three minutes after the men had left.

# A RIPPLE SONG

Once a ripple came to land
  In the golden sunset burning –
Lapped against a maiden's hand,
  By the ford returning.

*Dainty foot and gentle breast –*
Here, across, be glad and rest.
"Maiden, wait," the ripple saith.
*"Wait awhile, for I am Death!"*

"Where my lover calls I go –
  Shame it were to treat him coldly –
'Twas a fish that circled so,
  Turning over boldly."

*Dainty foot and tender heart,*
Wait the loaded ferry-cart.
"Wait, ah, wait!" the ripple saith;
*"Maiden, wait, for I am Death!"*

"When my lover calls I haste –
  Dame Disdain was never wedded!"
Ripple-ripple round her waist,
  Clear the current eddied.

*Foolish heart and faithful hand,*
*Little feet that touched no land.*
*Far away the ripple sped,*
*Ripple – ripple – running red!*

# THE KING'S ANKUS*

These are the Four that are never content, that have never
been filled since the Dews began –
Jacala's mouth, and the glut of the Kite, and the hands of the
Ape, and the Eyes of Man.

– *A Jungle Saying.*

Kaa, the big Rock Python, had changed his skin for perhaps the two-hundredth time since his birth; and Mowgli, who never forgot that he owed his life to Kaa for a night's work at Cold Lairs, which you may perhaps remember, went to congratulate him. Skin-changing always makes a snake moody and depressed till the new skin begins to shine and look beautiful. Kaa never made fun of Mowgli any more, but accepted him, as the other Jungle People did, for the Master of the Jungle, and brought him all the news that a python of his size would naturally hear. What Kaa did not know about the Middle Jungle, as they call it, – the life that runs close to the earth or under it, the boulder, burrow, and the tree-bole life, – might have been written upon the smallest of his scales.

That afternoon Mowgli was sitting in the circle of Kaa's great coils, fingering the flaked and broken old skin that lay all looped and twisted among the rocks just as Kaa had left it. Kaa had very courteously packed himself under Mowgli's broad, bare shoulders, so that the boy was really resting in a living arm-chair.

"Even to the scales of the eyes it is perfect," said Mowgli, under his breath, playing with the old skin. "Strange to see the covering of one's own head at one's own feet!"

"Ay, but I lack feet," said Kaa; "and since this is the custom of all my people, I do not find it strange. Does thy skin never feel old and harsh?"

* *Ankush,* an elephant-goad.

"Then go I and wash, Flathead; but, it is true, in the great heats I have wished I could slough my skin without pain, and run skinless."

"I wash, and *also* I take off my skin. How looks the new coat?"

Mowgli ran his hand down the diagonal checkerings of the immense back. "The Turtle is harder-backed, but not so gay," he said judgmatically. "The Frog, my name-bearer, is more gay, but not so hard. It is very beautiful to see – like the mottling in the mouth of a lily."

"It needs water. A new skin never comes to full colour before the first bath. Let us go bathe."

"I will carry thee," said Mowgli; and he stooped down, laughing, to lift the middle section of Kaa's great body, just where the barrel was thickest. A man might just, as well have tried to heave up a two-foot water-main; and Kaa lay still, puffing with quiet amusement. Then the regular evening game began – the Boy in the flush of his great strength, and the Python in his sumptuous new skin, standing up one against the other for a wrestling match – a trial of eye and strength. Of course, Kaa could have crushed a dozen Mowglis if he had let himself go; but he played carefully, and never loosed one-tenth of his power. Ever since Mowgli was strong enough to endure a little rough handling, Kaa had taught him this game, and it suppled his limbs as nothing else could. Sometimes Mowgli would stand lapped almost to his throat in Kaa's shifting coils, striving to get one arm free and catch him by the throat. Then Kaa would give way limply, and Mowgli, with both quick-moving feet, would try to cramp the purchase of that huge tail as it flung backward feeling for a rock or a stump. They would rock to and fro, head to head, each waiting for his chance, till the beautiful, statue-like group melted in a whirl of black-and-yellow coils and struggling legs and arms, to rise up again and again. "Now! now! now!" said Kaa, making feints with his head that even Mowgli's quick hand could not turn aside. "Look! I touch thee here, Little Brother! Here, and here! Are thy hands numb? Here again!"

The game always ended in one way – with a straight, driving blow of the head that knocked the boy over and over. Mowgli could never learn the guard for that lightning lunge, and, as Kaa said, there was not the least use in trying.

"Good hunting!" Kaa grunted at last; and Mowgli, as usual, was shot away half a dozen yards, gasping and laughing. He rose with his fingers full of grass, and followed Kaa to the wise snake's pet bathing-place – a deep, pitchy-black pool surrounded with rocks, and made interesting by sunken tree-stumps. The boy slipped in, Jungle-fashion, without a sound, and dived across; rose, too, without a sound, and turned on his back, his arms behind his head, watching the moon rising above the rocks, and breaking up her reflection in the water with his toes. Kaa's diamond-shaped head cut the pool like a razor, and came out to rest on Mowgli's shoulder. They lay still, soaking luxuriously in the cool water.

"It is *very* good," said Mowgli at last, sleepily. Now, in the Man-Pack, at this hour, as I remember, they laid them down upon hard pieces of wood in the inside of a mud-trap, and, having carefully shut out all the clean winds, drew foul cloth over their heavy heads and made evil songs through their noses. It is better in the Jungle."

A hurrying cobra slipped down over a rock and drank, gave them "Good hunting!" and went away.

"Sssh!" said Kaa, as though he had suddenly remembered something. "So the Jungle gives thee all that thou hast ever desired, Little Brother?"

"Not all," said Mowgli, laughing; "else there would be a new and strong Shere Khan to kill once a moon. Now, I could kill with my own hands, asking no help of buffaloes. And also I have wished the sun to shine in the middle of the Rains, and the Rains to cover the sun in the deep of summer; and also I have never gone empty but I wished that I had killed a goat; and also I have never killed a goat but I wished it had been buck; nor buck but I wished it had been nilgai. But thus do we feel, all of us."

"Thou hast no other desire?" the big snake demanded.

"What more can I wish? I have the Jungle, and the favour of the Jungle! Is there more anywhere between sunrise and sunset?"

"Now, the Cobra said — " Kaa began.

What cobra? He that went away just now said nothing. He was hunting."

"It was another."

"Hast thou many dealings with the Poison People? I give them their own path. They carry death in the fore-tooth, and that is not good – for they are so small. But what hood is this thou hast spoken with?"

Kaa rolled slowly in the water like a steamer in a beam sea. "Three or four moons since," said he, "I hunted in Cold Lairs, which place thou hast not forgotten. And the thing I hunted fled shrieking past the tanks and to that house whose side I once broke for thy sake, and ran into the ground."

"But the people of Cold Lairs do not live in burrows." Mowgli knew that Kaa was telling of the Monkey People.

"This thing was not living, but seeking to live," Kaa replied, with a quiver of his tongue. "He ran into a burrow that led very far. I followed, and having killed, I slept. When I waked I went forward."

"Under the earth?"

"Even so, coming at last upon a White Hood [a white cobra], who spoke of things beyond my knowledge, and showed me many things I had never before seen."

"New game? Was it good hunting?" Mowgli turned quickly on his side.

"It was no game, and would have broken all my teeth; but the White Hood said that a man – he spoke as one that knew the breed – that a man would give the breath under his ribs for only the sight of those things."

"We will look," said Mowgli. "I now remember that I was once a man."

"Slowly – slowly. It was haste killed the Yellow Snake that ate the sun. We two spoke together under the earth, and I spoke of thee, naming thee as a man. Said the White Hood (and he is indeed as old as the Jungle): 'it is long since I have seen a man. Let him come, and he shall see all these things, for the least of which very many men would die.' "

"That *must* be new game. And yet the Poison People do not tell us when game is afoot. They are an unfriendly folk."

"It is *not* game. It is – it is – I cannot say what it is."

"We will go there. I have never seen a White Hood, and I wish to see the other things. Did he kill them?"

"They are all dead things. He says he is the keeper of them all."

"Ah! As a wolf stands above meat he has taken to his own lair. Let us go."

Mowgli swam to bank, rolled on the grass to dry himself, and the two set off for Cold Lairs, the deserted city of which you may have heard. Mowgli was not the least afraid of the Monkey People in those days, but the Monkey People had the liveliest horror of Mowgli. Their tribes, however, were raiding in the Jungle, and so Cold Lairs stood empty and silent in the moonlight. Kaa led up to the ruins of the queens' pavilion that stood on the terrace, slipped over the rubbish, and dived down the half-choked staircase that went underground from the centre of the pavilion. Mowgli gave the snake-call, – "We be of one blood, ye and I," – and followed on his hands and knees. They crawled a long distance down a sloping passage that turned and twisted several times, and at last came to where the root of some great tree, growing thirty feet overhead, had forced out a solid stone in the wall. They crept through the gap, and found themselves in a large vault, whose domed roof had been also broken away by tree-roots so that a few streaks of light dropped down into the darkness.

"A safe lair," said Mowgli, rising to his firm feet, "but over-far to visit daily. And now what do we see?"

"Am I nothing?" said a voice in the middle of the vault; and Mowgli saw something white move till, little by little, there stood up the hugest cobra he had ever set eyes on – a creature nearly eight feet long, and bleached by being in darkness to an old ivory-white. Even the spectacle-marks of his spread hood had faded to faint yellow. His eyes were as red as rubies, and altogether he was most wonderful to see.

"Good hunting!" said Mowgli, who carried his manners with his knife, and that never left him.

"What of the city?" said the White Cobra, without answering the greeting. "What of the great, the walled city – the city of a hundred elephants and twenty thousand horses, and cattle past counting – the city of the King of Twenty Kings? I grow deaf here, and it is long since I heard their war-gongs."

"The Jungle is above our heads," said Mowgli. I know only Hathi and his sons among elephants. Bagheera has slain all the horses in one village, and – what is a King?"

"I told thee," said Kaa softly to the Cobra, – "I told thee, four moons ago, that thy city was not."

"The city – the great city of the forest whose gates are guarded by the King's towers – can never pass. They builded it before my father's father came from the egg, and it shall endure when my son's sons are as white as I! Salomdhi, son of Chandrabija, son of Viyeja, son of Yegasuri, made it in the days of Bappa Rawal. Whose cattle are *ye*?"

"It is a lost trail," said Mowgli, turning to Kaa. "I know not his talk."

"Nor I. He is very old. Father of Cobras, there is only the Jungle here, as it has been since the beginning."

"Then who is *he*," said the White Cobra, "sitting down before me, unafraid, knowing not the name of the King, talking our talk through a man's lips? Who is he with the knife and the snake's tongue?"

"Mowgli they call me," was the answer. "I am of the Jungle. The wolves are my people, and Kaa here is my brother. Father of Cobras, who art thou?"

"I am the Warden of the King's Treasure. Kurrun Raja builded the stone above me, in the days when my skin was dark, that I might teach death to those who came to steal. Then they let down the treasure through the stone, and I heard the song of the Brahmins my masters."

"Umm!" said Mowgli to himself. "I have dealt with one Brahmin already, in the Man-Pack, and – I know what I know. Evil comes here in a little."

"Five times since I came here has the stone been lifted, but always to let down more, and never to take away. There are no riches like these riches – the treasures of a hundred kings. But it is long and long since the stone was last moved, and I think that my city has forgotten."

"There is no city. Look up. Yonder are roots of the great trees tearing the stones apart. Trees and men do not grow together," Kaa insisted.

"Twice and thrice have men found their way here," the White Cobra answered savagely; "but they never spoke till I came upon them groping in the dark, and then they cried only a little time. But ye come with lies, Man and Snake both, and would have me believe the city is not, and that my wardship ends. Little do men change in the years. But I change never! Till the stone is lifted, and the Brahmins come down singing the songs that I know, and feed me with warm milk, and take me to the light again, I – I – *I*, and no other, am the Warden of the King's Treasure! The city is dead, ye say, and here are the roots of the trees? Stoop down, then, and take what ye will. Earth has no treasure like to these. Man with the snake's tongue, if thou canst go alive by the way that thou hast entered it, the lesser Kings will be thy servants!"

"Again the trail is lost," said Mowgli coolly. "Can any jackal have burrowed so deep and bitten this great White Hood? He is surely mad. Father of Cobras, I see nothing here to take away."

"By the Gods of the Sun and Moon, it is the madness of death upon the boy!" hissed the Cobra. "Before thine eyes close I will allow thee this favour. Look thou, and see what man has never seen before!"

"They do not do well in the Jungle who speak to Mowgli of favours," said the boy, between his teeth; "but the dark changes all, as I know. I will look, if that please thee."

He stared with puckered-up eyes round the vault, and then lifted up from the floor a handful of something that glittered.

"Oho!" said he, "this is like the stuff they play with in the Man-Pack: only this is yellow and the other was brown."

He let the gold pieces fall, and move forward. The floor of the vault was buried some five or six feet deep in coined gold and silver that had burst from the sacks it had been originally stored in, and, in the long years, the metal had packed and settled as sand packs at low tide. On it and in it and rising through it, as wrecks lift through the sand, were jewelled elephant-howdahs of embossed silver, studded with plates of hammered gold, and adorned with carbuncles and turquoises. There were palanquins and litters for carrying queens, framed and braced with silver and enamel, with jade-handled poles and amber curtain-rings; there were golden candlesticks hung with pierced emeralds that quivered on the branches; there were studded images, five feet high, of forgotten gods, silver with jewelled eyes; there were coats of mail, gold inlaid on steel, and fringed with rotted and blackened seed-pearls; there were helmets, crested and beaded with pigeon's-blood rubies; there were shields of lacquer, of tortoise-shell and rhinoceros-hide, strapped and bossed with red gold and set with emeralds at the edge; there were sheaves of diamond-hilted swords, daggers, and hunting-knives; there were golden sacrificial bowls and ladles, and portable altars of a shape that never sees the light of day; there were jade cups and bracelets; there were incense-burners, combs, and pots for perfume, henna, and eye-powder, all in embossed gold; there were nose-rings, armlets, head-bands, finger-rings, and girdles past any counting; there were belts, seven fingers broad, of square-cut diamonds and rubies, and wooden boxes, trebly clamped with iron, from which the wood had fallen away in powder, showing the pile of uncut star-sapphires, opals, cat's-eyes, sapphires, rubies, diamonds, emeralds, and garnets within.

The White Cobra was right. No mere money would begin to pay the value of this treasure, the sifted pickings of centuries of war, plunder, trade, and taxation. The coins alone were priceless, leaving out of count all the precious stones; and the dead weight of the gold and silver alone might be two or three hundred tons. Every native ruler in India to-day, however poor, has a hoard to which he is always adding; and though, once in a long while, some enlightened prince may send off forty or fifty bullock-cart loads of silver to be exchanged for Government securities, the bulk of them keep their treasure and the knowledge of it very closely to themselves.

But Mowgli naturally did not understand what these things meant. The knives interested him a little, but they did not balance so well as his own, and so he dropped them. At last he found something really fascinating laid on the front of a howdah half buried in the coins. It was a three-foot ankus, or elephant-goad – something like a small boat-hook. The top was one round, shining ruby, and eight inches of the handle below it were studded with rough turquoises close together, giving a most satisfactory grip. Below them was a rim of jade with a flower-pattern running round it – only the leaves were emeralds, and the blossoms were rubies sunk in the cool, green stone. The rest of the handle was a shaft of pure ivory, while the point – the spike and hook – was gold-inlaid steel with pictures of elephant-catching; and the pictures attracted Mowgli, who saw that they had something to do with his friend Hathi the Silent.

The White Cobra had been following him closely.

"Is this not worth dying to behold?" he said. Have I not done thee a great favour?"

"I do not understand," said Mowgli. "The things are hard and cold, and by no means good to eat. But this" – he lifted the ankus – "I desire to take away, that I may see it in the sun. Thou sayest they are all thine? Wilt thou give it to me, and I will bring thee frogs to eat?"

The White Cobra fairly shook with evil delight. "Assuredly I will give it," he said. "All that is here I will give thee – till thou goest away."

"But I go now. This place is dark and cold, and I wish to take the thorn-pointed thing to the Jungle."

"Look by thy foot! What is that there?"

Mowgli picked up something white and smooth. "It is the bone of a man's head," he said quietly. "And here are two more."

"They came to take the treasure away many years ago. I spoke to them in the dark, and they lay still."

"But what do I need of this that is called treasure? If thou wilt give me the ankus to take away, it is good hunting. If not, it is good hunting nonetheless. I do not fight with the Poison People, and I was also taught the Master-word of thy tribe."

"There is but one Master-word here. It is mine!"

Kaa flung himself forward with blazing eyes. "Who bade me bring the Man?" he hissed.

"I surely," the old Cobra lisped. "It is long since I have seen Man, and this Man speaks our tongue."

"But there was no talk of killing. How can I go to the Jungle and say that I have led him to his death?" said Kaa.

"I talk not of killing till the time. And as to thy going or not going, there is the hole in the wall. Peace, now, thou fat monkey-killer! I have but to touch thy neck, and the Jungle will know thee no longer. Never Man came here that went away with the breath under his ribs. I am the Warden of the Treasure of the King's City!"

"But, thou white worm of the dark, I tell thee there is neither king nor city! The Jungle is all about us!" cried Kaa.

"There is still the Treasure. But this can be done. Wait awhile, Kaa of the Rocks, and see the boy run. There is room for great sport here. Life is good. Run to and fro awhile, and make sport, boy!"

Mowgli put his hand on Kaa's head quietly.

"The white thing has dealt with men of the Man-Pack until now. He does not know me," he whispered. "He has asked for this hunting. Let him have it." Mowgli had been standing with the ankus held point down. He flung it from him quickly and it dropped crossways just behind the great snake's hood, pinning him to the floor. In a flash, Kaa's weight was upon the writhing body, paralysing it from hood to tail. The red eyes burned, and the six spare inches of the head struck furiously right and left.

"Kill!" said Kaa, as Mowgli's hand went to his knife.

"No," he said, as he drew the blade; "I will never kill again save for food. But look you, Kaa!" He caught the snake behind the hood, forced the mouth open with the blade of the knife, and showed the terrible poison-fangs of the upper jaw lying black and withered in the gum. The White Cobra had outlived his poison, as a snake will. "*Thuu*" ("It is dried up" – Literally, a rotted out tree-stump), said Mowgli; and motioning Kaa away, he picked up the ankus, setting the White Cobra free.

"The King's Treasure needs a new Warden, he said gravely. "Thuu, thou hast not done well. Run to and fro and make sport, Thuu!"

"I am ashamed. Kill me!" hissed the White Cobra.

"There has been too much talk of killing. We will go now. I take the thorn-pointed thing, Thuu, because I have fought and worsted thee."

"See, then, that the thing does not kill thee at last. It is Death! Remember, it is Death! There is enough in that thing to kill the men of all my city. Not long wilt thou hold it, Jungle Man, nor he who takes it from thee. They will kill, and kill, and kill for its sake! My strength is dried up, but the ankus will do my work. It is Death! It is Death! It is Death!"

Mowgli crawled out through the hole into the passage again, and the last that he saw was the White Cobra striking furiously with his harmless fangs at the stolid golden faces of the gods that lay on the floor, and hissing, "It is Death!"

They were glad to get to the light of day once more; and when they were back in their own Jungle and Mowgli made the ankus glitter in the morning light, he was almost as pleased as though he had found a bunch of new flowers to stick in his hair.

"This is brighter than Bagheera's eyes," he said delightedly, as he twirled the ruby. "I will show it to him; but what did the Thuu mean when he talked of death?"

"I cannot say. I am sorrowful to my tail's tail that he felt not thy knife. There is always evil at Cold Lairs – above ground or below. But now I am hungry. Dost thou hunt with me this dawn?" said Kaa.

"No; Bagheera must see this thing. Good hunting!" Mowgli danced off, flourishing the great ankus, and stopping from time to time to admire it, till he came to that part of the Jungle Bagheera chiefly used, and found him drinking after a heavy kill. Mowgli told him all his adventures from beginning to end, and Bagheera sniffed at the ankus between whiles. When Mowgli came to the White Cobra's last words, the Panther purred approvingly.

"Then the White Hood spoke the thing which is?" Mowgli asked quickly.

"I was born in the King's cages at Oodeypore, and it is in my stomach that I know some little of Man. Very many men would kill thrice in a night for the sake of that one big red stone alone."

"But the stone makes it heavy to the hand. My little bright knife is better; and – see! The red stone is not good to eat. Then *why* would they kill?"

"Mowgli, go thou and sleep. Thou hast lived among men, and — "

"I remember. Men kill because they are not hunting; – for idleness and pleasure. Wake again, Bagheera. For what use was this thorn-pointed thing made?"

Bagheera half opened his eyes – he was very sleepy – with a malicious twinkle.

"It was made by men to thrust into the head of the sons of Hathi, so that the blood should pour out. I have seen the like in the street of Oodeypore, before our cages. That thing has tasted the blood of many such as Hathi."

"But why do they thrust into the heads of elephants?"

"To teach them Man's Law. Having neither claws nor teeth, men make these things – and worse."

"Always more blood when I come near, even to the things the Man-Pack have made," said Mowgli disgustedly. He was getting a little tired of the weight of the ankus. "If I had known this, I would not have taken it. First it was Messua's blood on the thongs, and now it is Hathi's. I will use it no more. Look!"

The ankus flew sparkling, and buried itself point down thirty yards away, between the trees. "So my hands are clean of Death," said Mowgli, rubbing his palms on the fresh, moist earth. "The Thuu said Death would follow me. He is old and white and mad."

"White or black, or death or life, I am going to sleep, Little Brother. I cannot hunt all night and howl all day, as do some folk."

Bagheera went off to a hunting-lair that he knew, about two miles off. Mowgli made an easy way for himself up a convenient tree, knotted three or four creepers together, and in less time than it takes to tell was swinging in a hammock fifty feet above ground. Though he had no positive objection to strong daylight, Mowgli followed the custom of his friends, and used it as little as he could. When he waked among the very loud-voiced peoples that live in the trees, it was twilight once more, and he had been dreaming of the beautiful pebbles he had thrown away.

"At least I will look at the thing again," he said, and slid down a creeper to the earth; but Bagheera was before him. Mowgli could hear him snuffing in the half light.

"Where is the thorn-pointed thing?" cried Mowgli.

"A man has taken it. Here is the trail."

"Now we shall see whether the Thuu spoke truth. If the pointed thing is Death, that man will die. Let us follow."

"Kill first," said Bagheera. "An empty stomach makes a careless eye. Men go very slowly, and the Jungle is wet enough to hold the lightest mark."

They killed as soon as they could, but it was nearly three hours before they finished their meat and drink and buckled down to the trail. The Jungle People know that nothing makes up for being hurried over your meals.

"Think you the pointed thing will turn in the man's hand and kill him?" Mowgli asked. "The Thuu said it was Death."

"We shall see when we find," said Bagheera, trotting with his head low. "It is single-foot" (he meant that there was only one man), "and the weight of the thing has pressed his heel far into the ground."

"Hai! This is as clear as summer lightning," Mowgli answered; and they fell into the quick, choppy trail-trot in and out through the checkers of the moonlight, following the marks of those two bare feet.

"Now he runs swiftly," said Mowgli. "The toes are spread apart." They went on over some wet ground. "Now why does he turn aside here?"

"Wait!" said Bagheera, and flung himself forward with one superb bound as far as ever he could. The first thing to do when a trail ceases to explain itself is to cast forward without leaving, your own confusing foot-marks on the ground.

Bagheera turned as he landed, and faced Mowgli, crying, "Here comes another trail to meet him. It is a smaller foot, this second trail, and the toes turn inward."

Then Mowgli ran up and looked. "It is the foot of a Gond hunter," he said. "Look! Here he dragged his bow on the grass. That is why the first trail turned aside so quickly. Big Foot hid from Little Foot."

"That is true," said Bagheera. "Now, lest by crossing each other's tracks we foul the signs, let each take one trail. I am Big Foot, Little Brother, and thou art Little Foot, the Gond."

Bagheera leaped back to the original trail, leaving Mowgli stooping above the curious narrow track of the wild little man of the woods.

"Now," said Bagheera, moving step by step along the chain of footprints, "I, Big Foot, turn aside here. Now I hide me behind a rock and stand still," not daring to shift my feet. Cry thy trail, Little Brother."

"Now, I, Little Foot, come to the rock," said Mowgli, running up his trail. "Now, I sit down under the rock, leaning upon my right hand, and resting my bow between my toes. I wait long, for the mark of my feet is deep here."

"I also, said Bagheera, hidden behind the rock. I wait, resting the end of the thorn-pointed thing upon a stone. It slips, for here is a scratch upon the stone. Cry thy trail, Little Brother."

"One, two twigs and a big branch are broken here," said Mowgli, in an undertone. "Now, how shall I cry *that*? Ah! It is plain now. I, Little Foot, go away making noises and tramplings so that Big Foot may hear me." He moved away from the rock pace by pace among the trees, his voice rising in the distance as he approached a little cascade. "I – go – far – away – to – where – the – noise – of – falling-water –

covers – my – noise; and – here – I – wait. Cry thy trail, Bagheera, Big Foot!"

The panther had been casting in every direction to see how Big Foot's trail led away from behind the rock. Then he gave tongue:

"I come from behind the rock upon my knees, dragging the thorn-pointed thing. Seeing no one, I run. I, Big Foot, run swiftly. The trail is clear. Let each follow his own. I run!"

Bagheera swept on along the clearly-marked trail, and Mowgli followed the steps of the Gond. For some time there was silence in the Jungle.

"Where art thou, Little Foot?" cried Bagheera. Mowgli's voice answered him not fifty yards to the right.

"Um!" said the Panther, with a deep cough. "The two run side by side, drawing nearer!"

They raced on another half-mile, always keeping about the same distance, till Mowgli, whose head was not so close to the ground as Bagheera's, cried: "They have met. Good hunting – look! Here stood Little Foot, with his knee on a rock – and yonder is Big Foot indeed!"

Not ten yards in front of them, stretched across a pile of broken rocks, lay the body of a villager of the district, a long, small-feathered Gond arrow through his back and breast.

"Was the Thuu so old and so mad, Little Brother?" said Bagheera gently. "Here is one death, at least."

"Follow on. But where is the drinker of elephant's blood – the red-eyed thorn?"

"Little Foot has it – perhaps. It is single-foot again now."

The single trail of a light man who had been running quickly and bearing a burden on his left shoulder held on round a long, low spur of dried grass, where each footfall seemed, to the sharp eyes of the trackers, marked in hot iron.

Neither spoke till the trail ran up to the ashes of a camp-fire hidden in a ravine.

"Again!" said Bagheera, checking as though he had been turned into stone.

The body of a little wizened Gond lay with its feet in the ashes, and Bagheera looked inquiringly at Mowgli.

"That was done with a bamboo," said the boy, after one glance. "I have used such a thing among the buffaloes when I served in the Man-Pack. The Father of Cobras – I am sorrowful that I made a jest of him – knew the breed well, as I might have known. Said I not that men kill for idleness?"

"Indeed, they killed for the sake of the red and blue stones," Bagheera answered. "Remember, I was in the King's cages at Oodeypore."

"One, two, three, four tracks," said Mowgli, stooping over the ashes. "Four tracks of men with shod feet. They do not go so quickly as Gonds. Now, what evil had the little woodman done to them? See, they talked together, all five, standing up, before they killed him. Bagheera, let us go back. My stomach is heavy in me, and yet it heaves up and down like an oriole's nest at the end of a branch."

"It is not good hunting to leave game afoot. Follow!" said the panther. "Those eight shod feet have not gone far."

No more was said for fully an hour, as they worked up the broad trail of the four men with shod feet.

It was clear, hot daylight now, and Bagheera said, "I smell smoke."

Men are always more ready to eat than to run, Mowgli answered, trotting in and out between the low scrub bushes of the new Jungle they were exploring. Bagheera, a little to his left, made an indescribable noise in his throat.

"Here is one that has done with feeding," said he. A tumbled bundle of gay-coloured clothes lay under a bush, and round it was some spilt flour.

"That was done by the bamboo again," said Mowgli. "See! That white dust is what men eat. They have taken the kill from this one, – he carried their food, – and given him for a kill to Chil, the Kite."

"It is the third," said Bagheera.

"I will go with new, big frogs to the Father of Cobras, and feed him fat," said Mowgli to himself. "The drinker of elephant's blood is Death himself – but still I do not understand!"

"Follow!" said Bagheera.

They had not gone half a mile farther when they heard Ko, the Crow, singing the death-song in the top of a tamarisk under whose shade three men were lying. A half-dead fire smoked in the centre of the circle, under an iron plate which held a blackened and burned cake of unleavened bread. Close to the fire, and blazing in the sunshine, lay the ruby-and-turquoise ankus.

"The thing works quickly; all ends here," said Bagheera. "How did *these* die, Mowgli? There is no mark on any."

A Jungle-dweller gets to learn by experience as much as many doctors know of poisonous plants and berries. Mowgli sniffed the smoke that came up from the fire, broke off a morsel of the blackened bread, tasted it, and spat it out again.

"Apple of Death," he coughed. "The first must have made it ready in the food for *these*, who killed him, having first killed the Gond."

"Good hunting, indeed! The kills follow close," said Bagheera.

"Apple of Death" is what the Jungle call thorn-apple or *dhatura*, the readiest poison in all India.

"What now?" said the panther. "Must thou and I kill each other for yonder red-eyed slayer?"

"Can it speak?" said Mowgli in a whisper. Did I do it a wrong when I threw it away? Between us two it can do no wrong, for we do not desire what men desire. If it be left here, it will assuredly continue to kill men one after another as fast as nuts fall in a high wind. I have no love to men, but even I would not have them die six in a night."

"What matter? They are only men. They killed one another, and were well pleased," said Bagheera. "That first little woodman hunted well."

"They are cubs none the less; and a cub will drown himself to bite the moon's light on the water. The fault was mine," said Mowgli, who spoke as though he knew all about everything. "I will never again bring into the Jungle strange things – not though they be as beautiful as flowers. This" – he handled the ankus gingerly – "goes back to the Father of Cobras. But first we must sleep, and we cannot sleep near these sleepers. Also we must bury *him*, lest he run away and kill another six. Dig me a hole under that tree."

"But, Little Brother," said Bagheera, moving off to the spot, "I tell thee it is no fault of the blood-drinker. The trouble is with the men."

"All one," said Mowgli. "Dig the hole deep. When we wake I will take him up and carry him back."

* * * * *

Two nights later, as the White Cobra sat mourning in the darkness of the vault, ashamed, and robbed, and alone, the turquoise ankus whirled through the hole in the wall, and clashed on the floor of golden coins.

"Father of Cobras," said Mowgli (he was careful to keep the other side of the wall), "get thee a young and ripe one of thine own people to help thee guard the King's Treasure, so that no man may come away alive any more."

"Ah-ha! It returns, then. I said the thing was Death. How comes it that thou art still alive?" the old Cobra mumbled, twining lovingly round the ankus-haft.

"By the Bull that bought me, I do not know! That thing has killed six times in a night. Let him go out no more."

# THE SONG OF THE LITTLE HUNTER

Ere Mor the Peacock flutters, ere the Monkey People cry,
Ere Chil the Kite swoops down a furlong sheer,
Through the Jungle very softly flits a shadow and a sigh –
He is Fear, O Little Hunter, he is Fear!
Very softly down the glade runs a waiting, watching shade,
And the whisper spreads and widens far and near;
And the sweat is on thy brow, for he passes even now –
He is Fear, O Little Hunter, he is Fear!

Ere the moon has climbed the mountain, ere the rocks are ribbed with light,
When the downward-dipping trails are dank and drear,
Comes a breathing hard behind thee – *snuffle-snuffle* through the night –
It is Fear, O Little Hunter, it is Fear!
On thy knees and draw the bow; bid the shrilling arrow go;
In the empty, mocking thicket plunge the spear;
But thy hands are loosed and weak, and the blood has left thy cheek—
It is Fear, O Little Hunter, it is Fear!
When the heat-cloud sucks the tempest, when the slivered pine-trees fall,
When the blinding, blaring rain-squalls lash and veer;
Through the war-gongs of the thunder rings a voice more loud than all –
It is Fear, O Little Hunter, it is Fear!

Now the spates are banked and deep; now the footless boulders leap –

Now the lightning shows each littlest leaf-rib clear –
But thy throat is shut and dried, and thy heart against thy side
Hammers: Fear, O Little Hunter – this is Fear!

# QUIQUERN*

The People of the Eastern Ice, they are melting like the snow –
They beg for coffee and sugar; they go where the white men go.
The People of the Western Ice, they learn to steal and fight;
"They sell their furs to the trading-post: they sell their souls to the white.
The People of the Southern Ice, they trade with the whaler's crew;
Their women have many ribbons, but their tents are torn and few.
But the People of the Elder Ice, beyond the white man's ken –
Their spears are made of the narwhal-horn, and they are the last of the Men!

– *A translation of an Arctic folklore*

* * * * *

"HE HAS opened his eyes. Look!"

"Put him in the skin again. He will be a strong dog. On the fourth month we will name him."

"For whom?" said Amoraq.

Kadlu's eye rolled round the skin-lined snow-house till it fell on fourteen-year-old Kotuku sitting on the sleeping-bench, making a button out of walrus ivory. "Name him for me," said Kotuku, with a grin. "I shall need him one day."

Kadlu grinned back till his eyes were almost buried in the fat of his flat cheeks, and nodded to Amoraq, while the puppy's

* A legendary phantom dog appearing in the arctic fables.

fierce mother whined to see her baby wriggling far out of reach in the little sealskin pouch hung above the warmth of the blubber-lamp. Kotuku went on with his carving, and Kadlu threw a rolled bundle of leather dog-harnesses into a tiny little room that opened from one side of the house, slipped off his heavy deerskin hunting-suit, put it into a whalebone-net that hung above another lamp, and dropped down on the sleeping-bench to whittle at a piece of frozen seal-meat till Amoraq, his wife, should bring the regular dinner of boiled meat and blood-soup. He had been out since early dawn at the seal-holes, eight miles away, and had come home with three big seal. Half-way down the long, low snow passage or tunnel that led to the inner door of the house you could hear snappings and yelpings, as the dogs of his sleigh-team, released from the day's work, scuffled for warm places.

When the yelpings grew too loud Kotuku lazily rolled off the sleeping-bench, and picked up a whip with an eighteen-inch handle of springy whalebone, and twenty-five feet of heavy, plaited thong. He dived into the passage, where it sounded as though all the dogs were eating him alive; but that was no more than their regular grace before meals. When he crawled out at the far end, half a dozen furry heads followed him with their eyes as he went to a sort of gallows of whale-jawbones, from which the dog's meat was hung; split off the frozen stuff in big lumps with a broad-headed spear; and stood, his whip in one hand and the meat in the other. Each beast was called by name, the weakest first, and woe betide any dog that moved out of his turn; for the tapering lash would shoot out like thonged lightning, and flick away an inch or so of hair and hide. Each beast growled, snapped, choked once over his portion, and hurried back to the protection of the passage, while the boy stood upon the snow under the blazing Northern Lights and dealt out justice. The last to be served was the big black leader of the team, who kept order when the dogs were harnessed; and to him Kotuku gave a double allowance of meat as well as an extra crack of the whip.

"Ah!" said Kotuku, coiling up the lash," I have a little one over the lamp that will make a great many howlings. *Sarpok*! Get in!"

He crawled back over the huddled dogs, dusted the dry snow from his furs with the whalebone beater that Amoraq kept by the door, tapped the skin-lined roof of the house to shake off any icicles that might have fallen from the dome of snow above, and curled up on the bench. The dogs in the passage snored and whined in their sleep, the boy-baby in Amoraq's deep fur hood kicked and choked and gurgled, and the mother of the newly-named puppy lay at Kotuku's side, her eyes fixed on the bundle of sealskin, warm and safe above the broad yellow flame of the lamp.

And all this happened far away to the north, beyond Labrador, beyond Hudson's Strait, where the great tides heave the ice about, north of Melville Peninsula – north even of the narrow Fury and Hecla Straits – on the north shore of Baffin Land, where Bylot's Island stands above the ice of Lancaster Sound like a pudding-bowl wrong side up. North of Lancaster Sound there is little we know anything about, except North Devon and Ellesmere Land; but even there live a few scattered people, next door, as it were, to the very Pole.[1]

Kadlu was an Inuit,[2] – what you call an Esquimau, – and his tribe, some thirty persons all told, belonged to the Tununirmiut – "the country lying at the back of something." In the maps that desolate coast is written Navy Board Inlet, but the Inuit name is best, because the country lies at the very back of everything in the world. For nine months of the year there is only ice and snow, and gale after gale, with a cold that no one can realise who has never seen the thermometer even

1 The author has chosen the Arctic archipelago territory between Canada and Greenland, with its towering mountains and vast ice fields, for this story.
2 The Eskimo people of Canada.

at zero. For six months of those nine it is dark; and that is what makes it so horrible. In the three months of the summer it only freezes every other day and every night, and then the snow begins to weep off on the southerly slopes, and a few ground-willows put out their woolly buds, a tiny stonecrop or so makes believe to blossom, beaches of fine gravel and rounded stones run down to the open sea, and polished boulders and streaked rocks lift up above the granulated snow. But all that is gone in a few weeks, and the wild winter locks down again on the land; while at sea the ice tears up and down the offing, jamming and ramming, and splitting and hitting, and pounding and grounding, till it all freezes together, ten feet thick, from the land outward to deep water.

In the winter Kadlu would follow the seal to the edge of this land-ice, and spear them as they came up to breathe at their blow-holes. The seal must have open water to live and catch fish in, and in the deep of winter the ice would sometimes run eighty miles without a break from the nearest shore. In the spring he and his people retreated from the floes to the rocky mainland, where they put up tents of skins, and snared the sea-birds, or speared the young seal basking on the beaches. Later, they would go south into Baffin Land after the reindeer, and to get their year's store of salmon from the hundreds of streams and lakes of the interior; coming back north in September or October for the musk-ox hunting and the regular winter sealery. This travelling was done with dog-sleighs, twenty and thirty miles a day, or sometimes down the coast in big skin "woman-boats," when the dogs and the babies lay among the feet of the rowers, and the women sang songs as they glided from cape to cape over the glassy, cold waters. All the luxuries that the Tununirmiut knew came from the south – driftwood for sleigh-runners, rod-iron for harpoon-tips, steel knives, tin kettles that cooked food much better than the old soap-stone affairs, flint and steel, and even matches, as well as coloured ribbons for the women's hair, little cheap mirrors, and red cloth for the edging of deerskin dress-jackets. Kadlu traded the rich, creamy, twisted narwhal horn and musk-ox teeth (these are just as valuable as pearls) to the Southern Inuit, and they, in turn, traded with the whalers and the missionary-posts of Exeter and Cumberland Sounds; and so the chain went on, till a kettle picked up by a ship's cook in the Bhendy Bazaar* might end its days over a blubber-lamp somewhere on the cool side of the Arctic Circle.

Kadlu, being a good hunter, was rich in iron harpoons, snow-knives, bird-darts, and all the other things that make life easy up there in the great cold; and he was the head of his tribe, or, as they say, "the man who knows all about it by practice." This did not give him any authority, except now and then he could advise his friends to change their hunting-grounds; but Kotuku used it to domineer a little, in the lazy, fat Inuit fashion, over the other boys, when they came out at night to play ball in the moonlight, or to sing the Child's Song to the Aurora Borealis.

But at fourteen an Inuit feels himself a man, and Kotuku was tired of making snares for wild-fowl and kit-foxes, and most tired of all of helping the women to chew seal-and deer-skins (that supples them as nothing else can) the long day through, while the men were out hunting. He wanted to go into the *quaggi*, the Singing-House, when the hunters gathered there for their mysteries, and the *angekok*, the sorcerer, frightened them into the most delightful fits after the lamps were put out, and you could hear the Spirit of the Reindeer stamping on the roof; and when a spear was thrust out into the open black night it came back covered with hot blood. He wanted to throw his big boots into the net with the tired air of the head of a family, and to gamble with the hunters when they dropped in of an evening and played a sort of home-made roulette with a tin pot and a nail. There were

* A crowded market-place in Mumbai, India.

hundreds of things that he wanted to do, but the grown men laughed at him and said, "Wait till you have been in the buckle, Kotuku. Hunting is not *all* catching."

Now that his father had named a puppy for him, things looked brighter. An Inuit does not waste a good dog on his son till the boy knows something of dog-driving; and Kotuku was more than sure that he knew more than everything.

If the puppy had not had an iron constitution he would have died from over-stuffing and over-handling. Kotuku made him a tiny harness with a trace to it, and hauled him all over the house-floor, shouting: "*Aua! Ja aua*!" (Go to the right). *Choiachoi! Ja choiachoi*!" (Go to the left). "*Ohaha*!" (Stop). The puppy did not like it at all, but being fished for in this way was pure happiness beside being put to the sleigh for the first time. He just sat down on the snow, and played with the seal-hide trace that ran from his harness to the *pitu*, the big thong in the bows of the sleigh. Then the team started, and the puppy found the heavy ten-foot sleigh running up his back, and dragging him along the snow, while Kotuku laughed till the tears ran down his face. There followed days and days of the cruel whip that hisses like the wind over ice, and his companions all bit him because he did not know his work, and the harness chafed him, and he was dot allowed to sleep with Kotuku any more, but had to take the coldest place in the passage. It was a sad time for the puppy.

The boy learned, too, as fast as the dog; though a dog-sleigh is a heart-breaking thing to manage. Each beast is harnessed, the weakest nearest to the driver, by his own separate trace, which runs under his left fore-leg to the main thong, where it is fastened by a sort of button and loop which can be slipped by a turn of the wrist, thus freeing one dog at a time. This is very necessary, because young dogs often get the trace between their hind legs, where it cuts to the bone. And they one and all *will* go visiting their friends as they run, jumping in and out among the traces. Then they fight, and the result is more mixed than a wet fishing-line next morning. A great deal of trouble can be avoided by scientific use of the whip. Every Inuit boy prides himself as being a master of the long lash; but it is easy to flick at a mark on the ground, and difficult to lean forward and catch a shirking dog just behind the shoulders when the sleigh is going at full speed. If you call one dog's name for "visiting," and accidentally lash another, the two will fight it out at once, and stop all the others. Again, if you travel with a companion and begin to talk, or by yourself and sing, the dogs will halt, turn round, and sit down to hear what you have to say. Kotuku was run away from once or twice through forgetting to block the sleigh when he stopped; and he broke many lashings, and ruined a few thongs before he could be trusted with a full team of eight and the light sleigh. Then he felt himself a person of consequence, and on smooth, black ice, with a bold heart and a quick elbow, he smoked along over the levels as fast as a pack in full cry. He would go ten miles to the seal-holes, and when he was on the hunting-grounds he would twitch a trace loose from the *pitu*, and free the big black leader, who was the cleverest dog in the team. As soon as the dog had scented a breathing-hole, Kotuku would reverse the sleigh, driving a couple of sawed-off antlers, that stuck up like perambulator-handles from the back-rest, deep into the snow, so that the team could not get away. Then he would crawl forward inch by inch, and wait till the seal came up to breathe. Then he would stab down swiftly with his spear and running-line, and presently would haul his seal up to the lip of the ice, while the black leader came up and helped to pull the carcass across the ice to the sleigh. That was the time when the harnessed dogs yelled and foamed with excitement, and Kotuku laid the long lash like a red-hot bar across all their faces, till the carcass froze stiff. Going home was the heavy work. The loaded sleigh had to be humoured among the rough ice, and the dogs sat down and looked hungrily at the seal instead of pulling. At last they would strike the well-worn sleigh-road to the village, and *toodle-kiyi* along the ringing ice, heads down and tails up, while Kotuku struck up the "*Angutivaun tai-na tau-na-ne taina*" (The Song of the Returning Hunter), and voices hailed him from house to house under all that dim, star-litten sky.

When Kotuku the dog came to his full growth he enjoyed himself too. He fought his way up the team steadily, fight after fight, till one fine evening, over their food, he tackled the big, black leader (Kotuku the boy saw fair play), and made second dog of him, as they say. So he was promoted to the long thong of the leading dog, running five feet in advance of all the others: it was his bounden duty to stop all fighting, in harness or out of it, and he wore a collar of copper wire, very thick and heavy. On special occasions he was fed with cooked food inside the house, and sometimes was allowed to sleep on the bench with Kotuku. He was a good seal-dog, and would keep a musk-ox at bay by running round him and snapping at his heels. He would even – and this for a sleigh-dog is the last proof of bravery – he would even stand up to the gaunt Arctic wolf, whom all dogs of the North, as a rule, fear beyond anything that walks the snow. He and his master – they did not count the team of ordinary dogs as company – hunted together, day after day and night after night, fur-wrapped boy and savage, long-haired, narrow-eyed, white-fanged, yellow brute. All an Inuit has to do is to get food and skins for himself and his family. The women-folk make the skins into clothing, and occasionally help in trapping small game; but the bulk of the food – and they eat enormously – must be found by the men. If the supply fails there is no one up there to buy or beg or borrow from. The people must die.

An Inuit does not think of these chances till he is forced to. Kadlu, Kotuku, Amoraq, and the boy-baby who kicked about in Amoraq's fur hood and chewed pieces of blubber all day, were as happy together as any family in the world. They came of a very gentle race – an Inuit seldom loses his temper, and almost never strikes a child – who did not know exactly what telling a real lie meant, still less how to steal. They were content to spear their living out of the heart of the bitter, hopeless cold; to smile oily smiles, and tell queer ghost and fairy tales of evenings, and eat till they could eat no more, and sing the endless woman's song: "*Amna aya, aya amna, ah! ah*!" through the long lamp-lighted days as they mended their clothes and their hunting-gear.

But one terrible winter everything betrayed them. The Tununirmiut returned from the yearly salmon-fishing, and made their houses on the early ice to the north of Bylot's Island, ready to go after the seal as soon as the sea froze. But it was an early and savage autumn. All through September there were continuous gales that broke up the smooth seal-ice when it was only four or five feet thick, and forced it inland, and piled a great barrier, some twenty miles broad, of lumped and ragged and needly ice, over which it was impossible to draw the dog-sleighs. The edge of the floe off which the seal were used to fish in winter lay perhaps twenty miles beyond this barrier, and out of reach of the Tununirmiut. Even so, they might have managed to scrape through the winter on their stock of frozen salmon and stored blubber, and what the traps gave them, but in December one of their hunters came across a *tupik* (a skin-tent) of three women and a girl nearly dead, whose men had come down from the far North and been crushed in their little skin hunting-boats while they were out after the long-horned narwhal. Kadlu, of course, could only distribute the women among the huts of the winter village, for no Inuit dare refuse a meal to a stranger. He never knows when his own turn may come to beg. Amoraq took the girl, who was about fourteen, into her own house as a sort of servant. From the cut of her sharp-pointed hood, and the long diamond pattern of her white deer-skin leggings, they supposed she came from Ellesmere Land. She had never seen tin cooking-pots or wooden-shod sleighs before; but Kotuku the boy and Kotuku the dog were rather fond of her.

Then all the foxes went south, and even the wolverine, that growling, blunt-headed little thief of the snow, did not take the trouble to follow the line of empty traps that Kotuku set. The tribe lost a couple of their best hunters, who were badly crippled in a fight with a musk-ox, and this threw more work on the others. Kotuku went out, day after day, with a light hunting-sleigh and six or seven of the strongest dogs, looking till his eyes ached for some patch of clear ice where a seal might perhaps have scratched a breathing-hole. Kotuku the dog ranged far and wide, and in the dead stillness of the ice-fields Kotuku the boy could hear his half-choked whine of excitement, above a seal-hole three miles away, as plainly as though he were at his elbow. When the dog found a hole the boy would build himself a little, low snow wall to keep off the worst of the bitter wind, and there he would wait ten, twelve, twenty hours for the seal to come up to breathe, his eyes glued to the tiny mark he had made above the hole to guide the downward thrust of his harpoon, a little seal-skin mat under his feet, and his legs tied together in the *tutareang* (the buckle that the old hunters had talked about). This helps to keep a man's legs from twitching as he waits and waits and waits for the quick-eared seal to rise. Though there is no excitement in it, you can easily believe that the sitting still in the buckle with the thermometer perhaps forty degrees below zero is the hardest work an Inuit knows. When a seal was caught, Kotuku the dog would bound forward, his trace trailing behind him, and help to pull the body to the sleigh, where the tired and hungry dogs lay sullenly under the lee of the broken ice.

A seal did not go very far, for each mouth in the little village had a right to be filled, and neither bone, hide, nor sinew was wasted. The dogs' meat was taken for human use, and Amoraq fed the team with pieces of old summer skin-tents raked out from under the sleeping-bench, and they howled and howled again, and waked to howl hungrily. One could tell by the soap-stone lamps in the huts that famine was near. In good seasons, when blubber was plentiful, the light in the boat-shaped lamps would be two feet high – cheerful, oily, and yellow. Now it was a bare six inches: Amoraq carefully pricked down the moss wick, when an unwatched flame brightened for a moment, and the eyes of all the family followed her hand. The horror of famine up there in the great cold is not so much dying, as dying in the dark. All the Inuit dread the dark that presses on them without a break for six months in each year; and when the lamps are low in the houses the minds of people begin to be shaken and confused.

But worse was to come.

The underfed dogs snapped and growled in the passages, glaring at the cold stars, and snuffing into the bitter wind, night after night. When they stopped howling the silence fell down again as solid and heavy as a snowdrift against a door, and men could hear the beating of their blood in the thin passages of the ear, and the thumping of their own hearts, that sounded as loud as the noise of sorcerers' drums beaten across the snow. One night Kotuku the dog, who had been unusually sullen in harness, leaped up and pushed his head against Kotuku's knee. Kotuku patted him, but the dog still pushed blindly forward, fawning. Then Kadlu waked, and gripped the heavy wolf-like head, and stared into the glassy eyes. The dog whimpered and shivered between Kadlu's knees. The hair rose about his neck, and he growled as though a stranger were at the door; then he barked joyously, and rolled on the ground, and bit at Kotuku's boot like a puppy.

"What is it?" said Kotuku; for he was beginning to be afraid.

"The sickness," Kadlu answered. "It is the dog sickness." Kotuku the dog lifted his nose and howled and howled again.

"I have not seen this before. What will he do?" said Kotuku.

Kadlu shrugged one shoulder a little, and crossed the hut for his short stabbing-harpoon. The big dog looked at him, howled again, and slunk away down the passage, while the other dogs drew aside right and left to give him ample room. When he was out on the snow he barked furiously, as though on the trail of a musk-ox, and, barking and leaping and frisking, passed out of sight. His trouble was not hydrophobia, but simple, plain madness. The cold and the hunger, and, above all, the dark, had turned his head; and when the terrible dog-sickness once shows itself in a team, it spreads like wild-fire. Next hunting-day another dog sickened, and was killed then and there by Kotuku as he bit and struggled among the traces. Then the black second dog, who had been the leader in the old days, suddenly gave tongue on an imaginary reindeer-track, and when they slipped him from the pitu he flew at the throat of an ice-cliff, and ran away as his leader had done, his harness on his back. After that no one would take the dogs out again. They needed them for something else, and the dogs knew it; and though they were tied down and fed by hand, their eyes were full of despair and fear. To make things worse, the old women began to tell ghost-tales, and to say that they had met the spirits of the dead hunters lost that autumn, who prophesied all sorts of horrible things.

Kotuku grieved more for the loss of his dog than anything else; for though an Inuit eats enormously he also knows how to starve. But the hunger, the darkness, the cold, and the exposure told on his strength, and he began to hear voices inside his head, and to see people who were not there, out of the tail of his eye. One night – he had unbuckled himself after ten hours' waiting above a "blind" seal-hole, and was staggering back to the village faint and dizzy – he halted to lean his back against a boulder which happened to be supported like a rocking-stone on a single jutting point of ice. His weight disturbed the balance of the thing, it rolled over ponderously, and as Kotuku sprang aside to avoid it, slid after him, squeaking and hissing on the ice-slope.

That was enough for Kotuku. He had been brought up to believe that every rock and boulder had its owner (its inua), who was generally a one-eyed kind of a Woman-Thing called a *tornaq*, and that when a *tornaq* meant to help a man she rolled after him inside her stone house, and asked him whether he would take her for a guardian spirit. (In summer thaws the ice-propped rocks and boulders roll and slip all over the face of the land, so you can easily see how the idea of live stones arose.) Kotuku heard the blood beating in his ears as he had heard it all day, and he thought that was the *tornaq* of the stone speaking to him. Before he reached home he was quite certain that he had held a long conversation with her, and as all his people believed that this was quite possible, no one contradicted him.

"She said to me, 'I jump down, I jump down from my place on the snow,' " cried Kotuku, with hollow eyes, leaning forward in the half-lighted hut. "She said, 'I will be a guide.' She said, 'I will guide you to the good seal-holes.' To-morrow I go out, and the *tornaq* will guide me."

Then the *angekok*, the village sorcerer, came in, and Kotuku told him the tale a second time. It lost nothing in the telling.

"Follow the *tornait* [the spirits of the stones], and they will bring us food again," said the angekok.

Now the girl from the North had been lying near the lamp, eating very little and saying less for days past; but when Amoraq and Kadlu next morning packed and lashed a little hand-sleigh for Kotuku, and loaded it with his hunting-gear and as much blubber and frozen seal-meat as they could spare, she took the pulling-rope, and stepped out boldly at the boy's side.

"Your house is my house," she said, as the little bone-shod sleigh squeaked and bumped behind them in the awful Arctic night.

"My house is your house," said Kotuku; "but I think that we shall both go to Sedna together."

Now Sedna is the Mistress of the Underworld, and the Inuit believe that every one who dies must spend a year in her horrible country before going to Quadliparmiut, the Happy Place, where it never freezes and the fat reindeer trot up when you call.

Through the village people were shouting: "The *tornait* have spoken to Kotuku. They will show him open ice. He will bring us the seal again!" Their voices were soon swallowed up by the cold, empty dark, and Kotuku and the girl shouldered close together as they strained on the pulling-rope or humoured the sleigh through the ice in the direction of the Polar Sea. Kotuku insisted that the *tornaq* of the stone had told him to go north, and north they went under Tuktuqdjung the Reindeer – those stars that we call the Great Bear.

No European could have made five miles a day over the ice-rubbish and the sharp-edged drifts; but those two knew exactly the turn of the wrist that coaxes a sleigh round a hummock, the jerk that nearly lifts it out of an ice-crack, and the exact strength that goes to the few quiet strokes of the spear-head that make a path possible when everything looks hopeless.

The girl said nothing, but bowed her head, and the long wolverine-fur fringe of her ermine hood blew across her broad, dark face. The sky above them was an intense velvety black, changing to bands of Indian red on the horizon, where the great stars burned like street-lamps. From time to time a greenish wave of the Northern Lights would roll across the hollow of the high heavens, flick like a flag, and disappear; or a meteor would crackle from darkness to darkness, trailing a shower of sparks behind. Then they could see the ridged and furrowed surface of the floe tipped and laced with strange colours – red, copper, and bluish; but in the ordinary starlight everything turned to one frost-bitten gray. The floe, as you will remember, had been battered and tormented by the autumn gales till it was one frozen earthquake. There were gullies and ravines, and holes like gravel-pits, cut in ice; lumps and scattered pieces frozen down to the original floor of the floe; blotches of old black ice that had been thrust under the floe in some gale and heaved up again; roundish boulders of ice; saw-like edges of ice carved by the snow that flies before the wind; and sunken pits where thirty or forty acres lay below the level of the rest of the field. From a little distance you might have taken the lumps for seal or walrus, overturned sleighs or men on a hunting expedition, or even the great Ten-legged White Spirit-Bear himself; but in spite of these fantastic shapes, all on the very edge of starting into life, there was neither sound nor the least faint echo of sound. And through this silence and through this waste, where the sudden lights flapped and went out again, the sleigh and the two that pulled it crawled like things in a nightmare – a nightmare of the end of the world at the end of the world.

When they were tired Kotuku would make what the hunters call a "half-house," a very small snow hut, into which they would huddle with the travelling-lamp, and try to thaw out the frozen seal-meat. When they had slept, the march began again – thirty miles a day to get ten miles northward. The girl was always very silent, but Kotuku muttered to himself and broke out into songs he had learned in the

Singing-House – summer songs, and reindeer and salmon songs – all horribly out of place at that season. He would declare that he heard the *tornaq* growling to him, and would run wildly up a hummock, tossing his arms and speaking in loud, threatening tones. To tell the truth, Kotuku was very nearly crazy for the time being; but the girl was sure that he was being guided by his guardian spirit, and that everything would come right. She was not surprised, therefore, when at the end of the fourth march Kotuku, whose eyes were burning like fire-balls in his head, told her that his *tornaq* was following them across the snow in the shape of a two-headed dog. The girl looked where Kotuku pointed, and something seemed to slip into a ravine. It was certainly not human, but everybody knew that the *tornait* preferred to appear in the shape of bear and seal, and such like.

It might have been the Ten-legged White Spirit-Bear himself, or it might have been anything, for Kotuku and the girl were so starved that their eyes were untrustworthy. They had trapped nothing, and seen no trace of game since they had left the village; their food would not hold out for another week, and there was a gale coming. A Polar storm can blow for ten days without a break, and all that while it is certain death to be abroad. Kotuku laid up a snow-house large enough to take in the hand-sleigh (never be separated from your meat), and while he was shaping the last irregular block of ice that makes the key-stone of the roof, he saw a Thing looking at him from a little cliff of ice half a mile away. The air was hazy, and the Thing seemed to be forty feet long and ten feet high, with twenty feet of tail and a shape that quivered all along the outlines. The girl saw it too, but instead of crying aloud with terror, said quietly, "That is Quiquern. What comes after?"

"He will speak to me," said Kotuku; but the snow-knife trembled in his hand as he spoke, because however much a man may believe that he is a friend of strange and ugly spirits, he seldom likes to be taken quite at his word. Quiquern, too, is the phantom of a gigantic toothless dog without any hair, who is supposed to live in the far North, and to wander about the country just before things are going to happen. They may be pleasant or unpleasant things, but not even the sorcerers care to speak about Quiquern. He makes the dogs go mad. Like the Spirit-Bear, he has several extra pairs of legs, – six or eight, – and this Thing jumping up and down in the haze had more legs than any real dog needed.

Kotuku and the girl huddled into their hut quickly. Of course if Quiquern had wanted them, he could have torn it to pieces above their heads, but the sense of a foot-thick snow-wall between themselves and the wicked dark was great comfort. The gale broke with a shriek of wind like the shriek of a train, and for three days and three nights it held, never varying one point, and never lulling even for a minute. They fed the stone lamp between their knees, and nibbled at the half-warm seal-meat, and watched the black soot gather on the roof for seventy-two long hours. The girl counted up the food in the sleigh; there was not more than two days' supply, and Kotuku looked over the iron heads and the deer-sinew fastenings of his harpoon and his seal-lance and his bird-dart. There was nothing else to do.

"We shall go to Sedna soon – very soon," the girl whispered. "In three days we shall lie down and go. Will your *tornaq* do nothing? Sing her an *angekok's* song to make her come here."

He began to sing in the high-pitched howl of the magic songs, and the gale went down slowly. In the middle of his song the girl started, laid her mittened hand and then her head to the ice floor of the hut. Kotuku followed her example, and the two kneeled, staring into each other's eyes, and listening with every nerve. He ripped a thin sliver of whalebone from the rim of a bird-snare that lay on the sleigh, and, after straightening, set it upright in a little hole in the ice, firming it down with his mitten. It was almost as delicately adjusted as a compass-needle, and now instead of listening they watched. The thin rod quivered a little – the least little jar in the world; then it vibrated steadily for a few seconds, came to rest, and vibrated again, this time nodding to another point of the compass.

"Too soon!" said Kotuku. "Some big floe has broken far away outside."

The girl pointed at the rod, and shook her head. "It is the big breaking," she said. "Listen to the ground-ice. It knocks."

When they kneeled this time they heard the most curious muffled grunts and knockings, apparently under their feet. Sometimes it sounded as though a blind puppy were squeaking above the lamp; then as if a stone were being ground on hard ice; and again, like muffled blows on a drum; but all dragged out and made small, as though they travelled through a little horn a weary distance away.

"We shall not go to Sedna lying down," said Kotuku. "It is the breaking. The *tornaq* has cheated us. We shall die."

All this may sound absurd enough, but the two were face to face with a very real danger. The three days' gale had driven the deep water of Baffin's Bay southerly, and piled it on to the edge of the far-reaching land-ice that stretches from Bylot's Island to the west. Also, the strong current which sets east out of Lancaster Sound carried with it mile upon mile of what they call pack-ice – rough ice that has not frozen into fields; and this pack was bombarding the floe at the same time that the swell and heave of the storm-worked sea was weakening and undermining it. What Kotuku and the girl had been listening to were the faint echoes of that fight thirty or forty miles away, and the little tell-tale rod quivered to the shock of it.

Now, as the Inuit say, when the ice once wakes after its long winter sleep, there is no knowing what may happen, for solid floe-ice changes shape almost as quickly as a cloud. The gale was evidently a spring gale sent out of time, and anything was possible.

Yet the two were happier in their minds than before. If the floe broke up there would be no more waiting and suffering. Spirits, goblins, and witch-people were moving about on the racking ice, and they might find themselves stepping into Sedna's country side by side with all sorts of wild Things, the flush of excitement still on them. When they left the hut after the gale, the noise on the horizon was steadily growing, and the tough ice moaned and buzzed all round them.

"It is still waiting," said Kotuku.

On the top of a hummock sat or crouched the eight-legged Thing that they had seen three days before – and it howled horribly.

"Let us follow," said the girl. "It may know some way that does not lead to Sedna"; but she reeled from weakness as she took the pulling-rope. The Thing moved off slowly and clumsily across the ridges, heading always toward the westward and the land, and they followed, while the growling thunder at the edge of the floe rolled nearer and nearer. The floe's lip was split and cracked in every direction for three or four miles inland, and great pans of ten-foot-thick ice, from a few yards to twenty acres square, were jolting and ducking and surging into one another, and into the yet unbroken floe, as the heavy swell took and shook and spouted between them. This battering-ram ice was, so to speak, the first army that the sea was flinging against the floe. The incessant crash and jar of these cakes almost drowned the ripping sound of sheets of pack-ice driven bodily under the floe as cards are hastily pushed under a tablecloth. Where the water was shallow these sheets would be piled one atop of the other till the bottommost touched mud fifty feet down, and the discoloured sea banked behind the muddy ice till the increasing pressure drove all forward again. In addition to the floe and the pack-ice, the gale and the currents were bringing down true bergs, sailing mountains of ice, snapped off from the Greenland side of the water or the north shore of Melville Bay. They pounded in solemnly, the waves breaking white round them, and advanced on the floe like an old-time fleet under full sail. A berg that seemed ready to carry the world before it would ground helplessly in deep water, reel over, and wallow in a lather of foam and mud and flying frozen spray, while a much smaller and lower one would rip and ride into the flat floe, flinging tons of ice on either side, and cutting a track half a mile long before it was stopped. Some fell like swords, shearing a raw-edged canal; and others splintered into a shower of blocks, weighing scores of tons apiece, that whirled and skirted among the hummocks. Others, again, rose up bodily out of the water when they shoaled, twisted as though in pain, and fell solidly on their sides, while the sea threshed over their shoulders. This trampling and crowding and bending and buckling and arching of the ice into every possible shape was going on as far as the eye could reach all along the north line of the floe. From where Kotuku and the girl were, the confusion looked no more than an uneasy, rippling, crawling movement under the horizon; but it came toward them each moment, and they could hear, far away to landward a heavy booming, as it might have been the boom of artillery through a fog. That showed that the floe was being jammed home against the iron cliffs of Bylot's Island, the land to the southward behind them.

"This has never been before," said Kotuku, staring stupidly. "This is not the time. How can the floe break *now*?"

"Follow *that*! the girl cried, pointing to the Thing half limping, half running distractedly before them. They followed, tugging at the hand-sleigh, while nearer and nearer came the roaring march of the ice. At last the fields round them cracked and starred in every direction, and the cracks opened and snapped like the teeth of wolves. But where the Thing rested, on a mound of old and scattered ice-blocks some fifty feet high, there was no motion. Kotuku leaped forward wildly, dragging the girl after him, and crawled to the bottom of the mound. The talking of the ice grew louder and louder round them, but the mound stayed fast, and, as the girl looked at him, he threw his right elbow upward and outward, making the Inuit sign for land in the shape of an island. And land it was that the eight-legged, limping Thing had led them to – some granite-tipped, sand-beached islet off the coast, shod and sheathed and masked with ice so that no man could have told it from the floe, but at the bottom solid earth, and not shifting ice! The smashing and rebound of the floes as they grounded and splintered marked the borders of it, and a friendly shoal ran out to the northward, and turned aside the rush of the heaviest ice, exactly as a ploughshare turns over loam. There was danger, of course, that some heavily squeezed ice-field might shoot up the beach, and plane off the top of the islet bodily; but that did not trouble Kotuku and the girl when they made their snow-house and began to eat, and heard the ice hammer and skid along the beach. The Thing had disappeared, and Kotuku was talking excitedly about his power over spirits as he crouched round the lamp. In the middle of his wild sayings the girl began to laugh, and rock herself backward and forward.

Behind her shoulder, crawling into the hut crawl by crawl, there were two heads, one yellow and one black, that belonged to two of the most sorrowful and ashamed dogs that ever you saw. Kotuku the dog was one, and the black leader was the other. Both were now fat, well-looking, and quite restored to their proper minds, but coupled to each other in an extraordinary fashion. When the black leader ran off, you remember, his harness was still on him. He must have met Kotuku the dog, and played or fought with him, for his shoulder-loop had caught in the plaited copper wire of Kotuku's collar, and had drawn tight, so that neither could get at the trace to gnaw it apart, but each was fastened sidelong to his neighbour's neck. That, with the freedom of hunting on their own account, must have helped to cure their madness. They were very sober.

The girl pushed the two shamefaced creatures towards Kotuku, and, sobbing with laughter, cried, "That is Quiquern, who led us to safe ground. Look at his eight legs and double head!"

Kotuku cut them free, and they fell into his arms, yellow and black together, trying to explain how they had got their senses back again. Kotuku ran a hand down their ribs, which were round and well clothed. "They have found food," he said, with a grin. "I do not think we shall go to Sedna so soon. My *tornaq* sent these. The sickness has left them."

As soon as they had greeted Kotuku, these two, who had been forced to sleep and eat and hunt together for the past few weeks, flew at each other's throat, and there was a beautiful battle in the snow-house. "Empty dogs do not fight," Kotuku said. "They have found the seal. Let us sleep. We shall find food."

When they waked there was open water on the north beach of the island, and all the loosened ice had been driven landward. The first sound of the surf is one of the most delightful that the Inuit can hear, for it means that spring is on the road. Kotuku and the girl took hold of hands and smiled, for the clear, full roar of the surge among the ice reminded them of salmon and reindeer time and the smell of blossoming ground-willows. Even as they looked, the sea began to skim over between the floating cakes of ice, so intense was the cold; but on the horizon there was a vast red glare, and that was the light of the sunken sun. It was more like hearing him yawn in his sleep than seeing him rise, and the glare lasted for only a few minutes, but it marked the turn of the year. Nothing, they felt, could alter that.

Kotuku found the dogs fighting over a fresh-killed seal who was following the fish that a gale always disturbs. He was the first of some twenty or thirty seal that landed on the island in the course of the day, and till the sea froze hard there were hundreds of keen black heads rejoicing in the shallow free water and floating about with the floating ice.

It was good to eat seal-liver again; to fill the lamps recklessly with blubber, and watch the flame blaze three feet in the air; but as soon as the new sea-ice bore, Kotuku and the girl loaded the hand-sleigh, and made the two dogs pull as they had never pulled in their lives, for they feared what might have happened in their village. The weather was as pitiless as usual; but it is easier to draw a sleigh loaded with good food than to hunt starving. They left five-and-twenty seal carcasses buried in the ice of the beach, all ready for use, and hurried back to their people. The dogs showed them the way as soon as Kotuku told them what was expected, and though there was no sign of a landmark, in two days they were giving tongue outside Kadlu's house. Only three dogs answered them; the others had been eaten, and the houses were all dark. But when Kotuku shouted, "*Ojo*!" (boiled meat), weak voices replied, and when he called the muster of the village name by name, very distinctly, there were no gaps in it.

An hour later the lamps blazed in Kadlu's house; snow-water was heating; the pots were beginning to simmer, and the snow was dripping from the roof, as Amoraq made ready a meal for all the village, and the boy-baby in the hood chewed at a strip of rich nutty blubber, and the hunters slowly and methodically filled themselves to the very brim with seal-meat. Kotuku and the girl told their tale. The two dogs sat between them, and whenever their names came in, they cocked an ear apiece and looked most thoroughly ashamed of themselves. A dog who has once gone mad and recovered, the Inuit say, is safe against all further attacks.

"So the *tornaq* did not forget us," said Kotuku. The storm blew, the ice broke, and the seal swam in behind the fish that were frightened by the storm. Now the new seal-holes are not two days distant. Let the good hunters go to-morrow and bring back the seal I have speared – twenty-five seal buried in the ice. When we have eaten those we will all follow the seal on the floe."

"What do *you* do?" said the sorcerer in the same sort of voice as he used to Kadlu, richest of the Tununirmiut.

Kadlu looked at the girl from the North, and said quietly, "*We* build a house." He pointed to the north-west side of Kadlu's house, for that is the side on which the married son or daughter always lives.

The girl turned her hands palm upward, with a little despairing shake of her head. She was a foreigner, picked up starving, and could bring nothing to the housekeeping.

Amoraq jumped from the bench where she sat, and began to sweep things into the girl's lap – stone lamps, iron skin-scrapers, tin kettles, deer-skins embroidered with musk-ox teeth, and real canvas-needles such as sailors use – the finest dowry that has ever been given on the far edge of the Arctic Circle, and the girl from the North bowed her head down to the very floor.

"Also these!" said Kotuku, laughing and signing to the dogs, who thrust their cold muzzles into the girl's face.

"Ah," said the *angekok*, with an important cough, as though he had been thinking it all over. "As soon as Kotuku left the village I went to the Singing-House and sang magic. I sang all the long nights, and called upon the Spirit of the Reindeer. *My* singing made the gale blow that broke the ice and drew the two dogs toward Kotuku when the ice would have crushed his bones. *My* song drew the seal in behind the broken ice. My body lay still in the *quaggi*, but my spirit ran about on the ice, and guided Kotuku and the dogs in all the things they did. *I* did it."

Everybody was full and sleepy, so no one contradicted; and the angekok, by virtue of his office, helped himself to yet another lump of boiled meat, and lay down to sleep with the others in the warm, well-lighted, oil-smelling home.

* * * * *

Now Kotuku, who drew very well in the Inuit fashion, scratched pictures of all these adventures on a long, flat piece of ivory with a hole at one end. When he and the girl went north to Ellesmere Land in the year of the Wonderful Open Winter, he left the picture-story with Kadlu, who lost it in the shingle when his dog-sleigh broke down one summer on the beach of Lake Nettilling at Nikosiring, and there a Lake Inuit found it next spring and sold it to a man at Imigen who was interpreter on a Cumberland Sound whaler, and he sold it to Hans Olsen, who was afterward a quartermaster on board a big steamer that took tourists to the North Cape in Norway. When the tourist season was over, the steamer ran between London and Australia, stopping at Ceylon, and there Olsen sold the ivory to a Cingalese jeweller for two imitation sapphires. I found it under some rubbish in a house at Colombo, and have translated it from one end to the other.

# 'ANGUTIVAUN TAINA'

[This is a very free translation of the Song of the Returning Hunter, as the men used to sing it after seal-spearing. The Inuit always repeat things over and over again.]

Our gloves are stiff with the frozen blood,
Our furs with the drifted snow,
As we come in with the seal – the seal!
In from the edge of the floe.

*Au jana! Aua! Oha! Haq!*
And the yelping dog-teams go,
And the long whips crack, and the men come back,
Back from the edge of the floe!

We tracked our seal to his secret place,
We heard him scratch below,
We made our mark, and we watched beside,
Out on the edge of the floe.

We raised our lance when he rose to breathe,
We drove it downward – so!
And we played him thus, and we killed him thus,
Out on the edge of the floe.

Our gloves are glued with the frozen blood,
Our eyes with the drifting snow;
But we come back to our wives again,
Back from the edge of the floe!

*Au jana! Aua! Oha! Haq!*
*And the loaded dog-teams go,*
*And the wives can hear their men come back.*
*Back from the edge of the floe*!

# RED DOG

For our white and our excellent nights – for the nights of swift running.
Fair ranging, far seeing, good hunting, sure cunning!
For the smells of the dawning, untainted, ere dew has departed!
For the rush through the mist, and the quarry blind-started!
For the cry of our mates when the sambhur has wheeled and is standing at bay,
For the risk and the riot of night!
For the sleep at the lair-mouth by day,
It is met, and we go to the fight.
Bay! O bay!

It was after the letting in of the Jungle that the pleasantest part of Mowgli's life began. He had the good conscience that comes from paying debts; all the Jungle was his friend, and just a little afraid of him. The things that he did and saw and heard when he was wandering from one people to another, with or without his four companions, would make many many stories, each as long as this one. So you will never be told how he met the Mad Elephant of Mandla, who killed two-and-twenty bullocks drawing eleven carts of coined silver to the Government Treasury, and scattered the shiny rupees in the dust; how he fought Jacala, the Crocodile, all one long night in the Marshes of the North, and broke his skinning-knife on the brute's back-plates; how he found a new and longer knife round the neck of a man who had been killed by a wild boar, and how he tracked that boar and killed him as a fair price for the knife; how he was caught up once in the Great Famine, by the moving of the deer, and nearly crushed to death in the swaying hot herds; how he saved Hathi the Silent from being once more trapped in a pit with a stake at the bottom, and how, next day, he himself fell into a very cunning leopard-trap, and how Hathi broke the thick wooden bars to pieces above him; how he milked the wild buffaloes in the swamp, and how –

But we must tell one tale at a time. Father and Mother Wolf died, and Mowgli rolled a big boulder against the mouth of their cave, and cried the Death Song over them; Baloo grew very old and stiff, and even Bagheera, whose nerves were steel and whose muscles were iron, was a shade slower on the kill than he had been. Akela turned from gray to milky white with pure age; his ribs stuck out, and he walked as though he had been made of wood, and Mowgli killed for him. But the young wolves, the children of the disbanded Seeonee Pack, throve and increased, and when there were about forty of them, masterless, full-voiced, clean-footed five-year-olds, Akela told them that they ought to gather themselves together and follow the Law, and run under one head, as befitted the Free People.

This was not a question in which Mowgli concerned himself, for, as he said, he had eaten sour fruit, and he knew the tree it hung from; but when Phao, son of Phaona (his father was the Gray Tracker in the days of Akela's headship), fought his way to the leadership of the Pack, according to the Jungle Law, and the old calls and songs began to ring under the stars once more, Mowgli came to the Council Rock for memory's sake. When he chose to speak the Pack waited till he had finished, and he sat at Akela's side on the rock above Phao. Those were days of good hunting and good sleeping. No stranger cared to break into the jungles that belonged to Mowgli's people, as they called the Pack, and the young wolves grew fat and strong, and there were many cubs to bring to the Looking-over. Mowgli always attended a Looking-over, remembering the night when a black panther bought a naked brown baby into the pack, and the long call, "Look, look well, O Wolves," made his heart flutter. Otherwise, he would be far away in the Jungle with his four brothers, tasting, touching, seeing, and feeling new things.

One twilight when he was trotting leisurely across the ranges to give Akela the half of a buck that he had killed, while the Four jogged behind him, sparring a little, and tumbling one another over for joy of being alive, he heard a cry that had never been heard since the bad days of Shere Khan. It was what they call in the Jungle the *pheeal*, a hideous kind of shriek that the jackal gives when he is hunting behind a tiger, or when there is a big killing afoot. If you can imagine a mixture of hate, triumph, fear, and despair, with a kind of leer running through it, you will get some notion of the *pheeal* that rose and sank and wavered and quavered far away across the Waingunga. The Four stopped at once, bristling and growling. Mowgli's hand went to his knife, and he checked, the blood in his face, his eyebrows knotted.

"There is no Striped One dare kill here," he said at last.

"That is not the cry of the Forerunner," answered Gray Brother. "It is some great killing. Listen!"

It broke out again, half sobbing and half chuckling, just as though the jackal had soft human lips. Then Mowgli drew deep breath, and ran to the Council Rock, overtaking on his way hurrying wolves of the Pack. Phao and Akela were on the Rock together, and below them, every nerve strained, sat the others. The mothers and the cubs were cantering off to their lairs; for when the *pheeal* cries it is no time for weak things to be abroad.

They could hear nothing except the Waingunga rushing and gurgling in the dark, and the light evening winds among the tree-tops, till suddenly across the river a wolf called. It was no wolf of the Pack, for they were all at the Rock. The note changed to a long, despairing bay; and "Dhole!"[Wild dog] it said, "Dhole! dhole! dhole!" They heard tired feet on the rocks, and a gaunt wolf, streaked with red on his flanks, his right fore-paw useless, and his jaws white with foam, flung himself into the circle and lay gasping at Mowgli's feet.

"Good hunting! Under whose Headship?" said Phao gravely.

"Good hunting! Won-tolla am I," was the answer. He meant that he was a solitary wolf, fending for himself, his mate, and his cubs in some lonely lair, as do many wolves in the south. Won-tolla means an Outlier – one who lies out from any Pack. Then he panted, and they could see his heart-beats shake him backward and forward.

"What moves?" said Phao, for that is the question all the Jungle asks after the *pheeal* cries.

"The dhole, the dhole of the Dekkan – Red Dog, the Killer! They came north from the south saying the Dekkan was empty and killing out by the way. When this moon was new there were four to me – my mate and three cubs. She would teach them to kill on the grass plains, hiding to drive the buck, as we do who are of the open. At midnight I heard them together, full tongue on the trail. At the dawn-wind I found them stiff in the grass – four, Free People, four when this moon was new. Then sought I my Blood-Right and found the dhole."

"How many?" said Mowgli quickly; the Pack growled deep in their throats.

"I do not know. Three of them will kill no more, but at the last they drove me like the buck; on my three legs they drove me. Look, Free People!"

He thrust out his mangled fore-foot, all dark with dried blood. There were cruel bites low down on his side, and his throat was torn and worried.

"Eat," said Akela, rising up from the meat Mowgli had brought him, and the Outlier flung himself on it.

"This shall be no loss," he said humbly, when he had taken off the first edge of his hunger. "Give me a little strength, Free People, and I also will kill. My lair is empty that was full when this moon was new, and the Blood Debt is not all paid."

Phao heard his teeth crack on a haunch-bone and grunted approvingly.

"We shall need those jaws," said he. "Were there cubs with the dhole?"

"No, no. Red Hunters all: grown dogs of their Pack, heavy and strong for all that they eat lizards in the Dekkan."

What Won-tolla had said meant that the dhole, the red hunting-dog of the Dekkan, was moving to kill, and the Pack knew well that even the tiger will surrender a new kill to the dhole. They drive straight through the Jungle, and what they meet they pull down and tear to pieces. Though they are not as big nor half as cunning as the wolf, they are very strong and very numerous. The dhole, for instance, do not begin to call themselves a pack till they are a hundred strong; whereas forty wolves make a very fair pack indeed. Mowgli's wanderings had taken him to the edge of the high grassy downs of the Dekkan, and he had seen the fearless dholes sleeping and playing and scratching themselves in the little hollows and tussocks that they use for lairs. He despised and hated them because they did not smell like the Free People, because they did not live in caves, and, above all, because they had hair between their toes while he and his friends were clean-footed. But he knew, for Hathi had told him, what a terrible thing a dhole hunting-pack was. Even Hathi moves aside from their line, and until they are killed, or till game is scarce, they will go.

Akela knew something of the dholes, too, for he said to Mowgli quietly, "It is better to die in a Full Pack than leaderless and alone. This is good hunting, and – my last. But, as men live, thou hast very many more nights and days, Little Brother. Go north and lie down, and if any live after the dhole has gone by he shall bring thee word of the fight."

"Ah," said Mowgli, quite gravely, "must I go to the marshes and catch little fish and sleep in a tree, or must I ask help of the *Bandar-log* and crack nuts, while the Pack fight below?"

"It is to the death," said Akela. "Thou hast never met the dhole – the Red Killer. Even the Striped One — "

"*Aowa! Aowa*!" said Mowgli pettingly. "I have killed one striped ape, and sure am I in my stomach that Shere Khan would have left his own mate for meat to the dhole if he had winded a pack across three ranges. Listen now: There was a wolf, my father, and there was a wolf, my mother, and there was an old gray wolf (not too wise: he is white now) was my father and my mother. Therefore I – " he raised his voice, "I say that when the dhole come, and if the dhole come, Mowgli and the Free People are of one skin for that hunting; and I say, by the Bull that bought me – by the Bull Bagheera paid for me in the old days which ye of the Pack do not remember – *I* say, that the Trees and the River may hear and hold fast if I forget; *I* say that this my knife shall be as a tooth to the Pack – and I do not think it is so blunt. This is my Word which has gone from me."

"Thou dost not know the dhole, man with a wolf's tongue," said Won-tolla. "I look only to clear the Blood Debt against them ere they have me in many pieces. They move slowly, killing out as they go, but in two days a little strength will come back to me and I turn again for the Blood Debt. But for *ye*, Free People, my word is that ye go north and eat but little for a while till the dhole are gone. There is no meat in this hunting."

"Hear the Outlier!" said Mowgli with a laugh. Free People, we must go north and dig lizards and rats from the bank, lest by any chance we meet the dhole. He must kill out our hunting-grounds, while we lie hid in the north till it please him to give us our own again. He is a dog – and the pup of a dog – red, yellow-bellied, lairless, and haired between every toe! He counts his cubs six and eight at the litter, as though he were Chikai, the little leaping rat. Surely we must run away, Free People, and beg leave of the peoples of the north for the offal of dead cattle! Ye know the saying: 'North are the vermin; south are the lice. WE are the Jungle.' Choose ye, O choose. It is good hunting! For the Pack – for the Full Pack – for the lair and the litter; for the in-kill and the out-kill; for the mate that drives the doe and the little, little cub within the cave; it is met! – it is met! – it is met!"

The Pack answered with one deep, crashing bark that sounded in the night like a big tree falling. "It is met!" they cried.

"Stay with these," said Mowgli to the Four. We shall need every tooth. Phao and Akela must make ready the battle. I go to count the dogs."

"It is death!" Won-tolla cried, half rising. What can such a hairless one do against the Red Dog? Even the Striped One, remember — "

"Thou art indeed an Outlier," Mowgli called back; "but we will speak when the dholes are dead. Good hunting all!"

He hurried off into the darkness, wild with excitement, hardly looking where he set foot, and the natural consequence was that he tripped full length over Kaa's great coils where the python lay watching a deer-path near the river.

"Kssha!" said Kaa angrily. "Is this jungle-work, to stamp and tramp and undo a night's hunting – when the game are moving so well, too?"

"The fault was mine," said Mowgli, picking himself up. "Indeed I was seeking thee, Flathead, but each time we meet thou art longer and broader by the length of my arm. There is none like thee in the Jungle, wise, old, strong, and most beautiful Kaa."

"Now whither does *this* trail lead?" Kaa's voice was gentler. "Not a moon since there was a Manling with a knife threw stones at my head and called me bad little tree-cat names, because I lay asleep in the open."

"Ay, and turned every driven deer to all the winds, and Mowgli was hunting, and this same Flathead was too deaf to hear his whistle, and leave the deer-roads free," Mowgli answered composedly, sitting down among the painted coils.

"Now this same Manling comes with soft, tickling words to this same Flathead, telling him that he is wise and strong and beautiful, and this same old Flathead believes and makes a place, thus, for this same stone-throwing Manling, and – Art thou at ease now? Could Bagheera give thee so good a resting-place?"

Kaa had, as usual, made a sort of soft half-hammock of himself under Mowgli's weight. The boy reached out in the darkness, and gathered in the supple cable-like neck till Kaa's head rested on his shoulder, and then he told him all that had happened in the Jungle that night.

"Wise I may be," said Kaa at the end; "but deaf I surely am. Else I should have heard the *pheeal*. Small wonder the Eaters of Grass are uneasy. How many be the dhole?"

"I have not yet seen. I came hot-foot to thee. Thou art older than Hathi. But oh, Kaa," – here Mowgli wriggled with sheer joy, – "it will be good hunting. Few of us will see another moon."

"Dost *thou* strike in this? Remember thou art a Man; and remember what Pack cast thee out. Let the Wolf look to the Dog. *Thou* art a Man."

"Last year's nuts are this year's black earth," said Mowgli. "It is true that I am a Man, but it is in my stomach that this night I have said that I am a Wolf. I called the River and the Trees to remember. I am of the Free People, Kaa, till the dhole has gone by."

"Free People," Kaa grunted. "Free thieves! And thou hast tied thyself into the death-knot for the sake of the memory of the dead wolves? This is no good hunting."

"It is my Word which I have spoken. The Trees know, the River knows. Till the dhole have gone by my Word comes not back to me."

"*Ngssh*! This changes all trails. I had thought to take thee away with me to the northern marshes, but the Word – even the Word of a little, naked, hairless Manling – is the Word. Now I, Kaa, say — "

"Think well, Flathead, lest thou tie thyself into the death-knot also. I need no Word from thee, for well I know — "

"Be it so, then," said Kaa. "I will give no Word; but what is in thy stomach to do when the dhole come?"

"They must swim the Waingunga. I thought to meet them with my knife in the shallows, the Pack behind me; and so stabbing and thrusting, we a little might turn them down-stream, or cool their throats."

"The dhole do not turn and their throats are hot," said Kaa. "There will be neither Manling nor Wolf-cub when that hunting is done, but only dry bones."

"*Alala*! If we die, we die. It will be most good hunting. But my stomach is young, and I have not seen many Rains. I am not wise nor strong. Hast thou a better plan, Kaa?"

"I have seen a hundred and a hundred Rains. Ere Hathi cast his milk-tushes my trail was big in the dust. By the First Egg, I am older than many trees, and I have seen all that the Jungle has done."

"But *this* is new hunting," said Mowgli. "Never before have the dhole crossed our trail."

"What is has been. What will be is no more than a forgotten year striking backward. Be still while I count those my years."

For a long hour Mowgli lay back among the coils, while Kaa, his head motionless on the ground, thought of all that he had seen and known since the day he came from the egg. The light seemed to go out of his eyes and leave them like stale opals, and now and again he made little stiff passes with his head, right and left, as though he were hunting in his sleep. Mowgli dozed quietly, for he knew that there is nothing like sleep before hunting, and he was trained to take it at any hour of the day or night.

Then he felt Kaa's back grow bigger and broader below him as the huge python puffed himself out, hissing with the noise of a sword drawn from a steel scabbard.

"I have seen all the dead seasons," Kaa said at last, "and the great trees and the old elephants, and the rocks that were bare and sharp-pointed ere the moss grew. Art *thou* still alive, Manling?"

"It is only a little after moonset," said Mowgli. I do not understand — "

"*Hssh*! I am again Kaa. I knew it was but a little time. Now we will go to the river, and I will show thee what is to be done against the dhole."

He turned, straight as an arrow, for the main stream of the Waingunga, plunging in a little above the pool that hid the Peace Rock, Mowgli at his side.

"Nay, do not swim. I go swiftly. My back, Little Brother."

Mowgli tucked his left arm round Kaa's neck, dropped his right close to his body, and straightened his feet. Then Kaa breasted the current as he alone could, and the ripple of the checked water stood up in a frill round Mowgli's neck, and his feet were waved to and fro in the eddy under the python's lashing sides. A mile or two above the Peace Rock the Waingunga narrows between a gorge of marble rocks from eighty to a hundred feet high, and the current runs like a mill-race between and over all manner of ugly stones. But Mowgli did not trouble his head about the water; little water in the world could have given him a moment's fear. He was looking at the gorge on either side and sniffing uneasily, for there was a sweetish-sourish smell in the air, very like the smell of a big ant-hill on a hot day. Instinctively he lowered himself in the water, only raising his head to breathe from time to time, and Kaa came to anchor with a double twist of his tail round a sunken rock, holding Mowgli in the hollow of a coil, while the water raced on.

"This is the Place of Death," said the boy. "Why do we come here?"

"They sleep," said Kaa. "Hathi will not turn aside for the Striped One. Yet Hathi and the Striped One together turn aside for the dhole, and the dhole they say turn aside for nothing. And yet for whom do the Little People of the Rocks turn aside? Tell me, Master of the Jungle, who is the Master of the Jungle?"

"These," Mowgli whispered. "It is the Place of Death. Let us go."

"Nay, look well, for they are asleep. It is as it was when I was not the length of thy arm."

The split and weatherworn rocks of the gorge of the Waingunga had been used since the beginning of the Jungle by the Little People of the Rocks – the busy, furious, black wild bees of India; and, as Mowgli knew well, all trails turned off half a mile before they reached the gorge. For centuries the Little People had hived and swarmed from cleft to cleft, and swarmed again, staining the white marble with stale honey, and made their combs tall and deep in the dark of the inner caves, where neither man nor beast nor fire nor water had ever touched them. The length of the gorge on both sides was hung as it were with black shimmery velvet curtains, and Mowgli sank as he looked, for those were the clotted millions of the sleeping bees. There were other lumps and festoons and things like decayed tree-trunks studded on the face of the rock, the old combs of past years, or new cities built in the shadow of the windless gorge, and huge masses of spongy, rotten trash had rolled down and stuck among the trees and creepers that clung to the rock-face. As he listened he heard more than once the rustle and slide of a honey-loaded comb turning over or failing away somewhere in the dark galleries; then a booming of angry wings, and the sullen drip, drip, drip, of the wasted honey, guttering along till it lipped over some ledge in the open air and sluggishly trickled down on the twigs. There was a tiny little beach, not five feet broad, on one side of the river, and that was piled high with the rubbish of uncounted years. There were dead bees, drones, sweepings, and stale combs, and wings of marauding moths that had strayed in after honey, all tumbled in smooth piles of the finest black dust. The mere sharp smell of it was enough to frighten anything that had no wings, and knew what the Little People were.

Kaa moved up-stream again till he came to a sandy bar at the head of the gorge.

"Here is this season's kill," said he. "Look!"

On the bank lay the skeletons of a couple of young deer and a buffalo. Mowgli could see that neither wolf nor jackal had touched the hones, which were laid out naturally.

"They came beyond the line;, they did not know the Law," murmured Mowgli, "and the Little People killed them. Let us go ere they wake."

"They do not wake till the dawn," said Kaa. "Now I will tell thee. A hunted buck from the south, many, many Rains ago, came hither from the south, not knowing the Jungle, a Pack on his trail. Being made blind by fear, he leaped from above, the Pack running by sight, for they were hot and blind on the trail. The sun was high, and the Little People were many and very angry. Many, too, were those of the Pack who leaped into the Waingunga, but they were dead ere they took water. Those who did not leap died also in the rocks above. But the buck lived."

"How?"

"Because he came first, running for his life, leaping ere the Little People were aware, and was in the river when they gathered to kill. The Pack, following, was altogether lost under the weight of the Little People."

"The buck lived?" Mowgli repeated slowly.

"At least he did not die *then*, though none waited his coming down with a strong body to hold him safe against the water, as a certain old fat, deaf, yellow Flathead would wait for a Manling – yea, though there were all the dholes of the Dekkan on his trail. What is in thy stomach?"

Kaa's head was close to Mowgli's ear; and it was a little time before the boy whispered.

"It is to pull the very whiskers of Death, but – Kaa, thou art, indeed, the wisest of all the Jungle."

"So many have said. Look now, if the dhole follow thee — "

"As surely they will follow. Ho! ho! I have many little thorns under my tongue to prick into their hides."

"If they follow thee hot and blind, looking only at thy shoulders, those who do not die up above will take water either here or lower down, for the Little People will rise up and cover them. Now the Waingunga is hungry water, and they will have no Kaa to hold them, but will go down, such as live, to the shallows by the Seeonee Lairs, and there thy Pack may meet them by the throat."

"*Ahai*! *Eowawa*! Better could not be till the Rains fall in the dry season. There is now only the little matter of the run and the leap. I will make me known to the dholes, so that they shall follow me very closely."

"Hast thou seen the rocks above thee? From the landward side?"

"Indeed, no. That I had forgotten."

"Go look. It is all rotten ground, cut and full of holes. One of thy clumsy feet set down without seeing would end the hunt. See, I leave thee here, and for thy sake only I will carry word to the Pack that they may know where to look for the dhole. For myself, I am not of one skin with *any* wolf."

When Kaa disliked an acquaintance he could be more unpleasant than any of the Jungle People, except perhaps Bagheera. He swam down-stream, and opposite the Rock he came on Phao and Akela listening to the night noises.

"*Hssh*! Dogs," he said cheerfully. "The dholes will come down-stream. If ye be not afraid ye can kill them in the shallows."

"When come they?" said Phao. "And where is my Man-cub?" said Akela.

"They come when they come," said Kaa. "Wait and see. As for *thy* Man-cub, from whom thou hast taken a Word and so laid him open to Death, *thy* Man-cub is with *me*, and if he be not already dead the fault is none of thine, bleached dog! Wait here for the dhole, and he glad that the Man-cub and I strike on thy side."

Kaa flashed up-stream again, and moored himself in the middle of the gorge, looking upward at the line of the cliff. Presently he saw Mowgli's head move against the stars, and then there was a whizz in the air, the keen, clean *schloop* of a body falling feet first, and next minute the boy was at rest again in the loop of Kaa's body.

"It is no leap by night," said Mowgli quietly. "I have jumped twice as far for sport; but that is an evil place above – low bushes and gullies that go down very deep, all full of the Little People. I have put big stones one above the other by the side of three gullies. These I shall throw down with my feet in running, and the Little People will rise up behind me, very angry."

"That is Man's talk and Man's cunning," said Kaa. "Thou art wise, but the Little People are always angry."

"Nay, at twilight all wings near and far rest for a while. I will play with the dhole at twilight, for the dhole hunts best by day. He follows now Won-tolla's blood-trail."

"Chil does not leave a dead ox, nor the dhole the blood-trail," said Kaa.

"Then I will make him a new blood-trail, of his own blood, if I can, and give him dirt to eat. Thou wilt stay here, Kaa, till I come again with my dholes?"

"Ay, but what if they kill thee in the Jungle, or the Little People kill thee before thou canst leap down to the river?"

"When to-morrow comes we will kill for to-morrow," said Mowgli, quoting a Jungle saying; and again, "When I am dead it is time to sing the Death Song. Good hunting, Kaa!"

He loosed his arm from the python's neck and went down the gorge like a log in a freshet, paddling toward the far bank, where he found slack-water, and laughing aloud from sheer happiness. There was nothing Mowgli liked better than, as he himself said, "to pull the whiskers of Death," and make the Jungle know that he was their overlord. He had often, with Baloo's help, robbed bees' nests in single trees, and he knew that the Little People hated the smell of wild garlic. So he gathered a small bundle of it, tied it up with a bark string, and then followed Won-tolla's blood-trail, as it ran southerly from the Lairs, for some five miles, looking at the trees with his head on one side, and chuckling as he looked.

"Mowgli the Frog have I been," said he to himself; "Mowgli the Wolf have I said that I am. Now Mowgli the Ape must I be before I am Mowgli the Buck. At the end I shall be Mowgli the Man. Ho!" and he slid his thumb along the eighteen-inch blade of his knife.

Won-tolla's trail, all rank with dark blood-spots, ran under a forest of thick trees that grew close together and stretched away north-eastward, gradually growing thinner and thinner to within two miles of the Bee Rocks. From the last tree to the low scrub of the Bee Rocks was open country, where there was hardly cover enough to hide a wolf. Mowgli trotted along under the trees, judging distances between branch and branch, occasionally climbing up a trunk and taking a trial leap from one tree to another till he came to the open ground, which he studied very carefully for an hour. Then he turned, picked up Won-tolla's trail where he had left it, settled himself in a tree with an outrunning branch some eight feet from the ground, and sat still, sharpening his knife on the sole of his foot and singing to himself.

A little before mid-day, when the sun was very warm, he heard the patter of feet and smelt the abominable smell of the dhole-pack as they trotted pitilessly along Won-tolla's trail. Seen from above, the red dhole does not look half the size of a wolf, but Mowgli knew how strong his feet and jaws were. He watched the sharp bay head of the leader snuffing along the trail, and gave him "Good hunting!"

The brute looked up, and his companions halted behind him, scores and scores of red dogs with low-hung tails, heavy shoulders, weak quarters, and bloody mouths. The dholes are a very silent people as a rule, and they have no manners even in their own Jungle. Fully two hundred must have gathered below him, but he could see that the leaders sniffed hungrily on Won-tolla's trail, and tried to drag the Pack forward. That would never do, or they would be at the Lairs in broad daylight, and Mowgli meant to hold them under his tree till dusk.

"By whose leave do ye come here?" said Mowgli.

"All Jungles are our Jungle," was the reply, and the dhole that gave it bared his white teeth. Mowgli looked down with a smile, and imitated perfectly the sharp chitter-chatter of Chikai, the leaping rat of the Dekkan, meaning the dholes to understand that he considered them no better than Chikai. The Pack closed up round the tree-trunk and the leader bayed savagely, calling Mowgli a tree-ape. For an answer Mowgli stretched down one naked leg and wriggled his bare toes just above the leader's head. That was enough, and more than enough, to wake the Pack to stupid rage. Those who have hair between their toes do not care to be reminded of it. Mowgli caught his foot away as the leader leaped up, and said sweetly: Dog, red dog! Go back to the Dekkan and eat lizards. Go to Chikai thy brother – dog, dog – red, red dog! There is hair between every toe!" He twiddled his toes a second time.

"Come down ere we starve thee out, hairless ape!" yelled the Pack, and this was exactly what Mowgli wanted. He laid himself down along the branch, his cheek to the bark, his right arm free, and there he told the Pack what he thought and knew about them, their manners, their customs, their mates, and their puppies. There is no speech in the world so rancorous and so stinging as the language the Jungle People use to show scorn and contempt. When you come to think of it you will see how this must be so. As Mowgli told Kaa, he had many little thorns under his tongue, and slowly and deliberately he drove the dholes from silence to growls, from growls to yells, and from yells to hoarse slavery ravings. They tried to answer his taunts, but a cub might as well have tried to answer Kaa in a rage; and all the while Mowgli's right hand lay crooked at his side, ready for action, his feet locked round the branch. The big bay leader had leaped many times in the air, but Mowgli dared not risk a false blow. At last, made furious beyond his natural strength, he bounded up seven or eight feet clear of the ground. Then Mowgli's hand shot out like the head of a tree-snake, and gripped him by the scruff of his neck, and the branch shook with the jar as his weight fell back, almost wrenching Mowgli to the ground. But he never loosed his grip, and inch by inch he hauled the beast, hanging like a drowned jackal, up on the branch. With his left hand he reached for his knife and cut off the red, bushy tail, flinging the dhole back to earth again. That was all he needed. The Pack would not go forward on Won-tolla's trail now till they had killed Mowgli or Mowgli had killed them. He saw them settle down in circles with a quiver of the haunches that meant they were going to stay, and so he climbed to a higher crotch, settled his back comfortably, and went to sleep.

After three or four hours he waked and counted the Pack. They were all there, silent, husky, and dry, with eyes of steel. The sun was beginning to sink. In half an hour the Little People of the Rocks would be ending their labours, and, as you know, the dhole does not fight best in the twilight. "I did not need such faithful watchers," he said politely, standing up on a branch, "but I will remember this. Ye be true dholes, but to my thinking over much of one kind. For that reason I do not give the big lizard-eater his tail again. Art thou not pleased, Red Dog?"

"I myself will tear out thy stomach!" yelled the leader, scratching at the foot of the tree.

"Nay, but consider, wise rat of the Dekkan. There will now be many litters of little tailless red dogs, yea, with raw red stumps that sting when the sand is hot. Go home, Red Dog, and cry that an ape has done this. Ye will not go? Come, then, with me, and I will make you very wise!"

He moved, *Bandar-log* fashion, into the next tree, and so on into the next and the next, the Pack following with lifted hungry heads. Now and then he would pretend to fall, and the Pack would tumble one over the other in their haste to be at the death. It was a curious sight – the boy with the knife that shone in the low sunlight as it sifted through the upper branches, and the silent Pack with their red coats all aflame, huddling and following below. When he came to the last tree he took the garlic and rubbed himself all over carefully, and the dholes yelled with scorn. "Ape with a wolf's tongue, dost thou think to cover thy scent?" they said. "We follow to the death."

"Take thy tail," said Mowgli, flinging it back along the course he had taken. The Pack instinctively rushed after it. "And follow now – to the death."

He had slipped down the tree-trunk, and headed like the wind in bare feet for the Bee Rocks, before the dholes saw what he would do.

They gave one deep howl, and settled down to the long, lobbing canter that can at the last run down anything that runs. Mowgli knew their pack-pace to be much slower than that of the wolves, or he would never have risked a two-mile run in full sight. They were sure that the boy was theirs at last, and he was sure that he held them to play with as he pleased. All his trouble was to keep them sufficiently hot behind him to prevent their turning off too soon. He ran cleanly, evenly, and springily; the tailless leader not five yards behind him; and the Pack tailing out over perhaps a quarter of a mile of ground, crazy and blind with the rage of slaughter. So he kept his distance by ear, reserving his last effort for the rush across the Bee Rocks.

The Little People had gone to sleep in the early twilight, for it was not the season of late blossoming flowers; but as Mowgli's first foot-falls rang hollow on the hollow ground he heard a sound as though all the earth were humming. Then he ran as he had never run in his life before, spurned aside one – two – three of the piles of stones into the dark, sweet-smelling gullies; heard a roar like the roar of the sea in a cave; saw with the tail of his eye the air grow dark behind him; saw the current of the Waingunga far below, and a flat, diamond-shaped head in the water; leaped outward with all his strength, the tailless dhole snapping at his shoulder in mid-air, and dropped feet first to the safety of the river, breathless and triumphant. There was not a sting upon him, for the smell of the garlic had checked the Little People for just the few seconds that he was among them. When he rose Kaa's coils were steadying him and things were bounding over the edge of the cliff – great lumps, it seemed, of clustered bees falling like plummets; but before any lump touched water the bees flew upward and the body of a dhole whirled down-stream. Overhead they could hear furious short yells that were drowned in a roar like breakers – the roar of the wings of the Little People of the Rocks. Some of the dholes, too, had fallen into the gullies that communicated with the underground caves, and there choked and fought and snapped among the tumbled honeycombs, and at last, borne up, even when they were dead, on the heaving waves of bees beneath them, shot out of some hole in the river-face, to roll over on the black rubbish-heaps. There were dholes who had leaped short into the trees on the cliffs, and the bees blotted out their shapes; but the greater number of them, maddened by the stings, had flung themselves into the river; and, as Kaa said, the Waingunga was hungry water.

Kaa held Mowgli fast till the boy had recovered his breath.

"We may not stay here," he said. "The Little People are roused indeed. Come!"

Swimming low and diving as often as he could, Mowgli went down the river, knife in hand.

"Slowly, slowly," said Kaa. "One tooth does not kill a hundred unless it be a cobra's, and many of the dholes took water swiftly when they saw the Little People rise. *They* are unhurt"

"The more work for my knife, then. Phai! How the, Little People follow!" Mowgli sank again. The face of the water was blanketed with wild bees, buzzing sullenly and stinging all they found.

"Nothing was ever yet lost by silence," said Kaa – no sting could penetrate his scales – "and thou hast all the long night for the hunting. Hear them howl!"

Nearly half the pack had seen the trap their fellows rushed into, and turning sharp aside had flung themselves into the water where the gorge broke down in steep banks. Their cries of rage and their threats against the "tree-ape" who had brought them to their shame mixed with the yells and growls of those who had been punished by the Little People. To remain ashore was death, and every dhole knew it. Their pack was swept along the current, down to the deep eddies of the Peace Pool, but even there the angry Little People followed and forced them to the water again. Mowgli could hear the voice of the tailless leader bidding his people hold on and kill out every wolf in Seeonee. But he did not waste his time in listening.

"One kills in the dark behind us!" snapped a dhole. "Here is tainted water!"

Mowgli had dived forward like an otter, twitched a struggling dhole under water before he could open his mouth, and dark rings rose as the body plopped up, turning on its side. The dholes tried to turn, but the current prevented them, and the Little People darted at the heads and ears, and they could hear the challenge of the Seeonee Pack growing louder and deeper in the gathering darkness. Again Mowgli dived, and again a dhole went under, and rose dead, and again the clamour broke out at the rear of the pack; some howling that it was best to go ashore, others calling on their leader to lead them back to the Dekkan, and others bidding Mowgli show himself and he killed.

"They come to the fight with two stomachs and several voices," said Kaa. "The rest is with thy brethren below yonder, The Little People go back to sleep. They have chased us far. Now I, too, turn back, for I am not of one skin with any wolf. Good hunting, Little Brother, and remember the dhole bites low."

A wolf came running along the bank on three legs, leaping up and down, laying his head sideways close to the ground, hunching his back, and breaking high into the air, as though he were playing with his cubs. It was Won-tolla, the Outlier, and he said never a word, but continued his horrible sport beside the dholes. They had been long in the water now, and were swimming wearily, their coats drenched and heavy, their bushy tails dragging like sponges, so tired and shaken that they, too, were silent, watching the pair of blazing eyes that moved abreast.

"This is no good hunting," said one, panting.

"Good hunting!" said Mowgli, as he rose boldly at the brute's side, and sent the long knife home behind the shoulder, pushing hard to avoid his dying snap.

"Art thou there, Man-cub?" said Won-tolla across the water.

"Ask of the dead, Outlier," Mowgli replied. "Have none come down-stream? I have filled these dogs' mouths with dirt; I have tricked them in the broad daylight, and their leader lacks his tail, but here be some few for thee still. Whither shall I drive them?"

"I will wait," said Won-tolla. "The night is before me and I shall see well."

Nearer and nearer came the bay of the Seeonee wolves. "For the Pack, for the Full Pack it is met!" and a bend in the river drove the dholes forward among the sands and shoals opposite the Lairs.

Then they saw their mistake. They should have landed half a mile higher up, and rushed the wolves on dry ground. Now it was too late. The bank was lined with burning eyes, and except for the horrible *pheeal* that had never stopped since sundown, there was no sound in the Jungle. It seemed as though Won-tolla were fawning on them to come ashore; and "Turn and take hold!" said the leader of the dholes. The entire Pack flung themselves at the shore, threshing and squattering through the shoal water, till the face of the Waingunga was all white and torn, and the great ripples went from side to side, like bow-waves from a boat. Mowgli followed the rush, stabbing and slicing as the dholes, huddled together, rushed up the river-beach in one wave.

Then the long fight began, heaving and straining and splitting and scattering and narrowing and broadening along the red, wet sands, and over and between the tangled tree-roots, and through and among the bushes, and in and out of the grass clumps; for even now the dholes were two to one. But they met wolves fighting for all that made the Pack, and not only the short, high, deep-chested, white-tusked hunters of the Pack, but the anxious-eyed *lahinis* – the she-wolves of the lair, as the saying is – fighting for their litters, with here and there a yearling wolf, his first coat still half woolly, tugging and grappling by their sides. A wolf, you must know, flies at the throat or snaps at the flank, while a dhole, by preference, bites at the belly; so when the dholes were struggling out of the water and had to raise their heads, the odds were with the wolves. On dry land the wolves suffered; but in the water or ashore, Mowgli's knife came and went without ceasing. The Four had worried their way to his side. Gray Brother, crouched between the boy's knees, was protecting his stomach, while the others guarded his back and either side, or stood over him when the shock of a leaping, yelling dhole who had thrown himself full on the steady blade bore him down. For the rest, it was one tangled confusion – a locked and swaying mob that moved from right to left and from left to right along the bank; and also ground round and round slowly on its own centre. Here would be a heaving mound, like a water-blister in a whirlpool, which would break like a water-blister, and throw up four or five mangled dogs, each striving to get back to the centre; here would be a single wolf borne down by two or three dholes, laboriously dragging them forward, and sinking the while; here a yearling cub would he held up by the pressure round him, though he had been killed early, while his mother, crazed with dumb rage, rolled over and over, snapping, and passing on; and in the middle of the thickest press, perhaps, one wolf and one dhole, forgetting everything else, would be manoeuvring for first hold till they were whirled away by a rush of furious fighters. Once Mowgli passed Akela, a dhole on either flank, and his all but toothless jaws closed over the loins of a third; and once he saw Phao, his teeth set in the throat of a dhole, tugging the unwilling beast forward till the yearlings could finish him. But the bulk of the fight was blind flurry and smother in the dark; hit, trip, and tumble, yelp, groan, and worry-worry-worry, round him and behind him and above him.

As the night wore on, the quick, giddy-go-round motion increased. The dholes were cowed and afraid to attack the stronger wolves, but did not yet dare to run away. Mowgli felt that the end was coming soon, and contented himself with striking merely to cripple. The yearlings were growing bolder; there was time now and again to breathe, and pass a word to a friend, and the mere flicker of the knife would sometimes turn a dhole aside.

"The meat is very near the bone," Gray Brother yelled. He was bleeding from a score of flesh-wounds.

"But the bone is yet to he cracked," said Mowgli. "*Aowawa*! *Thus* do we do in the Jungle!" The red blade ran like a flame along the side of a dhole whose hind-quarters were hidden by the weight of a clinging wolf.

"My kill!" snorted the wolf through his wrinkled nostrils. "Leave him to me."

"Is thy stomach *still* empty, Outlier?" said Mowgli. Won-tolla was fearfully punished, but his grip had paralysed the dhole, who could not turn round and reach him.

"By the Bull that bought me," said Mowgli, with a bitter laugh, "it is the tailless one!" And indeed it was the big bay-coloured leader.

"It is not wise to kill cubs and *lahinis*," Mowgli went on philosophically, wiping the blood out of his eyes, "unless one has also killed the Outlier; and it is in my stomach that this Won-tolla kills thee."

A dhole leaped to his leader's aid; but before his teeth had found Won-tolla's flank, Mowgli's knife was in his throat, and Gray Brother took what was left.

"And thus do we do in the Jungle," said Mowgli.

Won-tolla said not a word, only his jaws were closing and closing on the backbone as his life ebbed. The dhole shuddered, his head dropped, and he lay still, and Won-tolla dropped above him.

"*Huh*! The Blood Debt is paid," said Mowgli. "Sing the song, Won-tolla."

"He hunts no more," said Gray Brother; "and Akela, too, is silent this long time."

"The bone is cracked!" thundered Phao, son of Phaona. "They go! Kill, kill out, O hunters of the Free People!"

Dhole after dhole was slinking away from those dark and bloody sands to the river, to the thick Jungle, up-stream or down-stream as he saw the road clear.

"The debt! The debt!" shouted Mowgli. "Pay the debt! They have slain the Lone Wolf! Let not a dog go!"

He was flying to the river, knife in hand, to check any dhole who dared to take water, when, from under a mound of nine dead, rose Akela's head and fore-quarters, and Mowgli dropped on his knees beside the Lone Wolf.

"Said I not it would be my last fight?" Akela gasped. "It is good hunting. And thou, Little Brother?"

"I live, having killed many."

"Even so. I die, and I would – I would die by thee, Little Brother."

Mowgli took the terrible scarred head on his knees, and put his arms round the torn neck.

"It is long since the old days of Shere Khan, and a Man-cub that rolled naked in the dust."

"Nay, nay, I am a wolf. I am of one skin with the Free People," Mowgli cried. "It is no will of mine that I am a man."

"Thou art a man, Little Brother, wolfling of my watching. Thou art a man, or else the Pack had fled before the dhole. My life I owe to thee, and to-day thou hast saved the Pack even as once I saved thee. Hast thou forgotten? All debts are paid now. Go to thine own people. I tell thee again, eye of my eye, this hunting is ended. Go to thine own people."

"I will never go. I will hunt alone in the Jungle. I have said it."

"After the summer come the Rains, and after the Rains comes the spring. Go back before thou art driven."

"Who will drive me?"

"Mowgli will drive Mowgli. Go back to thy people. Go to Man."

"When Mowgli drives Mowgli I will go," Mowgli answered.

"There is no more to say," said Akela. "Little Brother, canst thou raise me to my feet? I also was a leader of the Free People."

Very carefully and gently Mowgli lifted the bodies aside, and raised Akela to his feet, both arms round him, and the Lone Wolf drew a long breath, and began the Death Song that a leader of the Pack should sing when he dies. It gathered strength as he went on, lifting and lifting, and ringing far across the river, till it came to the last "Good hunting!" and Akela shook himself clear of Mowgli for an instant, and, leaping into the air, fell backward dead upon his last and most terrible kill.

Mowgli sat with his head on his knees, careless of anything else, while the remnant of the flying dholes were being overtaken and run down by the merciless *lahinis*. Little by little the cries died away, and the wolves returned limping, as their wounds stiffened, to take stock of the losses. Fifteen of the Pack, as well as half a dozen *lahinis*, lay dead by the river, and of the others not one was unmarked. And Mowgli sat through it all till the cold daybreak, when Phao's wet, red muzzle was dropped in his hand, and Mowgli drew back to show the gaunt body of Akela.

"Good hunting!" said Phao, as though Akela were still alive, and then over his bitten shoulder to the others: "Howl, dogs! A Wolf has died to-night!"

But of all the Pack of two hundred fighting dholes, whose boast was that all jungles were their Jungle, and that no living thing could stand before them, not one returned to the Dekkan to carry that word.

# CHIL'S SONG

[This is the song that Chil sang as the kites dropped down one after another to the river-bed, when the great fight was finished. Chil is good friends with everybody, but he is a cold-blooded kind of creature at heart, because he knows that almost everybody in the Jungle comes to him in the long-run.]

These were my companions going forth by night –
    (For *Chil! Look you, for Chil*!)

Now come I to whistle them the ending of the fight.
    (*Chil! Vanguards of Chil!*)

Word they gave me overhead of quarry newly slain,
Word I gave them underfoot of buck upon the plain.
Here's an end of every trail – they shall not speak again!

They that called the hunting-cry – they that followed fast –
    (For *Chil! Look you, for Chil*!)

They that bade the sambhur wheel, or pinned him as he
    passed –
    (*Chil! Vanguards of Chil*!)

They that lagged behind the scent – they that ran before,
They that shunned the level horn – they that overbore.
Here's an end of every trail – they shall not follow more.

These were my companions. Pity 'twas they died!
    (For *Chil! Look you, for Chil*!)

Now come I to comfort them that knew them in their pride.
    (*Chil! Vanguards of Chil*!)

Tattered flank and sunken eye, open mouth and red,
Locked and lank and lone they lie, the dead upon their dead.
Here's an end of every trail – and here my hosts are fed.

# THE SPRING RUNNING

Man goes to Man! Cry the challenge through the Jungle!
He that was our Brother goes away.
Hear, now, and judge, O ye People of the Jungle, –
Answer, who shall turn him – who shall stay?

Man goes to Man! He is weeping in the Jungle:
He that was our Brother sorrows sore!
Man goes to Man! (Oh, we loved him in the Jungle!)
To the Man-Trail where we may not follow more.

THE SECOND year after the great fight with Red Dog and the death of Akela, Mowgli must have been nearly seventeen years old. He looked older, for hard exercise, the best of good eating, and baths whenever he felt in the least hot or dusty, had given him strength and growth far beyond his age. He could swing by one hand from a top branch for half an hour at a time, when he had occasion to look along the tree-roads. He could stop a young buck in mid-gallop and throw him sideways by the head. He could even jerk over the big, blue wild boars that lived in the Marshes of the North. The Jungle People who used to fear him for his wits feared him now for his strength, and when he moved quietly on his own affairs the mere whisper of his coming cleared the wood-paths. And yet the look in his eyes was always gentle. Even when he fought, his eyes never blazed as Bagheera's did. They only grew more and more interested and excited; and that was one of the things that Bagheera himself did not understand.

He asked Mowgli about it, and the boy laughed and said. "When I miss the kill I am angry. When I must go empty for two days I am very angry. Do not my eyes talk then?"

"The mouth is hungry," said Bagheera, "but the eyes say nothing. Hunting, eating, or swimming, it is all one – like a stone in wet or dry weather." Mowgli looked at him lazily from under his long eyelashes, and, as usual, the panther's head dropped. Bagheera knew his master.

They were lying out far up the side of a hill overlooking the Waingunga, and the morning mists hung below them in bands of white and green. As the sun rose it changed into bubbling seas of red gold, churned off, and let the low rays stripe the dried grass on which Mowgli and Bagheera were resting. It was the end of the cold weather, the leaves and the trees looked worn and faded, and there was a dry, ticking rustle everywhere when the wind blew. A little leaf tap-tap-tapped furiously against a twig, as a single leaf caught in a current will. It roused Bagheera, for he snuffed the morning air with a deep, hollow cough, threw himself on his back, and struck with his fore-paws at the nodding leaf above.

"The year turns," he said. "The Jungle goes forward. The Time of New Talk is near. That leaf knows. It is very good."

"The grass is dry," Mowgli answered, pulling up a tuft. "Even Eye-of-the-Spring [that is a little trumpet-shaped, waxy red flower that runs in and out among the grasses] – even Eye-of-the Spring is shut, and . . . Bagheera, *is* it well for the Black Panther so to lie on his back and beat with his paws in the air, as though he were the tree-cat?"

"*Aowh*?" said Bagheera. He seemed to be thinking of other things.

"I say, is it well for the Black Panther so to mouth and cough, and howl and roll? Remember, we be the Masters of the Jungle, thou and I."

"Indeed, yes; I hear, Man-cub." Bagheera rolled over hurriedly and sat up, the dust on his ragged black flanks. (He was just casting his winter coat.) "We be surely the Masters of the Jungle! Who is so strong as Mowgli? Who so wise?" There was a curious drawl in the voice that made Mowgli turn to see whether by any chance the Black Panther were making fun of him, for the Jungle is full of words that sound like one thing, but mean another. "I said we be beyond question the Masters of the Jungle," Bagheera repeated. "Have I done wrong? I did not know that the Man-cub no longer lay upon the ground. Does he fly, then?"

Mowgli sat with his elbows on his knees, looking out across the valley at the daylight. Somewhere down in the woods below a bird was trying over in a husky, reedy voice the first few notes of his spring song. It was no more than a shadow of the liquid, tumbling call he would be pouring later, but Bagheera heard it.

"I said the Time of New Talk is near," growled the panther, switching his tail.

"I hear," Mowgli answered. "Bagheera, why dost thou shake all over? The sun is warm."

"That is Ferao, the scarlet woodpecker," said Bagheera. "*He* has not forgotten. Now I, too, must remember my song," and he began purring and crooning to himself, harking back dissatisfied again and again.

"There is no game afoot," said Mowgli lazily.

"Little Brother, are *both* thine ears stopped? That is no killing-word, but my song that I make ready against the need."

"I had forgotten. I shall know when the Time of New Talk is here, because then thou and the others all run away and leave me alone." Mowgli spoke rather savagely.

"But, indeed, Little Brother," Bagheera began, "we do not always — "

"I say ye do," said Mowgli, shooting out his forefinger angrily. "Ye *do* run away, and I, who am the Master of the Jungle, must needs walk alone. How was it last season, when I would gather sugar-cane from the fields of a Man-Pack? I sent a runner – I sent thee! – to Hathi, bidding him to come upon such a night and pluck the sweet grass for me with his trunk."

"He came only two nights later," said Bagheera, cowering a little; "and of that long, sweet grass that pleased thee so he gathered more than any Man-cub could eat in all the nights of the Rains. That was no fault of mine."

"He did not come upon the night when I sent him the word. No, he was trumpeting and running and roaring through the valleys in the moonlight. His trail was like the trail of three elephants, for he would not hide among the trees. He danced in the moonlight before the houses of the Man-Pack. I saw him, and yet he would not come to me; and I am the Master of the Jungle!"

"It was the Time of New Talk," said the panther, always very humble. "Perhaps, Little Brother, thou didst not that time call him by a Master-word? Listen to Ferao, and be happy!"

Mowgli's bad temper seemed to have boiled itself away. He lay back with his head on his arms, his eyes shut. "I do not know – nor do I care," he said sleepily. "Let us sleep, Bagheera. My stomach is heavy in me. Make me a rest for my head."

The panther lay down again with a sigh, because he could hear Ferao practising and repractising his song against the Springtime of New Talk, as they say.

In an Indian Jungle the seasons slide one into the other almost without division. There seem to be only two – the wet and the dry; but if you look closely below the torrents of rain and the clouds of char and dust you will find all four going round in their regular ring. Spring is the most wonderful, because she has not to cover a clean, bare field with new leaves and flowers, but to drive before her and to put away the hanging-on, over-surviving raffle of half-green things which the gentle winter has suffered to live, and to make the partly-dressed stale earth feel new and young once more. And this she does so well that there is no spring in the world like the Jungle spring.

There is one day when all things are tired, and the very smells, as they drift on the heavy air, are old and used. One cannot explain this, but it feels so. Then there is another day – to the eye nothing whatever has changed – when all the smells are new and delightful, and the whiskers of the Jungle People quiver to their roots, and the winter hair comes away from their sides in long, draggled locks. Then, perhaps, a little rain falls, and all the trees and the bushes and the bamboos and the mosses and the juicy-leaved plants wake with a noise of growing that you can almost hear, and under this noise runs, day and night, a deep hum. *That* is the noise of the spring – a vibrating boom which is neither bees, nor falling water, nor the wind in tree-tops, but the purring of the warm, happy world.

Up to this year Mowgli had always delighted in the turn of the seasons. It was he who generally saw the first Eye-of-the-Spring deep down among the grasses, and the first bank of spring clouds, which are like nothing else in the Jungle. His voice could be heard in all sorts of wet, star-lighted, blossoming places, helping the big frogs through their choruses, or mocking the little upside-down owls that hoot through the white nights. Like all his people, spring was the season he chose for his flittings – moving, for the mere joy of rushing through the warm air, thirty, forty, or fifty miles between twilight and the morning star, and coming back panting and laughing and wreathed with strange flowers. The Four did not follow him on these wild ringings of the Jungle, but went off to sing songs with other wolves. The Jungle People are very busy in the spring, and Mowgli could hear them grunting and screaming and whistling according to their kind. Their voices then are different from their voices at other times of the year, and that is one of the reasons why spring in the Jungle is called the Time of New Talk.

But that spring, as he told Bagheera, his stomach was changed in him. Ever since the bamboo shoots turned spotty-brown he had been looking forward to the morning when the smells should change. But when the morning came, and Mor the Peacock, blazing in bronze and blue and gold, cried it aloud all along the misty woods, and Mowgli opened his mouth to send on the cry, the words choked between his teeth, and a feeling came over him that began at his toes and ended in his hair – a feeling of pure unhappiness, so that he looked himself over to be sure that he had not trod on a thorn. Mor cried the new smells, the other birds took it over, and from the rocks by the Waingunga he heard Bagheera's hoarse scream – something between the scream of an eagle and the neighing of a horse. There was a yelling and scattering of *Bandar-log* in the new-budding branches above, and there stood Mowgli, his chest, filled to answer Mor, sinking in little gasps as the breath was driven out of it by this unhappiness.

He stared all round him, but he could see no more than the mocking *Bandar-log* scudding through the trees, and Mor, his tail spread in full splendour, dancing on the slopes below.

"The smells have changed," screamed Mor. "Good hunting, Little Brother! Where is thy answer?"

"Little Brother, good hunting!" whistled Chil the Kite and his mate, swooping down together. The two baffed under Mowgli's nose so close that a pinch of downy white feathers brushed away.

A light spring rain – elephant-rain they call it – drove across the Jungle in a belt half a mile wide, left the new leaves wet and nodding behind, and died out in a double rainbow and a light roll of thunder. The spring hum broke out for a minute, and was silent, but all the Jungle Folk seemed to be giving tongue at once. All except Mowgli.

"I have eaten good food," he said to himself. "I have drunk good water. Nor does my throat burn and grow small, as it did when I bit the blue-spotted root that Oo the Turtle said was clean food. But my stomach is heavy, and I have given very bad talk to Bagheera and others, people of the Jungle and my people. Now, too, I am hot and now I am cold, and now I am neither hot nor cold, but angry with that which I cannot see. *Huhu*! It is time to make a running! To-night I will cross the ranges; yes, I will make a spring running to the Marshes of the North, and back again. I have hunted too easily too long. The Four shall come with me, for they grow as fat as white grubs."

He called, but never one of the Four answered. They were far beyond earshot, singing over the spring songs – the Moon and Sambhur Songs – with the wolves of the pack; for in the spring-time the Jungle People make very little difference between the day and the night. He gave the sharp, barking note, but his only answer was the mocking *maiou* of the little spotted tree-cat winding in and out among the branches for early birds' nests. At this he shook all over with rage, and half drew his knife. Then he became very haughty, though there was no one to see him, and stalked severely down the hillside, chin up and eyebrows down. But never a single one of his people asked him a question, for they were all too busy with their own affairs.

"Yes," said Mowgli to himself, though in his heart he knew that he had no reason. "Let the Red Dhole come from the Dekkan, or the Red Flower dance among the bamboos, and all the Jungle runs whining to Mowgli, calling him great elephant-names. But now, because Eye-of-the-Spring is red, and Mor, forsooth, must show his naked legs in some spring dance, the Jungle goes mad as Tabaqui. . . . By the Bull that bought me! Am I the Master of the Jungle, or am I not? Be silent! What do ye here?"

A couple of young wolves of the Pack were cantering down a path, looking for open ground in which to fight. (You will remember that the Law of the Jungle forbids fighting where the Pack can see.) Their neck-bristles were as stiff as wire, and they bayed furiously, crouching for the first grapple. Mowgli leaped forward, caught one outstretched throat in either hand, expecting to fling the creatures backward as he had often done in games or Pack hunts. But he had never before interfered with a spring fight. The two leaped forward and dashed him aside, and without word to waste rolled over and over close locked.

Mowgli was on his feet almost before he fell, his knife and his white teeth were bared, and at that minute he would have killed both for no reason but that they were fighting when he wished them to be quiet, although every wolf has full right under the Law to fight. He danced round them with lowered shoulders and quivering hand, ready to send in a double blow when the first flurry of the scuffle should be over; but while he waited the strength seemed to ebb from his body, the knife-point lowered, and he sheathed the knife and watched.

"I have surely eaten poison," he sighed at last. Since I broke up the Council with the Red Flower – since I killed Shere Khan – none of the Pack could fling me aside. And these be only tail-wolves in the Pack, little hunters! My strength is gone from me, and presently I shall die. Oh, Mowgli, why dost thou not kill them both?"

The fight went on till one wolf ran away, and Mowgli was left alone on the torn and bloody ground, looking now at his knife, and now at his legs and arms, while the feeling of unhappiness he had never known before covered him as water covers a log.

He killed early that evening and ate but little, so as to be in good fettle for his spring running, and he ate alone because all the Jungle People were away singing or fighting. It was a perfect white night, as they call it. All green things seemed to have made a month's growth since the morning. The branch that was yellow-leaved the day before dripped sap when

Mowgli broke it. The mosses curled deep and warm over his feet, the young grass had no cutting edges, and all the voices of the Jungle boomed like one deep harp-string touched by the moon – the Moon of New Talk, who splashed her light full on rock and pool, slipped it between trunk and creeper, and sifted it through a million leaves. Forgetting his unhappiness, Mowgli sang aloud with pure delight as he settled into his stride. It was more like flying than anything else, for he had chosen the long downward slope that leads to the Northern Marshes through the heart of the main Jungle, where the springy ground deadened the fall of his feet. A man-taught man would have picked his way with many stumbles through the cheating moonlight, but Mowgli's muscles, trained by years of experience, bore him up as though he were a feather. When a rotten log or a hidden stone turned under his foot he saved himself, never checking his pace, without effort and without thought. When he tired of ground-going he threw up his hands monkey-fashion to the nearest creeper, and seemed to float rather than to climb up into the thin branches, whence he would follow a tree-road till his mood changed, and he shot downward in a long, leafy curve to the levels again. There were still, hot hollows surrounded by wet rocks where he could hardly breathe for the heavy scents of the night flowers and the bloom along the creeper buds; dark avenues where the moonlight lay in belts as regular as checkered marbles in a church aisle; thickets where the wet young growth stood breast-high about him and threw its arms round his waist; and hilltops crowned with broken rock, where he leaped from stone to stone above the lairs of the frightened little foxes. He would hear, very faint and far off, the *chug-drug* of a boar sharpening his tusks on a bole; and would come across the great gray brute all alone, scribing and rending the bark of a tall tree, his mouth dripping with foam, and his eyes blazing like fire. Or he would turn aside to the sound of clashing horns and hissing grunts, and dash past a couple of furious sambhur, staggering to and fro with lowered heads, striped with blood that showed black in the moonlight. Or at some rushing ford he would hear Jacala the Crocodile bellowing like a bull, or disturb a twined knot of the Poison People, but before they could strike he would be away and across the glistening shingle, and deep in the Jungle again.

So he ran, sometimes shouting, sometimes singing to himself, the happiest thing in all the Jungle that night, till the smell of the flowers warned him that he was near the marshes, and those lay far beyond his farthest hunting-grounds.

Here, again, a man-trained man would have sunk overhead in three strides, but Mowgli's feet had eyes in them, and they passed him from tussock to tussock and clump to quaking clump without asking help from the eyes in his head. He ran out to the middle of the swamp, disturbing the duck as he ran, and sat down on a moss-coated tree-trunk lapped in the black water. The marsh was awake all round him, for in the spring the Bird People sleep very lightly, and companies of them were coming or going the night through. But no one took any notice of Mowgli sitting among the tall reeds humming songs without words, and looking at the soles of his hard brown feet in case of neglected thorns. All his unhappiness seemed to have been left behind in his own Jungle, and he was just beginning a full-throat song when it came back again – ten times worse than before. To make things difficult, the moon began setting.

This time Mowgli was frightened. "It is here also!" he said half aloud. "It has followed me," and he looked over his shoulder to see whether the It were not standing behind him. "There is no one here." The night noises of the marsh went on, but never a bird or beast spoke to him, and the new feeling of misery grew.

"I have surely eaten poison," he said in an awe-stricken voice. "It must be that carelessly I have eaten poison, and my strength is going from me. I was afraid – and yet it was not *I* that was afraid – Mowgli was afraid when the two wolves fought. Akela, or even Phao, would have silenced them; yet Mowgli was afraid. That is true sign I have eaten poison. . . . But what do they care in the Jungle? They sing and howl and fight, and run in companies under the moon, and I – *Hai-mai*! – I am dying in the marshes, of that poison which I have eaten." He was so sorry for himself that he nearly wept. "And after," he went on, "they will find me lying in the black water. Nay, I will go back to my own Jungle, and I will die upon the Council Rock, and Bagheera, whom I love, if he is not screaming in the valley – Bagheera, perhaps, may watch by what is left for a little, lest Chil use me as he used Akela."

A large, warm tear splashed down on his knee, and, miserable as he was, Mowgli felt happy that he was so miserable, if you can understand that upside-down sort of happiness. "As Chil the Kite used Akela," he repeated, "on the night I saved the Pack from Red Dog." He was quiet for a little, thinking of the last words of the Lone Wolf, which you, of course, remember. "Now Akela said to me many foolish things before he died, for when we die our stomachs change. He said . . . None the less, I *am* of the Jungle!"

In his excitement, as he remembered the fight on Waingunga bank, he shouted the last words aloud, and a wild buffalo-cow among the reeds sprang to her knees, snorting, "Man!"

"*Uhh*!" said Mysah the Wild Buffalo (Mowgli could hear him turn in his wallow), "*that* is no man. It is only the hairless wolf of the Seeonee Pack. On such nights runs he to and fro."

"*Uhh*!" said the cow, dropping her head again to graze, "I thought it was Man."

"I say no. Oh, Mowgli, is it danger?" lowed Mysah.

"Oh, Mowgli, is it danger?" the boy called back mockingly. "That is all Mysah thinks for: Is it danger? But for

Mowgli, who goes to and fro in the Jungle by night, watching, what do ye care?"

"How loud he cries!" said the cow.

"Thus do they cry," Mysah answered contemptuously, "who, having torn up the grass, know not how to eat it."

"For less than this," Mowgli groaned to himself, for less than this even last Rains I had pricked Mysah out of his wallow, and ridden him through the swamp on a rush halter." He stretched a hand to break one of the feathery reeds, but drew it back with a sigh. Mysah went on steadily chewing the cud, and the long grass ripped where the cow grazed. "I will not die HERE," he said angrily. "Mysah, who is of one blood with Jacala and the pig, would see me. Let us go beyond the swamp and see what comes. Never have I run such a spring running – hot and cold together. Up, Mowgli!"

He could not resist the temptation of stealing across the reeds to Mysah and pricking him with the point of his knife. The great dripping bull broke out of his wallow like a shell exploding, while Mowgli laughed till he sat down.

"Say now that the hairless wolf of the Seeonee Pack once herded thee, Mysah," he called.

"Wolf! *thou*?" the bull snorted, stamping in the mud. "All the jungle knows thou wast a herder of tame cattle – such a man's brat as shouts in the dust by the crops yonder. *Thou* of the Jungle! What hunter would have crawled like a snake among the leeches, and for a muddy jest – a jackal's jest – have shamed me before my cow? Come to firm ground, and I will – I will . . ." Mysah frothed at the mouth, for Mysah has nearly the worst temper of any one in the Jungle.

Mowgli watched him puff and blow with eyes that never changed. When he could make himself heard through the pattering mud, he said: "What Man-Pack lair here by the marshes, Mysah? This is new Jungle to me."

"Go north, then," roared the angry bull, for Mowgli had pricked him rather sharply. "It was a naked cow-herd's jest. Go and tell them at the village at the foot of the marsh."

"The Man-Pack do not love jungle-tales, nor do I think, Mysah, that a scratch more or less on thy hide is any matter for a council. But I will go and look at this village. Yes, I will go. Softly now. It is not every night that the Master of the Jungle comes to herd thee."

He stepped out to the shivering ground on the edge of the marsh, well knowing that Mysah would never charge over it and laughed, as he ran, to think of the bull's anger.

"My strength is not altogether gone," he said. It may be that the poison is not to the bone. There is a star sitting low yonder." He looked at it between his half-shut hands. "By the Bull that bought me, it is the Red Flower – the Red Flower that I lay beside before – before I came even to the first Seeonee Pack! Now that I have seen, I will finish the running."

The marsh ended in a broad plain where a light twinkled. It was a long time since Mowgli had concerned himself with the doings of men, but this night the glimmer of the Red Flower drew him forward.

"I will look," said he, "as I did in the old days, and I will see how far the Man-Pack has changed."

Forgetting that he was no longer in his own Jungle, where he could do what he pleased, he trod carelessly through the dew-loaded grasses till he came to the hut where the light stood. Three or four yelping dogs gave tongue, for he was on the outskirts of a village.

"Ho!" said Mowgli, sitting down noiselessly, after sending back a deep wolf-growl that silenced the curs. "What comes will come. Mowgli, what hast thou to do any more with the lairs of the Man-Pack?" He rubbed his mouth, remembering where a stone had struck it years ago when the other Man-Pack had cast him out.

The door of the hut opened, and a woman stood peering out into the darkness. A child cried, and the woman said over her shoulder, "Sleep. It was but a jackal that waked the dogs. In a little time morning comes."

Mowgli in the grass began to shake as though he had fever. He knew that voice well, but to make sure he cried softly, surprised to find how man's talk came back, "Messua! O Messua!"

"Who calls?" said the woman, a quiver in her voice.

"Hast thou forgotten?" said Mowgli. His throat was dry as he spoke.

"If it be *thou*, what name did I give thee? Say!" She had half shut the door, and her hand was clutching at her breast.

"Nathoo! Ohé, Nathoo!" said Mowgli, for, as you remember, that was the name Messua gave him when he first came to the Man-Pack.

"Come, my son," she called, and Mowgli stepped into the light, and looked full at Messua, the woman who had been good to him, and whose life he had saved from the Man-Pack so long before. She was older, and her hair was gray, but her eyes and her voice had not changed. Woman-like, she expected to find Mowgli where she had left him, and her eyes travelled upward in a puzzled way from his chest to his head, that touched the top of the door.

"My son," she stammered; and then, sinking to his feet: "But it is no longer my son. It is a Godling of the Woods! *Ahai*!"

As he stood in the red light of the oil-lamp, strong, tall, and beautiful, his long black hair sweeping over his shoulders, the knife swinging at his neck, and his head crowned with a wreath of white jasmine, he might easily have been mistaken for some wild god of a jungle legend. The child half asleep on a cot sprang up and shrieked aloud with terror. Messua turned to soothe him, while Mowgli stood still, looking in at the water-jars and the cooking-pots, the grain-bin, and all the other human belongings that he found himself remembering so well.

"What wilt thou eat or drink?" Messua murmured. "This is all thine. We owe our lives to thee. But art thou him I called Nathoo, or a Godling, indeed?"

"I am Nathoo," said Mowgli, "I am very far from my own place. I saw this light, and came hither. I did not know thou wast here."

"After we came to Khanhiwara," Messua said timidly, "the English would have helped us against those villagers that sought to burn us. Rememberest thou?"

"Indeed, I have not forgotten."

"But when the English Law was made ready, we went to the village of those evil people, and it was no more to be found."

"That also I remember," said Mowgli, with a quiver of his nostril.

"My man, therefore, took service in the fields, and at last – for, indeed, he was a strong man – we held a little land here. It is not so rich as the old village, but we do not need much – we two."

"Where is he the man that dug in the dirt when he was afraid on that night?"

"He is dead – a year."

"And he?" Mowgli pointed to the child.

"My son that was born two Rains ago. If thou art a Godling, give him the Favour of the Jungle, that he may be safe among thy – thy people, as we were safe on that night."

She lifted up the child, who, forgetting his fright, reached out to play with the knife that hung on Mowgli's chest, and Mowgli put the little fingers aside very carefully.

"And if thou art Nathoo whom the tiger carried away," Messua went on, choking, "he is then thy younger brother. Give him an elder brother's blessing."

"*Hai-mai*! What do I know of the thing called a blessing? I am neither a Godling nor his brother, and – O mother, mother, my heart is heavy in me." He shivered as he set down the child.

"Like enough," said Messua, bustling among the cooking-pots. "This comes of running about the marshes by night. Beyond question, the fever had soaked thee to the marrow." Mowgli smiled a little at the idea of anything in the Jungle hurting him. "I will make a fire, and thou shalt drink warm milk. Put away the jasmine wreath: the smell is heavy in so small a place."

Mowgli sat down, muttering, with his face in his hands. All manner of strange feelings that he had never felt before were running over him, exactly as though he had been poisoned, and he felt dizzy and a little sick. He drank the warm milk in long gulps, Messua patting him on the shoulder from time to time, not quite sure whether he were her son Nathoo of the long ago days, or some wonderful Jungle being, but glad to feel that he was at least flesh and blood.

"Son," she said at last, – her eyes were full of pride, – "have any told thee that thou art beautiful beyond all men?"

"Hah?" said Mowgli, for naturally he had never heard anything of the kind. Messua laughed softly and happily. The look in his face was enough for her.

"I am the first, then? It is right, though it comes seldom, that a mother should tell her son these good things. Thou art very beautiful. Never have I looked upon such a man."

Mowgli twisted his head and tried to see over his own hard shoulder, and Messua laughed again so long that Mowgli, not knowing why, was forced to laugh with her, and the child ran from one to the other, laughing too.

"Nay, thou must not mock thy brother," said Messua, catching him to her breast. "When thou art one-half as fair we will marry thee to the youngest daughter of a king, and thou shalt ride great elephants."

Mowgli could not understand one word in three of the talk here; the warm milk was taking effect on him after his long run, so he curled up and in a minute was deep asleep, and Messua put the hair back from his eyes, threw a cloth over him, and was happy. Jungle-fashion, he slept out the rest of that night and all the next day; for his instincts, which never wholly slept, warned him there was nothing to fear. He waked at last with a bound that shook the hut, for the cloth over his face made him dream of traps; and there he stood, his hand on his knife, the sleep all heavy in his rolling eyes, ready for any fight.

Messua laughed, and set the evening meal before him. There were only a few coarse cakes baked over the smoky fire, some rice, and a lump of sour preserved tamarinds – just enough to go on with till he could get to his evening kill. The smell of the dew in the marshes made him hungry and restless. He wanted to finish his spring running, but the child insisted on sitting in his arms, and Messua would have it that his long, blue-black hair must he combed out. So she sang, as she combed, foolish little baby-songs, now calling Mowgli her son, and now begging him to give some of his jungle power to the child. The hut door was closed, but Mowgli heard a sound he knew well, and saw Messua's jaw drop with horror as a great gray paw came under the bottom of the door, and Gray Brother outside whined a muffled and penitent whine of anxiety and fear.

"Out and wait! Ye would not come when I called," said Mowgli in Jungle-talk, without turning his head, and the great gray paw disappeared.

"Do not – do not bring thy – thy servants with thee," said Messua. "I – we have always lived at peace with the Jungle."

"It is peace," said Mowgli, rising. "Think of that night on the road to Khanhiwara. There were scores of such folk before thee and behind thee. But I see that even in springtime the Jungle People do not always forget. Mother, I go."

Messua drew aside humbly – he was indeed a wood-god, she thought; but as his hand was on the door the mother in her made her throw her arms round Mowgli's neck again and again.

"Come back!" she whispered. "Son or no son, come back, for I love thee – Look, he too grieves."

The child was crying because the man with the shiny knife was going away.

"Come back again," Messua repeated. "By night or by day this door is never shut to thee."

Mowgli's throat worked as though the cords in it were being pulled, and his voice seemed to be dragged from it as he answered, "I will surely come back."

"And now," he said, as he put by the head of the fawning wolf on the threshold, "I have a little cry against thee, Gray Brother. Why came ye not all four when I called so long ago?"

"So long ago? It was but last night. I – we – were singing in the Jungle the new songs, for this is the Time of New Talk. Rememberest thou?"

"Truly, truly."

"And as soon as the songs were sung," Gray Brother went on earnestly, "I followed thy trail. I ran from all the others and followed hot-foot. But, O Little Brother, what hast *thou* done, eating and sleeping with the Man-Pack?"

"If ye had come when I called, this had never been," said Mowgli, running much faster.

"And now what is to be?" said Gray Brother.

Mowgli was going to answer when a girl in a white cloth came down some path that led from the outskirts of the village. Gray Brother dropped out of sight at once, and Mowgli backed noiselessly into a field of high-springing crops. He could almost have touched her with his hand when the warm, green stalks closed before his face and he disappeared like a ghost. The girl screamed, for she thought she had seen a spirit, and then she gave a deep sigh. Mowgli parted the stalks with his hands and watched her till she was out of sight.

"And now I do not know," he said, sighing in his turn. "*Why* did ye not come when I called?"

"We follow thee – we follow thee," Gray Brother mumbled, licking at Mowgli's heel. "We follow thee always, except in the Time of the New Talk."

"And would ye follow me to the Man-Pack?" Mowgli whispered.

"Did I not follow thee on the night our old Pack cast thee out? Who waked thee lying among the crops?"

"Ay, but again?"

"Have I not followed thee to-night?"

"Ay, but again and again, and it may be again, Gray Brother?"

Gray Brother was silent. When he spoke he growled to himself, "The Black One spoke truth."

"And he said?"

"Man goes to Man at the last. Raksha, our mother, said — "

"So also said Akela on the night of Red Dog," Mowgli muttered.

"So also says Kaa, who is wiser than us all."

"What dost thou say, Gray Brother?"

"They cast thee out once, with bad talk. They cut thy mouth with stones. They sent Buldeo to slay thee. They would have thrown thee into the Red Flower. Thou, and not I, hast said that they are evil and senseless. Thou, and not I – I follow my own people – didst let in the Jungle upon them. Thou, and not I, didst make song against them more bitter even than our song against Red Dog."

"I ask thee what *thou* sayest?"

They were talking as they ran. Gray Brother cantered on a while without replying, and then he said, – between bound and bound as it were, – "Man-cub – Master of the Jungle – Son of Raksha, Lair-brother to me – though I forget for a little while in the spring, thy trail is my trail, thy lair is my lair, thy kill is my kill, and thy death-fight is my death-fight. I speak for the Three. But what wilt thou say to the Jungle?"

"That is well thought. Between the sight and the kill it is not good to wait. Go before and cry them all to the Council Rock, and I will tell them what is in my stomach. But they may not come – in the Time of New Talk they may forget me."

"Hast thou, then, forgotten nothing?" snapped Gray Brother over his shoulder, as he laid himself down to gallop, and Mowgli followed, thinking.

At any other season the news would have called all the Jungle together with bristling necks, but now they were busy hunting and fighting and killing and singing. From one to another Gray Brother ran, crying, "The Master of the Jungle goes back to Man! Come to the Council Rock." And the happy, eager People only answered, "He will return in the summer heats. The Rains will drive him to lair. Run and sing with us, Gray Brother."

"But the Master of the Jungle goes back to Man," Gray Brother would repeat.

"*Eee – Yoawa*? Is the Time of New Talk any less sweet for that?" they would reply. So when Mowgli, heavy-hearted, came up through the well-remembered rocks to the place where he had been brought into the Council, he found only the

Four, Baloo, who was nearly blind with age, and the heavy, cold-blooded Kaa coiled around Akela's empty seat.

"Thy trail ends here, then, Manling?" said Kaa, as Mowgli threw himself down, his face in his hands. "Cry thy cry. We be of one blood, thou and I – man and snake together."

"Why did I not die under Red Dog?" the boy moaned. "My strength is gone from me, and it is not any poison. By night and by day I hear a double step upon my trail. When I turn my head it is as though one had hidden himself from me that instant. I go to look behind the trees and he is not there. I call and none cry again; but it is as though one listened and kept back the answer. I lie down, but I do not rest. I run the spring running, but I am not made still. I bathe, but I am not made cool. The kill sickens me, but I have no heart to fight except I kill. The Red Flower is in my body, my bones are water – and – I know not what I know."

"What need of talk?" said Baloo slowly, turning his head to where Mowgli lay. "Akela by the river said it, that Mowgli should drive Mowgli back to the Man-Pack. I said it. But who listens now to Baloo? Bagheera – where is Bagheera this night? – He knows also. It is the Law."

"When we met at Cold Lairs, Manling, I knew it," said Kaa, turning a little in his mighty coils. "Man goes to Man at the last, though the Jungle does not cast him out."

The Four looked at one another and at Mowgli, puzzled but obedient.

"The Jungle does not cast me out, then?" Mowgli stammered.

Gray Brother and the Three growled furiously, beginning, "So long as we live none shall dare — " But Baloo checked them.

"I taught thee the Law. It is for me to speak," he said; "and, though I cannot now see the rocks before me, I see far.

Little Frog, take thine own trail; make thy lair with thine own blood and pack and people; but when there is need of foot or tooth or eye, or a word carried swiftly by night, remember, Master of the Jungle, the Jungle is thine at call."

"The Middle Jungle is thine also," said Kaa. I speak for no small people."

"*Hai-mai*, my brothers," cried Mowgli, throwing up his arms with a sob. "I know not what I know! I would not go; but I am drawn by both feet. How shall I leave these nights?"

"Nay, look up, Little Brother," Baloo repeated. There is no shame in this hunting. When the honey is eaten we leave the empty hive."

"Having cast the skin," said Kaa, "we may not creep into it afresh. It is the Law."

"Listen, dearest of all to me," said Baloo. There is neither word nor will here to hold thee back. Look up! Who may question the Master of the Jungle? I saw thee playing among the white pebbles yonder when thou wast a little frog; and Bagheera, that bought thee for the price of a young bull newly killed, saw thee also. Of that Looking Over we two only remain; for Raksha, thy lair-mother, is dead with thy lair-father; the old Wolf-Pack is long since dead; thou knowest whither Shere Khan went, and Akela died among the dholes, where, but for thy wisdom and strength, the second Seeonee Pack would also have died. There remains nothing but old bones. It is no longer the Man-cub that asks leave of his Pack, but the Master of the Jungle that changes his trail. Who shall question Man in his ways?"

"But Bagheera and the Bull that bought me," said Mowgli. "I would not — "

His words were cut short by a roar and a crash in the thicket below, and Bagheera, light, strong, and terrible as always, stood before him.

"*Therefore*," he said, stretching out a dripping right paw, "I did not come. It was a long hunt, but he lies dead in the bushes now – a bull in his second year – the Bull that frees thee, Little Brother. All debts are paid now. For the rest, my word is Baloo's word." He licked Mowgli's foot. "Remember, Bagheera loved thee," he cried, and bounded away. At the foot of the hill he cried again long and loud, "Good hunting on a new trail, Master of the Jungle! Remember, Bagheera loved thee."

"Thou hast heard," said Baloo. "There is no more. Go now; but first come to me. O wise Little Frog, come to me!"

"It is hard to cast the skin," said Kaa as Mowgli sobbed and sobbed, with his head on the blind bear's side and his arms round his neck, while Baloo tried feebly to lick his feet.

"The stars are thin," said Gray Brother, snuffing at the dawn wind. "Where shall we lair to-day? For from now, we follow new trails."

* * * * *

And this is the last of the Mowgli stories.

# THE OUTSONG

[This is the song that Mowgli heard behind him in the Jungle till he came to Messua's door again.]

## Baloo

For the sake of him who showed
One wise Frog the Jungle-Road,
Keep the Law the Man-Pack make –
For thy blind old Baloo's sake!
Clean or tainted, hot or stale,
Hold it as it were the Trail,
Through the day and through the night,
Questing neither left nor right.
For the sake of him who loves
Thee beyond all else that moves,
When thy Pack would make thee pain,
Say: "Tabaqui sings again."
When thy Pack would work thee ill,
Say: "Shere Khan is yet to kill."
When the knife is drawn to slay,
Keep the Law and go thy way.
(Root and honey, palm and spathe,
Guard a cub from harm and scathe!)
*Wood and Water, Wind and Tree,*
*Jungle-Favour go with thee!*

## Kaa

Anger is the egg of Fear –
Only lidless eyes are clear.
Cobra-poison none may leech.

Even so with Cobra-speech.
Open talk shall call to thee
Strength, whose mate is Courtesy.
Send no lunge beyond thy length;
Lend no rotten bough thy strength.
Gauge thy gape with buck or goat,
Lest thine eye should choke thy throat,
After gorging, wouldst thou sleep?
Look thy den is hid and deep,
Lest a wrong, by thee forgot,
Draw thy killer to the spot.
East and West and North and South,
Wash thy hide and close thy mouth.
(Pit and rift and blue pool-brim,
Middle-Jungle follow him!)
*Wood and Water, Wind and Tree,*
*Jungle-Favour go with thee!*

## Bagheera

In the cage my life began;
Well I know the worth of Man.
By the Broken Lock that freed –
Man-cub, 'ware the Man-cub's breed!
Scenting-dew or starlight pale,
Choose no tangled tree-cat trail.
Pack or council, hunt or den,
Cry no truce with Jackal-Men.
Feed them silence when they say:
"Come with us an easy way."
Feed them silence when they seek
Help of thine to hurt the weak.
Make no bandar's boast of skill;
Hold thy peace above the kill.

Let nor call nor song nor sign
Turn thee from thy hunting-line.
(Morning mist or twilight clear,
Serve him, Wardens of the Deer!)
*Wood and Water, Wind and Tree,*
*Jungle-Favour go with thee*!

## The Three

On the trail that thou must tread
To the thresholds of our dread,
Where the Flower blossoms red;
Through the nights when thou shalt lie
Prisoned from our Mother-sky,
Hearing us, thy loves, go by;
In the dawns when thou shalt wake
To the toil thou canst not break,
Heartsick for the Jungle's sake:
Wood and Water, Wind and Tree,
*Wisdom, Strength, and Courtesy,*
*Jungle-Favour go with thee*!

## The End

# SELECTED SHORT STORIES

# CONTENTS

# 1

# *The Courting of Dinah Shadd*

What did the colonel's lady think?
   Nobody never knew.
Somebody asked the sergeant's wife
   An' she told 'em true.
When you git to a man in the case
   They're like a row o' pins,
For the colonel's lady an' Judy O'Grady
   Are sisters under their skins.

*Barrack-Room Ballads*

ALL DAY I had followed at the heels of a pursuing army engaged on one of the finest battles that ever camp of exercise beheld. Thirty thousand troops had, by the wisdom of the Government of India, been turned loose over a few thousand square miles of country to practise in peace what they would never attempt in war. Consequently cavalry charged unshaken infantry at the trot. Infantry captured artillery by frontal attacks delivered in line of quarter columns, and mounted infantry skirmished up to the wheels of an armoured train which carried nothing more deadly than a twenty-five pounder Armstrong, two Nordenfeldts, and a few score volunteers all cased in three-eighths-inch boiler-plate. Yet it was a very lifelike camp. Operations did not cease at sundown; nobody knew the country and nobody spared man or horse. There was unending cavalry scouting and almost unending forced work over broken ground. The Army of the South had finally pierced the centre of the Army of the North, and was pouring through the gap hot-foot to capture a city of strategic importance. Its front extended fanwise, the sticks being represented by regiments strung out along the line of route backwards to the divisional transport columns and all the lumber that trails behind an army on the move. On its right the broken left of the Army of the North was flying in mass, chased by the Southern horse and hammered by the Southern guns till these had been pushed far beyond the limits of their last support. Then the flying sat down to rest, while the elated commandant of the pursuing force telegraphed that he held all in check and observation.

Unluckily he did not observe that three miles to his right flank a flying column of Northern horse with a detachment of Gurkhas and British troops had been pushed round as fast as the failing light allowed, to cut across the entire rear of the Southern Army – to break, as it were, all the ribs of the fan where they converged by striking at the transport, reserve ammunition, and artillery supplies. Their instructions were to go in, avoiding the few scouts who might not have been drawn off by the pursuit, and create sufficient excitement to impress the Southern Army with the wisdom of guarding their own flank and rear before they captured cities. It was a pretty manoeuvre, neatly carried out.

Speaking for the second division of the Southern Army, our first intimation of the attack was at twilight, when the artillery were labouring in deep sand, most of the escort were trying to help them out, and the main body of the infantry had gone on. A Noah's Ark of elephants, camels, and the mixed menagerie of an Indian transport-train bubbled and squealed behind the guns, when there appeared from nowhere in particular British infantry to the extent of three companies, who sprang to the heads of the gun-horses and brought all to a standstill amid oaths and cheers.

'How's that, umpire?' said the major commanding the attack, and with one voice the drivers and limber gunners answered 'Hout!' while the colonel of artillery sputtered.

'All your scouts are charging our main body,' said the major. 'Your flanks are unprotected for two miles. I think we've broken the back of this division. And listen – there go the Gurkhas!'

A weak fire broke from the rear-guard more than a mile away, and was answered by cheerful howlings. The Gurkhas, who should have swung clear of the second division, had stepped on its tail in the dark, but drawing off hastened to reach the next line of attack, which lay almost parallel to us five or six miles away.

Our column swayed and surged irresolutely – three batteries, the divisional ammunition reserve, the baggage, and a section of the hospital and bearer corps. The commandant ruefully promised to report himself 'cut up' to the nearest umpire and, commending his cavalry and all other cavalry to the special care of Eblis, toiled on to resume touch with the rest of the division.

'We'll bivouac here tonight,' said the major. 'I have a notion that the Gurkhas will get caught. They may want us to re-form on. Stand easy till the transport gets away.'

A hand caught my beast's bridle and led him out of the choking dust; a larger hand deftly canted me out of the saddle; and two of the hugest hands in the world received me sliding. Pleasant is the lot of the special correspondent who falls into such hands as those of Privates Mulvaney, Ortheris, and Learoyd.

'An' that's all right,' said the Irishman calmly. 'We thought we'd find you somewheres here by. Is there anything av yours in the transport? Orth'ris'll fetch ut out'

Ortheris did 'fetch ut out', from under the trunk of an elephant, in the shape of a servant and an animal both laden with medical comforts. The little man's eyes sparkled.

'If the brutil an' licentious soldiery av these parts gets sight av the thruck,' said Mulvaney, making practised investigation, 'they'll loot ev'rything. They're bein' fed on iron-filin's an' dog-biscuit these days, but glory's no compensation for a bellyache. Praise be, we're here to protect you, sorr. Beer, sausage, bread (soft an' that's a cur'osity), soup in a tin, whisky by the smell av ut, an' fowls! Mother av Moses, but ye take the field like a confectioner! 'Tis scand'lus.'

' 'Ere's a orficer,' said Ortheris significantly. 'When the sergent's done lushin' the privit may clean the pot.'

I bundled several things into Mulvaney's haversack before the major's hand fell on my shoulder and he said tenderly, 'Requisitioned for the Queen's service. Wolseley was quite wrong about special correspondents: they are the soldier's best friends. Come and take pot luck with us tonight.'

And so it happened amid laughter and shoutings that my well-considered commissariat melted away to reappear later at the mess table, which was a waterproof sheet spread on the ground. The flying column had taken three days' rations with it, and there be few things nastier than Government rations – especially when Government is experimenting with German toys. Erbswurst, tinned beef of surpassing tinniness, compressed vegetables, and meat-biscuits may be nourishing, but what Thomas Atkins needs is bulk in his inside. The major, assisted by his brother officers, purchased goats for the camp, and so made the experiment of no effect. Long before the fatigue-party sent to collect brushwood had returned, the men were settled down by their valises, kettles and pots had appeared from the surrounding country, and were dangling over fires as the kid and the compressed vegetable bubbled together; there rose a cheerful clinking of mess-tins; outrageous demands for 'a little more stuffin' with that there liver-wing'; and gust on gust of chaff as pointed as a bayonet and as delicate as a gun-butt.

'The boys are in a good temper,' said the major. 'They'll be singing presently. Well, a night like this is enough to keep them happy.'

Over our heads burned the wonderful Indian stars, which are not all pricked in on one plane, but, preserving an orderly perspective, draw the eye through the velvet darkness of the void up to the barred doors of heaven itself. The earth was a grey shadow more unreal than the sky. We could hear her breathing lightly in the pauses between the howling of the jackals, the movement of the wind in the tamarisks, and the fitful mutter of musketry fire leagues away to the left. A native woman from some unseen hut began to sing, the mail-train thundered past on its way to Delhi, and a roosting crow cawed drowsily. Then there was a belt-loosening silence about the fires, and the even breathing of the crowded earth took up the story.

The men, full fed, turned to tobacco and song – their officers with them. The subaltern is happy who can win the approval of the musical critics in his regiment, and is honoured among the more intricate step-dancers. By him, as by him who plays cricket cleverly, Thomas Atkins will stand in time of need, when he will let a better officer go on alone. The ruined tombs of forgotten Mussulman saints heard *The ballad of Agra Town, The Buffalo Battery, Marching to Kabul, The Long, Long Indian Day, The Place where the Punkah-coolie Died,* and that crashing chorus which announces,

> Youth's daring spirit, manhood's fire,
> Firm hand and eagle eye,
> Must he acquire, who would aspire
> To see the grey boar die.

Today, of all those jovial thieves who appropriated my commissariat and lay and laughed round that waterproof sheet, not one remains. They went to camps that were not of exercise and to battles without umpires. Burma, the Sudan, and the frontier – fever and fight – took them in their time.

I drifted across to the men's fires in search of Mulvaney, whom I found strategically greasing his feet by the blaze. There is nothing particularly lovely in the sight of a private thus engaged after a long day's march, but when you reflect on the exact proportion of the 'might, majesty, dominion, and power' of the British Empire which stands on those feet you take an interest in the proceedings.

'There's a blister, bad luck to ut, on the heel,' said Mulvaney. 'I can't touch ut. Prick ut out, little man.'

Ortheris took out his housewife, eased the trouble with a needle, stabbed Mulvaney in the calf with the same weapon, and was swiftly kicked into the fire.

'I've bruk the best av my toes over you, ye grinnin' child av disruption,' said Mulvaney, sitting cross-legged and nursing his feet; then seeing me, 'Oh, ut's you, sorr! Be welkim, an' take that maraudin' scutt's place. Jock, hold him down on the cindhers for a bit.'

But Ortheris escaped and went elsewhere, as I took possession of the hollow he had scraped for himself and lined with his greatcoat. Learoyd on the other side of the fire grinned affably and in a minute fell fast asleep.

'There's the height av politeness for you,' said Mulvaney, lighting his pipe with a flaming branch. 'But Jock's eaten half a box av your sardines at wan gulp, an' I think the tin too. What's the best wid you, sorr, an' how did you happen to be on the losin' side this day whin we captured you?'

'The Army of the South is winning all along the line,' I said.

'Then that line's the hangman's rope, savin' your presence. You'll learn tomorrow how we rethreated to dhraw thim on before we made thim trouble, an' that's what a woman does. By the same tokin, we'll be attacked before the dawnin' an' ut would be betther not to slip your boots. How do I know that? By the light av pure reason. Here are three companies av us ever so far inside av the enemy's flank an' a crowd av roarin', tarin', squealin' cavalry gone on just to turn out the whole hornet's nest av them. Av course the enemy will pursue, by brigades like as not, an' thin we'll have to run for ut. Mark my words. I am av the opinion av Polonius whin he said, "Don't fight wid ivry scutt for the pure joy av fightin', but if you do, knock the nose av him first an' frequint." We ought to ha' gone on an' helped the Gurkhas.'

'But what do you know about Polonius?' I demanded. This was a new side of Mulvaney's character.

'All that Shakespeare iver wrote an' a dale more that the gallery shouted,' said the man of war, carefully lacing his boots. 'Did I not tell you av Silver's theatre in Dublin whin I was younger than I am now an' a patron av the drama? Ould Silver wud never pay actor-man or woman their just dues, an' by consequince his comp'nies was collapsible at the last minut. Thin the bhoys wud clamour to take a part, an' oft as not ould Silver made them pay for the fun. Faith, I've seen Hamlut played wid a new black eye an' the queen as full as a cornucopia. I remimber wanst Hogin that 'listed in the Black Tyrone an' was shot in South Africa, he sejuced ould Silver into givin' him Hamlut's part instid av me that had a fine fancy for rhetoric in those days. Av course I wint into the gallery an' began to fill the pit wid other people's hats, an' I passed the time av day to Hogin walkin' through Denmark like a hamstrung mule wid a pall on his back. "Hamlut," sez I, "there's a hole in your heel. Pull up your shtockin's, Hamlut," sez I. "Hamlut, Hamlut, for the love av decincy dhrop that skull an' pull up your shtockin's." The whole house begun to tell him that. He stopped his soliloquishms mid-between. "My shtockin's may be comin' down or they may not," sez he, screwin' his eye into the gallery, for well he knew who I was. "But afther this performince is over me an' the Ghost'll trample the tripes out av you, Terence, wid your ass's bray!" An' that's how I come to know about Hamlut. Eyah! Those days, those days! Did you iver have onendin' devilmint an' nothin' to pay for it in your life, sorr?'

'Never, without having to pay,' I said.

'That's thrue! 'Tis mane whin you considher on ut; but ut's the same wid horse or fut. A headache if you dhrink, an' a bellyache if you eat too much, an' a heartache to kape all down. Faith, the beast only gets the colic, an' he's the lucky man.'

He dropped his head and stared into the fire, fingering his moustache the while. From the far side of the bivouac the voice of Corbet-Nolan, senior subaltern of B company, uplifted itself in an ancient and much appreciated song of sentiment, the men moaning melodiously behind him.

'The north wind blew coldly, she drooped
from that hour,
My own little Kathleen, my sweet little Kathleen,
Kathleen, my Kathleen, Kathleen O'Moore!'

With forty-five O's in the last word: even at that distance you might have cut the soft South Irish accent with a shovel.

'For all we take we must pay, but the price is cruel high,' murmured Mulvaney when the chorus had ceased.

'What's the trouble?' I said gently, for I knew that he was a man of an inextinguishable sorrow.

'Hear now,' said he. 'Ye know what I am now. *I* know what I mint to be at the beginnin' av my service. I've tould you time an' again, an' what I have not Dinah Shadd has. An' what am I? Oh, Mary Mother av Hiven, an ould dhrunken, untrustable baste av a privit that has seen the reg'ment change out from colonel to drummer-boy, not wanst or twice, but scores av times! Ay, scores! An' me not so near gettin' promotion as in the first! An' me livin' on an' kapin' clear av clink, not by my own good conduck, but the kindness av some orf'cer-bhoy young enough to be son to me! Do I not know ut? Can I not tell whin I'm passed over at p'rade, tho' I'm rockin' full av liquor an' ready to fall all in wan piece, such as even a suckin' child might see, bekaze, "Oh, 'tis only ould Mulvaney!" An' whin I'm let off in ord'ly-room through some thrick of the tongue an' a ready answer an' the ould man's mercy, is ut smilin' I feel whin I fall away an' go back to Dinah Shadd, thryin' to carry ut all off as a joke? Not I! 'Tis hell to me, dumb hell through ut all; an' next time whin the fit comes I will be as bad again. Good cause the reg'ment has to know me for the best soldier in ut. Better cause have I to know mesilf for the worst man. I'm only fit to tache the new drafts what I'll niver learn myself; an' I am sure, as tho' I heard ut, that the minut wan av these pink-eyed recruities gets away from my "Mind ye now" an' "Listen to this, Jim, bhoy" – sure I am that the sergint houlds me up to him for a warnin'. So I tache, as they say at musketry instruction, by direct and ricochet fire. Lord be good to me, for I have stud some throuble!'

'Lie down and go to sleep,' said I, not being able to comfort or advise. 'You're the best man in the regiment, and, next to Ortheris, the biggest fool. Lie down and wait till we're attacked. What force will they turn out? Guns, think you?'

'Try that wid your lorrds an' ladies, twistin' an turnin' the talk, tho' you mint ut well. Ye cud say nothin' to help me, an' yet ye niver knew what cause I had to be what I am.'

'Begin at the beginning and go on to the end,' I said royally. 'But rake up the fire a bit first.'

I passed Ortheris's bayonet for a poker.

'That shows how little we know what we do,' said Mulvaney, putting it aside. 'Fire takes all the heart out av the steel, an' the next time, may be, that our little man is fighting for his life his bradawl'll break, an' so you'll ha' killed him, manin' no more than to kape yourself warm. 'Tis a recruity's thrick that. Pass the clanin'-rod, sorr.'

I snuggled down abashed; and after an interval the voice of Mulvaney began.

'Did I iver tell you how Dinah Shadd came to be wife av mine?'

I dissembled a burning anxiety that I had felt for some months – ever since Dinah Shadd, the strong, the patient, and the infinitely tender, had of her own good love and free will washed a shirt for me, moving in a barren land where washing was not.

'I can't remember,' I said casually. 'Was it before or after you made love to Annie Bragin, and got no satisfaction?'

The story of Annie Bragin is written in another place. It is one of the many less respectable, episodes in Mulvaney's chequered career.

'Before – before – long before, was that business av Annie Bragin an' the corp'ril's ghost. Niver woman was the worse for me whin I had married Dinah. There's a time for all things, an' I know how to kape all things in place – barrin' the dhrink, that kapes me in my place wid no hope av comin' to be aught else.'

'Begin at the beginning,' I insisted. 'Mrs Mulvaney told me that you married her when you were quartered in Krab Bokhar barracks.'

'An' the same is a cesspit,' said Mulvaney piously. 'She spoke thrue, did Dinah. 'Twas this way. Talkin' av that, have ye iver fallen in love, sorr?'

I preserved the silence of the damned. Mulvaney continued –

'Thin I will assume that ye have not. *I* did. In the days av my youth, as I have more than wanst tould you, I was a man that filled the eye an' delighted the sowl av women. Niver man was hated as I have bin. Niver man was loved as I – no, not within half a day's march av ut! For the first five years av my service, whin I was what I wud give my sowl to be now, I tuk whatever was within my reach an' digested ut – an' that's more than most men can say. Dhrink I tuk, an' ut did me no harm. By the Hollow av Hiven, I cud play wid four women at wanst, an' kape them from findin' out anythin' about the other three, an' smile like a full-blown marigold through ut all. Dick Coulhan, av the battery we'll have down on us tonight, could drive his team no better than I mine, an' I hild the worser cattle! An' so I lived, an' so I was happy till afther that business wid Annie Bragin – she that turned me off as cool as a meat-safe, an' taught me where I stud in the mind av an honest woman. 'Twas no sweet dose to swallow.

'Afther that I sickened awhile an' tuk thought to my reg'mental work; conceiting mesilf I wud study an' be a sargint, an' a major-gineral twinty minutes afther that. But on top av my ambitiousness there was an empty place in my sowl, an' me own opinion av mesilf cud not fill ut. Sez I to mesilf, "Terence, you're a great man an' the best set-up in the reg'mint. Go on an' get promotion." Sez mesilf to me, "What for?" Sez I to mesilf, "For the glory av ut!" Sez mesilf to me, "Will that fill these two strong arrums av yours, Terence?" – "Go to the devil," sez I to mesilf. "Go to the married lines," sez mesilf to me. " 'Tis the same thing," sez I to mesilf. "Av you're the same man, ut is," said mesilf to me; an' wid that I considhered on ut a long while. Did you iver feel that way, sorr?'

I snored gently, knowing that if Mulvaney were uninterrupted he would go on. The clamour from the bivouac fires beat up to the stars, as the rival singers of the companies were pitted against each other.

'So I felt that way an' a bad time ut was. Wanst, bein' a fool, I wint into the married lines more for the sake av spakin' to our ould colour-sergint Shadd than for any thruck wid womenfolk. I was a corp'ril then – rejuced aftherwards, but a corp'ril then. I've got a photograft av mesilf to prove ut. "You'll take a cup av tay wid us?" sez Shadd. "I will that," I sez, "tho' tay is not my divarsion."

' " 'Twud be better for you if ut were," sez ould Mother Shadd, an' she had ought to know, for Shadd, in the ind av his service, dhrank bungfull each night.

'Wid that I tuk off my gloves – there was pipeclay in thim, so that they stud alone – an' pulled up my chair, lookin' round at the china ornaments an' bits av things in the Shadds' quarters. They were things that belonged to a man, an' no camp-kit, here today an' dishipated next. "You're comfortable in this place, sergint," sez I. " 'Tis the wife that did ut, boy," sez he, pointin' the stem av his pipe to ould Mother Shadd, an' she smacked the top av his bald head apon the compliment. "That manes you want money," sez she.

'An' thin – an' thin whin the kettle was to be filled, Dinah came in – my Dinah – her sleeves rowled up to the elbow an' her hair in a winkin' glory over her forehead, the big blue eyes beneath twinklin' like stars on a frosty night, an' the tread av her two feet lighter than waste-paper from the colonel's basket in ord'ly-room whin ut's emptied. Bein' but a shlip av a girl she went pink at seein' me, an' I twisted me moustache an' looked at a picture forninst the wall. Niver show a woman that ye care the snap av a finger for her, an' begad she'll come bleatin' to your boot-heels!'

'I suppose that's why you followed Annie Bragin till everybody in the married quarters laughed at you,' said I, remembering that unhallowed wooing and casting off the disguise of drowsiness.

'I'm layin' down the gin'ral theory av the attack,' said Mulvaney, driving his boot into the dying fire. 'If you read the *Soldier's Pocket Book,* which niver any soldier reads, you'll see that there are exceptions. Whin Dinah was out av the door (an' 'twas as tho' the sunlight had shut too) – "Mother av Hiven, sergint," sez I, "but is that your daughter?" – "I've believed that way these eighteen years," sez ould Shadd, his eyes twinklin', "but Mrs Shadd has her own opinion, like iv'ry woman." – " 'Tis wid yours this time, for a mericle," sez Mother Shadd. "Thin why in the name av fortune did I niver see her before?" sez I. "Bekaze you've been thrapesin' round wid the married women these three years past. She was a bit av a child till last year, an' she shot up wid the spring," sez ould Mother Shadd. "I'll thrapese no more," sez I. "D'you mane that?" sez ould Mother Shadd, lookin' at me sideways like a hen looks at a hawk whin the chickens are runnin' free. "Try me, an' tell," sez I. Wid that I pulled on my gloves, dhrank off the tay, an' went out av the house as stiff as at gin'ral p'rade, for well I knew that Dinah Shadd's eyes were in the small av my back out av the scullery window. Faith! that was the only time I mourned I was not a cav'l'ry man for the pride av the spurs to jingle.

'I wint out to think, an' I did a powerful lot av thinkin', but ut all came round to that shlip av a girl in the dotted blue dhress, wid the blue eyes an' the sparkil in them. Thin I kept off canteen, an' I kept to the married quarthers, or near by, on the chanst av meetin' Dinah. Did I meet her? Oh, my time past, did I not; wid a lump in my throat as big as my valise an' my heart goin' like a farrier's forge on a Saturday morning? 'Twas "Good-day to ye, Miss Dinah," an "Good-day t'you, corp'ril," for a week or two, and divil a bit further could I get bekaze av the respect I had to that girl that I cud ha' broken betune finger an' thumb.'

Here I giggled as I recalled the gigantic figure of Dinah Shadd when she handed me my shirt.

'Ye may laugh,' grunted Mulvaney. 'But I'm speakin' the trut', an' 'tis you that are in fault. Dinah was a girl that wud ha' taken the imperiousness out av the Duchess av Clonmel in those days. Flower hand, foot av shod air, an' the eyes av the livin' mornin' she had that is my wife today – ould Dinah, and niver aught else than Dinah Shadd to me.

' 'Twas after three weeks standin' off an' on, an' niver makin' headway excipt through the eyes, that a little drummer-boy grinned in me face whin I had admonished him wid the buckle av my belt for riotin' all over the place. "An' I'm not the only wan that doesn't kape to barricks," sez he. I tuk him by the scruff av his neck – my heart was hung on a hair-thrigger those days, you will onderstand – an' "Out wid ut," sez I, "or I'll lave no bone av you unbreakable." – "Speak to Dempsey," sez he howlin'. "Dempsey which?" sez I, "ye unwashed limb av Satan." – "Av the Bobtailed Dhragoons," sez he. "He's seen her home from her aunt's house in the civil lines four times this fortnight." – "Child!" sez I, dhroppin' him, "your tongue's stronger than your body. Go to your quarters. I'm sorry I dhressed you down."

'At that I went four ways to wanst huntin' Dempsey. I was mad to think that wid all my airs among women I shud ha' been chated by a basin-faced fool av a cav'lryman not fit to trust on a trunk. Presintly I found him in our lines – the Bobtails was quartered next us – an' a tallowy, topheavy son av a she-mule he was wid his big brass spurs an' his plastrons on his epigastrons an' all. But he niver flinched a hair.

' "A word wid you, Dempsey," sez I. "You've walked wid Dinah Shadd four times this fortnight gone.'

' "What's that to you?" sez he. "I'll walk forty times more, an' forty on top av that, ye shovel-futted clod-breakin' infantry lance-corp'ril."

'Before I cud gyard he had his gloved fist home on my cheek an' down I went full-sprawl. "Will that content you?" sez he, blowin' on his knuckles for all the world like a Scots

Greys orf'cer. "Content!" sez I. "For your own sake, man, take off your spurs, peel your jackut, an' onglove. 'Tis the beginnin' av the overture; stand up!"

'He stud all he know, but he niver peeled his jacket, an' his shoulders had no fair play. I was fightin' for Dinah Shadd an' that cut on my cheek. What hope had he forninst me? "Stand up," sez I, time an' again whin he was beginnin' to quarter the ground an' gyard high an' go large. "This isn't ridin' school," I sez. "O man, stand up an' let me get in at ye." But whin I saw he wud be runnin' about, I grup his shtock in my left an' his waist-belt in my right an' swung him clear to my right front, head undher, he hammerin' my nose till the wind was knocked out av him on the bare ground. "Stand up," sez I, "or I'll kick your head into your chest!" and I wud ha' done ut too, so ragin' mad I was.

' "My collar-bone's bruk," sez he. "Help me back to lines. I'll walk wid her no more." So I helped him back.'

'And was his collar-bone broken?' I asked, for I fancied that only Learoyd could neatly accomplish that terrible throw.

'He pitched on his left shoulder-point. Ut was. Next day the news was in both barricks, an' whin I met Dinah Shadd wid a cheek on me like all the reg'mintal tailor's samples there was no "Good-mornin', corp'ril," or aught else. "An' what have I done, Miss Shadd," sez I, very bould, plantin' mesilf forninst her, "that ye should not pass the time of day?"

' "Ye've half-killed rough-rider Dempsey," sez she, her dear blue eyes fillin' up.

' "May be," sez I. "Was he a friend av yours that saw ye home four times in the fortnight?"

‘ “Yes,” sez she, but her mouth was down at the corners. “An’ – an’ what’s that to you?” she sez.

‘ “Ask Dempsey,” sez I, purtendin’ to go away.

‘ “Did you fight for me then, ye silly man?” she sez, tho’ she knew ut all along.

‘ “Who else?” sez I, an’ I tuk wan pace to the front.

‘ “I wasn’t worth ut,” sez she, fingerin’ in her apron.

‘ “That’s for me to say,” sez I. “Shall I say ut?”

‘ “Yes,” sez she in a saint’s whisper, an’ at that I explained mesilf; and she tould me what ivry man that is a man, an’ many that is a woman, hears wanst in his life.

‘ “But what made ye cry at startin’, Dinah, darlin’?” sez I.

‘ “Your – your bloody cheek,” sez she, duckin’ her little head down on my sash (I was on duty for the day) an’ whimperin’ like a sorrowful angil.

‘Now a man cud take that two ways. I tuk ut as pleased me best an’ my first kiss wid ut. Mother av Innocence! but I kissed her on the tip av the nose an’ undher the eye; an’ a girl that lets a kiss come tumbleways like that has never been kissed before. Take note av that, sorr. Thin we wint hand in hand to ould Mother Shadd like two little childher, an’ she said ’twas no bad thing, an’ ould Shadd nodded behind his pipe, an’ Dinah ran away to her own room. That day I throd on rollin’ clouds. All earth was too small to hould me. Begad, I cud ha’ hiked the sun out av the sky for a live coal to my pipe, so magnificent I was. But I tuk recruities at squad-drill instid, an’ began wid general battalion advance whin I shud ha’ been balance-steppin’ them. Eyah! that day! that day!’

A very long pause. 'Well?' said I.

' 'Twas all wrong,' said Mulvaney, with an enormous sigh. 'An' I know that ev'ry bit av ut was my own foolishness. That night I tuk maybe the half av three pints – not enough to turn the hair of a man in his natural senses. But I was more than half drunk wid pure joy, an' that canteen beer was so much whisky to me. I can't tell how it came about, but *bekaze* I had no thought for anywan except Dinah, *bekaze* I hadn't slipped her little white arms from my neck five minuts, *bekaze* the breath of her kiss was not gone from my mouth, I must go through the married lines on my way to quarters, an' I must stay talkin' to a redheaded Mullingar heifer av a girl, Judy Sheehy, that was daughter to Mother Sheehy, the wife of Nick Sheehy, the canteen-sergint – the Black Curse av Shielygh be on the whole brood that are above groun' this day!

' "An' what are ye houldin' your head that high for, corp'ril?" sez Judy. "Come in an' thry a cup av tay," she sez, standin' in the doorway. Bein' an ontrustable fool, an' thinkin' av anything but tay, I wint.

' "Mother's at canteen," sez Judy, smoothin' the hair av hers that was like red snakes, an' lookin' at me corner-ways out av her green cats' eyes. "Ye will not mind, corp'ril?"

' "I can endure," sez I; ould Mother Sheehy bein' no divarsion av mine, nor her daughter too. Judy fetched the tea things an' put thim on the table, leanin' over me very close to get thim square. I dhrew back, thinkin' av Dinah.

' "Is ut afraid you are av a girl alone?" sez Judy.

' "No," sez I. "Why should I be?"

' "That rests wid the girl," sez Judy, dhrawin' her chair next to mine.

' "Thin there let ut rest," sez I; an' thinkin' I'd been a trifle onpolite, I sez, "The tay's not quite sweet enough for my taste. Put your little finger in the cup, Judy. 'Twill make ut necthar."

' "What's necthar?" sez she.

' "Somethin' very sweet," sez I; an' for the sinful life av me I cud not help lookin' at her out av the corner av my eye, as I was used to look at a woman.

' "Go on wid ye, corp'ril," sez she. "You're a flirrt."

' "On me sowl I'm not," sez I.

' "Then you're a cruel handsome man, an' that's worse," sez she, heaving big sighs an' lookin' crossways.

' "You know your own mind," sez I.

' " 'Twud be better for me if I did not," she sez.

' "There's a dale to be said on both sides av that," sez I, unthinkin'.

' "Say your own part av ut, then, Terence, darlin'," sez she, "for begad I'm thinkin' I've said too much or too little for an honest girl," an' wid that she put her arms round my neck an' kissed me.

' "There's no more to be said afther that," sez I, kissin' her back again – Oh the mane scutt that I was, my head ringin' wid Dinah Shadd! How does ut come about, sorr, that when a man has put the comether on wan woman, he's sure bound to put it on another? 'Tis the same thing at musketry. Wan day ivry shot goes wide or into the bank, an' the next, lay high lay low, sight or snap, ye can't get off the bull's-eye for ten shots runnin'.'

'That only happens to a man who has had a good deal of experience. He does it without thinking,' I replied.

'Thankin' you for the complimint, sorr, ut may be so. But I'm doubtful whether you mint ut for a complimint. Hear now; I sat there wid Judy on my knee tellin' me all manner av nonsinse an' only sayin' "yes" an' "no" when I'd much better ha' kept tongue betune teeth. An' that was not an hour afther I had left Dinah! What I was thinkin' av I cannot say. Presindy, quiet as a cat, ould Mother Sheehy came in velvet-dhrunk. She had her daughter's red hair, but 'twas bald in patches, an' I cud see in her wicked ould face, clear as lightnin', what Judy wud be twenty years to come. I was for jumpin' up, but Judy niver moved.

' "Terence has promust, mother," sez she, an' the could sweat bruk out all over me. Ould Mother Sheehy sat down of a heap an' began playin' wid the cups. "Thin you're a well-matched pair," she sez very thick. "For he's the biggest rogue that iver spoiled the Queen's shoe-leather," an' –

' "I'm off, Judy," sez I. "Ye should not talk nonsinse to your mother. Get her to bed, girl."

' "Nonsinse!" sez the ould woman, prickin' up her ears like a cat an' grippin' the table edge. " 'Twill be the most nonsinsical nonsinse for you, ye grinnin' badger, if nonsinse 'tis. Git clear, you. I'm goin' to bed."

'I ran out into the dhark, my head in a stew an' my heart sick, but I had sinse enough to see that I'd brought ut all on mysilf. "It's this to pass the time av day to a panjandhrum av hellcats," sez I. "What I've said, an' what I've not said do not matther. Judy an' her dam will hould me for a promust man, an' Dinah will give me the go, an' I desarve ut. I will go an' get dhrunk," sez I, "an' forget about ut, for 'tis plain I'm not a marrin' man."

'On my way to canteen I ran against Lascelles, colour-sergeant that was av E Comp'ny, a hard, hard man, wid a torment av a wife. "You've the head av a drowned man on your shoulders," sez he, "an' you're goin' where you'll get a worse wan. Come back," sez he. "Let me go," sez I. "I've thrown my luck over the wall wid my own hand!" – "Then that's not the way to get ut back again," sez he. "Have out wid your throuble, ye fool-bhoy." An' I tould him how the matther was.

'He sucked in his lower lip. "You've been thrapped," sez he. "Ju Sheehy wud be the betther for a man's name to hers as soon as can. An' ye thought ye'd put the comether on her – that's the natural vanity of the baste. Terence, you're a big born fool, but you're not bad enough to marry into that comp'ny. If you said anythin', an' for all your protestations I'm sure ye did – or did not, which is worse – eat ut all – lie like the father of all lies, but come out av ut free av Judy. Do I not know what ut is to marry a woman that was the very spit an' image av Judy whin she was young? I'm gettin' old an' I've larnt patience, but you, Terence, you'd raise hand on Judy an' kill her in a year. Never mind if Dinah gives you the go, you've desarved ut; never mind if the whole reg'mint laughs you all day. Get shut av Judy an' her mother. They can't dhrag you to church, but if they do, they'll dhrag you to hell. Go back to your quarters and lie down," sez he. Thin over his shoulder, "You *must* ha' done with thim."

'Next day I wint to see Dinah, but there was no tucker in me as I walked. I knew the throuble wud come soon enough widout any handlin' av mine, an' I dreaded ut sore.

'I heard Judy callin' me, but I hild straight on to the Shadds' quarthers, an' Dinah wud ha' kissed me but I put her back.

' "Whin all's said, darlin'," sez I, "you can give ut me if ye will, tho' I misdoubt 'twill be so easy to come by then."

'I had scarce begun to put the explanation into shape before Judy an' her mother came to the door. I think there was a verandah, but I'm forgettin'.

' "Will ye not step in?" sez Dinah, pretty and polite, though the Shadds had no dealin's with the Sheehys. Old Mother Shadd looked up quick, an' she was the fust to see the throuble; for Dinah was her daughter.

' "I'm pressed for time today," sez Judy as bould as brass, "an' I've only come for Terence – my promust man. 'Tis strange to find him here the day afther the day."

'Dinah looked at me as though I had hit her, an' I answered straight.

' "There was some nonsinse last night at the Sheehys' quarthers, an' Judy's carryin' on the joke, darlin'," sez I.

' "At the Sheehys' quarthers?" sez Dinah very slow, an' Judy cut in wid: "He was there from nine till ten, Dinah Shadd, an' the betther half av that time I was sittin' on his knee, Dinah Shadd. Ye may look and ye may look an' ye may look me up an' down, but ye won't look away that Terence is my promust man. Terence, darlin', 'tis time for us to be comin' home."

'Dinah Shadd niver said word to Judy. "Ye left me at half-past eight," she sez to me, "an' I niver thought that ye'd leave me for Judy – promises or no promises. Go back wid her, you that have to be fetched by a girl! I'm done with you," sez she, and she ran into her own room, her mother followin'. So I was alone wid those two women and at liberty to spake my sentiments.

' "Judy Sheehy," sez I, "if you made a fool av me betune the lights you shall not do ut in the day. I niver promised you words or lines."

' "You lie," sez ould Mother Sheehy, "an' may ut choke you where you stand!" She was far gone in dhrink.

' "An' tho' ut choked me where I stud I'd not change," sez I. "Go home, Judy. I take shame for a decent girl like you dhraggin' your mother out bare-headed on this errand. Hear now, and have ut for an answer. I gave my word to Dinah Shadd yesterday, an', more blame to me, I was wid you last night talkin' nonsinse but nothin' more. You've chosen to thry to hould me on ut. I will not be held thereby for anythin' in the world. Is that enough?"

'Judy wint pink all over. "An' I wish you joy av the perjury," sez she, duckin' a curtsey. "You've lost a woman that would ha' wore her hand to the bone for your pleasure; an' 'deed, Terence, ye were not thrapped . . ." Lascelles must ha' spoken plain to her. "I am such as Dinah is – 'deed I am! Ye've lost a fool av a girl that'll niver look at you again, an' ye've lost what ye niver had – your common honesty. If you manage your men as you manage your love-makin', small wondher they call you the worst corp'ril in the comp'ny. Come away, mother," sez she.

'But divil a fut would the ould woman budge! "D'you hould by that?" sez she, peerin' up under her thick grey eyebrows.

' "Ay, an' wud," sez I, "tho' Dinah gave me the go twinty times. I'll have no thruck with you or yours," sez I. "Take your child away, ye shameless woman."

' "An' am I shameless?" sez she, bringin' her hands up above her head. "Thin what are you, ye lyin', schamin', weak-kneed, dhirty-souled son av a sutler? Am *I* shameless? Who put the open shame on me an' my child that we shud go beggin' through the lines in the broad daylight for the broken word of a man? Double portion of my shame be on you, Terence Mulvaney, that think yourself so strong! By Mary and the saints, by blood and water an' by ivry sorrow that came into the world since the beginnin', the black blight fall on you and yours, so that you may niver be free from pain for another when ut's not your own! May your heart bleed in your breast drop by drop wid all your friends laughin' at the bleedin'! Strong you think yourself? May your strength be a curse to you to dhrive you into the divil's hands against your own will! Clear-eyed you are? May your eyes see clear evry step av the dark path you take till the hot cindhers av hell put thim out! May the ragin' dry thirst in my own ould bones go to you that you shall niver pass bottle full nor glass empty. God preserve the light av your onderstandin' to you, my jewel av a bhoy, that ye may niver forget what you mint to be an' do, whin you're wallowin' in the muck! May ye see the betther and follow the worse as long as there's breath in your body; an' may ye die quick in a strange land, watchin' your death before ut takes you, an' onable to stir hand or foot!"

'I heard a scufflin' in the room behind, and thin Dinah Shadd's hand dhropped into mine like a rose-leaf into a muddy road.

' "The half av that I'll take," sez she, "an' more too if I can. Go home, ye silly talkin' woman – go home an' confess."

' "Come away! Come away!" sez Judy, pullin' her mother by the shawl. " 'Twas none av Terence's fault. For the love av Mary stop the talkin'!"

' "An' you!" said ould Mother Sheehy, spinnin' round forninst Dinah. "Will ye take the half av that man's load? Stand off from him, Dinah Shadd, before he takes you down too – you that look to be a quarthermaster-sergeant's wife in five years. You look too high, child. You shall *wash* for the quarthermaster-sergeant, whin he plases to give you the job out av charity; but a privit's wife you shall be to the end, an' evry sorrow of a privit's wife you shall know and niver a joy but wan, that shall go from you like the running tide from a rock. The pain av bearin' you shall know but niver the pleasure av giving the breast; an' you shall put away a man-child into the common ground wid niver a priest to say a prayer over him, an' on that man-child ye shall think ivry day av your life. Think long, Dinah Shadd, for you'll niver have another tho' you pray till your knees are bleedin'. The mothers av childer shall mock you behind your back when you're wringing over the wash-tub. You shall know what ut is to help a dhrunken husband home an' see him go to the gyard-room. Will that plase you, Dinah Shadd, that won't be seen talkin' to my daughter? You shall talk to worse than Judy before all's over. The sergints' wives shall look down on you contemptuous, daughter av a sergint, an' you shall cover ut all up wid a smiling face whin your heart's burstin'. Stand off av him, Dinah Shadd, for I've put the Black Curse of Shielygh upon him an' his own mouth shall make ut good."

'She pitched forward on her head an' began foamin' at the mouth. Dinah Shadd ran out wid water, an' Judy dhragged the ould woman into the verandah till she sat up.

' "I'm old an' forlore," she sez, thremblin' an' cryin', "and 'tis like I say a dale more than I mane."

' "When you're able to walk – go," says ould Mother Shadd. "This house has no place for the likes av you that have cursed my daughter."

' "Eyah!" said the ould woman. "Hard words break no bones, an' Dinah Shadd 'll kape the love av her husband till my bones are green corn. Judy darlin', I misremember what I came here for. Can you lend us the bottom av a taycup av tay, Mrs Shadd?"

'But Judy dhragged her off cryin' as tho' her heart wud break. An' Dinah Shadd an' I, in ten minutes we had forgot ut all.'

'Then why do you remember it now?' said I.

'Is ut like I'd forget? Ivry word that wicked ould woman spoke fell thrue in my life aftherwards, an' I cud ha' stud ut all – stud ut all – excipt when my little Shadd was born. That was on the line av march three months afther the regiment was taken with cholera. We were betune Umballa an' Kalka thin, an' I was on picket. Whin I came off duty the women showed me the child, an' ut turned on uts side an' died as I looked. We buried him by the road, an' Father Victor was a day's march behind wid the heavy baggage, so the comp'ny captain read a prayer. An' since then I've been a childless man, an' all else that ould Mother Sheehy put upon me an' Dinah Shadd. What do you think, sorr?'

I thought a good deal, but it seemed better then to reach out for Mulvaney's hand. The demonstration nearly cost me the use of three fingers. Whatever he knows of his weaknesses, Mulvaney is entirely ignorant of his strength.

'But what do you think?' he repeated, as I was straightening out the crushed fingers.

My reply was drowned in yells and outcries from the next fire, where ten men were shouting for 'Orth'ris', 'Privit Orth'ris', 'Mistah Or – ther – ris!' 'Deah boy', 'Cap'n Orth'ris', 'Field-marshal Orth'ris', 'Stanley, you pen'north o' pop come 'ere to your own comp'ny!' And the cockney, who had been delighting another audience with recondite and Rabelaisian yarns, was shot down among his admirers by the major force.

'You've crumpled my dress-shirt 'orrid,' said he, 'an' I shan't sing no more to this 'ere bloomin' drawin'-room.'

Learoyd, roused by the confusion, uncoiled himself, crept behind Ortheris, and slung him aloft on his shoulders.

'Sing, ye bloomin' hummin' bird!' said he, and Ortheris, beating time on Learoyd's skull, delivered himself, in the raucous voice of the Ratcliffe Highway, of this song –

'My girl she give me the go onst,  
When I was a London lad,  
An' I went on the drink for a fortnight,  
An' then I went to the bad.  
The Queen she give me a shillin'  
To fight for 'er over the seas;  
But Guv'ment built me a fever-trap,  
An' Injia give me disease.

*Chorus*

Ho! don't you 'eed what a girl says,
An' don't you go for the beer;
But I was an ass when I was at grass,
An' that is why I'm here.

I fired a shot at a Afghan,
The beggar 'e fired again,
An' I lay on my bed with a 'ole in my 'ed,
An' missed the next campaign!
I up with my gun at a Burman
Who carried a bloomin' *dah,*
But the cartridge stuck and the bay'nit bruk,
An' all I got was the scar.

*Chorus*

Ho! don't you aim at a Afghan,
When you stand on the skyline clear
An' don't you go for a Burman
If none o' your friends is near.

I served my time for a corp'ral,
An' wetted my stripes with pop,
For I went on the bend with a intimate friend,
An' finished the night in the "shop".
I served my time for a sergeant;
The colonel 'e sez, "No!
The most you'll see is a full CB."*
An'. . . very next night 'twas so.

* Confined to Barracks.

*Chorus*

Ho! don't you go for a corp'ral
    Unless your 'ed is clear;
But I was an ass when I was at grass,
    An' that is why I'm 'ere.

I've tasted the luck o' the army
    In barrack an' camp an' clink,
An' I lost my tip through the bloomin' trip
    Along o' the women an' drink.
I'm down at the heel o' my service,
    An' when I am laid on the shelf,
My very wust friend from beginning to end
    By the blood of a mouse was myself!

*Chorus*

Ho! don't you 'eed what a girl says,
    An' don't you go for the beer;
But I was an ass when I was at grass
    An' that is why I'm 'ere.'

'Ay, listen to our little man now, singin' an' shoutin' as tho' trouble had niver touched him. D' you remember when he went mad with the home-sickness?' said Mulvaney, recalling a never-to-be-forgotten season when Ortheris waded through the deep waters of affliction and behaved abominably. 'But he's talkin' bitter truth, though. Eyah!

My very worst frind from beginnin' to ind
By the blood av a mouse was mesilf!'

When I woke I saw Mulvaney, the night-dew gemming his moustache, leaning on his rifle at picket, lonely as Prometheus on his rock, with I know not what vultures tearing his liver.

# 2

# *On Greenhow Hill*

To Love's low voice she lent a careless ear;
Her hand within his rosy fingers lay,
A chilling weight. She would not turn or hear;
But with averted face went on her way.
But when pale Death, all featureless and grim,
Lifted his bony hand, and beckoning
Held out his cypress-wreath, she followed him,
And Love was left forlorn and wondering,
That she who for his bidding would not stay,
At Death's first whisper rose and went away.

*Rivals*

'*OHÉ, AHMED Din! Shafiz Ullah ahoo!* Bandur Khan, where are you? Come out of the tents, as I have done, and fight against the English. Don't kill your own kin! Come out to me!'

The deserter from a native corps was crawling round the outskirts of the camp, firing at intervals, and shouting invitations to his old comrades. Misled by the rain and the darkness, he came to the English wing of the camp, and with his yelping and rifle-practice disturbed the men. They had been making roads all day, and were tired.

Ortheris was sleeping at Learoyd's feet. 'Wot's all that?' he said thickly. Learoyd snored, and a Snider bullet ripped its way through the tent wall. The men swore. 'It's that bloomin' deserter from the Aurangabadis,' said Ortheris. 'Git up, someone, an' tell 'im 'e's come to the wrong shop.'

'Go to sleep, little man,' said Mulvaney, who was steaming nearest the door. 'I can't arise an' expaytiate with him. 'Tis rainin' entrenchin' tools outside.'

' 'Tain't because you bloomin' can't. It's 'cause you bloomin' won't, ye long, limp, lousy, lazy beggar, you. 'Ark to 'im 'owlin'!'

'Wot's the good of argifying? Put a bullet into the swine!' 'E's keepin' us awake!' said another voice.

A subaltern shouted angrily, and a dripping sentry whined from the darkness –

' 'Tain't no good, sir. I can't see 'im. 'E's 'idin' somewhere down'ill.'

Ortheris tumbled out of his blanket. 'Shall I try to get 'im, sir?' said he.

'No,' was the answer. 'Lie down. I won't have the whole camp shooting all round the clock. Tell him to go and pot his friends.'

Ortheris considered for a moment. Then, putting his head under the tent wall, he called, as a 'bus conductor calls in a block, ' 'Igher up, there! 'Igher up!'

The men laughed, and the laughter was carried downwind to the deserter, who, hearing that he had made a mistake, went off to worry his own regiment half a mile away. He was received with shots; the Aurangabadis were very angry with him for disgracing their colours.

'An' that's all right,' said Ortheris, withdrawing his head as he heard the hiccough of the Sniders in the distance. 'S'elp me Gawd, tho', that man's not fit to live – messin' with my beauty sleep this way.'

'Go out and shoot him in the morning, then,' said the subaltern incautiously. 'Silence in the tents now. Get your rest, men.'

Ortheris lay down with a happy little sigh, and in two minutes there was no sound except the rain on the canvas and the all-embracing and elemental snoring of Learoyd.

The camp lay on a bare ridge of the Himalayas, and for a week had been waiting for a flying column to make connection. The nightly rounds of the deserter and his friends had become a nuisance.

In the morning the men dried themselves in hot sunshine and cleaned their grimy accoutrements. The native regiment was to take its turn of road-making that day while the Old Regiment loafed.

'I'm goin' to lay for a shot at that man,' said Ortheris, when he had finished washing out his rifle. ' 'E comes up the watercourse every evenin' about five o'clock. If we go and lie out on the north 'ill a bit this afternoon we'll get 'im.'

'You're a bloodthirsty little mosquito,' said Mulvaney, blowing blue clouds into the air. 'But I suppose I will have to come wid you. Fwhere's Jock?'

'Gone out with the Mixed Pickles, 'cause 'e thinks 'isself a bloomin' marksman,' said Ortheris with scorn.

The 'Mixed Pickles' were a detachment of picked shots, generally employed in clearing spurs of hills when the enemy were too impertinent. This taught the young officers how to handle men, and did not do the enemy much harm. Mulvaney and Ortheris strolled out of camp, and passed the Aurangabadis going to their road-making.

'You've got to sweat today,' said Ortheris genially. 'We're going to get your man. You didn't knock 'im out last night by any chance, any of you?'

'No. The pig went away mocking us. I had one shot at him,' said a private. 'He's my cousin, and *I* ought to have cleared our dishonour. But good luck to you.'

They went cautiously to the north hill, Ortheris leading, because, as he explained, 'this is a long-range show, an' I've got to do it.' His was an almost passionate devotion to his rifle, whom, by barrack-room report, he was supposed to kiss every night before turning in. Charges and scuffles he held in contempt, and, when they were inevitable, slipped between Mulvaney and Learoyd, bidding them to fight for his skin as well as their own. They never failed him. He trotted along, questing like a hound on a broken trail, through the wood of the north hill. At last he was satisfied, and threw himself down on the soft pine-needled slope that commanded a clear view of the watercourse and a brown, bare hillside beyond it. The trees made a scented darkness in which an army corps could have hidden from the sun-glare without.

' 'Ere's the tail o' the wood,' said Ortheris. ' 'E's got to come up the watercourse, 'cause it gives 'im cover. We'll lay 'ere. 'Tain't not 'arf so bloomin' dusty neither.'

He buried his nose in a clump of scentless white violets. No one had come to tell the flowers that the season of their strength was long past, and they had bloomed merrily in the twilight of the pines.

'This is something like,' he said luxuriously. 'Wot a 'evinly clear drop for a bullet acrost. How much d'you make it, Mulvaney?'

'Seven hunder. Maybe a trifle less, bekaze the air's so thin.'

*Wop! wop! wop!* went a volley of musketry on the rear face of the north hill.

'Curse them Mixed Pickles firin' at nothin'! They'll scare 'arf the country.'

'Thry a sightin' shot in the middle of the row,' said Mulvaney, the man of many wiles. 'There's a red rock yonder he'll be sure to pass. Quick!'

Ortheris ran his sight up to six hundred yards and fired. The bullet threw up a feather of dust by a clump of gentians at the base of the rock.

'Good enough!' said Ortheris, snapping the scale down. 'You snick your sights to mine or a little lower. You're always firin' high. But remember, first shot to me. O Lordy! but it's a lovely afternoon.'

The noise of the firing grew louder, and there was a tramping of men in the wood. The two lay very quiet, for they knew that the British soldier is desperately prone to fire at anything that moves or calls. Then Learoyd appeared, his tunic ripped across the breast by a bullet, looking ashamed of himself. He flung down on the pine needles, breathing in snorts.

'One o' them damned gardeners o' th' Pickles,' said he, fingering the rent. 'Finn' to th' right flank, when he knowed I was there. If I knew who he was I'd 'a' rippen the hide offan him. Look at ma tunic!'

'That's the spishil trustability av a marksman. Train him to hit a fly wid a stiddy rest at seven hunder, an' he loose on anythin' he sees or hears up to th' mile. You're well out av that fancy-firin' gang, Jock. Stay here.'

'Bin firin' at the bloomin' wind in the bloomin' treetops,' said Ortheris with a chuckle. 'I'll show you some firin' later on.'

They wallowed in the pine-needles, and the sun warmed them where they lay. The Mixed Pickles ceased firing, and returned to camp, and left the wood to a few scared apes. The watercourse lifted up its voice in the silence, and talked foolishly to the rocks. Now and again the dull thump of a blasting charge three miles away told that the Aurangabadis were in difficulties with their road-making. The men smiled as they listened and lay still, soaking in the warm leisure. Presently Learoyd, between the whiffs of his pipe –

'Seems queer – about 'im yonder – desertin' at all.'

' 'E'll be a bloomin' side queerer when I've done with 'im,' said Ortheris. They were talking in whispers, for the stillness of the wood and the desire of slaughter lay heavy upon them.

'I make no doubt he had his reasons for desertin'; but, my faith! I make less doubt ivry man has good reason for killin' him,' said Mulvaney.

'Happen there was a lass tewed up wi' it. Men do more than more for th' sake of a lass.'

'They make most av us 'list. They've no manner av right to make us desert.'

'Ah; they make us 'list, or their fathers do,' said Learoyd softly, his helmet over his eyes.

Ortheris's brows contracted savagely. He was watching the valley. 'If it's a girl I'll shoot the beggar twice over, an' second time for bein' a fool. You're blasted sentimental all of a sudden. Thinkin' o' your last near shave?'

'Nay, lad; ah was but thinkin' o' what has happened.'

'An' fwhat has happened, ye lumberin' child av calamity, that you're lowing like a cow-calf at the back av the pasture, an' suggestin' invidious excuses for the man Stanley's goin' to kill. Ye'll have to wait another hour yet, little man. Spit it out, Jock, an' bellow melojus to the moon. It takes an earthquake or a bullet graze to fetch aught out av you. Discourse, Don Juan! The a-moors av Lotharius Learoyd! Stanley, kape a rowlin' rig'mental eye on the valley.'

'It's along o' yon hill there,' said Learoyd, watching the bare sub-Himalayan spur that reminded him of his Yorkshire moors. He was speaking more to himself than his fellows. 'Ay,' said he, 'Rumbolds Moor stands up ower Skipton town, an' Greenhow Hill stands up ower Pately Brig. I reckon you've never heeard tell o' Greenhow Hill, but yon bit o' bare stuff if there was nobbut a white road windin' is like ut; strangely like. Moors an' moors an' moors, wi' never a tree for shelter, an' grey houses wi' flagstone rooves, and pewits cryin', an' a windhover goin' to and fro just like these kites. And cold! A wind that cuts you like a knife. You could tell Greenhow Hill folk by the red-apple colour o' their cheeks an' nose tips, and their blue eyes, driven into pin-points by the wind. Miners mostly, burrowin' for lead i' th' hillsides, followin' the trail of th' ore vein same as a field-rat. It was the roughest minin' I ever seen. Yo'd come on a bit o' creakin' wood windlass like a well-head, an' you was let down i' th' bight of a rope, fendin' yoursen off the side wi' one hand, carryin' a candle stuck in a lump o' clay with t'other, an' clickin' hold of a rope with t'other hand.'

'An' that's three of them,' said Mulvaney. 'Must be a good climate in those parts.'

Learoyd took no heed.

'An' then yo' came to a level, where you crept on your hands and knees through a mile o' windin' drift, an' you come out into a cave-place as big as Leeds Townhall, with a engine pumpin' water from workin's 'at went deeper still. It's a queer country, let alone minin', for the hill is full of those natural caves, an' the rivers an' the becks drops into what they call pot-holes, an' come out again miles away.'

'Wot was you doin' there?' said Ortheris.

'I was a young chap then, an' mostly went wi' 'osses, leadin' coal and lead ore; but at th' time I'm tellin' on I was drivin' the wagon-team i' th' big sumph. I didn't belong to that countryside by rights. I went there because of a little difference at home, an' at fust I took up wi' a rough lot. One night we'd been drinkin', an' I must ha' hed more than I could stand, or happen th' ale was none so good. Though i' them days, By for God, I never seed bad ale.' He flung his arms over his head, and gripped a vast handful of white violets. 'Nah,' said he, 'I never seed the ale I could not drink, the bacca I could not smoke, nor the lass I could not kiss. Well, we mun have a race home, the lot on us. I lost all th' others, an' when I was climbin' ower one of them walls built o' loose stones, I comes down into the ditch, stones and all, an' broke my arm. Not as I knawed much about it, for I fell on th' back of my head, an' was knocked stupid like. An' when I come to mysen it were mornin', an' I were lyin' on the settle i' Jesse Roantree's house-place, an' 'Liza Roantree was settin' sewin'. I ached all ovver, and my mouth were like a lime-kiln. She gave me a drink out of a china mug wi' gold letters – "A Present from Leeds" – as I looked at many and many a time at after. "Yo're to lie still while Dr Warbottom comes, because your arm's broken, and father has sent a lad to fetch him. He found yo' when he was goin' to work, an' carried you here on his back," sez she. "Oa!" sez I, an' I shet my eyes, for I felt ashamed o' mysen. "Father's gone to his work these three hours, an' he said he'd tell 'em to get somebody to drive the tram." The clock ticked, an' a bee corned in the house, an' they rung i' my head like mill-wheels. An' she give me another drink an' settled the pillow. "Eh, but yo're young to be getten drunk an' such like, but yo' won't do it again, will yo'?" – "Noa," sez I, "I wouldn't if she'd not but stop they mill-wheels clatterin'." '

'Faith, it's a good thing to be nursed by a woman when you're sick!' said Mulvaney. 'Dir' cheap at the price av twenty broken heads.'

Ortheris turned to frown across the valley. He had not been nursed by many women in his life.

'An' men Dr Warbottom comes ridin' up, an' Jesse Roantree along with 'im. He was a high-larned doctor, but he talked wi' poor folk same as theirsens. "What's ta bin agaate on naa?" he sings out. "Brekkin' tha thick head?" An' he felt me all ovver. "That's none broken. Tha' nobbut knocked a bit sillier than ordinary, an' that's daaft eneaf." An' soa he went on, callin' me all the names he could think on, but settin' my arm, wi'Jesse's help, as careful as could be. "Yo' mun let the big oaf bide here a bit, Jesse," he says, when he hed strapped me up an' given me a dose o' physic, "an' you an' 'Liza will tend him, though he's scarcelins worth the trouble. An' tha'll lose ma work," sez he, "an' tha'll be upon th' Sick Club for a couple o' months an' more. Doesn't tha think tha's a fool?" '

'But whin was a young man, high or low, the other av a fool, I'd like to know?' said Mulvaney. 'Sure, folly's the only safe way to wisdom, for I've thried it.'

'Wisdom!' grinned Ortheris, scanning his comrades with uplifted chin. 'You're bloomin' Solomons, you two, ain't you?'

Learoyd went calmly on, with a steady eye like an ox chewin the cud.

'And that was how I comed to know 'Liza Roantree. There's some tunes as she used to sing – aw, she were always singin' – that fetches Greenhow Hill before my eyes as fair as yon brow across there. And she would learn me to sing bass, an' I was to go to th' chapel wi' 'em, where Jesse and she led the singin', th' old man playin' the fiddle. He was a strange chap, old Jesse, fair mad wi' music, an' he made me promise to learn the big fiddle when my arm was better. It belonged to him, and it stood up in a big case alongside o' th' eight-day clock, but Willie Satterthwaite, as played it in the chapel, had getten deaf as a doorpost, and it vexed Jesse, as he had to rap him ower his head wi' th' fiddlestick to make him give ower sawin' at th' right time.

'But there was a black drop in it all, an' it was a man in a black coat that brought it. When th' Primitive Methodist preacher came to Greenhow, he would always stop wi' Jesse Roantree, an' he laid hold of me from th' beginning. It seemed I wor a soul to be saved, and he meaned to do it. At th' same time I jealoused 'at he were keen o' savin' 'Liza Roantree's soul as well, and I could ha' killed him many a time. An' this went on till one day I broke out, an' borrowed th' brass for a drink from 'Liza. After fower days I come back, wi' my tail between my legs, just to see 'Liza again. But Jesse were at home an' th' preacher – th' Reverend Amos Barraclough. 'Liza said naught, but a bit o' red come into her face as were white of a regular thing. Says Jesse, tryin' his best to be civil, "Nay, lad, it's like this. You've getten to choose which way it's goin' to be. I'll ha' nobody across ma doorstep as goes a-drinkin', an' borrows my lass's money to spend i' their drink. Ho'd tha tongue, 'Liza," sez he, when she wanted to put in a word 'at I were welcome to th' brass, and she were none afraid that I wouldn't pay it back. Then the Reverend cuts in, seein' as Jesse were losin' his temper, an' they fair beat me among them. But it were 'Liza, as looked an' said naught, as did more than either o' their tongues, an' soa I concluded to get converted.'

'Fwhat!' shouted Mulvaney. Then, checking himself, he said softly, 'Let be! Let be! Sure the Blessed Virgin is the mother of all religion an' most women; an' there's a dale av piety in a girl if the men would only let ut stay there. I'd ha' been converted myself under the circumstances.'

'Nay, but,' pursued Learoyd with a blush, 'I meaned it.'

Ortheris laughed as loudly as he dared, having regard to his business at the time.

'Ay, Ortheris, you may laugh, but you didn't know yon preacher Barraclough – a little white-faced chap, wi' a voice as 'ud wile a bird off an a bush, and a way o' layin' hold of folks as made them think they'd never had a live man for a friend before. You never saw him, an' – an' – you never seed 'Liza Roantree – never seed 'Liza Roantree . . . Happen it was as much 'Liza as th' preacher and her father, but anyways they all meaned it, an' I was fair shamed o' mysen, an' so I become what they called a changed character. And when I think on, it's hard to believe as yon chap going to prayer-meetin's, chapel, and class-meetin's were me. But I never had naught to say for mysen, though there was a deal o' shoutin', and old Sammy Strother, as were almost clemmed to death and doubled up with the rheumatics, would sing out, "Joyful! Joyful!" and 'at it were better to go up to heaven in a coal-basket than down to hell i' a coach an' six. And he would put his poor old claw on my shoulder, sayin', "Doesn't tha feel it, tha great lump? Doesn't tha feel it?" An' sometimes I thought I did, and then again I thought I didn't, an' how was that?'

'The iverlastin' nature av mankind,' said Mulvaney. 'An', furthermore, I misdoubt you were built for the Primitive Methodians. They're a new corps anyways. I hold by the Ould Church, for she's the mother of them all – ay, an' the father, too. I like her bekaze she's most remarkable regimental in her fittings. I may die in Honolulu, Nova Zambra, or Cape Cayenne, but wherever I die, me bein' fwhat I am, an' a priest handy, I go under the same orders an' the same words an' the same unction as tho' the Pope himself come down from the roof av St Peter's to see me off. There's neither high nor low, nor broad nor deep, nor betwixt nor between wid her, an' that's what I like. But mark you, she's no manner av Church for a wake man, bekaze she takes the body and the soul av him, onless he has his proper work to do. I remember when my father died that was three months comin' to his grave; begad he'd ha' sold the shebeen above our heads for ten minutes' quittance of purgathory. An' he did all he could. That's why I say ut takes a strong man to deal with the Ould Church, an' for that reason you'll find so many women go there. An' that sames a conundrum.'

'Wot's the use o' worrittin' 'bout these things?' said Ortheris. 'You're bound to find all out quicker nor you want to, any'ow.' He jerked the cartridge out of the breech-block into the palm of his hand. ' 'Ere's my chaplain,' he said, and made the venomous black-headed bullet bow like a marionette.' 'E's goin' to teach a man all about which is which, an' wot's true, after all, before sundown. But wot 'appened after that, Jock?'

'There was one thing they boggled at, and almost shut th' gate i' my face for, and that were my dog Blast, th' only one saved out o' a litter o' pups as was blowed up when a keg o' minin' powder loosed off in th' store-keeper's hut. They liked his name no better than his business, which were fightin' every dog he comed across; a rare good dog, wi' spots o' black and pink on his face, one ear gone, and lame o' one side wi' being driven in a basket through an iron roof, a matter of half a mile.

'They said I mun give him up 'cause he were worldly and low; and would I let mysen be shut out of heaven for the sake on a dog? "Nay," says I, "if th' door isn't wide enough for th' pair on us, we'll stop outside, for we'll none be parted." And th' preacher spoke up for Blast, as had a likin' for him from th' first – I reckon that was why I come to like th' preacher – and wouldn't hear o' changin' his name to Bless, as some o' them wanted. So th' pair on us became reg'lar chapel-members. But it's hard for a young chap o' my build to cut traces from the world, th' flesh, an' the devil all uv a heap. Yet I stuck to it for a long time, while th' lads as used to stand about th' town-end an' lean ower th' bridge, spittin' into th' beck o' a Sunday, would call after me, "Sitha, Learoyd, when's ta bean to preach, 'cause we're comin' to hear tha." – "Ho'd tha jaw. He hasn't getten th' white choaker on ta morn," another lad would say, and I had to double my fists hard i' th' bottom of my Sunday coat, and say to mysen, "If 'twere Monday and I warn't a member o' the Primitive Methodists, I'd leather all th' lot of yond'." That was th' hardest of all – to know that I could fight and I mustn't fight.'

Sympathetic grunts from Mulvaney.

'So what wi' singin', practisin', and class-meetin's, and th' big fiddle, as he made me take between my knees, I spent a deal o' time i' Jesse Roantree's house-place. But often as I was there, th' preacher fared to me to go oftener, and both th' old man an' th' young woman were pleased to have him. He lived i' Pately Brig, as were a goodish step off, but he come. He come all the same. I liked him as well or better as any man I'd ever seen i' one way, and yet I hated him wi' all my heart i' t'other, and we watched each other like cat and mouse, but civil as you please, for I was on my best behaviour, and he was that fair and open that I was bound to be fair with him. Rare good company he was, if I hadn't wanted to wring his cliver little neck half of the time. Often and often when he was goin' from Jesse's I'd set him a bit on the road.'

'See 'im 'ome, you mean?' said Ortheris.

'Ay. It's a way we have i' Yorkshire o' seein' friends off. Yon was a friend as I didn't want to come back, and he didn't want me to come back neither, and so we'd walk together towards Pately, and then he'd set me back again, and there we'd be wal two o'clock i' the mornin' settin' each other to an' fro like a blasted pair o' pendulums twixt hill and valley, long after th' light had gone out i' 'Liza's window, as both on us had been looking at, pretending to watch the moon.'

'Ah!' broke in Mulvaney, 'ye'd no chanst against the maraudin' psalm-singer. They'll take the airs an' the graces instid av the man nine times out av ten, an' they only find the blunder later – the wimmen.'

'That's just where yo're wrong,' said Learoyd, reddening under the freckled tan of his cheeks. 'I was th' first wi 'Liza, an' yo'd think that were enough. But th' parson were a steady-gaited sort o' chap, and Jesse were strong o' his side, and all th' women i' the congregation dinned it to 'Liza 'at she were fair fond to take up wi' a wastrel ne'er-do-weel like me, as was scarcelins respectable an' a fighting dog at his heels. It was all very well for her to be doing me good and saving my soul, but she must mind as she didn't do herself harm. They talk o' rich folk bein' stuck up an' genteel, but for cast-iron pride o' respectability there's naught like poor chapel folk. It's as cold as th' wind o' Greenhow Hill – ay, and colder, for 'twill never change. And now I come to think on it, one at strangest things I know is 'at they couldn't abide th' thought o' soldiering. There's a vast o' fightin' i' th' Bible, and there's a deal of Methodists i' th' army; but to hear chapel folk talk yo'd think that soldierin' were next door, an' t'other side, to hangin'. I' their meetin's all their talk is o' fightin'. When Sammy Strother were stuck for summat to say in his prayers, he'd sing out, "Th' sword o' th' Lord and o' Gideon." They were allus at it about puttin' on th' whole armour o' righteousness, an' fightin' the good fight o' faith. And then, atop o' 't all, they held a prayer-meetin' ower a young chap as wanted to 'list, and nearly deafened him, till he picked up his hat and fair ran away. And they'd tell tales in th' Sunday-school o' bad lads as had been thumped and brayed for bird-nesting o' Sundays and playin' truant o' weekdays, and how they took to wrestlin', dog-fightin', rabbit-runnin', and drinkin', till at last, as if 'twere a hepitaph on a gravestone, they damned him across th' moors wi', "an' then he went and 'listed for a soldier," an' they'd all fetch a deep breath, and throw up their eyes like a hen drinkin'.'

'Fwhy is ut?' said Mulvaney, bringing down his hand on his thigh with a crack. 'In the name av God, fwhy is ut? I've seen ut, tu. They cheat an' they swindle an' they lie an' they slander, an' fifty things fifty times worse; but the last an' the worst by their reckonin' is to serve the Widdy* honest. It's like the talk av childer – seein' things all round.'

'Plucky lot of fightin' good fights of whatsername they'd do if we didn't see they had a quiet place to fight in. And such fightin' as theirs is! Cats on the tiles. T'other callin' to which to come on. I'd give a month's pay to get some o' them broad-backed beggars in London sweatin' through a day's road-makin' an' a night's rain. They'd carry on a deal afterwards – same as we're supposed to carry on. I've bin turned out of a measly 'arf-license pub down Lambeth way, full o' greasy kebmen, 'fore now,' said Ortheris with an oath.

* Queen Victoria.

'Maybe you were dhrunk,' said Mulvaney soothingly.

'Worse nor that. The Forders were drunk, *I* was wearin' the Queen's uniform.'

'I'd no particular thought to be a soldier i' them days,' said Learoyd, still keeping his eye on the bare hill opposite, 'but this sort o' talk put it i' my head. They was so good, th' chapel folk, that they tumbled ower t'other side. But I stuck to it for 'Liza's sake, specially as she was learning me to sing the bass part in a horotorio as Jesse were gettin' up. She sung like a throstle hersen, and we had practisin's night after night for a matter of three months.'

'I know what a horotorio is,' said Ortheris pertly. 'It's a sort of chaplain's sing-song – words all out of the Bible, and hullabaloojah choruses.'

'Most Greenhow Hill folks played some instrument or t'other, an' they all sung so you might have heard them miles away, and they were so pleased wi' the noise they made they didn't fair to want anybody to listen. The preacher sung high seconds when he wasn't playin' the flute, an' they set me, as hadn't got far with big fiddle, against Willie Satterthwaite, to jog his elbow when he had to get a' gate playin'. Old Jesse was happy if ever a man was, for he were th' conductor an' th' first fiddle an' th' leadin' singer, beatin' time wi' his fiddle-stick, till at times he'd rap with it on the table, and cry out, "Now, you mun all stop; it's my turn." And he'd face round to his front, fair sweating wi' pride, to sing th' tenor solos. But he were grandest i' th' choruses, waggin' his head, flinging his arms round like a windmill, and singin' hisself black in the face. A rare singer were Jesse.

'Yo' see, I was not o' much account wi' 'em all exceptin' to 'Liza Roantree, and I had a deal o' time settin' quiet at meetings and horotorio practises to hearken their talk, and if it were strange to me at beginnin', it got stranger still at after, when I was shut on it, and could study what it meaned.

'Just after th' horotorios came off, 'Liza, as had allus been weakly like, was took very bad. I walked Dr Warbottom's horse up and down a deal of times while he were inside, where they wouldn't let me go, though I fair ached to see her.

' "She'll be better i' noo, lad – better i' noo," he used to say. "Tha mun ha' patience." Then they said if I was quiet I might go in, and th' Reverend Amos Barraclough used to read to her lyin' propped up among th' pillows. Then she began to mend a bit, and they let me carry her on to th' settle, and when it got warm again she went about same as afore. Th' preacher and me and Blast was a deal together i' them days, and i' one way we was rare good comrades. But I could ha' stretched him time and again with a good will. I mind one day he said he would like to go down into th' bowels o' th' earth, and see how th' Lord had builded th' framework o' th' everlastin' hills. He were one of them chaps as had a gift o' sayin' things. They rolled off the tip of his clever tongue, same as Mulvaney here, as would ha' made a rare good preacher if he had nobbut given his mind to it. I lent him a suit o' miner's kit as almost buried th' little man, and his white face down i' th' coat-collar and hat-flap looked like the face of a boggart, and he cowered down i' th' bottom o' the wagon. I was drivin' a tram as led up a bit of an incline up to th' cave where the engine was pumpin', and where th' ore was brought up and put into th' wagons as went down o' themselves, me puttin' th' brake on and th' horses a-trottin' after. Long as it was daylight we were good friends, but when we got fair into th' dark, and could nobbut see th' day shinin' at the hole like a lamp at a street-end, I feeled downright wicked. Ma religion dropped all away from me when I looked back at him as were always comin' between me and 'Liza. The talk was 'at they were to be wed when she got better, an' I couldn't get her to say yes or nay to it. He began to sing a hymn in his dun voice, and I came out wi' a chorus mat was all cussin' an' swearin' at my horses, an' I began to know how I hated him. He were such a little chap, too. I could drop him wi' one hand down Garstang's Copper-hole – a place where th' beck slithered ower th' edge on a rock, and fell wi' a bit of a whisper into a pit as no rope i' Greenhow could plump.'

Again Learoyd rooted up the innocent violets. 'Ay, he should see th' bowels o' th' earth an' never naught else. I could take him a mile or two along th' drift, and leave him wi' his candle doused to cry hallelujah, wi' none to hear him and say amen. I was to lead him down th' ladder-way to th' drift where Jesse Roantree was workin', and why shouldn't he slip on th' ladder, wi' my feet on his fingers till they loosed grip, and I put him down wi' my heel? If I went fust down th' ladder I could click hold on him and chuck him over my head, so as he should go squshin' down the shaft, breakin' his bones at ev'ry timberin' as Bill Appleton did when he was fresh, and hadn't a bone left when he wrought to th' bottom. Niver a blasted leg to walk from Pately. Niver an arm to put round 'Liza Roantree's waist. Niver no more – niver no more.'

The thick lips curled back over the yellow teeth, and that flushed face was not pretty to look upon. Mulvaney nodded sympathy, and Ortheris, moved by his comrade's passion, brought up the rifle to his shoulder, and searched the hillside for his quarry, muttering ribaldry about a sparrow, a spout, and a thunderstorm. The voice of the watercourse supplied the necessary small talk till Learoyd picked up his story.

'But it's none so easy to kill a man like yon. When I'd given up my horses to th' lad as took my place and I was showin' th' preacher th' workin's, shoutin' into his ear across th' clang o' th' pumpin' engines, I saw he were afraid o' naught; and when the lamplight showed his black eyes, I could feel as he was masterin' me again. I were no better nor Blast chained up short and growlin' i' the depths of him while a strange dog went safe past.

' "Th'art a coward and a fool," I said to mysen; an' I wrestled i' my mind again' him till, when we come to Garstang's Copper-hole, I laid hold o' the preacher and lifted him up over my head and held him into the darkest on it. "Now, lad," I says, "it's to be one or t'other on us – thee or me – for 'Liza Roantree. Why, isn't thee afraid for thysen?" I says, for he were still i' my arms as a sack. "Nay; I'm but afraid for thee, my poor lad, as knows naught," says he. I set him down on th' edge, an' th' beck run stiller, an' there was no more buzzin' in my head like when th' bee come through th' window o' Jesse's house. "What dost tha mean?" says I.

' "I've often thought as thou ought to know," says he, "but 'twas hard to tell thee. 'Liza Roantree's for neither on us, nor for nobody o' this earth. Dr Warbottom says – and he knows her, and her mother before her – that she is in a decline, and she cannot live six months longer. He's known it for many a day. Steady, John! Steady!" says he. And that weak little man pulled me further back and set me again' him, and talked it all over quiet and still, me turnin' a bunch o' candles in my hand, and counting them ower and ower again as I listened. A deal on it were th' regular preachin' talk, but there were a vast lot as made me begin to think as he were more of a man than I'd ever given him credit for, till I were cut as deep for him as I were for mysen.

'Six candles we had, and we crawled and climbed all that day while they lasted, and I said to mysen, " 'Liza Roantree hasn't six months to live." And when we came into th' daylight again we were like dead men to look at, an' Blast come behind us without so much as waggin' his tail. When I saw 'Liza again she looked at me a minute and says, "Who's telled tha? For I see tha knows." And she tried to smile as she kissed me, and I fair broke down.

'Yo'see, I was a young chap i' them days, and had seen naught o' life, let alone death, as is allus a-waitin'. She telled me as Dr Warbottom said as Greenhow air was too keen, and they were goin' to Bradford, to Jesse's brother David, as worked i' a mill, and I mun hold up like a man and a Christian, and she'd pray for me. Well, and they went away, and the preacher that same back end o' th' year were appointed to another circuit, as they call it, and I were left alone on Greenhow Hill.

'I tried, and I tried hard, to stick to th' chapel, but 'tweren't th' same thing at after. I hadn't 'Liza's voice to follow i' th' singin', nor her eyes a'shinin' acrost their heads. And i' th' class-meetings they said as I mun have some experiences to tell, and I hadn't a word to say for mysen.

'Blast and me moped a good deal, and happen we didn't behave ourselves over well, for they dropped us and wondered however they'd come to take us up. I can't tell how we got through th' time, while i' th' winter I gave up my job and went to Bradford. Old Jesse were at th' door o' th' house, in a long street o' little houses. He'd been sendin' th' children 'way as were clatterin' their clogs in th' causeway, for she were asleep.

' "Is it thee?" he says, "but you're not to see her. I'll none have her wakened for a nowt like thee. She's goin' fast, and she mun go in peace. Thou'lt never be good for naught i' th' world, and as long as thou lives thou'll never play the big fiddle. Get away, lad, get away!" So he shut the door softly i' my face.

'Nobody never made Jesse my master, but it seemed to me he was about right, and I went away into the town and knocked up against a recruiting sergeant. The old tales o' th' chapel folk came buzzin' into my head. I was to get away, and this were th' regular road for the likes o' me. I 'listed there and then, took th' Widow's shillin', and had a bunch o' ribbons pinned i' my hat.

'But next day I found my way to David Roantree's door, and Jesse came to open it. Says he, "Thou's come back again wi' th' devil's colours flyin' – thy true colours, as I always telled thee."

'But I begged and prayed of him to let me see her nobbut to say goodbye, till a woman calls down th' stairway, "She says John Learoyd's to come up." Th' old man shifts aside in a flash, and lays his hand on my arm, quite gentle like. "But thou'lt be quiet, John," says he, "for she's rare and weak. Thou was allus a good lad."

'Her eyes were all alive wi' light, and her hair was thick on the pillow round her, but her cheeks were thin – thin to frighten a man that's strong. "Nay, father, yo mayn't say th' devil's colours. Them ribbons is pretty." An' she held out her hands for th' hat, an' she put all straight as a woman will wi' ribbons. "Nay, but what they're pretty," she says. "Eh, but I'd ha' liked to see thee i' thy red coat, John, for thou was allus my own lad – my very own lad, and none else."

'She lifted up her arms, and they come round my neck i' a gentle grip, and they slacked away, and she seemed fainting. "Now yo' mun get away, lad," says Jesse, and I picked up my hat and I came downstairs.

'Th' recruiting sergeant were waitin' for me at th' corner public-house. "Yo've seen your sweetheart?" says he. "Yes, I've seen her," says I. "Well, we'll have a quart now, and you'll do your best to forget her," says he, bein' one o' them smart, bustlin' chaps. "Ay, sergeant," says I. "Forget her." And I've been forgettin' her ever since.'

He threw away the wilted clump of white violets as he spoke. Ortheris suddenly rose to his knees, his rifle at his shoulder, and peered across the valley in the clear afternoon light. His chin cuddled the stock, and there was a twitching of the muscles of the right cheek as he sighted; Private Stanley Ortheris was engaged on his business. A speck of white crawled up the watercourse.

'See that beggar? . . . Got 'im.'

Seven hundred yards away, and a full two hundred down the hillside, the deserter of the Aurangabadis pitched forward, rolled down a red rock, and lay very still, with his face in a clump of blue gentians, while a big raven flapped out of me pine wood to make investigation.

'That's a clean shot, little man,' said Mulvaney.

Learoyd thoughtfully watched the smoke clear away. 'Happen there was a lass tewed up wi' him, too,' said he.

Ortheris did not reply. He was staring across the valley, with the smile of the artist who looks on the completed work.

# 3
# *At the End of the Passage*

The sky is lead and our faces are red,
    And the gates of Hell are opened and riven,
    And the winds of Hell are loosened and driven,
And the dust flies up in the face of Heaven,
    And the clouds come down in a fiery sheet,
Heavy to raise and hard to be borne.
    And the soul of man is turned from his meat,
Turned from the trifles for which he has striven,
    Sick in his body, and heavy hearted,
And his soul flies up like the dust in the sheet,
    Breaks from his flesh and is gone and departed,
As the blasts they blow on the cholera-horn.

*Himalayan*

FOUR MEN, each entitled to 'life, liberty, and the pursuit of happiness', sat at a table playing whist. The thermometer marked – for them – one hundred and one degrees of heat. The room was darkened till it was only just possible to distinguish the pips of the cards and the very white faces of the players. A tattered, rotten punkah of whitewashed calico was puddling the hot air and whining dolefully at each stroke. Outside lay gloom of a November day in London. There was neither sky, sun, nor horizon – nothing but a brown purple haze of heat. It was as though the earth were dying of apoplexy.

From time to time clouds of tawny dust rose from the ground without wind or warning, flung themselves tablecloth-wise among the tops of the parched trees, and came down again. Then a whirling dust-devil would scutter across the plain for a couple of miles, break, and fall outward, though there was nothing to check its flight save a long low line of piled railway-sleepers white with the dust, a cluster of huts made of mud, condemned rails, and canvas, and the one squat four-roomed bungalow that belonged to the assistant engineer in charge of a section of the Gaudhari State line then under construction.

The four, stripped to the thinnest of sleeping-suits, played whist crossly, with wranglings as to leads and returns. It was not the best kind of whist, but they had taken some trouble to arrive at it. Mottram of the Indian Survey had ridden thirty and railed one hundred miles from his lonely post in the desert since the night before; Lowndes of the Civil Service, on special duty in the political department, had come as far to escape for an instant the miserable intrigues of an impoverished native State whose king alternately fawned and blustered for more money from the pitiful revenues contributed by hard-wrung peasants and despairing camel-breeders; Spurstow, the doctor of the line, had left a cholera-stricken camp of coolies to look after itself for forty-eight hours while he associated with white men once more. Hummil, the assistant engineer, was the host. He stood fast and received his friends thus every Sunday if they could come in. When one of them failed to appear, he would send a telegram to his last address, in order that he might know whether the defaulter were dead or alive. There are very many places in the East where it is not good or kind to let your acquaintances drop out of sight even for one short week.

The players were not conscious of any special regard for each other. They squabbled whenever they met; but they ardently desired to meet, as men without water desire to drink. They were lonely folk who understood the dread meaning of loneliness. They were all under thirty years of age – which is too soon for any man to possess that knowledge.

'Pilsener?' said Spurstow, after the second rubber, mopping his forehead.

'Beer's out, I'm sorry to say, and there's hardly enough soda-water for tonight,' said Hummil.

'What filthy bad management!' Spurstow snarled.

'Can't help it. I've written and wired; but the trains don't come through regularly yet. Last week the ice ran out – as Lowndes knows.'

'Glad I didn't come. I could ha' sent you some if I had known, though. Phew! it's too hot to go on playing bumblepuppy.' This with a savage scowl at Lowndes, who only laughed. He was a hardened offender.

Mottram rose from the table and looked out of a chink in the shutters.

'What a sweet day!' said he.

The company yawned all together and betook themselves to an aimless investigation of all Hummil's possessions – guns, tattered novels, saddlery, spurs, and the like. They had fingered them a score of times before, but there was really nothing else to do.

'Got anything fresh?' said Lowndes.

'Last week's *Gazette of India,* and a cutting from a home paper. My father sent it out. It's rather amusing.'

'One of those vestrymen that call 'emselves MPs again, is it?' said Spurstow, who read his newspapers when he could get them.

'Yes. Listen to this. It's to your address, Lowndes. The man was making a speech to his constituents, and he piled it on. Here's a sample, "And I assert unhesitatingly that the Civil Service in India is the preserve – the pet preserve – of the aristocracy of England. What does the democracy – what do the masses – get from that country, which we have step by step fraudulently annexed? I answer, nothing whatever. It is farmed with a single eye to their own interests by the scions of the aristocracy. They take good care to maintain their lavish scale of incomes, to avoid or stifle any enquiries into the nature and conduct of their administration, while they themselves force the unhappy peasant to pay with the sweat of his brow for all the luxuries in which they are lapped." ' Hummil waved the cutting above his head.' 'Ear! 'ear!' said his audience.

Then Lowndes, meditatively, 'I'd give – I'd give three months' pay to have that gentleman spend one month with me and see how the free and independent native prince works things. Old Timbersides' – this was his flippant title for an honoured and decorated feudatory prince – 'has been wearing my life out this week past for money. By Jove, his latest performance was to send me one of his women as a bribe!'

'Good for you! Did you accept it?' said Mottram.

'No. I rather wish I had, now. She was a pretty little person, and she yarned away to me about the horrible destitution among the king's womenfolk. The darlings haven't had any new clothes for nearly a month, and the old man wants to buy a new drag from Calcutta – solid silver railings and silver lamps, and trifles of that kind. I've tried to make him understand that he has played the deuce with the revenues for the last twenty years and must go slow. He can't see it.'

'But he has the ancestral treasure-vaults to draw on. There must be three millions at least in jewels and coin under his palace,' said Hummil.

'Catch a native king disturbing the family treasure! The priests forbid it except as the last resort. Old Timbersides has added something like a quarter of a million to the deposit in his reign.'

'Where the mischief does it all come from?' said Mottram.

'The country. The state of the people is enough to make you sick. I've known the tax-men wait by a milch-camel till the foal was born and then hurry off the mother for arrears. And what can I do? I can't get the court clerks to give me any accounts; I can't raise anything more than a fat smile from the commander-in-chief when I find out the troops are three months in arrears; and old Timbersides begins to weep when I speak to him. He has taken to the King's Peg heavily – liqueur brandy for whisky, and Heidsieck for soda-water.'

'That's what the Rao of Jubela took to. Even a native can't last long at that,' said Spurstow. 'He'll go out'

'And a good thing, too. Then I suppose we'll have a council of regency, and a tutor for the young prince, and hand him back his kingdom with ten years' accumulations.'

'Whereupon that young prince, having been taught all the vices of the English, will play ducks and drakes with the money and undo ten years' work in eighteen months. I've seen that business before,' said Spurstow. 'I should tackle the king with a light hand if I were you, Lowndes. They'll hate you quite enough under any circumstances.'

'That's all very well. The man who looks on can talk about the light hand; but you can't clean a pig-stye with a pen dipped in rose-water. I know my risks; but nothing has happened yet. My servant's an old Pathan, and he cooks for me. They are hardly likely to bribe him, and I don't accept food from my true friends, as they call themselves. Oh, but it's weary work! I'd sooner be with you, Spurstow. There's shooting near your camp.'

'Would you? I don't think it. About fifteen deaths a day don't incite a man to shoot anything but himself. And the worst of it is that the poor devils look at you as though you ought to save them. Lord knows, I've tried everything. My last attempt was empirical, but it pulled an old man through. He was brought to me apparently past hope, and I gave him gin and Worcester sauce with cayenne. It cured him; but I don't recommend it.'

'How do the cases run generally?' said Hummil.

'Very simply indeed. Chlorodyne, opium pill, chlorodyne, collapse, nitre, bricks to the feet, and then – the burning-ghaut. The last seems to be the only thing that stops the trouble. It's black cholera, you know. Poor devils! But, I will say, little Bunsee Lal, my apothecary, works like a demon. I've recommended him for promotion if he comes through it all alive.'

'And what are your chances, old man?' said Mottram.

'Don't know; don't care much; but I've sent the letter in. What are you doing with yourself generally?'

'Sitting under a table in the tent and spitting on the sextant to keep it cool,' said the man of the survey. 'Washing my eyes to avoid ophthalmia, which I shall certainly get, and trying to make a sub-surveyor understand that an error of five degrees in an angle isn't quite so small as it looks. I'm altogether alone, y' know, and shall be till the end of the hot weather.'

'Hummil's the lucky man,' said Lowndes, flinging himself into a long chair. 'He has an actual roof – torn as to the ceiling-cloth, but still a roof – over his head. He sees one train daily. He can get beer and soda-water and ice 'em when God is good. He has books, pictures' – they were torn from the *Graphic* – 'and the society of the excellent sub-contractor Jevins, besides the pleasure of receiving us weekly.'

Hummil smiled grimly. 'Yes, I'm the lucky man, I suppose. Jevins is luckier.'

'How? Not – '

'Yes. Went out. Last Monday.'

'By his own hand?' said Spurstow quickly, hinting the suspicion that was in everybody's mind. There was no cholera near Hummil's section. Even fever gives a man at least a week's grace, and sudden death generally implied self-slaughter.

'I judge no man this weather,' said Hummil. 'He had a touch of the sun, I fancy; for last week, after you fellows had left, he came into the verandah and told me that he was going home to see his wife, in Market Street, Liverpool, that evening.

'I got the apothecary in to look at him, and we tried to make him lie down. After an hour or two he rubbed his eyes and said he believed he had had a fit – hoped he hadn't said anything rude. Jevins had a great idea of bettering himself socially. He was very like Chucks in his language.'

'Well?'

'Then he went to his own bungalow and began cleaning a rifle. He told the servant that he was going to shoot buck in the morning. Naturally he fumbled with the trigger, and shot himself through the head – accidentally. The apothecary sent in a report to my chief, and Jevins is buried somewhere out there. I'd have wired to you, Spurstow, if you could have done anything.'

'You're a queer chap,' said Mottram. 'If you'd killed the man yourself you couldn't have been more quiet about the business.'

'Good Lord! what does it matter?' said Hummil calmly. 'I've got to do a lot of his overseeing work in addition to my own. I'm the only person that suffers. Jevins is out of it – by pure accident, of course, but out of it. The apothecary was going to write a long screed on suicide. Trust a babu to drivel when he gets the chance.'

'Why didn't you let it go in as suicide?' said Lowndes.

'No direct proof. A man hasn't many privileges in this country, but he might at least be allowed to mishandle his own rifle. Besides, someday I may need a man to smother up an accident to myself. Live and let live. Die and let die.'

'You take a pill,' said Spurstow, who had been watching Hummil's white face narrowly. 'Take a pill, and don't be an ass. That sort of talk is skittles. Anyhow, suicide is shirking your work. If I were Job ten times over, I should be so interested in what was going to happen next that I'd stay on and watch.'

'Ah! I've lost that curiosity,' said Hummil.

'Liver out of order?' said Lowndes feelingly.

'No. Can't sleep. That's worse.'

'By Jove, it is!' said Mottram. 'I'm that way every now and then, and the fit has to wear itself out. What do you take for it?'

'Nothing. What's the use? I haven't had ten minutes' sleep since Friday morning.'

'Poor chap! Spurstow, you ought to attend to this,' said Mottram. 'Now you mention it, your eyes are rather gummy and swollen.'

Spurstow, still watching Hummil, laughed lightly. 'I'll patch him up, later on. Is it too hot, do you think, to go for a ride?'

'Where to?' said Lowndes wearily. 'We shall have to go away at eight, and there'll be riding enough for us then. I hate a horse when I have to use him as a necessity. Oh, heavens! what is there to do?'

'Begin whist again, at chick points [a 'chick' is supposed to be eight shillings] and a gold mohur on the rub,' said Spurstow promptly.

'Poker. A month's pay all round for the pool – no limit – and fifty-rupee raises. Somebody would be broken before we got up,' said Lowndes.

'Can't say that it would give me any pleasure to break any man in this company,' said Mottram. 'There isn't enough excitement in it, and it's foolish.' He crossed over to the worn and battered little camp-piano – wreckage of a married household that had once held the bungalow – and opened the case.

'It's used up long ago,' said Hummil. 'The servants have picked it to pieces.'

The piano was indeed hopelessly out of order, but Mottram managed to bring the rebellious notes into a sort of agreement, and there rose from the ragged keyboard something that might once have been the ghost of a popular music-hall song. The men in the long chairs turned with evident interest as Mottram banged the more lustily.

'That's good!' said Lowndes. 'By Jove! the last time I heard that song was in '79, or thereabouts, just before I came out.'

'Ah!' said Spurstow with pride, 'I was home in '80.' And he mentioned a song of the streets popular at that date.

Mottram executed it roughly. Lowndes criticised and volunteered emendations. Mottram dashed into another ditty, not of the music-hall character, and made as if to rise.

'Sit down,' said Hummil. 'I didn't know that you had any music in your composition. Go on playing until you can't think of anything more. I'll have that piano tuned up before you come again. Play something festive.'

Very simple indeed were the tunes to which Mottram's art and the limitations of the piano could give effect, but the men listened with pleasure, and in the pauses talked all together of what they had seen or heard when they were last at home. A dense dust-storm sprung up outside, and swept roaring over the house, enveloping it in the choking darkness of midnight, but Mottram continued unheeding, and the crazy tinkle reached the ears of the listeners above the flapping of the tattered ceiling-cloth.

In the silence after the storm he glided from the more directly personal songs of Scotland, half humming them as he played, into the Evening Hymn.

'Sunday,' said he, nodding his head.

'Go on. Don't apologise for it,' said Spurstow.

Hummil laughed long and riotously. 'Play it, by all means. You're full of surprises today. I didn't know you had such a gift of finished sarcasm. How does that thing go?'

Mottram took up the tune.

'Too slow by half. You miss the note of gratitude,' said Hummil. 'It ought to go to the "Grasshopper's Polka" – this way.' And he chanted, *prestissimo* –

> 'Glory to thee, my God, this night,
> For all the blessings of the light.

That shows we really feel our blessings. How does it go on? –

> If in the night I sleepless lie,
> My soul with sacred thoughts supply;
> May no ill dreams disturb my rest –

Quicker, Mottram! –

> Or powers of darkness me molest!'

'Bah! what an old hypocrite you are!'

'Don't be an ass,' said Lowndes. 'You are at full liberty to make fun of anything else you like, but leave that hymn alone. It's associated in my mind with the most sacred recollections – '

'Summer evenings in the country – stained-glass window – light going out, and you and she jamming your heads together over one hymn-book,' said Mottram.

'Yes, and a fat old cockchafer hitting you in the eye when you walked home. Smell of hay, and a moon as big as a bandbox sitting on the top of a haycock; bats – roses – milk and midges,' said Lowndes.

'Also mothers. I can just recollect my mother singing me to sleep with that when I was a little chap,' said Spurstow.

The darkness had fallen on the room. They could hear Hummil squirming in his chair.

'Consequently,' said he testily, 'you sing it when you are seven fathom deep in Hell! It's an insult to the intelligence of the Deity to pretend we're anything but tortured rebels.'

'Take *two* pills,' said Spurstow, 'that's tortured liver.'

'The usually placid Hummil is in a vile bad temper. I'm sorry for his coolies tomorrow,' said Lowndes, as the servants brought in the lights and prepared the table for dinner.

As they were settling into their places about the miserable goat-chops, and the smoked tapioca pudding, Spurstow took occasion to whisper to Mottram, 'Well done, David!'

'Look after Saul, then,' was the reply.

'What are you two whispering about?' said Hummil suspiciously.

'Only saying that you are a damned poor host. This fowl can't be cut,' returned Spurstow with a sweet smile. 'Call this a dinner?'

'I can't help it. You don't expect a banquet, do you?'

Throughout that meal Hummil contrived laboriously to insult directly and pointedly all his guests in succession, and at each insult Spurstow kicked the aggrieved persons under the table; but he dared not exchange a glance of intelligence with either of them. Hummil's face was white and pinched, while his eyes were unnaturally large. No man dreamed for a moment of resenting his savage personalities, but as soon as the meal was over they made haste to get away.

'Don't go. You're just getting amusing, you fellows. I hope I haven't said anything that annoyed you. You're such touchy devils.' Then, changing the note into one of almost abject entreaty, Hummil added, 'I say, you surely aren't going?'

'In the language of the blessed Jorrocks, where I dines I sleeps,' said Spurstow. 'I want to have a look at your coolies tomorrow, if you don't mind. You can give me a place to lie down in, I suppose?'

The others pleaded the urgency of their several duties next day, and, saddling up, departed together, Hummil begging them to come next Sunday. As they jogged off, Lowndes unbosomed himself to Mottram –

' . . . And I never felt so like kicking a man at his own table in my life. He said I cheated at whist, and reminded me

I was in debt! Told you you were as good as a liar to your face! You aren't half indignant enough over it'

'Not I,' said Mottram. 'Poor devil! Did you ever know old Hummy behave like that before or within a hundred miles of it?'

'That's no excuse. Spurstow was hacking my shin all the time, so I kept a hand on myself. Else I should have – '

'No, you wouldn't. You'd have done as Hummy did about Jevins; judge no man this weather. By Jove! the buckle of my bridle is hot in my hand! Trot out a bit, and 'ware rat-holes.'

Ten minutes' trotting jerked out of Lowndes one very sage remark when he pulled up, sweating from every pore –

'Good thing Spurstow's with him tonight.'

'Ye–es. Good man, Spurstow. Our roads turn here. See you again next Sunday, if the sun doesn't bowl me over.'

'S'pose so, unless old Timbersides' finance minister manages to dress some of my food. Good-night, and – God bless you!'

'What's wrong now?'

'Oh, nothing.' Lowndes gathered up his whip, and, as he flicked Mottram's mare on the flank, added, 'You're not a bad little chap – that's all.' And the mare bolted half a mile across the sand, on the word.

In the assistant engineer's bungalow Spurstow and Hummil smoked the pipe of silence together, each narrowly watching the other. The capacity of a bachelor's establishment is as elastic as its arrangements are simple. A servant cleared away the dining-room table, brought in a couple of rude native bedsteads made of tape strung on a light wood frame, flung a square of cool Calcutta matting over each, set them side by side, pinned two towels to the punkah so that their fringes should just sweep clear of the sleeper's nose and mouth, and announced that the couches were ready.

The men flung themselves down, ordering the punkah-coolies by all the powers of Hell to pull. Every door and window was shut, for the outside air was that of an oven. The atmosphere within was only $104^0$, as the thermometer bore witness, and heavy with the foul smell of badly-trimmed kerosene lamps; and this stench, combined with that of native tobacco, baked brick, and dried earth, sends the heart of many a strong man down to his boots, for it is the smell of the Great Indian Empire when she turns herself for six months into a house of torment. Spurstow packed his pillows craftily so that he reclined rather than lay, his head at a safe elevation above his feet. It is not good to sleep on a low pillow in the hot weather if you happen to be of thick-necked build, for you may pass with lively snores and gugglings from natural sleep into the deep slumber of heat-apoplexy.

'Pack your pillows,' said the doctor sharply, as he saw Hummil preparing to lie down at full length.

The night-light was trimmed; the shadow of the punkah wavered across the room, and the '*flick*' of the punkah-towel and the soft whine of the rope through the wall-hole followed it. Then the punkah flagged, almost ceased. The sweat poured from Spurstow's brow. Should he go out and harangue the coolie? It started forward again with a savage jerk, and a pin came out of the towels. When this was replaced, a tomtom in the coolie-lines began to beat with the steady throb of a swollen artery inside some brain-fevered skull. Spurstow turned on his side and swore gently. There was no movement on Hummil's part. The man had composed himself as rigidly as a corpse, his hands clinched at his sides. The respiration was too hurried for any suspicion of sleep. Spurstow looked at the set face. The jaws were clinched, and there was a pucker round the quivering eyelids.

'He's holding himself as tightly as ever he can,' thought Spurstow. 'What in the world is the matter with him? – Hummil!'

'Yes,' in a thick constrained voice.

'Can't you get to sleep?'

'No.'

'Head hot? Throat feeling bulgy? or how?'

'Neither, thanks. I don't sleep much, you know.'

'Feel pretty bad?'

'Pretty bad, thanks. There is a tomtom outside, isn't there? I thought it was my head at first . . . Oh, Spurstow, for pity's sake give me something that will put me asleep – sound asleep – if it's only for six hours!' He sprang up, trembling from head to foot. 'I haven't been able to sleep naturally for days, and I can't stand it! – I can't stand it!'

'Poor old chap!'

'That's no use. Give me something to make me sleep. I tell you I'm nearly mad. I don't know what I say half my time. For three weeks I've had to think and spell out every word that has come through my lips before I dared say it. Isn't that enough to drive a man mad? I can't see things correctly now, and I've lost my sense of touch. My skin aches – my skin aches! Make me sleep. Oh, Spurstow, for the love of God make me sleep sound. It isn't enough merely to let me dream. Let me sleep!'

'All right, old man, all right. Go slow; you aren't half as bad as you think.'

The flood-gates of reserve once broken, Hummil was clinging to him like a frightened child. 'You're pinching my arm to pieces.'

'I'll break your neck if you don't do something for me. No, I didn't mean that. Don't be angry, old fellow.' He wiped the sweat off himself as he fought to regain composure. 'I'm a bit restless and off my oats, and perhaps you could recommend some sort of sleeping mixture – bromide of potassium.'

'Bromide of skittles! Why didn't you tell me this before? Let go of my arm, and I'll see if there's anything in my cigarette-case to suit your complaint.' Spurstow hunted among his day-clothes, turned up the lamp, opened a little silver cigarette-case, and advanced on the expectant Hummil with the daintiest of fairy squirts.

'The last appeal of civilisation,' said he, 'and a thing I hate to use. Hold out your arm. Well, your sleeplessness hasn't ruined your muscle; and what a thick hide it is! Might as well inject a buffalo subcutaneously. Now in a few minutes the morphia will begin working. Lie down and wait.'

A smile of unalloyed and idiotic delight began to creep over Hummil's face. 'I think,' he whispered, 'I think I'm going off now. Gad! it's positively heavenly! Spurstow, you must give me that case to keep; you – ' The voice ceased as the head fell back.

'Not for a good deal,' said Spurstow to the unconscious form. 'And now, my friend, sleeplessness of your kind being very apt to relax the moral fibre in little matters of life and death, I'll just take the liberty of spiking your guns.'

He padded into Hummil's saddle-room in his bare feet and uncased a twelve-bore rifle, an express, and a revolver. Of the first he unscrewed the nipples and hid them in the bottom of a saddlery-case; of the second he abstracted the lever, kicking it behind a big wardrobe. The third he merely opened, and knocked the doll-head bolt of the grip up with the heel of a riding-boot.

'That's settled,' he said, as he shook the sweat off his hands. 'These little precautions will at least give you time to turn. You have too much sympathy with gun-room accidents.'

And as he rose from his knees, the thick muffled voice of Hummil cried in the doorway, 'You fool!'

Such tones they use who speak in the lucid intervals of delirium to their friends a little before they die.

Spurstow started, dropping the pistol. Hummil stood in the door – way, rocking with helpless laughter.

'That was awf'ly good of you, I'm sure,' he said, very slowly, feeling for his words. 'I don't intend to go out by my own hand at present. I say, Spurstow, that stuff won't work. What shall I do? What shall I do?' And panic terror stood in his eyes.

'Lie down and give it a chance. Lie down at once.'

'I daren't. It will only take me half-way again, and I shan't be able to get away this time. Do you know it was all I could do to come out just now? Generally I am as quick as lightning; but you had clogged my feet. I was nearly caught.'

'Oh yes, I understand. Go and lie down.'

'No, it isn't delirium; but it was an awfully mean trick to play on me. Do you know I might have died?'

As a sponge rubs a slate clean, so some power unknown to Spurstow had wiped out of Hummil's face all that stamped it for the face of a man, and he stood at the doorway in the expression of his lost innocence. He had slept back into terrified childhood.

'Is he going to die on the spot?' thought Spurstow. Then, aloud, 'All right, my son. Come back to bed, and tell me all about it. You couldn't sleep; but what was all the rest of the nonsense?'

'A place – a place down there,' said Hummil, with simple sincerity. The drug was acting on him by waves, and he was flung from the fear of a strong man to the fright of a child as his nerves gathered sense or were dulled.

'Good God! I've been afraid of it for months past, Spurstow. It has made every night hell to me; and yet I'm not conscious of having done anything wrong.'

'Be still, and I'll give you another dose. We'll stop your nightmares, you unutterable idiot!'

'Yes, but you must give me so much that I can't get away. You must make me quite sleepy – not just a little sleepy. It's so hard to run then.'

'I know it; I know it. I've felt it myself. The symptoms are exactly as you describe.'

'Oh, don't laugh at me, confound you! Before this awful sleeplessness came to me I've tried to rest on my elbow and put a spur in the bed to sting me when I fell back. Look!'

'By Jove! the man has been rowelled like a horse! Ridden by the nightmare with a vengeance! And we all thought him sensible enough. Heaven send us understanding! You like to talk, don't you?'

'Yes, sometimes. Not when I'm frightened. *Then* I want to run. Don't you?'

'Always. Before I give you your second dose try to tell me exactly what your trouble is.'

Hummil spoke in broken whispers for nearly ten minutes, whilst Spurstow looked into the pupils of his eyes and passed his hand before them once or twice.

At the end of the narrative the silver cigarette-case was produced, and the last words that Hummil said as he fell back for the second time were, 'Put me quite to sleep; for if I'm caught I die – I die!'

'Yes, yes; we all do that sooner or later – thank Heaven who has set a term to our miseries,' said Spurstow, settling the cushions under the head. 'It occurs to me that unless I drink something I shall go out before my time. I've stopped sweating, and – I wear a seventeen-inch collar.' He brewed himself scalding hot tea, which is an excellent remedy against heat-apoplexy if you take three or four cups of it in time. Then he watched the sleeper.

'A blind face that cries and can't wipe its eyes, a blind face that chases him down corridors! H'm! Decidedly, Hummil ought to go on leave as soon as possible; and, sane or otherwise, he undoubtedly did rowel himself most cruelly. Well, Heaven send us understanding!'

At midday Hummil rose, with an evil taste in his mouth, but an unclouded eye and a joyful heart.

'I was pretty bad last night, wasn't I?' said he.

'I have seen healthier men. You must have had a touch of the sun. Look here: if I write you a swingeing medical certificate, will you apply for leave on the spot?'

'No.'

'Why not? You want it.'

'Yes, but I can hold on till the weather's a little cooler.'

'Why should you, if you can get relieved on the spot?'

'Burkett is the only man who could be sent; and he's a born fool.'

'Oh, never mind about the line. You aren't so important as all that. Wire for leave, if necessary.'

Hummil looked very uncomfortable.

'I can hold on till the Rains,' he said evasively.

'You can't. Wire to headquarters for Burkett.'

'I won't. If you want to know why, particularly, Burkett is married, and his wife's just had a kid, and she's up at Simla, in the cool, and Burkett has a very nice billet that takes him into Simla from Saturday to Monday. That little woman isn't at all well. If Burkett was transferred she'd try to follow him. If she left the baby behind she'd fret herself to death. If she came – and Burkett's one of those selfish little beasts who are always talking about a wife's place being with her husband – she'd die. It's murder to bring a woman here just now. Burkett hasn't the physique of a rat. If he came here he'd go out; and I know she hasn't any money, and I'm pretty sure she'd go out too. I'm salted in a sort of way, and I'm not married. Wait till the Rains, and then Burkett can get thin down here. It'll do him heaps of good.'

'Do you mean to say that you intend to face – what you have faced, till the Rains break?'

'Oh, it won't be so bad, now you've shown me a way out of it. I can always wire to you. Besides, now I've once got into the way of sleeping, it'll be all right. Anyhow, I shan't put in for leave. That's the long and me short of it.'

'My great Scott! I thought all that sort of thing was dead and done with.'

'Bosh! You'd do the same yourself. I feel a new man, thanks to that cigarette-case. You're going over to camp now, aren't you?'

'Yes; but I'll try to look you up every other day, if I can.'

'I'm not bad enough for that. I don't want you to bother. Give the coolies gin and ketchup.'

'Then you feel all right?'

'Fit to fight for my life, but not to stand out in the sun talking to you. Go along, old man, and bless you!'

Hummil turned on his heel to face the echoing desolation of his bungalow, and the first thing he saw standing in the verandah was the figure of himself. He had met a similar apparition once before, when he was suffering from overwork and the strain of the hot weather.

'This is bad – already,' he said, rubbing his eyes. 'If the thing slides away from me all in one piece, like a ghost, I shall know it is only my eyes and stomach that are out or order. If it walks – my head is going.'

He approached the figure, which naturally kept at an unvarying distance from him, as is the use of all spectres that are born of overwork. It slid through the house and dissolved into swimming specks within the eyeball as soon as it reached the burning light of the garden. Hummil went about his business till even. When he came in to dinner he found himself sitting at the table. The vision rose and walked out hastily. Except that it cast no shadow it was in all respects real.

No living man knows what that week held for Hummil. An increase of the epidemic kept Spurstow in camp among the coolies, and all he could do was to telegraph to Mottram, bidding him go to the bungalow and sleep there. But Mottram was forty miles away from the nearest telegraph, and knew nothing of anything save the needs of the survey till he met, early on Sunday morning, Lowndes and Spurstow heading towards Hummil's for the weekly gathering.

'Hope the poor chap's in a better temper,' said the former, swinging himself off his horse at the door. 'I suppose he isn't up yet.'

'I'll just have a look at him,' said the doctor. 'If he's asleep there's no need to wake him.'

And an instant later, by the tone of Spurstow's voice calling upon them to enter, the men knew what had happened. There was no need to wake him.

The punkah was still being pulled over the bed, but Hummil had departed this life at least three hours.

The body lay on its back, hands clinched by the side, as Spurstow had seen it lying seven nights previously. In the staring eyes was written terror beyond the expression of any pen.

Mottram, who had entered behind Lowndes, bent over the dead and touched the forehead lightly with his lips. 'Oh, you lucky, lucky devil!' he whispered.

But Lowndes had seen the eyes, and withdrew shuddering to the other side of the room.

'Poor chap! poor old chap! And the last time I met him I was angry. Spurstow, we should have watched him. Has he – ?'

Deftly Spurstow continued his investigations, ending by a search round the room.

'No, he hasn't,' he snapped. 'There's no trace of anything. Call the servants.'

They came, eight or ten of them, whispering and peering over each other's shoulders.

'When did your Sahib go to bed?' said Spurstow.

'At eleven or ten, we think,' said Hummil's personal servant.

'He was well then? But how should you know?'

'He was not ill, as far as our comprehension extended. But he had slept very little for three nights. This I know, because I saw him walking much, and specially in the heart of the night'

As Spurstow was arranging the sheet, a big straight-necked hunting-spur tumbled on the ground. The doctor groaned. The personal servant peeped at the body.

'What do you think, Chuma?' said Spurstow, catching the look on the dark face.

'Heaven-born, in my poor opinion, this that was my master has descended into the Dark Places, and there has been caught because he was not able to escape with sufficient speed. We have the spur for evidence that he fought with Fear. Thus have I seen men of my race do with thorns when a spell was laid upon them to overtake them in their sleeping hours and they dared not sleep.'

'Chuma, you're a mud-head. Go out and prepare seals to be set on the Sahib's property.'

'God has made the Heaven-born. God has made me. Who are we, to enquire into the dispensations of God? I will bid the other servants hold aloof while you are reckoning the tale of the Sahib's property. They are all thieves, and would steal.'

'As far as I can make out, he died from – oh, anything; stoppage of the heart's action, heat-apoplexy, or some other visitation,' said Spurstow to his companions. 'We must make an inventory of his effects, and so on.'

'He was scared to death,' insisted Lowndes. 'Look at those eyes! For pity's sake don't let him be buried with them open!'

'Whatever it was, he's clear of all the trouble now,' said Mottram softly.

Spurstow was peering into the open eyes.

'Come here,' said he. 'Can you see anything there?'

'I can't face it!' whimpered Lowndes. 'Cover up the face! Is there any fear on earth that can turn a man into that likeness? It's ghastly. Oh, Spurstow, cover it up!'

'No fear – on earth,' said Spurstow. Mottram leaned over his shoulder and looked intently.

'I see nothing except some grey blurs in the pupil. There can be nothing there, you know.'

'Even so. Well, let's think. It'll take half a day to knock up any sort of coffin; and he must have died at midnight. Lowndes, old man, go out and tell the coolies to break ground next to Jevins's grave. Mottram, go round the house with Chuma and see that the seals are put on things. Send a couple of men to me here, and I'll arrange.'

The strong-armed servants when they returned to their own kind told a strange story of the doctor Sahib vainly trying to call their master back to life by magic arts – to wit, the holding of a little green box that clicked to each of the dead man's eyes, and of a bewildered muttering on the part of the doctor Sahib, who took the little green box away with him.

The resonant hammering of a coffin-lid is no pleasant thing to hear, but those who have experience maintain that much more terrible is the soft swish of the bed-linen, the reeving and unreeving of the bed-tapes, when he who has fallen by the roadside is apparelled for burial, sinking gradually as the tapes are tied over, till the swaddled shape touches the floor and there is no protest against the indignity of hasty disposal.

At the last moment Lowndes was seized with scruples of conscience. 'Ought you to read the service – from beginning to end?' said he to Spurstow.

'I intend to. You're my senior as a civilian. You can take it if you like.'

'I didn't mean that for a moment. I only thought if we could get a chaplain from somewhere – I'm willing to ride anywhere – and give poor Hummil a better chance. That's all.'

'Bosh!' said Spurstow, as he framed his lips to the tremendous words that stand at the head of the burial service.

* * * * *

After breakfast they smoked a pipe in silence to the memory of the dead. Then Spurstow said absently –

' 'Tisn't in medical science.'

'What?'

'Things in a dead man's eye.'

'For goodness' sake leave that horror alone!' said Lowndes. 'I've seen a native die of pure fright when a tiger chivied him. I know what killed Hummil.'

'The deuce you do! I'm going to try to see.' And the doctor retreated into the bathroom with a Kodak camera. After a few minutes there was the sound of something being hammered to pieces, and he emerged, very white indeed.

'Have you got a picture?' said Mottram. 'What does the thing look like?'

'It was impossible, of course. You needn't look, Mottram. I've torn up the films. There was nothing there. It was impossible.'

'That,' said Lowndes, very distinctly, watching the shaking hand striving to relight the pipe, 'is a damned lie.'

Mottram laughed uneasily. 'Spurstow's right,' he said. 'We're all in such a state now that we'd believe anything. For pity's sake let's try to be rational.'

There was no further speech for a long time. The hot wind whistled without, and the dry trees sobbed. Presently the daily train, winking brass, burnished steel, and spouting steam, pulled up panting in the intense glare. 'We'd better go on on that,' said Spurstow. 'Go back to work I've written my certificate. We can't do any more good here, and work'll keep our wits together. Come on.'

No one moved. It is not pleasant to face railway journeys at midday in June. Spurstow gathered up his hat and whip, and, turning in the doorway, said –

'There may be Heaven – there must be Hell.
Meantime, there is our life here. We-ell?'

Neither Mottram nor Lowndes had any answer to the question.

# 4

# *The Limitations of Pambé Serang*

If you consider the circumstances of the case, it was the only thing that he could do. But Pambé Serang has been hanged by the neck till he is dead, and Nurkeed is dead also.

Three years ago, when the Elsass-Lothringen steamer *Saarbruck* was coaling at Aden and the weather was very hot indeed, Nurkeed, the big fat Zanzibar stoker who fed the second right furnace thirty feet down in the hold, got leave to go ashore. He departed a 'Seedee boy', as they call the stokers; he returned the full-blooded Sultan of Zanzibar – His Highness Sayyid Burgash, with a bottle in each hand. Then he sat on the fore-hatch grating, eating salt fish and onions, and singing the songs of a far country. The food belonged to Pambé, the Serang or head man of the lascar sailors. He had just cooked it for himself, turned to borrow some salt, and when he came back Nurkeed's dirty black fingers were spading into the rice.

A serang is a person of importance, far above a stoker, though the stoker draws better pay. He sets the chorus of 'Hya! Hulla! Hee-ah! Heh!' when the captain's gig is pulled up to the davits; he heaves the lead too; and sometimes, when all the ship is lazy, he puts on his whitest muslin and a big red sash, and plays with the passengers' children on the quarter-deck. Then the passengers give him money, and he saves it all up for an orgy at Bombay or Calcutta, or Pulu Penang.

'Ho! you fat black barrel, you're eating my food!' said Pambé, in the other lingua franca that begins where the Levant tongue stops, and runs from Port Said eastward till east is west, and the sealing-brigs of the Kurile Islands gossip with the strayed Hakodate junks.

'Son of Eblis, monkey-face, dried shark's liver, pig-man, I am the Sultan Sayyid Burgash, and the commander of all this ship. Take away your garbage,' and Nurkeed thrust the empty pewter rice-plate into Pambé's hand.

Pambé beat it into a basin over Nurkeed's woolly head. Nurkeed drew his sheath-knife and stabbed Pambé in the leg. Pambé drew *his* sheath-knife; but Nurkeed dropped down into the darkness of the hold and spat through the grating at Pambé, who was staining the clean fore-deck with his blood.

Only the white moon saw these things; for the officers were looking after the coaling, and the passengers were tossing in their close cabins. 'All right,' said Pambé – and went forward to tie up his leg – 'we will settle the account later on.'

He was a Malay born in India: married once in Burma, where his wife had a cigar-shop on the Shwe-Dagon road; once in Singapore, to a Chinese girl; and once in Madras, to a Mahomedan woman who sold fowls. The English sailor cannot, owing to postal and telegraph facilities, marry as profusely as he used to do; but native sailors can, being uninfluenced by the barbarous inventions of the Western savage. Pambé was a good husband when he happened to remember the existence of a wife; but he was also a very good Malay; and it is not wise to offend a Malay, because he does not forget anything. Moreover, in Pambé's case blood had been drawn and food spoiled.

Next morning Nurkeed rose with a blank mind. He was no longer Sultan of Zanzibar, but a very hot stoker. So he went on deck and opened his jacket to the morning breeze, till a sheath-knife came like a flying-fish and stuck into the woodwork of the cook's galley half an inch from his right armpit. He ran down below before his time, trying to remember what he could have said to the owner of the weapon. At noon, when all the ship's lascars were feeding, Nurkeed advanced into their midst, and, being a placid man with a large regard for his own skin, he opened negotiations, saying, 'Men of the ship, last night I was drunk, and this morning I know that I behaved unseemly to someone or another of you. Who was that man, that I may meet him face to face and say that I was drunk?'

Pambé measured the distance to Nurkeed's naked breast. If he sprang at him he might be tripped up, and a blind blow at the chest sometimes only means a gash on the breast-bone. Ribs are difficult to thrust between unless the subject be asleep. So he said nothing; nor did the other lascars. Their faces immediately dropped all expression, as is the custom of the Oriental when there is killing on the carpet or any chance of trouble. Nurkeed looked long at the white eyeballs. He was only an African, and could not read characters. A big sigh – almost a groan – broke from him, and he went back to the furnaces. The lascars took up the conversation where he had interrupted it. They talked of the best methods of cooking rice.

Nurkeed suffered considerably from lack of fresh air during the run to Bombay. He only came on deck to breathe when all the world was about; and even then a heavy block once dropped from a derrick within a foot of his head, and an apparently firm-lashed grating on which he set his foot began to turn over with the intention of dropping him on the cased cargo fifteen feet below; and one insupportable night the sheath-knife dropped from the fo'c's'le, and this time it drew blood. So Nurkeed made complaint; and, when the *Saarbruck* reached Bombay, fled and buried himself among eight hundred thousand people, and did not sign articles till the ship had been a month gone from the port. Pambé waited too; but his Bombay wife grew clamorous, and he was forced to sign in the *Spicheren* to Hongkong, because he realised that all play and no work gives Jack a ragged shirt. In the foggy China seas he thought a great deal of Nurkeed, and, when Elsass-Lothringen steamers lay in port with the *Spicheren,* enquired after him and found he had gone to England via the Cape, on the *Gravelotte.* Pambé came to England on the *Worth.* The *Spicheren* met her by the Nore Light. Nurkeed was going out with the *Spicheren* to the Calicut coast.

'Want to find a friend, my trap-mouthed coal-scuttle?' said a gentleman in the mercantile service. 'Nothing easier. Wait at the Nyanza Docks till he comes. Everyone comes to the Nyanza Docks. Wait, you poor heathen.' The gentleman spoke truth. There are three great doors in the world where, if you stand long enough, you shall meet anyone you wish. The head of the Suez Canal is one, but there Death comes also; Charing Cross Station is the second – for inland work; and the Nyanza Docks is the third. At each of these places are men and women looking eternally for those who will surely come. So Pambé waited at the docks. Time was no object to him; and the wives could wait, as he did from day to day, week to week, and month to month, by the Blue Diamond funnels, the Red Dot smoke-stacks, the Yellow Streaks, and the nameless dingy gypsies of the sea that loaded and unloaded, jostled, whistled, and roared in the everlasting fog. When money failed, a kind gentleman told Pambé to become a Christian; and Pambé became one with great speed, getting his religious teachings between ship and ship's arrival, and six or seven shillings a week for distributing tracts to mariners. What the faith was Pambé did not in the least care; but he knew if he said 'Native Ki-lis-ti-an, Sar' to men with long black coats he might get a few coppers; and the tracts were vendible at a little public-house that sold shag by the 'dottel', which is even smaller weight than the 'half-screw', which is less than the half-ounce, and a most profitable retail trade.

But after eight months Pambé fell sick with pneumonia, contracted from long standing still in slush; and much against his will he was forced to lie down in his two-and-sixpenny room raging against Fate.

The kind gentleman sat by his bedside, and grieved to find that Pambé talked in strange tongues, instead of listening to good books, and almost seemed to become a benighted heathen again – till one day he was roused from semi-stupor by a voice in the street by the dock-head. 'My friend – he,' whispered Pambé. 'Call now – call Nurkeed. Quick! God has sent him!'

'He wanted one of his own race,' said the kind gentleman; and, going out, he called 'Nurkeed!' at the top of his voice. An excessively coloured man in a rasping white shirt and brand-new slops, a shining hat, and a breast-pin, turned round. Many voyages had taught Nurkeed how to spend his money and made him a citizen of the world.

'Hi! Yes!' said he, when the situation was explained. 'Command him – black nigger – when I was in the

*Saarbruck.* Ole Pambé, good ole Pambé. Damn lascar. Show him up, Sar,' and he followed into the room. One glance told the stoker what the kind gentleman had overlooked. Pambé was desperately poor. Nurkeed drove his hands deep into his pockets, then advanced with clenched fists on the sick, shouting, 'Hya, Pambé. Hya! Hee-ah! Hulla! Heh! Takilo! Takilo! Make fast aft, Pambé. You know, Pambé. You know me. Dekho, jee! Look! Damn big fat lazy lascar!'

Pambé beckoned with his left hand. His right was under his pillow. Nurkeed removed his gorgeous hat and stooped over Pambé till he could catch a faint whisper. 'How beautiful!' said the kind gentleman. 'How these Orientals love like children!'

'Spit him out,' said Nurkeed, leaning over Pambé yet more closely.

'Touching the matter of that fish and onions – ' said Pambé – and sent the knife home under the edge of the rib-bone upwards and forwards.

There was a thick sick cough, and the body of the African slid slowly from the bed, his clutching hands letting fall a shower of silver pieces that ran across the room.

'Now I can die!' said Pambé.

But he did not die. He was nursed back to life with all the skill that money could buy, for the Law wanted him; and in the end he grew sufficiently healthy to be hanged in due and proper form.

Pambé did not care particularly; but it was a sad blow to the kind gentleman.

# 5

# *The Disturber of Traffic*

From the wheel and the drift of Things
    Deliver us, good Lord;
And we will meet the wrath of kings,
    The faggot, and the sword.

Lay not Thy toil before our eyes,
    Nor vex us with Thy wars,
Lest we should feel the straining skies
    O'ertrod by trampling stars.

A veil 'twixt us and Thee, dread Lord,
    A veil 'twixt us and Thee:
Lest we should hear too clear, too clear,
    And unto madness see!

*Miriam Cohen*

THE BROTHERS of the Trinity order that none unconnected with their service shall be found in or on one of their Lights during the hours of darkness; but their servants can be made to think otherwise. If you are fair-spoken and take an interest in their duties, they will allow you to sit with them through the long night and help to scare the ships into mid-channel.

Of the English south-coast Lights, that of St Cecilia-under-the-Cliff is the most powerful, for it guards a very foggy coast. When the sea-mist veils all, St Cecilia turns a hooded head to the sea and sings a song of two words once every minute. From the land that song resembles the bellowing of a brazen bull; but off-shore they understand, and the steamers grunt gratefully in answer.

Fenwick, who was on duty one night, lent me a pair of black glass spectacles, without which no man can look at the Light unblinded, and busied himself in last touches to the lenses before twilight fell. The width of the English Channel beneath us lay as smooth and as many-coloured as the inside of an oyster shell. A little Sunderland cargo-boat had made her signal to Lloyd's Agency, half a mile up the coast, and was lumbering down to the sunset, her wake lying white behind her. One star came out over the cliffs, the waters turned to lead colour, and St Cecilia's Light shot out across the sea in eight long pencils that wheeled slowly from right to left, melted into one beam of solid light laid down directly in front of the tower, dissolved again into eight, and passed away. The light-frame of the thousand lenses circled on its rollers, and the compressed-air engine that drove it hummed like a bluebottle under a glass. The hand of the indicator on the wall pulsed from mark to mark. Eight pulse-beats timed one half-revolution of the Light; neither more nor less.

Fenwick checked the first few revolutions carefully; he opened the engine's feed-pipe a trifle, looked at the racing governor, and again at the indicator, and said: 'She'll do for the next few hours. We've just sent our regular engine to London, and this spare one's not by any manner so accurate.'

'And what would happen if the compressed air gave out?' I asked.

'We'd have to turn the flash by hand, keeping an eye on the indicator. There's a regular crank for that. But it hasn't happened yet. We'll need all our compressed air tonight.'

'Why?' said I. I had been watching him for not more than a minute.

'Look,' he answered, and I saw that the dead sea-mist had risen out of the lifeless sea and wrapped us while my back had been turned. The pencils of the Light marched staggeringly across tilted floors of white cloud. From the balcony round the light-room the white walls of the lighthouse ran down into swirling, smoking space. The noise of the tide coming in very lazily over the rocks was choked down to a thick drawl.

'That's the way our sea-fogs come,' said Fenwick, with an air of ownership. 'Hark, now, to that little fool calling out 'fore he's hurt.'

Something in the mist was bleating like an indignant calf; it might have been half a mile or half a hundred miles away.

'Does he suppose we've gone to bed?' continued Fenwick. 'You'll hear us talk to him in a minute. He knows puffickly where he is, and he's carrying on to be told like if he was insured.'

'Who is "he"?'

'That Sunderland boat, o' course. Ah!'

I could hear a steam-engine hiss down below in the mist where the dynamos that fed the Light were clacking together. Then there came a roar that split the fog and shook the lighthouse.

'GIT-*toot!*' blared the fog-horn of St Cecilia. The bleating ceased.

'Little fool!' Fenwick repeated. Then, listening: 'Blest if that aren't another of them! Well, well, they always say that a fog do draw the ships of the sea together. They'll be calling all night, and so'll the siren. We're expecting some tea-ships up-Channel. . . If you put my coat on that chair, you'll feel more so-fash, sir.'

It is no pleasant thing to thrust your company upon a man for the night. I looked at Fenwick, and Fenwick looked at me; each gauging the other's capacities for boring and being bored. Fenwick was an old, clean-shaven, grey-haired man who had followed the sea for thirty years, and knew nothing of the land except the lighthouse in which he served. He fenced cautiously to find out the little that I knew and talked down to my level, till it came out that I had met a captain in the merchant service who had once commanded a ship in which Fenwick's son had served; and further, that I had seen some places that Fenwick had touched at. He began with a dissertation on pilotage in the Hugli. I had been privileged to know a Hugli pilot intimately. Fenwick had only seen the imposing and masterful breed from a ship's chains, and his intercourse had been cut down to 'Quarter less five', and remarks of a strictly business-like nature. Hereupon he ceased to talk down to me, and became so amazingly technical that I was forced to beg him to explain every other sentence. This set him fully at his ease; and then we spoke as men together, each too interested to think of anything except the subject in hand. And that subject was wrecks, and voyages, and old-time trading, and ships cast away in desolate seas, steamers we both had known, their merits and demerits, lading, Lloyd's, and, above all, Lights. The talk always came back to Lights: Lights of the Channel; Lights on forgotten islands, and men forgotten on them; Light-ships – two months' duty and one month's leave – tossing on kinked cables in ever troubled tideways; and Lights that men had seen where never lighthouse was marked on the charts.

Omitting all those stories, and omitting also the wonderful ways by which he arrived at them, I tell here, from Fenwick's mouth, one that was not the least amazing. It was delivered in pieces between the roller-skate rattle of the revolving lenses, the bellowing of the fog-horn below, the answering calls from the sea, and the sharp tap of reckless night-birds that flung themselves at the glasses. It concerned a man called Dowse, once an intimate friend of Fenwick, now a waterman at Portsmouth, believing that the guilt of blood is on his head, and finding no rest either at Portsmouth or Gosport Hard.

* * * * *

'. . . And if anybody was to come to you and say, "I know the Java currents," don't you listen to him; for those currents is never yet known to mortal man. Sometimes they're here, sometimes they're there, but they never runs less than five knots an hour through and among those islands of the Eastern Archipelagus. There's reverse currents in the Gulf of Boni – and that's up north in Celebes – that no man can explain; and through all those Java passages from the Bali Narrows, Dutch Gut, and Ombay, which I take it is the safest, they chop and they change, and they banks the tides fust on one shore and then on another, till your ship's tore in two. I've come through the Bali Narrows, stern first, in the heart o' the south-east monsoon, with a sou'-sou'-west wind blowing atop of the northerly flood, and our skipper said he wouldn't do it again, not for all Jamrach's. You've heard o'Jamrach's, sir?'

'Yes; and was Dowse stationed in the Bali Narrows?' I said.

'No; he was not at Bali, but much more east o' them passages, and that's Flores Strait, at the east end o' Flores. It's all on the way south to Australia when you're running through that Eastern Archipelagus. Sometimes you go through Bali Narrows if you're full-powered, and sometimes through Flores Strait, so as to stand south at once, and fetch round Timor, keeping well clear o' the Sahul Bank. Elseways, if you aren't full-powered, why it stands to reason you go round by the Ombay Passage, keeping careful to the north side. You understand that, sir?'

I was not full-powered, and judged it safer to keep to the north side – of Silence.

'And on Flores Strait, in the fairway between Adonare Island and the mainland, they put Dowse in charge of a screw-pile Light called the Wurlee Light. It's less than a mile across the head of Flores Strait. Then it opens out to ten or twelve mile for Solor Strait, and then it narrows again to a three-mile gut, with a toplin' flamin' volcano by it. That's old Loby Toby by Loby Toby Strait, and if you keep his Light and the Wurlee Light in a line you won't take much harm, not on the darkest night. That's what Dowse told me, and I can well believe him, knowing these seas myself; but you must ever be mindful of the currents. And there they put Dowse, since he was the only man that that Dutch Government which owns Flores could find that would go to Wurlee and tend a fixed Light. Mostly they uses Dutch and Italians; Englishmen being said to drink when alone. I never could rightly find out what made Dowse accept of that position, but accept he did, and used to sit for to watch the tigers come out of the forests to hunt for crabs and such like round about the lighthouse at low tide. The water was always warm in those parts, as I know well, and uncommon sticky, and it ran with the tides as thick and smooth as hogwash in a trough. There was another man along with Dowse in the Light, but he wasn't rightly a man. He was a Kling. No, nor yet a Kling he wasn't, but his skin was in little flakes and cracks all over, from living so much in the salt water as was his usual custom. His hands was all webby-foot, too. He was called, I remember Dowse saying now, an Orange-Lord, on account of his habits. You've heard of an Orange-Lord, sir?'

'Orang-Laut?' I suggested.

'That's the name,' said Fenwick, smacking his knee. 'An Orang-Laut, of course, and his name was Challong; what they call a sea-gypsy. Dowse told me that that man, long hair and all, would go swimming up and down the straits just for something to do; running down on one tide and back again with the other, swimming side-stroke, and the tides going tremenjus strong. Elseways he'd be skipping about the beach along with the tigers at low tide, for he was most part a beast; or he'd sit in a little boat praying to old Loby Toby of an evening when the volcano was spitting red at the south end of the strait. Dowse told me that he wasn't a companionable man, like you and me might have been to Dowse.

'Now I can never rightly come at what it was that began to ail Dowse after he had been there a year or something less. He was saving of all his pay and tending to his Light, and now and again he'd have a fight with Challong and tip him off the Light into the sea. Then, he told me, his head began to feel streaky from looking at the tide so long. He said there was long streaks of white running inside it; like wall-paper that hadn't been properly pasted up, he said. The streaks, they would run with the tides, north and south, twice a day, accordin' to them currents, and he'd lie down on the planking – it was a screw-pile Light – with his eye to a crack and watch the water streaking through the piles just so quiet as hogwash. He said the only comfort he got was at slack water. Then the streaks in his head went round and round like a sampan in a tide-rip; but that was heaven, he said, to the other kind of streaks – the straight ones that looked like arrows on a wind-chart, but much more regular, and that was the trouble of it. No more he couldn't ever keep his eyes off the tides that ran up and down so strong, but as soon as ever he looked at the high hills standing all along Flores Strait for rest and comfort his eyes would be pulled down like to the nesty streaky water; and when they once got there he couldn't pull them away again till the tide changed. He told me all this himself, speaking just as though he was talking of somebody else.'

'Where did you meet him?' I asked.

'In Portsmouth harbour, a-cleaning the brasses of a Ryde boat, but I'd known him off and on through following the sea for many years. Yes, he spoke about himself very curious, and all as if he was in the next room laying there dead. Those streaks, they preyed upon his intellecks, he said; and he made up his mind, every time that the Dutch gunboat that attends to the Lights in those parts come along, that he'd ask to be took off. But as soon as she did come something went click in his throat, and he was so took up with watching her masts, because they ran longways, in the contrary direction to his streaks, that he could never say a word until she was gone away and her masts was under sea again. Then, he said, he'd cry by the hour; and Challong swum round and round the Light, laughin' at him and splashin' water with his webby-foot hands. At last he took it into his pore sick head that the ships, and particularly the steamers that came by – there wasn't many of them – made the streaks, instead of the tides as was natural. He used to sit, he told me, cursing every boat that come along – sometimes a junk, sometimes a Dutch brig, and now and again a steamer rounding Flores Head and poking about in the mouth of the strait. Or there'd come a boat from Australia running north past old Loby Toby hunting for a fair current, but never throwing out any papers that Challong might pick up for Dowse to read. Generally speaking, the steamers kept more westerly, but now and again they came looking for Timor and the west coast of Australia. Dowse used to shout to them to go round by the Ombay Passage, and not to come streaking past him, making the water all streaky, but it wasn't likely they'd hear. He says to himself after a month, "I'll give them one more chance," he says. "If the next boat don't attend to my just representations," – he says he remembers using those very words to Challong – "I'll stop the fairway."

'The next boat was a Two-streak cargo-boat very anxious to make her northing. She waddled through under old Loby Toby at the south end of the strait, and she passed within a quarter of a mile of the Wurlee Light at the north end, in seventeen fathom o' water, the tide against her. Dowse took the trouble to come out with Challong in a little prow that they had – all bamboos and leakage – and he lay in the fairway waving a palm branch, and, so he told me, wondering why and what for he was making this fool of himself. Up come the Two-streak boat, and Dowse shouts: "Don't you come this way again, making my head all streaky! Go round by Ombay, and leave me alone." Someone looks over the port bulwarks and shies a banana at Dowse, and that's all. Dowse sits down in the bottom of the boat and cries fit to break his heart. Then he says, "Challong, what am I a-crying for?" and they fetches up by the Wurlee Light on the half-flood.

' "Challong," he says, "there's too much traffic here, and that's why the water's so streaky as it is. It's the junks and the brigs and the steamers that do it," he says; and all the time he was speaking he was thinking, "Lord, Lord, what a crazy fool I am!" Challong said nothing, because he couldn't speak a word of English except say "damn", and he said that where you or me would say "yes". Dowse lay down on the planking of the Light with his eye to the crack, and he saw the muddy water streaking below, and he never said a word till slack water, because the streaks kept him tongue-tied at such times. At slack water he says, "Challong, we must buoy this fairway for wrecks," and he holds up his hands several times, showing that dozens of wrecks had come about in the fairway; and Challong says, "Damn."

'That very afternoon he and Challong rows to Wurlee, the village in the woods that the Light was named after, and buys canes – stacks and stacks of canes, and coir rope thick and fine, all sorts – and they sets to work making square floats by lashing of the canes together. Dowse said he took longer over those floats than might have been needed, because he rejoiced in the corners, they being square, and the streaks in his head all running longways. He lashed the canes together, criss-cross and thwartways – any way but longways – and they made up twelve-foot-square floats, like rafts. Then he stepped a twelve-foot bamboo or a bundle of canes in the centre, and to the head of that he lashed a big six-foot W letter, all made of canes, and painted the float dark green and the W white, as a wreck-buoy should be painted. Between them two they makes a round dozen of these new kind of wreck-buoys, and it was a two months' job. There was no big traffic, owing to it being on the turn of the monsoon, but what there was Dowse cursed at, and the streaks in his head, they ran with the tides, as usual.

'Day after day, so soon as a buoy was ready, Challong would take it out, with a big rock that half sunk the prow and a bamboo grapnel, and drop it dead in the fairway. He did this day or night, and Dowse could see him of a clear night, when the sea brimed, climbing about the buoys with the sea-fire dripping off him. They was all put into place, twelve of them, in seventeen-fathom water; not in a straight line, on account of a well-known shoal there, but slantways, and two, one behind the other, mostly in the centre of the fairway. You must keep the centre of those Java currents, for currents at the side is different, and in narrow water, before you can turn a spoke, you get your nose took round and rubbed upon the rocks and the woods. Dowse knew that just as well as any skipper. Likeways he knew that no skipper daren't run through uncharted wrecks in a six-knot current. He told me he used to lie outside the Light watching his buoys ducking and dipping so friendly with the tide; and the motion was comforting to him on account of its being different from the run of the streaks in his head.

'Three weeks after he'd done his business up comes a steamer through Loby Toby Straits, thinking she'd run into Flores Sea before night. He saw her slow down; then she backed. Then one man and another come up on the bridge, and he could see there was a regular pow-wow, and the flood was driving her right on to Dowse's wreck-buoys. After that she spun round and went back south, and Dowse nearly killed himself with laughing. But a few weeks after that a couple of junks came shouldering through from the north, arm in arm, like junks go. It takes a good deal to make a Chinaman understand danger. They junks set well in the current, and went down the fairway, right among the buoys, ten knots an hour, blowing horns and banging tin pots all the time. That made Dowse very angry; he having taken so much trouble to stop the fairway. No boats run Flores Straits by night, but it seemed to Dowse that if junks 'd do that in the day, the Lord knew but what a steamer might trip over his buoys at night; and he sent Challong to run a coir rope between three of the buoys in the middle of the fairway, and he fixed naked lights of coir steeped in oil to that rope. The tides was the only things that moved in those seas, for the airs was dead still till they began to blow, and *then* they would blow your hair off. Challong tended those lights every night after the junks had been so impident – four lights in about a quarter of a mile hung up in iron skillets on the rope; and when they was alight – and coir burns well, very like a lamp wick – the fairway seemed more madder than anything else in the world. First there was the Wurlee Light, then these four queer lights, that couldn't be riding-lights, almost flush with the water, and behind them, twenty mile off, but the biggest light of all, there was the red top of old Loby Toby volcano. Dowse told me that he used to go out in the prow and look at his handiwork, and it made him scared, being like no lights that ever was fixed.

'By and by some more steamers came along, snorting and snifting at the buoys, but never going through, and Dowse says to himself: "Thank goodness I've taught them not to come streaking through my water. Ombay Passage is good enough for them and the like of them." But he didn't remember how quick that sort of news spreads among the shipping. Every steamer that fetched up by those buoys told another steamer and all the port officers concerned in those seas that there was something wrong with Flores Straits that hadn't been charted yet. It was block-buoyed for wrecks in the fairway, they said, and no sort of passage to use. Well, the Dutch, of course they didn't know anything about it. They thought our Admiralty Survey had been there, and they thought it very queer but neighbourly. You understand us English are always looking up marks and lighting seaways all the world over, never asking with your leave or by your leave, seeing that the sea concerns us more than anyone else. So the news went to and back from Flores to Bali, and Bali to Probolingo, where the railway is that runs to Batavia. All through the Java seas everybody got the word to keep clear o' Flores Straits, and Dowse, he was left alone except for such steamers and small craft as didn't know. They'd come up and look at the straits like a bull over a gate, but those nodding wreck-buoys scared them away. By and by the Admiralty Survey ship – the *Britomarte* I think she was – lay in Macassar Roads off Fort Rotterdam, alongside of the *Amboina,* a dirty little Dutch gunboat that used to clean there; and the Dutch captain says to our captain, "What's wrong with Flores Straits?" he says.

' "Blowed if I know," says our captain, who'd just come up from the Angelica Shoal.

' "Then why did you go and buoy it?" says the Dutchman.

' "Blowed if I have," says our captain. "That's your lookout."

' "Buoyed it is," says the Dutch captain, "according to what they tell me; and a whole fleet of wreck-buoys, too."

' "Gummy!" says our captain. "It's a dorg's life at sea, anyway. I must have a look at this. You come along after me as soon as you can," and down he skimmed that very night, round the heel of Celebes, three days' steam to Flores Head, and he met a Two-streak liner, very angry, backing out of the head of the strait; and the merchant captain gave our Survey ship something of his mind for leaving wrecks uncharted in those narrow waters and wasting his company's coal.

' "It's no fault o' mine," says our captain.

' "I don't care whose fault it is," says the merchant captain, who had come aboard to speak to him just at dusk. "The fairway's choked with wreck enough to knock a hole through a dock-gate. I saw their big ugly masts sticking up just under my forefoot Lord ha' mercy on us!" he says, spinning round. "The place is like Regent Street of a hot summer night"

'And so it was. They two looked at Flores Straits, and they saw lights one after the other stringing across the fairway. Dowse, he had seen the steamers hanging there before dark, and he said to Challong: "We'll give 'em something to remember. Get all the skillets and iron pots you can and hang them up alongside o' the regular four lights. We must teach 'em to go round by the Ombay Passage, or they'll be streaking up our water again!" Challong took a header off the lighthouse, got aboard the little leaking prow, with his coir soaked in oil and all the skillets he could muster, and he began to show his lights, four regulation ones and half a dozen new lights hung on that rope which was a little above the water. Then he went to all the spare buoys with all his spare coir, and hung a skillet-flare on every pole that he could get at – about seven poles. So you see, taking one with another, there was the Wurlee Light, four lights on the rope between the three centre fairway wreck-buoys that was hung out as a usual custom, six or eight extry ones that Challong had hung up on the same rope, and seven dancing flares that belonged to seven wreck-buoys – eighteen or twenty lights in all crowded into a mile of seventeen-fathom water, where no tide 'd ever let a wreck rest for three weeks, let alone ten or twelve wrecks, as the flares showed.

'The Admiralty captain, he saw the lights come out one after another, same as the merchant-skipper did who was standing at his side, and he said –

' "There's been an international catastrophe here or elseways," and then he whistled. "I'm going to stand on and off all night till the Dutchman comes," he says.

' "I'm off," says the merchant skipper. "My owners don't wish for me to watch illuminations. That strait's choked with wreck, and I shouldn't wonder if a typhoon hadn't driven half the junks o' China there." With that he went away; but the Survey ship, she stayed all night at the head o' Flores Strait, and the men admired of the lights till the lights was burning out, and then they admired more than ever.

'A little bit before morning the Dutch gunboat come flustering up, and the two ships stood together watching the lights burn out and out, till there was nothing left 'cept Flores Straits, all green and wet, and a dozen wreck-buoys, and Wurlee Light.

'Dowse had slept very quiet that night, and got rid of his streaks by means of thinking of the angry steamers outside. Challong was busy, and didn't come back to his bunk till late. In the grey early morning Dowse looked out to sea, being, as he said, in torment, and saw all the navies of the world riding outside Flores Strait fairway in a half-moon, seven miles from wing to wing, most wonderful to behold. Those were the words he used to me time and again in telling the tale.

'Then, he says, he heard a gun fired with a most tremenjus explosion, and all them great navies crumbled to little pieces of clouds, and there was only two ships remaining, and a man-o'-war's boat rowing to the Light, with the oars going sideways instead o' longways as the morning tides, ebb or flow, would continually run.

' "What the devil's wrong with this strait?" says a man in the boat as soon as they was in hailing distance. "Has the whole English Navy sunk here, or what?"

' "There's nothing wrong," says Dowse, sitting on the platform outside the Light, and keeping one eye very watchful on the streakiness of the tide, which he always hated, 'specially in the mornings. "You leave me alone and I'll leave you alone. Go round by the Ombay Passage, and don't cut up my water. You're making it streaky." All the time he was saying that he kept on thinking to himself, "Now that's foolishness – now that's nothing but foolishness", and all the time he was holding tight to the edge of the platform in case the streakiness of the tide should carry him away.

'Somebody answers from the boat, very soft and quiet, "We're going round by Ombay in a minute, if you'll just come and speak to our captain and give him his bearings."

'Dowse, he felt very highly flattered, and he slipped into the boat, not paying any attention to Challong. But Challong swum along to the ship after the boat. When Dowse was in the boat, he found, so he says, he couldn't speak to the sailors 'cept to call them "white mice with chains about their neck", and Lord knows he hadn't seen or thought o' white mice since he was a little bit of a boy with them in his hankerchief. So he kept himself quiet, and so they come to the Survey ship; and the man in the boat hails the quarterdeck with something that Dowse could not rightly understand, but there was one word he spelt out again and again – m-a-d, mad – and he heard someone behind him saying of it backwards. So he had two words – m-a-d, mad, d-a-m, damn; and he put they two words together as he come on the quarterdeck, and he says to the captain very slowly, "I be damned if I am mad," but all the time his eye was held like by the coils of rope on the belaying pins, and he followed those ropes up and up with his eye till he was quite lost and comfortable among the rigging, which ran criss-cross, and slopeways, and up and down, and any way but straight along under his feet north and south. The deck-seams, they ran *that* way, and Dowse daresn't look at them. They was the same as the streaks of the water under the planking of the lighthouse.

'Then he heard the captain talking to him very kind, and for the life of him he couldn't tell why; and what he wanted to tell the captain was that Flores Strait was too streaky, like bacon, and the steamers only made it worse; but all he could do was to keep his eye very careful on the rigging and sing –

I saw a ship a-sailing,
A-sailing on the sea;
And oh, it was all lading
With pretty things for me!

Then he remembered that was foolishness, and he started off to say about the Ombay Passage, but all he said was: "The captain was a duck – meaning no offence to you, sir – but there was something on his back that I've forgotten.

And when the ship began to move
The captain says, 'Quack-quack!' "

'He notices the captain turns very red and angry, and he says to himself, "My foolish tongue's run away with me again. I'll go forward," and he went forward, and catched the reflection of himself in the binnacle brasses; and he saw that he was standing there and talking mother-naked in front of all them sailors, and he ran into the fo'c's'le howling most grievous. He must ha' gone naked for weeks on the Light, and Challong o' course never noticed it. Challong was swimmin' round and round the ship, sayin' "damn" for to please the men and to be took aboard, because he didn't know any better.

'Dowse didn't tell what happened after this, but seemingly our Survey ship lowered two boats and went over to Dowse's buoys. They took one sounding, and then finding it was all correct they cut the buoys that Dowse and Challong had made, and let the tide carry 'em out through the Loby Toby end of the strait; and the Dutch gunboat, she sent two men ashore to take care o' the Wurlee Light, and the *Britomarte,* she went away with Dowse, leaving Challong to try to follow them, a-calling "damn – damn" all among the wake of the screw, and half heaving himself out of water and joining his webby-foot hands together. He dropped astern in five minutes, and I suppose he went back to the Wurlee Light. You can't drown an Orange-Lord, not even in Flores Strait on flood-tide.

'Dowse come across me when he came to England with the Survey ship, after being more than six months in her, and cured of his streaks by working hard and not looking over the side nore than he could help. He told me what I've told you, sir, and he was very much ashamed of himself; but the trouble on his mind was to know whether he hadn't sent something or other to the bottom with his buoyings and his lightings and such like. He put it to me many times, and each time more and more sure he was that something had happened in the straits because of him. I think that distracted him, because I found him up at Fratton one day, in a red jersey, a-praying before the Salvation Army, which had produced him in their papers as a Reformed Pirate. They knew from his mouth that he had committed evil on the deep waters – that was what he told them – and piracy, which no one does now except Chineses, was all they knew of. I says to him: "Dowse, don't be a fool. Take off that jersey and come along with me." He says:

"Fenwick, I'm a-saving of my soul; for I do believe that I have killed more men in Flores Strait than Trafalgar." I says: "A man that thought he'd seen all the navies of the earth standing round in a ring to watch his foolish false wreck-buoys" (those was my very words I used) "ain't fit to have a soul, and if he did he couldn't kill a louse with it. John Dowse, you was mad then, but you are a damn sight madder now. Take off that there jersey!"

'He took it off and come along with me, but he never got rid o' that suspicion that he'd sunk some ships a-cause of his foolishnesses at Flores Straits; and now he's a wherryman from Portsmouth to Gosport, where the tides run crossways and you can't row straight for ten strokes together. . . So late as all this! Look!'

Fenwick left his chair, passed to the Light, touched something that clicked, and the glare ceased with a suddenness that was pain. Day had come, and the Channel needed St Cecilia no longer. The sea-fog rolled back from the cliffs in trailed wreaths and dragged patches, as the sun rose and made the dead sea alive and splendid. The stillness of the morning held us both silent as we stepped on the balcony. A lark went up from the cliffs behind St Cecilia, and we smelt a smell of cows in the lighthouse pastures below.

Then we were both at liberty to thank the Lord for another day of clean and wholesome life.

# 6

# *'The Finest Story in the World'*

Or ever the knightly years were gone
  With the old world to the grave,
I was a king in Babylon
  And you were a Christian slave.

*W. E. Henley*

HIS NAME was Charlie Mears; he was the only son of his mother who was a widow, and he lived in the north of London, coming into the City every day to work in a bank. He was twenty years old and was full of aspirations. I met him in a public billiard-saloon where the marker called him by his first name, and he called the marker 'Bullseye'. Charlie explained, a little nervously, that he had only come to the place to look on, and since looking on at games of skill is not a cheap amusement for the young, I suggested that Charlie should go back to his mother.

That was our first step towards better acquaintance. He would call on me sometimes in the evenings instead of running about London with his fellow-clerks; and before long, speaking of himself as a young man must, he told me of his aspirations, which were all literary. He desired to make himself an undying name chiefly through verse, though he was not above sending stories of love and death to the penny-in-the-slot journals. It was my fate to sit still while Charlie read me poems of many hundred lines, and bulky fragments of plays that would surely shake the world. My reward was his unreserved confidence, and the self-revelations and troubles of a young man are almost as holy as those of a maiden. Charlie had never fallen in love, but was anxious to do so on the first opportunity; he believed in all things good and all things honourable, but at the same time, was curiously careful to let me see that he knew his way about the world as befitted a bank-clerk on twenty-five shillings a week. He rhymed 'dove' with 'love' and 'moon' with 'June', and devoutly believed that they had never so been rhymed before. The long lame gaps in his plays he filled up with hasty words of apology and description, and swept on, seeing all that he intended to do so clearly that he esteemed it already done, and turned to me for applause.

I fancy that his mother did not encourage his aspirations; and I know that his writing-table at home was the edge of his washstand. This he told me almost at the outset of our acquaintance – when he was ravaging my bookshelves, and a little before I was implored to speak the truth as to his chances of 'writing something really great, you know'. Maybe I encouraged him too much for, one night, he called on me, his eyes flaming with excitement, and said breathlessly:

'Do you mind – can you let me stay here and write all this evening? I won't interrupt you, I won't really. There's no place for me to write in at my mother's.'

'What's the trouble?' I said, knowing well what that trouble was.

'I've a notion in my head that would make the most splendid story that was ever written. Do let me write it out here. It's *such* a notion!'

There was no resisting the appeal. I set him a table; he hardly thanked me, but plunged into his work at once. For half an hour the pen scratched without stopping. Then Charlie sighed and tugged his hair. The scratching grew slower, there were more erasures, and at last ceased. The finest story in the world would not come forth.

'It looks such awful rot now,' he said mournfully. 'And yet it seemed so good when I was thinking about it. What's wrong?'

I could not dishearten him by saying the truth. So I answered: 'Perhaps you don't feel in the mood for writing.'

'Yes I do – except when I look at this stuff. Ugh!'

'Read me what you've done,' I said.

He read, and it was wondrous bad, and he paused at all the specially turgid sentences, expecting a little approval; for he was proud of those sentences, as I knew he would be.

'It needs compression,' I suggested cautiously.

'I hate cutting my things down. I don't think you could alter a word here without spoiling the sense. It reads better aloud than when I was writing it.'

'Charlie, you're suffering from an alarming disease afflicting a numerous class. Put the thing by, and tackle it again in a week.'

'I want to do it at once. What do you think of it?'

'How can I judge from a half-written tale? Tell me the story as it lies in your head.'

Charlie told, and in the telling there was everything that his ignorance had so carefully prevented from escaping into the written word. I looked at him, wondering whether it were possible that he did not know the originality, the power of the notion that had come in his way? It was distinctly a Notion among notions. Men had been puffed up with pride by ideas not a tithe as excellent and practicable. But Charlie babbled on serenely, interrupting the current of pure fancy with samples of horrible sentences that he purposed to use. I heard him out to the end. It would be folly to allow his thought to remain in his own inept hands, when I could do so much with it. Not all that could be done indeed; but, oh so much!

'What do you think?' he said at last. 'I fancy I shall call it "The Story of a Ship".'

'I think the idea's pretty good; but you won't be able to handle it for ever so long. Now I – '

'Would it be of any use to you? Would you care to take it? I should be proud,' said Charlie promptly.

There are few things sweeter in this world than the guileless, hotheaded, intemperate, open admiration of a junior. Even a woman in her blindest devotion does not fall into the gait of the man she adores, tilt her bonnet to the angle at which he wears his hat, or interlard her speech with his pet oaths. And Charlie did all these things. Still it was necessary to salve my conscience before I possessed myself of Charlie's thoughts.

'Let's make a bargain. I'll give you a fiver for the notion,' I said.

Charlie became a bank-clerk at once.

'Oh, that's impossible. Between two pals, you know, if I may call you so, and speaking as a man of the world,

I couldn't. Take the notion if it's any use to you. I've heaps more.'

He had – none knew this better than I – but they were the notions of other men.

'Look at it as a matter of business – between men of the world,' I returned. 'Five pounds will buy you any number of poetry books. Business is business, and you may be sure I shouldn't give that price unless – '

'Oh, if you put it *that* way,' said Charlie, visibly moved by the thought of the books. The bargain was clinched with an agreement that he should at unstated intervals come to me with all the notions that he possessed, should have a table of his own to write at, and unquestioned right to inflict upon me all his poems and fragments of poems. Then I said, 'Now tell me how you came by this idea.'

'It came by itself.' Charlie's eyes opened a little.

'Yes, but you told me a great deal about the hero that you must have read before somewhere.'

'I haven't any time for reading, except when you let me sit here, and on Sundays I'm on my bicycle or down the river all day. There's nothing wrong about the hero, is there?'

'Tell me again and I shall understand clearly. You say that your hero went pirating. How did he live?'

'He was on the lower deck of this ship-thing that I was telling you about.'

'What sort of ship?'

'It was the kind rowed with oars, and the sea spurts through the oar-holes, and the men row sitting up to their knees in water. Then there's a bench running down between the two lines of oars, and an overseer with a whip walks up and down the bench to make the men work.'

'How do you know that?'

'It's in the tale. There's a rope running overhead, looped to the upper-deck, for the overseer to catch hold of when the ship rolls. When the overseer misses the rope once and falls among the rowers, remember the hero laughs at him and gets licked for it. He's chained to his oar of course – the hero.'

'How is he chained?'

'With an iron band round his waist fixed to the bench he sits on, and a sort of handcuff on his left wrist chaining him to the oar. He's on the lower deck where the worst men are sent, and the only light comes from the hatchways and through the oar-holes. Can't you imagine the sunlight just squeezing through between the handle and the hole and wobbling about as the ship moves?'

'I can, but I can't imagine your imagining it.'

'How could it be any other way? Now you listen to me. The long oars on the upper deck are managed by four men to each bench, the lower ones by three, and the lowest of all by two. Remember it's quite dark on the lowest deck and all the men there go mad. When a man dies at his oar on that deck he isn't thrown overboard, but cut up in his chains and stuffed through the oar-hole in little pieces.'

'Why?' I demanded amazed, not so much at the information as the tone of command in which it was flung out.

'To save trouble and to frighten the others. It needs two overseers to drag a man's body up to the top deck; and if the men at the lower deck oars were left alone, of course they'd stop rowing and try to pull up the benches by all standing up together in their chains.'

'You've a most provident imagination. Where have you been reading about galleys and galley-slaves?'

'Nowhere that I remember. I row a little when I get the chance. But, perhaps, if you say so, I may have read something.'

He went away shortly afterwards to deal with booksellers, and I wondered how a bank-clerk aged twenty could put into my hands with a profligate abundance of detail, all given with absolute assurance, the story of extravagant and bloodthirsty adventure, riot, piracy, and death in unnamed seas. He had led his hero a desperate dance through revolt against the overseers, to command of a ship of his own, and at last to the establishment of a kingdom on an island 'somewhere in the sea, you know'; and, delighted with my paltry five pounds, had gone out to buy the notions of other men, that these might teach him how to write. I had the consolation of knowing that this notion was mine by right of purchase, and I thought that I could make something of it.

When next he came to me he was drunk – royally drunk on many poets for the first time revealed to him. His pupils were dilated, his words tumbled over each other, and he wrapped himself in quotations – as a beggar would enfold himself in the purple of emperors. Most of all was he drunk with Longfellow.

'Isn't it splendid? Isn't it superb?' he cried, after hasty greetings. 'Listen to this –

"Wouldst thou" – so the helmsman answered,
"Know the secret of the sea?
Only those who brave its dangers
Comprehend its mystery."

By gum!

"Only those who brave its dangers
Comprehend its mystery,"'

he repeated twenty times, walking up and down the room and forgetting me. 'But *I* can understand it too,' he said to himself. 'I don't know how to thank you for that fiver. And this; listen –

"I remember the black wharves and the slips
And the sea-tides tossing free;
And the Spanish sailors with bearded lips,
And the beauty and mystery of the ships,
And the magic of the sea."

I haven't braved any dangers, but I feel as if I knew all about it.'

'You certainly seem to have a grip of the sea. Have you ever seen it?'

'When I was a little chap I went to Brighton once; we used to live in Coventry, though, before we came to London. I never saw it,

"When descends on the Atlantic
The gigantic
Storm-wind of the Equinox." '

He shook me by the shoulder to make me understand the passion that was shaking himself.

'When that storm comes,' he continued, 'I think that all the oars in the ship that I was talking about get broken, and the rowers have their chests smashed in by the oar-heads bucking. By the way, have you done anything with that notion of mine yet?'

'No. I was waiting to hear more of it from you. Tell me how in the world you're so certain about the fittings of the ship. You know nothing of ships.'

'I don't know. It's as real as anything to me until I try to write it down. I was thinking about it only last night in bed, after you had lent me *Treasure Island*; and I made up a whole lot of new things to go into the story.'

'What sort of things?'

'About the food the men ate; rotten figs and black beans and wine in a skin bag, passed from bench to bench.'

'Was the ship built so long ago as *that*?'

'As what? I don't know whether it was long ago or not. It's only a notion, but sometimes it seems just as real as if it was true. Do I bother you with talking about it?'

'Not in the least. Did you make up anything else?'

'Yes, but it's nonsense.' Charlie flushed a little.

'Never mind; let's hear about it.'

'Well, I was thinking over the story, and after a while I got out of bed and wrote down on a piece of paper the sort of stuff the men might be supposed to scratch on their oars with the edges of their handcuffs. It seemed to make the thing more life-like. It *is* so real to me, y'know.'

'Have you the paper on you?'

'Ye–es, but what's the use of showing it? It's only a lot of scratches. All the same, we might have 'em reproduced in the book on the front page.'

'I'll attend to those details. Show me what your men wrote.'

He pulled out of his pocket a sheet of notepaper, with a single line of scratches upon it, and I put this carefully away.

'What is it supposed to mean in English?' I said.

'Oh, I don't know. I mean it to mean, "I'm beastly tired." It's great nonsense,' he repeated, 'but all those men in the ship seem as real as real people to me. Do do something to the notion soon; I should like to see it written and printed.'

'But all you've told me would make a long book.'

'Make it then. You've only to sit down and write it out'

'Give me a little time. Have you any more notions?'

'Not just now. I'm reading all the books I've bought. They're splendid.'

When he had left I looked at the sheet of notepaper with the inscription upon it. Then I took my head tenderly between both hands, to make certain that it was not coming off or turning round. Then . . . but there seemed to be no interval between quitting my rooms and finding myself arguing with a policeman outside a door marked *Private* in a corridor of the British Museum. All I demanded, as politely as possible, was 'the Greek antiquity man'. The policeman knew nothing except the rules of the Museum, and it became necessary to forage through all the houses and offices inside the gates. An elderly gentleman called away from his lunch put an end to my search by holding the notepaper between finger and thumb and sniffing at it scornfully.

'What does this mean? H'mm,' said he. 'So far as I can ascertain it is an attempt to write extremely corrupt Greek on the part' – here he glared at me with intention – 'of an extremely illiterate – ah – person.' He read slowly from the paper, '*Pollock, Erckmann, Tauchnitz, Henniker*' – four names familiar to me.

'Can you tell me what the corruption is supposed to mean – the gist of the thing?' I asked.

'I have been – many times – overcome with weariness in this particular employment. That is the meaning.' He returned me the paper, and I fled without a word of thanks, explanation, or apology.

I might have been excused for forgetting much. To me of all men had been given the chance to write the most marvellous tale in the world, nothing less than the story of a Greek galley-slave, as told by himself. Small wonder that his dreaming had seemed real to Charlie. The Fates that are so careful to shut the doors of each successive life behind us had, in this case, been neglectful, and Charlie was looking, though that he did not know, where never man had been permitted to look with full knowledge since Time began. Above all, he was absolutely ignorant of the knowledge sold to me for five pounds; and he would retain that ignorance, for bank-clerks do not understand metempsychosis, and a sound commercial education does not include Greek. He would supply me – here I capered among the dumb gods of Egypt and laughed in their battered faces – with material to make my tale sure – so sure that the world would hail it as an impudent and vamped fiction. And I – I alone would know that it was absolutely and literally true. I –I alone held this jewel to my hand for the cutting and polishing! Therefore I danced again among the gods of the Egyptian court till a policeman saw me and took steps in my direction.

It remained now only to encourage Charlie to talk, and here there was no difficulty. But I had forgotten those accursed books of poetry. He came to me time after time, as useless as a surcharged phonograph – drunk on Byron, Shelley, or Keats. Knowing now what the boy had been in his past lives, and desperately anxious not to lose one word of his babble, I could not hide from him my respect and interest. He misconstrued both into respect for the present soul of Charlie Mears, to whom life was as new as it was to Adam, and interest in his readings; and stretched my patience to breaking point by reciting poetry – not his own now, but that of others. I wished every English poet blotted out of the memory of mankind. I blasphemed the mightiest names of song because they had drawn Charlie from the path of direct narrative, and would, later, spur him to imitate them; but I choked down my impatience until the first flood of enthusiasm should have spent itself and the boy returned to his dreams.

'What's the use of my telling you what *I* think, when these chaps wrote things for the angels to read?' he growled, one evening. 'Why don't you write something like theirs?'

'I don't think you're treating me quite fairly,' I said, speaking under strong restraint.

'I've given you the story,' he said shortly, re-plunging into 'Lara'.

'But I want the details.'

'The things I make up about that damned ship that you call a galley? They're quite easy. You can just make 'em up for yourself. Turn up the gas a little, I want to go on reading.'

I could have broken the gas globe over his head for his amazing stupidity. I could indeed make up things for myself did I only know what Charlie did not know that he knew. But since the doors were shut behind me I could only wait his youthful pleasure and strive to keep him in good temper. One minute's want of guard might spoil a priceless revelation: now and again he would toss his books aside – he kept them in my rooms, for his mother would have been shocked at the waste of good money had she seen them – and launched into his sea-dreams. Again I cursed all the poets of England. The plastic mind of the bank-clerk had been overlaid, coloured, and distorted by that which he had read, and the result as delivered was a confused tangle of other voices most like the mutter and hum through a City telephone in the busiest part of the day.

He talked of the galley – his own galley had he but known it – with illustrations borrowed from the 'Bride of Abydos'. He pointed the experiences of his hero with quotations from 'The Corsair', and threw in deep and desperate moral reflections from 'Cain' and 'Manfred', expecting me to use them all. Only when the talk turned on Longfellow were the jarring cross-currents dumb, and I knew that Charlie was speaking the truth as he remembered it.

'What do you think of this?' I said one evening, as soon as I understood the medium in which his memory worked best, and, before he could expostulate, read him nearly the whole of 'The Saga of King Olaf.

He listened open-mouthed, flushed, his hands drumming on the back of the sofa where he lay, till I came to the Song of Einar Tamberskelver and the verse –

'Einar then, the arrow taking
    From the loosened string,
Answered, "That was Norway breaking
    'Neath thy hand, O King."'

He gasped with pure delight of sound.

'That's better than Byron, a little?' I ventured.

'Better! Why it's *true*! How could he have known?'

I went back and repeated –

' "What was that?" said Olaf, standing
    On the quarter-deck,
"Something heard I like the stranding
    Of a shattered wreck." '

'How could he have known how the ships crash and the oars rip out and go *z-zzp* all along the line? Why only the other night. . . But go back, please, and read "The Skerry of Shrieks" again.'

'No, I'm tired. Let's talk. What happened the other night?'

'I had an awful dream about that galley of ours. I dreamed I was drowned in a fight. You see we ran alongside another ship in harbour. The water was dead still except where our oars whipped it up. You know where I always sit in the galley?' He spoke haltingly at first, under a fine English fear of being laughed at.

'No. That's news to me,' I answered meekly, my heart beginning to beat.

'On the fourth oar from the bow on the right side on the upper deck There were four of us at that oar, all chained. I remember watching the water and trying to get my handcuffs off before the row began. Then we closed up on the other ship, and all their fighting men jumped over our bulwarks, and my bench broke and I was pinned down with the three other fellows on top of me, and the big oar jammed across our backs.'

'Well?' Charlie's eyes were alive and alight. He was looking at the wall behind my chair.

'I don't know how we fought. The men were trampling all over my back, and I lay low. Then our rowers on the left side – tied to their oars, you know – began to yell and back water. I could hear the water sizzle, and we spun round like a cockchafer, and I knew, lying where I was, that there was a galley coming up bow-on to ram us on the left side. I could just lift up my head and see her sail over the bulwarks. We wanted to meet her bow to bow, but it was too late. We could only turn a little bit because the galley on our right had hooked herself on to us and stopped our moving. Then, by gum! there was a crash! Our left oars began to break as the other galley, the moving one y'know, stuck her nose into them. Then the lower-deck oars shot up through the deck planking, butt first, and one of them jumped clear up into the air and came down again close at my head.'

'How was that managed?'

'The moving galley's bow was plunking them back through their own oar-holes, and I could hear no end of a shindy in the decks below. Then her nose caught us nearly in the middle, and we tilted sideways, and the fellows in the right-hand galley unhitched their hooks and ropes, and threw things on to our upper deck – arrows, and hot pitch or something that stung – and we went up and up and up on the left side, and the right side dipped, and I twisted my head round and saw the water stand still as it topped the right bulwarks, and men it curled over and crashed down on the whole lot of us on the right side, and I felt it hit my back, and I woke.'

'One minute, Charlie. When the sea topped the bulwarks, what did it look like?' I had my reasons for asking. A man of my acquaintance had once gone down with a leaking ship in a still sea, and had seen the water-level pause for an instant ere it fell on the deck.

'It looked just like a banjo-string drawn tight, and it seemed to stay there for years,' said Charlie.

Exactly! The other man had said: 'It looked like a silver wire laid down along the bulwarks, and I thought it was never going to break.' He had paid everything except the bare life for this little valueless piece of knowledge, and I had travelled ten thousand weary miles to meet him and take his knowledge at second hand. But Charlie, the bank-clerk on twenty-five shillings a week, who had never been out of sight of a made road, knew it all. It was no consolation to me that once in his lives he had been forced to die for his gains. I also must have died scores of times, but behind me, because I could have used my knowledge, the doors were shut.

'And then?' I said, trying to put away the devil of envy.

'The funny thing was, though, in all the row I didn't feel a bit astonished or frightened. It seemed as if I'd been in a good many fights, because I told my next man so when the row began. But that cad of an overseer on my deck wouldn't unloose our chains and give us a chance. He always said that we'd all be set free after a battle, but we never were; we never were.' Charlie shook his head mournfully.

'What a scoundrel!'

'I should say he was. He never gave us enough to eat, and sometimes we were so thirsty that we used to drink salt-water. I can taste that saltwater still.'

'Now tell me something about the harbour where the fight was fought.'

'I didn't dream about that. I know it was a harbour, though, because we were tied up to a ring on a white wall and all the face of the stone under water was covered with wood to prevent our ram getting chipped when the tide made us rock.'

'That's curious. Our hero commanded the galley, didn't he?'

'Didn't he just! He stood by the bows and shouted like a good 'un. He was the man who killed the overseer.'

'But you were all drowned together, Charlie, weren't you?'

'I can't make that fit quite,' he said, with a puzzled look. 'The galley must have gone down with all hands, and yet I fancy that the hero went on living afterwards. Perhaps he climbed into the attacking ship. I wouldn't see that, of course. I was dead, you know.'

He shivered slightly and protested that he could remember no more.

I did not press him further, but to satisfy myself that he lay in ignorance of the workings of his own mind, deliberately introduced him to Mortimer Collins's *Transmigration,* and gave him a sketch of the plot before he opened the pages.

'What rot it all is!' he said frankly, at the end of an hour. 'I don't understand his nonsense about the Red Planet Mars and the King, and the rest of it. Chuck me the Longfellow again.'

I handed him the book and wrote out as much as I could remember of his description of the sea-fight, appealing to him from time to time for confirmation of fact or detail. He would answer without raising his eyes from the book, as assuredly as though all his knowledge lay before him on the printed page. I spoke under the normal key of my voice that the current might not be broken, and I knew that he was not aware of what he was saying, for his thoughts were out on the sea with Longfellow.

'Charlie,' I asked, 'when the rowers on the galleys mutinied how did they kill their overseers?'

'Tore up the benches and brained 'em. That happened when a heavy sea was running. An overseer on the lower deck slipped from the centre plank and fell among the rowers. They choked him to death against the side of the ship with their chained hands quite quietly, and it was too dark for the other overseer to see what had happened. When he asked, he was pulled down too and choked, and the lower deck fought their way up deck by deck, with the pieces of the broken benches banging behind 'em. How they howled!'

'And what happened after that?'

'I don't know. The hero went away – red hair and red beard and all. That was after he had captured our galley, I think.'

The sound of my voice irritated him, and he motioned slightly with his left hand as a man does when interruption jars.

'You never told me he was red-headed before, or that he captured your galley,' I said, after a discreet interval.

Charlie did not raise his eyes.

'He was as red as a red bear,' said he abstractedly. 'He came from the north; they said so in the galley when he looked for rowers – not slaves, but free men. Afterwards – years and years afterwards – news came from another ship, or else he came back – '

His lips moved in silence. He was rapturously retasting some poem before him.

'Where had he been, then?' I was almost whispering that the sentence might come gently to whichever section of Charlie's brain was working on my behalf.

'To the Beaches – the Long and Wonderful Beaches!' was the reply after a minute of silence.

'To Furdurstrandi?' I asked, tingling from head to foot.

'Yes, to Furdurstrandi,' he pronounced the word in a new fashion. 'And I too saw – ' The voice failed.

'Do you know what you have said?' I shouted incautiously.

He lifted his eyes, fully roused now. 'No!' he snapped. 'I wish you'd let a chap go on reading. Hark to this –

But Othere, the old sea captain,
He neither paused nor stirred
    Till the king listened, and then
    Once more took up his pen
And wrote down every word.

And to the King of the Saxons
In witness of the truth
    Raising his noble head,
    He stretched his brown hand and said,
"Behold this walrus tooth."

By Jove, what chaps those must have been, to go sailing all over the shop never knowing where they'd fetch the land! Hah!'

'Charlie,' I pleaded, 'if you'll only be sensible for a minute or two I'll make our hero in our tale every inch as good as Othere.'

'Umph! Longfellow wrote that poem. I don't care about writing things any more. I want to read.' He was thoroughly out of tune now, and raging over my own ill-luck, I left him.

Conceive yourself at the door of the world's treasure-house guarded by a child – an idle, irresponsible child playing knuckle-bones – on whose favour depends the gift of the key, and you will imagine one-half my torment. Till that evening Charlie had spoken nothing that might not lie within the experiences of a Greek galley-slave. But now, or there was no virtue in books, he had talked of some desperate adventure of the Vikings, of Thorfin Karlsefne's sailing to Wineland, which is America, in the ninth or tenth century. The battle in the harbour he had seen; and his own death he had described. But this was a much more startling plunge into the past. Was it possible that he had skipped half a dozen lives, and was then dimly remembering some episode of a thousand years later? It was a maddening jumble, and the worst of it was that Charlie Mears in his normal condition was the last person in the world to clear it up. I could only wait and watch, but I went to bed that night full of the wildest imaginings. There was nothing that was not possible if Charlie's detestable memory only held good.

I might rewrite the Saga of Thorfin Karlsefne as it had never been written before, might tell the story of the first discovery of America, myself the discoverer. But I was entirely at Charlie's mercy, and so long as there was a three-and-sixpenny Bohn volume within his reach Charlie would not tell. I dared not curse him openly; I hardly dared jog his memory, for I was dealing with the experiences of a thousand years ago, told through the mouth of a boy of today; and a boy of today is affected by every change of tone and gust of opinion, so that he must lie even when he most desires to speak the truth.

I saw no more of Charlie for nearly a week. When next I met him it was in Gracechurch Street with a bill-book chained to his waist. Business took him over London Bridge, and I accompanied him. He was very full of the importance of that book and magnified it. As we passed over the Thames we paused to look at a steamer unloading great slabs of white and brown marble. A barge drifted under the steamer's stern and a lonely ship's cow in that barge bellowed. Charlie's face changed from the face of the bank-clerk to that of an unknown and – though he would not have believed this – a much shrewder man. He flung out his arm across the parapet of the bridge and laughing very loudly, said –

'When they heard *our* bulls bellow the Skroelings ran away!'

I waited only for an instant, but the barge and the cow had disappeared under the bows of the steamer before I answered.

'Charlie, what do you suppose are Skroelings?'

'Never heard of 'em before. They sound like a new kind of seagull. What a chap you are for asking questions!' he replied. 'I have to go to the cashier of the Omnibus Company yonder. Will you wait for me and we can lunch somewhere together? I've a notion for a poem.'

'No, thanks. I'm off. You're sure you know nothing about Skroelings?'

'Not unless he's been entered for the Liverpool Handicap.' He nodded and disappeared in the crowd.

Now it is written in the Saga of Eric the Red or that of Thorfin Karlsefne, that nine hundred years ago when Karlsefne's galleys came to Leif's booths, which Leif had erected in the unknown land called Markland, which may or may not have been Rhode Island, the Skroelings – and the Lord He knows who these may or may not have been – came to trade with the Vikings, and ran away because they were frightened at the bellowing of the cattle which Thorfin had brought with him in the ships. But what in the world could a Greek slave know of that affair? I wandered up and down among the streets trying to unravel the mystery and the more I considered it the more baffling it grew. One thing only seemed certain, and that certainty took away my breath for the moment. If I came to full knowledge of anything at all, it would not be one life of the soul in Charlie Mears's body, but half a dozen – half a dozen several and separate existences spent on blue water in the morning of the world!

Then I reviewed the situation.

Obviously if I used my knowledge I should stand alone and unapproachable until all men were as wise as myself. That would be something, but, manlike, I was ungrateful. It seemed bitterly unfair that Charlie's memory should fail me when I needed it most. Great Powers Above – I looked up at them through the fog-smoke – did the Lords of Life and Death know what this meant to me? Nothing less than eternal fame of the best kind, that comes from One, and is shared by one alone. I would be content – remembering Clive, I stood astounded at my own moderation – with the mere right to tell one story, to work out one little contribution to the light literature of the day. If Charlie were permitted full recollection for one hour – for sixty short minutes – of existences that had extended over a thousand years, I would forgo all profit and honour from all that I should make of his speech. I would take no share in the commotion that would follow throughout the particular corner of the earth that calls itself 'the world'. The thing should be put forth anonymously. Nay, I would make other men believe that they had written it. They would hire bull-hided self-advertising Englishmen to bellow it abroad. Preachers would found a fresh conduct of life upon it, swearing that it was new and that they had lifted the fear of death from all mankind. Every Orientalist in Europe would patronise it discursively with Sanskrit and Pali texts. Terrible women would invent unclean variants of the men's belief for the elevation of their sisters. Churches and religions would war over it. Between the hailing and restarting of an omnibus I foresaw the scuffles that would arise among half a dozen denominations all professing 'the doctrine of the True Metempsychosis as applied to the world and the New Era'; and saw, too, the respectable English newspapers shying, like frightened kine, over the beautiful simplicity of the tale. The mind leaped forward a hundred – two hundred – a thousand years. I saw with sorrow that men would mutilate and garble the story; that rival creeds would turn it upside down till, at last, the western world which clings to the dread of death more closely than the hope of life, would set it aside as an interesting superstition and stampede after some faith so long forgotten that it seemed altogether new. Upon this I changed the terms of the bargain that I would make with the Lords of Life and Death. Only let me know, let me write, the story with sure knowledge that I wrote the truth, and I would burn the manuscript as a solemn sacrifice. Five minutes after the last line was written I would destroy it all. But I must be allowed to write it with absolute certainty.

There was no answer. The flaming colours of an Aquarium poster caught my eye, and I wondered whether it would be wise or prudent to lure Charlie into the hands of the professional mesmerist then, and whether, if he were under his power, he would speak of his past lives. If he did, and if people believed him . . . but Charlie would be frightened and flustered, or made conceited by the interviews. In either case he would begin to lie through fear or vanity. He was safest in my own hands.

'They are very funny fools, your English,' said a voice at my elbow, and turning round I recognised a casual acquaintance, a young Bengali law student, called Grish Chunder, whose father had sent him to England to become civilised. The old man was a retired native official, and on an income of five pounds a month contrived to allow his son two hundred pounds a year, and the run of his teeth in a city where he could pretend to be the cadet of a royal house, and tell stories of the brutal Indian bureaucrats who ground the faces of the poor.

Grish Chunder was a young, fat, full-bodied Bengali, dressed with scrupulous care in frock coat, tall hat, light trousers, and tan gloves. But I had known him in the days when the brutal Indian Government paid for his university education, and he contributed cheap sedition to the *Sachi Durpan,* and intrigued with the wives of his fourteen-year-old schoolmates.

'That is very funny and very foolish,' he said, nodding at the poster. 'I am going down to the Northbrook Club. Will you come too?'

I walked with him for some time. 'You are not well,' he said. 'What is there on your mind? You do not talk.'

'Grish Chunder, you've been too well educated to believe in a God, haven't you?'

'Oah, yes, *here*! But when I go home I must conciliate popular superstition, and make ceremonies of purification, and my women will anoint idols.'

'And hang up *tulsi* and feast the *purohit,* and take you back into caste again, and make a good *khuttri* of you again, you advanced Freethinker. And you'll eat *desi* food, and like it all, from the smell in the courtyard to the mustard oil over you.'

'I shall very much like it,' said Grish Chunder unguardedly. 'Once a Hindu – always a Hindu. But I like to know what the English think they know.'

'I'll tell you something that one Englishman knows. It's an old tale to you.'

I began to tell the story of Charlie in English but Grish Chunder put a question in the vernacular, and the history went forward naturally in the tongue best suited for its telling. After all, it could never have been told in English. Grish Chunder heard me, nodding from time to time, and then came up to my rooms, where I finished the tale.

*'Beshak,'* he said philosophically. '*Lekin darwaza band hai.* (Without doubt; but the door is shut.) I have heard of this remembering of previous existences among my people. It is of course an old tale with us, but, to happen to an Englishman – a cow-fed *Mlechh* – an outcast. By Jove, that is *most* peculiar!'

'Outcast yourself, Grish Chunder! You eat cow-beef every day. Let's think the thing over. The boy remembers his incarnations.'

'Does he know that?' said Grish Chunder quietly, swinging his legs as he sat on my table. He was speaking in his English now.

'He does not know anything. Would I speak to you if he did? Go on!'

'There is no going on at all. If you tell that to your friends they will say you are mad and put it in the papers. Suppose, now, you prosecute for libel.'

'Let's leave that out of the question entirely. Is there any chance of his being made to speak?'

'There is a chance. Oah, yess! But *if* he spoke it would mean that all this world would end now – *instanto* – fall down on your head. These things are not allowed, you know. As I said, the door is shut.'

'Not a ghost of a chance?'

'How can there be? You are a Christi-án, and it is forbidden to eat, in your books, of the Tree of Life, or else you would never die. How shall you all fear death if you all know what your friend does not know that he knows? I am afraid to be kicked, but I am not afraid to die, because I know what I know. You are not afraid to be kicked, but you are afraid to die. If you were not, by God! you English would be all over the shop in an hour, upsetting the balances of power, and making commotions. It would not be good. But no fear. He will remember a little and a little less, and he will call it dreams. Then he will forget altogether. When I passed my First Arts Examination in Calcutta that was all in the cram-book on Wordsworth. "Trailing clouds of glory", you know.'

'This seems to be an exception to the rule.'

'There are no exceptions to rules. Some are not so hard-looking as others, but they are all the same when you touch. If this friend of yours said so-and-so and so-and-so, indicating that he remembered all his lost lives, or one piece of a lost life, he would not be in the bank another hour. He would be what you call sacked because he was mad, and they would send him to an asylum for lunatics. You can see that, my friend.'

'Of course I can, but I wasn't thinking of him. His name need never appear in the story.'

'Ah! I see. That story will never be written. You can try.'

'I am going to.'

'For your own credit and for the sake of money, *of* course?'

'No. For the sake of writing the story. On my honour that will be all.'

'Even then there is no chance. You cannot play with the gods. It is a very pretty story now. As they say, Let it go on that – I mean at that. Be quick; he will not last long.'

'How do you mean?'

'What I say. He has never, so far, thought about a woman.'

'Hasn't he, though!' I remembered some of Charlie's confidences.

'I mean no woman has thought about him. When that comes; *bus – hogya* – all up! I know. There are millions of women here. Housemaids, for instance. They kiss you behind doors.'

I winced at the thought of my story being ruined by a housemaid. And yet nothing was more probable.

Grish Chunder grinned.

'Yes – also pretty girls – cousins of his house, and perhaps *not* of his house. One kiss that he gives back again and remembers will cure all this nonsense, or else – '

'Or else what? Remember he does not know that he knows.'

'I know that. Or else, if nothing happens he will become immersed in the trade and the financial speculation like the rest. It must be so. You can see that it must be so. But the woman will come first, *I* think.'

There was a rap at the door, and Charlie charged in impetuously. He had been released from office, and by the look in his eyes I could see that he had come over for a long talk; most probably with poems in his pockets. Charlie's poems were very wearying, but sometimes they led him to speak about the galley.

Grish Chunder looked at him keenly for a minute.

'I beg your pardon,' Charlie said uneasily, 'I didn't know you had anyone with you.'

'I am going,' said Grish Chunder.

He drew me into the lobby as he departed.

'That is your man,' he said quickly. 'I tell you he will never speak all you wish. That is rot – bosh. But he would be most good to make to see things. Suppose now we pretend that it was only play' – I had never seen Grish Chunder so excited – 'and pour the ink-pool into his hand. Eh, what do you think? I tell you that he could see *anything* that a man could see. Let me get the ink and the camphor. He is a seer and he will tell us very many things.'

'He may be all you say, but I'm not going to trust him to your gods and devils.'

'It will not hurt him. He will only feel a little stupid and dull when he wakes up. You have seen boys look into the ink-pool before.'

'That is the reason why I am not going to see it any more. You'd better go, Grish Chunder.'

He went, insisting far down the staircase that it was throwing away my only chance of looking into the future.

This left me unmoved, for I was concerned for the past, and no peering of hypnotised boys into mirrors and ink-pools would help me to that. But I recognised Grish Chunder's point of view and sympathised with it.

'What a big black brute that was!' said Charlie, when I returned to him. 'Well, look here, I've just done a poem; did it instead of playing dominoes after lunch. May I read it?'

'Let me read it to myself.'

'Then you miss the proper expression. Besides, you always make my things sound as if the rhymes were all wrong.'

'Read it aloud, then. You're like the rest of 'em.'

Charlie mouthed me his poem, and it was not much worse than the average of his verses. He had been reading his books faithfully, but he was not pleased when I told him that I preferred my Longfellow undiluted with Charlie.

Then we began to go through the MS line by line, Charlie parrying every objection and correction with:

'Yes, that may be better, but you don't catch what I'm driving at.'

Charlie was, in one way at least, very like one kind of poet.

There was a pencil scrawl at the back of the paper, and 'What's that?' I said.

'Oh, that's not poetry at all. It's some rot I wrote last night before I went to bed, and it was too much bother to hunt for rhymes; so I made it a sort of blank verse instead.'

Here is Charlie's 'blank verse':

We pulled for you when the wind was against us and

the sails were low.

*Will you never let us go?*

We ate bread and onions when you took towns, or ran aboard quickly when you were beaten back by the foe,

The captains walked up and down the deck in fair weather singing songs, but we were below.

We fainted with our chins on the oars and you did not see that we were idle for we still swung to and fro.

*Will you never let us go?*

The salt made the oar-handles like shark-skin; our knees were cut to the bone with salt cracks; our hair was stuck to our foreheads; and our lips were cut to our gums, and you whipped us because we could not row.

*Will you never let us go?*

But in a little time we shall run out of the portholes as the water runs along the oar-blade, and though you tell the others to row after us you will never catch us till you catch the oar-thresh and tie up the winds in the belly of the sail. Aho!

*Will you never let us go?*

'H'm. What's oar-thresh, Charlie?'

'The water washed up by the oars. That's the sort of song they might sing in the galley y' know. Aren't you ever going to finish that story and give me some of the profits?'

'It depends on yourself. If you had only told me more about your hero in the first instance it might have been finished by now. You're so hazy in your notions.'

'I only want to give you the general notion of it – the knocking about from place to place and the fighting and all that. Can't you fill in the rest yourself? Make the hero save a girl on a pirate-galley and marry her or do something.'

'You're a really helpful collaborator. I suppose the hero went through some few adventures before he married.'

'Well then, make him a very artful card – a low sort of man – a sort of political man who went about making treaties and breaking them – a black-haired chap who hid behind the mast when the fighting began.'

'But you said the other day that he was red-haired.'

'I couldn't have. Make him black-haired of course. You've no imagination.'

Seeing that I had just discovered the entire principles upon which the half-memory falsely called imagination is based, I felt entitled to laugh, but forbore for the sake of the tale.

'You're right. *You're* the man with imagination. A black-haired chap in a decked ship,' I said.

'No, an open ship – like a big boat.'

This was maddening.

'Your ship has been built and designed, closed and decked in; you said so yourself,' I protested.

'No, no, not that ship. That was open or half-decked because – By Jove, you're right You made me think of the hero as a red-haired chap. Of course if he were red, the ship would be an open one with painted sails.'

Surely, I thought, he would remember now that he had served in two galleys at least – in a three-decked Greek one under the black-haired 'political man', and again in a Viking's open sea-serpent under the man 'red as a red bear' who went to Markland. The devil prompted me to speak.

'Why, "of course", Charlie?' said I.

'I don't know. Are you making fun of me?'

The current was broken for the time being. I took up a note-book and pretended to make many entries in it.

'It's a pleasure to work with an imaginative chap like yourself,' I said, after a pause. 'The way that you've brought out the character of the hero is simply wonderful.'

'Do you think so?' he answered, with a pleased flush. 'I often tell myself that there's more in me man my mo – than people think.'

'There's an enormous amount in you.'

'Then, won't you let me send an essay on "The Ways of Bank-Clerks" to *Tit-Bits,* and get the guinea prize?'

'That wasn't exactly what I meant, old fellow: perhaps it would be better to wait a little and go ahead with the galley story.'

'Ah, but I sha'n't get the credit of that. *Tit-Bits* would publish my name and address if I win. What are you grinning at? They *would.*'

'I know it. Suppose you go for a walk. I want to look through my notes about our story.'

Now this reprehensible youth who left me, a little hurt and put back, might for aught he or I knew have been one of the crew of the *Argo* – had been certainly slave or comrade to Thorfin Karlsefne. Therefore he was deeply interested in guinea competitions. Remembering what Grish Chunder had said I laughed aloud. The Lords of Life and Death would never allow Charlie Mears to speak with full knowledge of his pasts, and I must even piece out what he had told me with my own poor inventions while Charlie wrote of the ways of bank-clerks.

I got together and placed on one file all my notes; and the net result was not cheering. I read them a second time. There was nothing that might not have been compiled at second-hand from other people's books – except, perhaps, the story of the fight in the harbour. The adventures of a Viking had been written many times before; the history of a Greek galley-slave was no new thing, and though I wrote both, who could challenge or confirm the accuracy of my details? I might as well tell a tale of two thousand years hence. The Lords of Life and Death were as cunning as Grish Chunder had hinted. They would allow nothing to escape that might trouble or make easy the minds of men. Though I was convinced of this, yet I could not leave the tale alone. Exaltation followed reaction, not once, but twenty times in the next few weeks. My moods varied with the March sunlight and flying clouds. By night or in the beauty of a spring morning I perceived that I could write that tale and shift continents thereby. In the wet windy afternoons, I saw that the tale might indeed be written, but would be nothing more than a faked, false-varnished, sham-rusted piece of Wardour Street work in the end. Then I blessed Charlie in many ways – though it was no fault of his. He seemed to be busy with prize competitions, and I saw less and less of him as the weeks went by and the earth cracked and grew ripe to spring, and the buds swelled in their sheaths. He did not care to read or talk of what he had read, and there was a new ring of self-assertion in his voice. I hardly cared to remind him of the galley when we met; but Charlie alluded to it on every occasion, always as a story from which money was to be made.

'I think I deserve twenty-five per cent, don't I, at least?' he said, with beautiful frankness. 'I supplied all the ideas, didn't I?'

This greediness for silver was a new side to his nature. I assumed that it had been developed in the City, where Charlie was picking up the curious nasal drawl of the underbred City man.

'When the thing's done we'll talk about it. I can't make anything of it at present. Red-haired or black-haired heroes are equally difficult.'

He was sitting by the fire staring at the red coals. '*I* can't understand what you find so difficult. It's all as clear as mud to me,' he replied. A jet of gas puffed out between the bars, took light, and whistled softly. 'Suppose we take the red-haired hero's adventures first, from the time that he came south to my galley and captured it and sailed to the Beaches.'

I knew better now than to interrupt Charlie. I was out of reach of pen and paper, and dared not move to get them lest I should break the current. The gas-jet puffed and whinnied, Charlie's voice dropped almost to a whisper, and he told a tale of the sailing of an open galley to Furdurstrandi, of sunsets on the open sea, seen under the curve of the one sail evening after evening when the galley's beak was notched into the centre of the sinking disc, and 'we sailed by that for we had no other guide,' quoth Charlie. He spoke of a landing on an island and explorations in its woods, where the crew killed three men whom they found asleep under the pines. Their ghosts, Charlie said, followed the galley, swimming and choking in the water, and the crew cast lots and threw one of their number overboard as a sacrifice to the strange gods whom they had offended. Then they ate sea-weed when their provisions failed, and their legs swelled, and their leader, the red-haired man, killed two rowers who mutinied, and after a year spent among the woods they set sail for their own country, and a wind that never failed carried them back so safely that they all slept at night. This, and much more, Charlie told. Sometimes the voice fell so low that I could not catch the words, though every nerve was on the strain. He spoke of their leader, the red-haired man, as a pagan speaks of his God; for it was he who cheered them and slew them impartially as he thought best for their needs; and it was he who steered them for three days among floating ice, each floe crowded with strange beasts that 'tried to sail with us,' said Charlie, 'and we beat them back with the handles of the oars.'

The gas-jet went out, a burnt coal gave way, and the fire settled with a tiny crash to the bottom of the grate. Charlie ceased speaking, and I said no word.

'By Jove!' he said at last, shaking his head. 'I've been staring at the fire till I'm dizzy. What was I going to say?'

'Something about the galley book.'

'I remember now. It's twenty-five per cent of the profits, isn't it?'

'It's anything you like when I've done the tale.'

'I wanted to be sure of that. I must go now. I've – I've an appointment.' And he left me.

Had not my eyes been held I might have known that that broken muttering over the fire was the swan-song of Charlie Mears. But I thought it the prelude to fuller revelation. At last and at last I should cheat the Lords of Life and Death!

When next Charlie came to me I received him with rapture. He was nervous and embarrassed, but his eyes were very full of light, and his lips a little parted.

'I've done a poem,' he said; and then, quickly: 'It's the best I've ever done. Read it.' He thrust it into my hand and retreated to the window.

I groaned inwardly. It would be the work of half an hour to criticise – that is to say, praise – the poem sufficiently to please Charlie. Then I had good reason to groan, for Charlie, discarding his favourite centipede metres, had launched into shorter and choppier verse, and verse with a motive at the back of it. This is what I read:

The day is most fair, the cheery wind
    Halloos behind the hill,
Where he bends the wood as seemeth good,
    And the sapling to his will!
Riot, O wind; there is that in my blood
    That would not have thee still!

She gave me herself, O Earth, O Sky;
    Grey sea, she is mine alone!
Let the sullen boulders hear my cry,
    And rejoice tho' they be but stone!

Mine! I have won her, O good brown earth,
    Make merry! 'Tis hard on Spring;
Make merry; my love is doubly worth
    All worship your fields can bring!
Let the hind that tills you feel my mirth
    At the early harrowing!

'Yes, it's the early harrowing, past a doubt,' I said, with a dread at my heart. Charlie smiled, but did not answer.

Red cloud of the sunset, tell it abroad;
    I am victor. Greet me, O Sun,
Dominant master and absolute lord
    Over the soul of one!

'Well?' said Charlie, looking over my shoulder.

I thought it far from well, and very evil indeed, when he silently laid a photograph on the paper – the photograph of a girl with a curly head and a foolish slack mouth.

'Isn't it – isn't it wonderful?' he whispered, pink to the tips of his ears, wrapped in the rosy mystery of first love. 'I didn't know; I didn't think – it came like a thunderclap.'

'Yes. It comes like a thunderclap. Are you very happy, Charlie?'

'My God – she – she loves me!' He sat down repeating the last words to himself. I looked at the hairless face, the narrow shoulders already bowed by desk-work, and wondered when, where, and how he had loved in his past lives.

'What will your mother say?' I asked cheerfully.

'I don't care a damn what she says!'

At twenty the things for which one does not care a damn should, properly, be many, but one must not include mothers in the list. I told him this gently; and he described Her, even as Adam must have described to the newly-named beasts the glory and tenderness and beauty of Eve. Incidentally I learned that She was a tobacconist's assistant with a weakness for pretty dress, and had told him four or five times already that She had never been kissed by a man before.

Charlie spoke on and on, and on; while I, separated from him by thousands of years, was considering the beginnings of things. Now I understood why the Lords of Life and Death shut the doors so carefully behind us. It is that we may not remember our first and most beautiful wooings. Were this not so, our world would be without inhabitants in a hundred years.

'Now, about that galley story,' I said still more cheerfully, in a pause in the rush of the speech.

Charlie looked up as though he had been hit. 'The galley – what galley? Good heavens, don't joke, man! This is serious! You don't know how serious it is!'

Grish Chunder was right. Charlie had tasted the love of woman that kills remembrance, and the finest story in the world would never be written.

# 7

# *The Record of Badalia Herodsfoot*

The year's at the spring
And day's at the dawn;
Morning's at seven;
The hillside's dew-pearled;
The lark's on the wing;
The snail's on the thorn:
God's in His heaven –
All's right with the world!

*Pippa Passes*

THIS IS not that Badalia whose spare names were Joanna, Pugnacious, and M'Canna, as the song says, but another and a much nicer lady.

In the beginning of things she had been unregenerate; had worn the heavy fluffy fringe which is the ornament of the costermonger's girl, and there is a legend in Gunnison Street that on her wedding-day she, a flare-lamp in either hand, danced dances on a discarded lover's winkle-barrow, till a policeman interfered, and then Badalia danced with the Law amid shoutings. Those were her days of fatness, and they did not last long, for her husband after two years took to himself another woman, and passed out of Badalia's life, over Badalia's senseless body; for he stifled protest with blows. While she was enjoying her widow-hood the baby that the husband had not taken away died of croup, and Badalia was altogether alone. With rare fidelity she listened to no proposals for a second marriage according to the customs of Gunnison Street, which do not differ from those of the Barralong. 'My man,' she explained to her suitors,' 'e'll come back one o' these days, an' then, like as not, 'e'll take an' kill me if I was livin' 'long o' you. You don't know Tom; I do. Now you go. I can do for myself – not 'avin' a kid.' She did for herself with a mangle, some tending of babies, and an occasional sale of flowers. This latter trade is one that needs capital, and takes the vendor very far westward, insomuch that the return journey from, let us say, the Burlington Arcade to Gunnison Street, E., is an excuse for drink, and then, as Badalia pointed out, 'You come 'ome with your shawl 'arf off of your back, an' your bonnick under your arm, and the price of nothing-at-all in your pocket, let alone a slop takin' care o' you.' Badalia did not drink, but she knew her sisterhood, and gave them rude counsel. Otherwise she kept herself to herself, and meditated a great deal upon Tom Herodsfoot, her husband, who would come back someday, and the baby who would never return. In what manner these thoughts wrought upon her mind will not be known.

Her entry into society dates from the night when she rose literally under the feet of the Reverend Eustace Hanna, on the landing of No. 17 Gunnison Street, and told him that he was a fool without discernment in the dispensation of his district charities.

'You give Lascar Loo custids,' said she, without the formality of introduction; 'give her pork-wine. Garn! Give 'er blankits. Garn 'ome! 'Er mother, she eats 'em all, and drinks the blankits. Gits 'em back from the shop, she does, before you come visiting again, so as to 'ave 'em all handy an' proper; an' Lascar Loo she sez to you, "Oh, my mother's that good to me!" she do. Lascar Loo 'ad better talk so, bein' sick abed, 'r else 'er mother would kill 'er. Garn! you're a bloomin' gardener – you an' yer custids! Lascar Loo don't never smell of 'em even.'

Thereon the curate, instead of being offended, recognised in the heavy eyes under the fringe the soul of a fellow-worker, and so bade Badalia mount guard over Lascar Loo, when the next jelly or custard should arrive, to see that the invalid actually ate it. This Badalia did, to the disgust of Lascar Loo's mother, and the sharing of a black eye between the three; but Lascar Loo got her custard, and coughing heartily, rather enjoyed the fray.

Later on, partly through the Reverend Eustace Hanna's swift recognition of her uses, and partly through certain tales poured out with moist eyes and flushed cheeks by Sister Eva, youngest and most impressionable of the Little Sisters of the Red Diamond, it came to pass that Badalia, arrogant, fluffy-fringed, and perfectly unlicensed in speech, won a recognised place among such as labour in Gunnison Street.

These were a mixed corps, zealous or hysterical, faint-hearted or only very wearied of battle against misery, according to their lights. The most part were consumed with small rivalries and personal jealousies, to be retailed confidentially to their own tiny cliques in the pauses between wresding with death for the body of a moribund laundress, or scheming for further mission-grants to resole a consumptive compositor's very consumptive boots. There was a rector that lived in dread of pauperising the poor, would fain have held bazaars for fresh altar-cloths, and prayed in secret for a large new brass bird, with eyes of red glass, fondly believed to be carbuncles. There was Brother Victor, of the Order of Little Ease, who knew a great deal about altar-cloths, but kept his knowledge in the background while he strove to propitiate Mrs Jessel, the Secretary of the Tea Cup Board, who had money to dispense, but hated Rome – even though Rome would, on its honour, do no more than fill the stomach, leaving the dazed soul to the mercies of Mrs Jessel. There were all the Little Sisters of the Red Diamond, daughters of the horseleech, crying 'Give' when their own charity was exhausted, and pitifully explaining to such as demanded an account of their disbursements in return for one half-sovereign, that relief-work in a bad district can hardly be systematised on the accounts' side without expensive duplication of staff. There was the Reverend Eustace Hanna, who worked impartially with Ladies' Committees, Androgynous Leagues and Guilds, Brother Victor, and anybody else who could give him money, boots, or blankets, or that more precious help that allows itself to be directed by those who know. And all these people learned, one by one, to consult Badalia on matters of personal character, right to relief, and hope of eventual reformation in Gunnison Street. Her answers were seldom cheering, but she possessed special knowledge and complete confidence in herself.

'I'm Gunnison Street,' she said to the austere Mrs Jessel. 'I know what's what, I do, an' they don't want your religion, mum, not a single – Excuse me. It's all right when they comes to die, mum, but till they die what they wants is things to eat. The men they'll shif' for themselves. That's why Nick Lapworth sez to you that 'e wants to be confirmed an' all that. 'E won't never lead no new life, nor 'is wife won't get no good out o' all the money you gives 'im. No more you can't pauperise them as 'asn't things to begin with. They're bloomin' well pauped. The women they can't shif for themselves – 'specially bein' always confined. 'Ow should they? They wants things if they can get 'em anyways. If not they dies, and a good job too, for women is cruel put upon in Gunnison Street.'

'Do you believe that – that Mrs Herodsfoot is altogether a proper person to trust funds to?' said Mrs Jessel to the curate after this conversation. 'She seems to be utterly godless in her speech at least.'

The curate agreed. She was godless according to Mrs Jessels views, but did not Mrs Jessel think that since Badalia knew Gunnison Street and its needs, as none other knew it, she might in a humble way be, as it were, the scullion of charity from purer sources, and that if, say, the Tea Cup Board could give a few shillings a week, and the Little Sisters of the Red Diamond a few more, and, yes, he himself could raise yet a few more, the total, not at all likely to be excessive, might be handed over to Badalia to dispense among her associates. Thus Mrs Jessel herself would be set free to attend more directly to the spiritual wants of certain large-limbed hulking men who sat picturesquely on the lower benches of her gatherings and sought for truth – which is quite as precious as silver, when you know the market for it.

'She'll favour her own friends,' said Mrs Jessel. The curate refrained from mirth, and, after wise flattery, carried his point. To her un-bounded pride Badalia was appointed the dispenser of a grant – a weekly trust, to be held for the benefit of Gunnison Street.

'I don't know what we can get together each week,' said the curate to her. 'But here are seventeen shillings to start with. You do what you like with them among your people, only let me know how it goes so that we shan't get muddled in the accounts. D'you see?'

'Ho yuss! 'Taint much though, is it?' said Badalia, regarding the white coins in her palm. The sacred fever of the administrator, only known to those who have tasted power, burned in her veins. 'Boots is boots, unless they're give you, an' then they ain't fit to wear unless they're mended top an' bottom; an' jellies is jellies; an' I don't think anything o' that cheap pork-wine, but it all comes to something. It'll go quicker 'n a quartern of gin – seventeen bob. An' I'll keep a book – same as I used to do before Tom went an' took up 'long o' that pan-faced slut in Hennessy's Rents. We was the only barrer that kep' regular books, me an' – 'im.'

She bought a large copy-book – her unschooled handwriting demanded room – and in it she wrote the story of her war; boldly, as befits a general, and for no other eyes than her own and those of the Reverend Eustace Hanna. Long ere the pages were full the mottled cover had been soaked in kerosene – Lascar Loo's mother, defrauded of her percentage on her daughter's custards, invaded Badalia's room in 17 Gunnison Street, and fought with her to the damage of the lamp and her own hair. It was hard, too, to carry the precious 'pork-wine' in one hand and the book in the other through an eternally thirsty land; so red stains were added to those of the oil. But the Reverend Eustace

Hanna, looking at the matter of the book, never objected. The generous scrawls told their own tale, Badalia every Saturday night supplying the chorus between the written statements thus –

*Mrs Hikkey, very ill brandy 3d. Cab for hospital, she had to go,: 1s. Mrs Poone confined. In money for tea (she took it, I know, sir) 6d. Met her husband out looking for work.*

'I slapped 'is face for a bone-idle beggar! 'E won't get no work becos 'e's – excuse me, sir. Won't you go on?' The curate continued –

*Mrs Vincent. Confid. No linning for baby. Most untidy. In money: 2s. 6d. Some cloths from Miss Evva.*

'Did Sister Eva do that?' said the curate very softly. Now charity was Sister Eva's bounden duty, yet to one man's eyes each act of her daily toil was a manifestation of angelic grace and goodness – a thing to perpetually admire.

'Yes, sir. She went back to the Sisters' 'Ome an' took 'em off 'er own bed. Most beautiful marked too. Go on, sir. That makes up four and thruppence.'

*Mrs Junnet to keep good fire coals is up: 7d.*

*Mrs Lockhart took a baby to nurse to earn a triffle but mother can't pay husband summons over and over. He won't help. Cash 2s. 2d. Worked in a ketchin but had to leave.*

*Fire, tea, and shin of beef: 1s.7½d.*

'There was a fight there, sir,' said Badalia. 'Not me, sir. 'Er 'usband, o' course 'e come in at the wrong time, was wishful to 'ave the beef, so I calls up the next floor an' down comes that mulatter man wot sells the sword-stick canes, top o' Ludgate-'ill. "Muley," sez I, "you big black beast, you, take an' kill this big white beast 'ere." I knew I couldn't stop Tom Lockart 'alf drunk, with the beef in 'is 'ands. "I'll beef 'm," sez Muley, an' 'e did it, with that pore woman a-cryin' in the next room, an' the top banisters on that landin' is broke out, but she got 'er beef-tea, an' Tom 'e's got 'is gruel. Will you go on, sir?'

'No, I think it will be all right. I'll sign for the week,' said the curate. One gets so used to these things profanely called human documents.

'Mrs Churner's baby's got diptheery,' said Badalia, turning to go.

'Where's that? The Churners of Painter's Alley, or the other Churners in Houghton Street?'

'Houghton Street. The Painter's Alley people, they're sold out an' left.'

'Sister Eva's sitting one night a week with old Mrs Probyn in Houghton Street – isn't she?' said the curate uneasily.

'Yes; but she won't sit no longer. *I've* took up Mrs Probyn. I can't talk 'er no religion, but she don't want it; an' Miss Eva she don't want no diptheery, tho' she sez she does. Don't *you* be afraid for Miss Eva.'

'But – but you'll get it, perhaps.'

'Like as not.' She looked the curate between the eyes, and her own eyes flamed under the fringe. 'Maybe I'd like to get it, for aught you know.'

The curate thought upon these words for a little time till he began to think of Sister Eva in the grey cloak with the white bonnet ribbons under the chin. Then he thought no more of Badalia.

What Badalia thought was never expressed in words, but it is known in Gunnison Street that Lascar Loo's mother, sitting blind drunk on her own doorstep, was that night captured and wrapped up in the war-cloud of Badalia's wrath, so that she did not know whether she stood on her head or her heels, and after being soundly bumped on every particular stair up to her room, was set down on Badalia's bed, there to whimper and quiver till the dawn, protesting that all the world was against her, and calling on the names of children long since slain by dirt and neglect. Badalia, snorting, went out to war, and since the hosts of the enemy were many, found enough work to keep her busy till the dawn.

As she had promised, she took Mrs Probyn into her own care, and began by nearly startling the old lady into a fit with the announcement that 'there ain't no God like as not, an' if there *is* it don't matter to you or me, an' any'ow you take this jelly.' Sister Eva objected to being shut off from her pious work in Houghton Street, but Badalia insisted, and by fair words and the promise of favours to come so prevailed on three or four of the more sober men of the neighbourhood, that they blockaded the door whenever Sister Eva attempted to force an entry, and pleaded the diphtheria as an excuse. 'I've got to keep 'er out o' 'arm's way,' said Badalia, 'an' out she keeps. The curick won't care a – for me, but – he wouldn't any'ow.'

The effect of that quarantine was to shift the sphere of Sister Eva's activity to other streets, and notably those most haunted by the Reverend Eustace Hanna and Brother Victor, of the Order of Little Ease. There exists, for all their human bickerings, a very close brotherhood in the ranks of those whose work lies in Gunnison Street. To begin with, they have seen pain – pain that no word or deed of theirs can alleviate – life born into Death, and Death crowded down by unhappy life. Also they understand the full significance of drink, which is a knowledge hidden from very many well-meaning people, and some of them have fought with the beasts at Ephesus. They meet at unseemly hours in unseemly places, exchange a word or two of hasty counsel, advice, or suggestion, and pass on to their appointed toil, since time is precious and lives hang in the balance of five minutes. For many, the gas-lamps are their sun, and the Covent Garden wains the chariots of the twilight. They have all in their station begged for money, so that the freemasonry of the mendicant binds them together.

To all these influences there was added in the case of two workers that thing which men have agreed to call Love. The chance that Sister Eva might catch diphtheria did not enter into the curate's head till Badalia had spoken. Then it seemed a thing intolerable and monstrous that she should be exposed not only to this risk, but any accident whatever of the streets. A wain coming round a corner might kill her; the rotten staircases on which she trod daily and nightly might collapse and maim her; there was danger in the tottering coping-stones of certain crazy houses that he knew well; danger more deadly within those houses. What if one of a thousand drunken men crushed out that precious life? A woman had once flung a chair at the curate's head. Sister Eva's arm would not be strong enough to ward off a chair. There were also knives that were quick to fly. These and other considerations cast the soul of the Reverend Eustace Hanna into torment that no leaning upon Providence could relieve. God was indubitably great and terrible – one had only to walk through Gunnison Street to see that much – but it would be better, vastly better, that Eva should have the protection of his own arm. And the world that was not too busy to watch might have seen a woman, not too young, light-haired and light-eyed, slightly assertive in her speech, and very limited in such ideas as lay beyond the immediate sphere of her duty, where the eyes of the Reverend Eustace Hanna turned to follow the footsteps of a Queen crowned in a little grey bonnet with white ribbons under the chin.

If that bonnet appeared for a moment at the bottom of a courtyard, or nodded at him on a dark staircase, then there was hope yet for Lascar Loo, living on one lung and the memory of past excesses, hope even for whining sodden Nick Lapworth, blaspheming, in the hope of money, over the pangs of a 'true conversion this time, s'elp me Gawd, sir'. If that bonnet did not appear for a day, the mind of the curate was filled with lively pictures of horror, visions of stretchers, a crowd at some villainous crossing, and a policeman – he could see that policeman – jerking out over his shoulder the details of the accident, and ordering the man who would have set his body against the wheels – heavy dray wheels, he could see them – to 'move on'. Then there was less hope for the salvation of Gunnison Street and all in it.

This agony Brother Victor beheld one day when he was coming from a death-bed. He saw the light in the eye, the relaxing muscles of the mouth, and heard a new ring in the voice that had told flat all the forenoon. Sister Eva had turned into Gunnison Street after a forty-eight hours' eternity of absence. She had not been run over. Brother Victor's heart must have suffered in some human fashion, or he would never have seen what he saw. But the Law of his Church made suffering easy. His duty was to go on with his work until he died, even as Badalia went on. She, magnifying her office, faced the drunken husband; coaxed the doubly shiftless, thriftless girl-wife into a little forethought, and begged clothes when and where she could for the scrofulous babes that multiplied like the green scum on the untopped water-cisterns.

The story of her deeds was written in the book that the curate signed weekly, but she never told him any more of fights and tumults in the street. 'Mis' Eva does 'er work 'er way. I does mine mine. But I do more than Mis' Eva ten times over, an' "Thank yer, Badalia," sez 'e, "that'll do for this week." I wonder what Tom's doin' now long o' that – other woman. Seems like as if I'd go an' look at 'im one o' these days. But I'd cut 'er liver out – couldn't 'elp myself. Better not go, p'raps.'

Hennessy's Rents lay more than two miles from Gunnison Street, and were inhabited by much the same class of people. Tom had established himself there with Jenny Wabstow, his new woman, and for weeks lived in great fear of Badalia's suddenly descending upon him. The prospect of actual fighting did not scare him; but he objected to the police-court that would follow, and the orders for maintenance and other devices of a law that cannot understand the simple rule that 'when a man's tired of a woman 'e ain't such a bloomin' fool as to live with 'er no more, an' that's the long an' short of it'. For some months his new wife wore very well, and kept Tom in a state of decent fear and consequent orderliness. Also work was plentiful. Then a baby was born, and, following the law of his kind, Tom, little interested in the children he helped to produce, sought distraction in drink. He had confined himself, as a rule, to beer, which is stupefying and comparatively innocuous: at least, it clogs the legs, and though the heart may ardently desire to kill, sleep comes swiftly, and the crime often remains undone. Spirits, being more volatile, allow both the flesh and the soul to work together – generally to the inconvenience of others. Tom discovered that there was merit in whisky – if you only took enough of it – cold. He took as much as he could purchase or get given him, and by the time that his woman was fit to go abroad again, the two rooms of their household were stripped of many valuable articles. Then the woman spoke her mind, not once, but several times, with point, fluency, and metaphor; and Tom was indignant at being deprived of peace at the end of his day's work, which included much whisky. He therefore withdrew himself from the solace and companionship of Jenny Wabstow, and she therefore pursued him with more metaphors. At the last, Tom would turn round and hit her – sometimes across the head, and sometimes across the breast, and the bruises furnished material for discussion on doorsteps among such women as had been treated in like manner by their husbands. They were not few.

But no very public scandal had occurred till Tom one day saw fit to open negotiations with a young woman for matrimony according to the laws of free selection. He was getting very tired of Jenny, and the young woman was earning enough from flower-selling to keep him in comfort, whereas Jenny was expecting another baby, and most unreasonably expected consideration on this account. The shapelessness of her figure revolted him, and he said as much in the language of his breed. Jenny cried till Mrs Hart, lineal descendant, and Irish of the 'mother to Mike of the donkey-cart', stopped her on her own staircase and whispered: 'God be good to you, Jenny, my woman, for I see how 'tis with you.' Jenny wept more than ever, and gave Mrs Hart a penny and some kisses, while Tom was conducting his own wooing at the corner of the street.

The young woman, prompted by pride, not by virtue, told Jenny of his offers, and Jenny spoke to Tom that night. The altercation began in their own rooms, but Tom tried to escape; and in the end all Hennessy's Rents gathered themselves upon the pavement and formed a court to which Jenny appealed from time to time, her hair loose on her neck, her raiment in extreme disorder, and her steps astray from drink. 'When your man drinks, you'd better drink too! It don't 'urt so much when 'e 'its you then,' says the Wisdom of the Women. And surely they ought to know.

'Look at 'im!' shrieked Jenny. 'Look at 'im, standin' there without any word to say for himself, that 'ud smitch off and leave me an' never so much as a shillin' lef be'ind! You call yourself a man – you call yourself the bleedin' shadow of a man? I've seen better men than you made outer chewed paper and spat out afterwards. Look at 'im!' 'E's been drunk since Thursday last, an' 'e'll be drunk s' long's 'e can get drink. 'E's took all I've got, an' me – an' me – as you see – '

A murmur of sympathy from the women.

'Took it all, he did, an' atop of his blasted pickin' an' stealin' – yes, you, you thief – 'e goes off an' tries to take up long o' that' – here followed a complete and minute description of the young woman. Luckily, she was not on the spot to hear.' 'E'll serve 'er as 'e served me! 'E'll drink every bloomin' copper she makes an' then leave 'er alone, same as 'e done me! O women, look you, I've bore 'im one an' there's another on the way, an' 'e'd up an' leave me as I am now – the stinkin' dorg. An' you *may* leave me. I don't want none o' your leavin's. Go away. Get away!' The hoarseness of passion overpowered the voice. The crowd attracted a policeman as Tom began to slink away.

'Look at 'im,' said Jenny, grateful for the new listener. 'Ain't there no law for such as 'im? 'E's took all my money, 'e's beat me once, twice an' over. 'E's swine drunk when 'e ain't mad drunk, an' now, an' now 'e's trying to pick up along o' another woman. 'Im I give up a four times better man for. Ain't there no law?'

'What's the matter now? You go into your 'ouse. I'll see to the man. 'As 'e been 'itting you?' said the policeman.

' 'Ittin' me? 'E's cut my 'eart in two, an' 'e stands there grinnin' as tho' 'twas all a play to 'im.'

'You go on into your 'ouse an' lie down a bit.'

'I'm a married woman, I tell you, an' I'll 'ave my 'usband!'

'I ain't done her no bloomin' 'arm,' said Tom from the edge of the crowd. He felt that public opinion was running against him.

'You ain't done me any bloomin' good, you dorg. I'm a married woman, I am, an' I won't 'ave my 'usband took from me.'

'Well, if you *are* a married woman, cover your breasts,' said the policeman soothingly. He was used to domestic brawls.

'Shan't – thank you for your impidence. Look 'ere!' She tore open her dishevelled bodice and showed such crescent-shaped bruises as are made by a well-applied chair-back. 'That's what 'e done to me acause my heart wouldn't break quick enough! 'E's tried to get in an' break it. Look at that, Tom, that you gave me last night; an' I made it up with you. But that was before I knew what you were tryin' to do long o' that woman – '

'D'you charge 'im?' said the policeman. ' 'E'll get a month for it, per'aps.'

'No,' said Jenny firmly. It was one thing to expose her man to the scorn of the street, and another to lead him to jail.

'Then you go in an' lie down, and you' – this to the crowd – 'pass along the pavement, there. Pass along. 'Taint nothing to laugh at' To Tom, who was being sympathised with by his friends, 'It's good for you she didn't charge you, but mind this now, the next time,' etc.

Tom did not at all appreciate Jenny's forbearance, nor did his friends help to compose his mind. He had whacked the woman because she was a nuisance. For precisely the same reason he had cast about for a new mate. And all his kind acts had ended in a truly painful scene in the street, a most unjustifiable exposure by and of his woman, and a certain loss of caste – this he realised dimly – among his associates. Consequently, all women were nuisances, and consequently whisky was a good thing. His friends condoled with him. Perhaps he had been more hard on his woman than she deserved, but her disgraceful conduct under provocation excused all offence.

'I wouldn't 'ave no more to do with 'er – a woman like that there,' said one comforter.

'Let 'er go an' dig for her bloomin' self. A man wears 'isself out to 'is bones shovin' meat down their mouths, while they sit at 'ome easy all day; an' the very fust time, mark you, you 'as a bit of a difference, an very proper too for a man as *is* a man, she ups an' 'as you out into the street, callin' you Gawd knows what all. What's the good o' that, I arx you?' So spoke the second comforter.

The whisky was the third, and his suggestion struck Tom as the best of all. He would return to Badalia his wife. Probably she would have been doing something wrong while he had been away, and he could then vindicate his authority as a husband. Certainly she would have money. Single women always seemed to possess the pence that God and the Government denied to hard-working men. He refreshed himself with more whisky. It was beyond any doubt that Badalia would have done something wrong. She might even have married another man. He would wait till the new husband was out of the way, and, after kicking Badalia, would get money and a long absent sense of satisfaction. There is much virtue in a creed or a law, but when all is prayed and suffered, drink is the only thing that will make clean all a man's deeds in his own eyes. Pity it is that the effects are not permanent.

Tom parted with his friends, bidding them tell Jenny that he was going to Gunnison Street, and would return to her arms no more. Because this was the devil's message, they remembered and severally delivered it, with drunken distinctness, in Jenny's ears. Then Tom took more drink till his drunkenness rolled back and stood off from him as a wave rolls back and stands off the wreck it will swamp. He reached the traffic-polished black asphalt of a side-street and trod warily among the reflections of the shop-lamps that burned in gulfs of pitchy darkness, fathoms beneath his boot-heels. He was very sober indeed. Looking down his past, he beheld that he was justified of all his actions so entirely and perfectly that if Badalia had in his absence dared to lead a blameless life he would smash her for not having gone wrong.

Badalia at that moment was in her own room after the regular nightly skirmish with Lascar Loo's mother. To a reproof as stinging as a Gunnison Street tongue could make it, the old woman, detected for the hundredth time in the theft of the poor delicacies meant for the invalid, could only cackle and answer –

'D'you think Loo's never bilked a man in 'er life? She's dyin' now – on'y she's so cunning long about it. Me! I'll live for twenty years yet.'

Badalia shook her, more on principle than in any hope of curing her, and thrust her into the night, where she collapsed on the pavement and called upon the devil to slay Badalia.

He came upon the word in the shape of a man with a very pale face who asked for her by name. Lascar Loo's mother remembered. It was Badalia's husband – and the return of a husband to Gunnison Street was generally followed by beatings.

'Where's my wife?' said Tom. 'Where's my slut of a wife?'

'Upstairs an' be – to her,' said the old woman, falling over on her side. ' 'Ave you come back for 'er, Tom?'

'Yes. 'Oo's she took up while I bin gone?'

'All the bloomin' curicks in the parish. She's that set up you wouldn't know 'er.'

' 'Strewth she is!'

'Oh, yuss. Mor'n that, she's always round an' about with them sniffin' Sisters of Charity an' the curick. Mor'n that, 'e gives 'er money – pounds an' pounds a week. Been keepin' her that way for months, 'e 'as. No wonder you wouldn't 'ave nothin' to do with 'er when you left. An' she keeps me outer the food-stuff they gets for me lyin' dyin' out 'ere like a dorg. She's been a blazin' bad un has Badalia since you left.'

'Got the same room still, 'as she?' said Tom, striding over Lascar Loo's mother, who was picking at the chinks between the pave-stones.

'Yes, but so fine you wouldn't know it.'

Tom went up the stairs and the old lady chuckled. Tom was angry. Badalia would not be able to bump people for some time to come, or to interfere with the heaven-appointed distribution of custards.

Badalia, undressing to go to bed, heard feet on the stair that she knew well. Ere they stopped to kick at her door she had, in her own fashion, thought over very many things.

'Tom's back,' she said to herself. 'An' I'm glad . . . spite o' the curick an' everythink.'

She opened the door, crying his name.

The man pushed her aside.

'I don't want none o' your kissin's an' slaverin's. I'm sick of 'em,' said he.

'You ain't 'ad so many neither to make you sick these two years past.'

'I've 'ad better. Got any money?'

'On'y a little – orful little.'

'That's a – lie, an' you know it'

' 'Taint – and, oh Tom, what's the use o' talkin' money the minute you come back? Didn't you like Jenny? I knowed you wouldn't.'

'Shut your 'ead. Ain't you got enough to make a man drunk fair?'

'You don't want bein' made more drunk any. You're drunk a'ready. You come to bed, Tom.'

'To you?'

'Ay, to me. Ain't I nothin' – spite o'Jenny?'

She put out her arms as she spoke. But the drink held Tom fast.

'Not for me,' said he, steadying himself against the wall. 'Don't I know 'ow you've been goin' on while I was away, yah!'

'Arsk about!' said Badalia indignantly, drawing herself together. ' 'Oo sez anythink agin me 'ere?'

' 'Oo sez? Wy, everybody. I ain't come back more'n a minute fore I finds you've been with the curick Gawd knows where. Wot curick was 'e?'

'The curick that's 'ere always,' said Badalia hastily. She was thinking of anything rather than the Revd Eustace Hanna at that moment. Tom sat down gravely in the only chair in the room. Badalia continued her arrangements for going to bed.

'Pretty thing that,' said Tom, 'to tell your own lawful married 'usband – an' I guv five bob for the weddin'-ring. Curick that's 'ere always! Cool as brass you are. Ain't you got no shame? Ain't 'e under the bed now?'

'Tom, you're bleedin' drunk. I ain't done nothin' to be 'shamed of.'

'You! You don't know wot shame is. But I ain't come 'ere to mess with you. Give me wot you've got, an' then I'll dress you down an' go to Jenny.'

'I ain't got nothin' 'cept some coppers an' a shillin' or so.'

'Wot's that about the curick keepin' you on five poun' a week?'

' 'Oo told you that?'

'Lascar Loo's mother, lyin' on the pavemint outside, an' more honest than you'll ever be. Give me wot you've got!'

Badalia passed over to a little shell pin-cushion on the mantelpiece, drew thence four shillings and threepence – the lawful earnings of her trade – and held them out to the man who was rocking in his chair and surveying the room with wide-opened, rolling eyes.

'That ain't five poun',' said he drowsily.

'I ain't got no more. Take it an' go – if you won't stay.'

Tom rose slowly, gripping the arms of the chair. 'Wot about the curick's money that 'e guv you?' said he. 'Lascar Loo's mother told me. You give it over to me now, or I'll make you.'

'Lascar Loo's mother don't know anything about it.'

'She do, an' more than you want her to know.'

'She don't. I've bumped the 'eart out of 'er, and I can't give you the money. Anythin' else but that, Tom, an' everythin' else but that, Tom, I'll give willin' and true. 'Taint my money. Won't the dollar be enough? That money's my trust. There's a book along of it too.'

'Your trust? Wot are you doin' with any trust that your 'usband don't know of? You an' your trust! Take you that!'

Tom stepped towards her and delivered a blow of the clenched fist across the mouth. 'Give me wot you've got,' said he, in the thick, abstracted voice of one talking in dreams.

'I won't,' said Badalia, staggering to the washstand. With any other man than her husband she would have fought savagely as a wild cat; but Tom had been absent two years, and, perhaps, a little timely submission would win him back to her. None the less, the weekly trust was sacred.

The wave that had so long held back descended on Tom's brain. He caught Badalia by the throat and forced her to her knees. It seemed just to him in that hour to punish an erring wife for two years of wilful desertion; and the more, in that she had confessed her guilt by refusing to give up the wage of sin.

Lascar Loo's mother waited on the pavement without for the sounds of lamentation, but none came. Even if Tom had released her gullet Badalia would not have screamed.

'Give it up, you slut!' said Tom. 'Is that 'ow you pay me back for all I've done?'

'I can't. 'Tain't my money. Gawd forgive you, Tom, for wot you're – ,' the voice ceased as the grip tightened, and Tom heaved Badalia against the bed. Her forehead struck the bedpost, and she sank, half kneeling, on the floor. It was impossible for a self-respecting man to refrain from kicking her: so Tom kicked with the deadly intelligence born of whisky. The head drooped to the floor, and Tom kicked at that till the crisp tingle of hair striking through his nailed boot with the chill of cold water, warned him that it might be as well to desist.

'Where's the curick's money, you kep' woman?' he whispered in the blood-stained ear. But there was no answer – only a rattling at the door, and the voice of Jenny Wabstow crying ferociously, 'Come out o' that, Tom, an' come 'ome with me! An' you, Badalia, I'll tear your face off its bones!'

Tom's friends had delivered their message, and Jenny, after the first flood of passionate tears, rose up to follow Tom, and, if possible, to win him back. She was prepared even to endure an exemplary whacking for her performances in Hennessy's Rents. Lascar Loo's mother guided her to the chamber of horrors, and chuckled as she retired down the staircase. If Tom had not banged the soul out of Badalia, there would at least be a royal fight between that Badalia and Jenny. And Lascar Loo's mother knew well that Hell has no fury like a woman fighting above the life that is quick in her.

Still there was no sound audible in the street. Jenny swung back the unbolted door, to discover her man stupidly regarding a heap by the bed. An eminent murderer has remarked that if people did not die so untidily, most men, and all women, would commit at least one murder in their lives. Tom was reflecting on the present untidiness, and the whisky was fighting with the clear current of his thoughts.

'Don't make that noise,' he said. 'Come in quick.'

'My Gawd!' said Jenny, checking like a startled wild beast. 'What's all this 'ere? You ain't – '

'Dunno. 'Spose I did it.'

'Did it! You done it a sight too well this time.'

'She was aggravatin',' said Tom thickly, dropping back into the chair. 'That aggravatin' you'd never believe. Livin' on the fat o' the land among these aristocratic parsons an' all. Look at them white cuttings on the bed. *We* ain't got no white cuttings. What I want to know is – ' The voice died as Badalia's had died, but from a different cause. The whisky was tightening its grip after the accomplished deed, and Tom's eyes were beginning to close. Badalia on the floor breathed heavily.

'No, nor like to 'ave,' said Jenny. 'You've done for 'er this time. You go!'

'Not me. She won't hurt. Do 'er good. I'm goin' to sleep. Look at those there clean sheets! Aint you comin' too?'

Jenny bent over Badalia, and there was intelligence in the battered woman's eyes – intelligence and much hate.

'I never told 'im to do such,' Jenny whispered. ' 'Twas Tom's own doin' – none o' mine. Shall I get 'im took, dear?'

The eyes told their own story. Tom, who was beginning to snore, must not be taken by the Law.

'Go,' said Jenny. 'Get out! Get out of 'ere.'

'You – told – me – that – this afternoon,' said the man very sleepily. 'Lemme go asleep.'

'That wasn't nothing. You'd only 'it me. This time it's murder – murder – murder! Tom, you've killed 'er now.' She shook the man from his rest, and understanding with cold terror filled his fuddled brain.

'I done it for your sake, Jenny,' he whimpered feebly, trying to take her hand.

'You killed 'er for the money, same as you would ha' killed me. Get out o' this. Lay 'er on the bed first, you brute!'

They lifted Badalia on to the bed, and crept forth silently.

'I can't be took along o' you – and if you was took you'd say I made you do it, an' try to get me 'anged. Go away – anywhere outer 'ere,' said Jenny, and she dragged him down the stairs.

'Goin' to look for the curick?' said a voice from the pavement. Lascar Loo's mother was still waiting patiently to hear Badalia squeal.

'Wot curick?' said Jenny swiftly. There was a chance of salving her conscience yet in regard to the bundle upstairs.

' 'Anna – 63 Roomer Terrace – close 'ere,' said the old woman. She had never been favourably regarded by the curate. Perhaps, since, Badalia had not squealed, Tom preferred smashing the man to the woman. There was no accounting for tastes.

Jenny thrust her man before her till they reached the nearest main road. 'Go away, now,' she gasped. 'Go off anywheres, but don't come back to me. I'll never go with you again; an', Tom – Tom, d'you 'ear me? – clean your boots.'

Vain counsel. The desperate thrust of disgust which she bestowed upon him sent him staggering face-down into the kennel, where a policeman showed interest in his welfare.

'Took for a common drunk. Gawd send they don't look at 'is boots! 'Anna, 63 Roomer Terrace!' Jenny settled her hat and ran.

The excellent housekeeper of the Roomer Chambers still remembers how there arrived a young person, blue-lipped and gasping, who cried only: 'Badalia, 17 Gunnison Street. Tell the curick to come at once – at once – at once!'

and vanished into the night. This message was borne to the Revd Eustace Hanna, then enjoying his beauty-sleep. He saw there was urgency in the demand, and unhesitatingly knocked up Brother Victor across the landing. As a matter of etiquette, Rome and England divided their cases in the district according to the creeds of the sufferers; but Badalia was an institution, and not a case, and there was no district-relief etiquette to be considered. 'Something has happened to Badalia,' the curate said, 'and it's your affair as well as mine. Dress and come along.'

'I am ready,' was the answer. 'Is there any hint of what's wrong?'

'Nothing beyond a runaway-knock and a call.'

'Then it's a confinement or a murderous assault. Badalia wouldn't wake us up for anything less. I'm qualified for both, thank God.'

The two men raced to Gunnison Street, for there were no cabs abroad, and under any circumstances a cab-fare means two days' good firing for such as are perishing with cold. Lascar Loo's mother had gone to bed, and the door was naturally on the latch. They found considerably more than they had expected in Badalia's room, and the Church of Rome acquitted itself nobly with bandages, while the Church of England could only pray to be delivered from the sin of envy. The Order of Little Ease, recognising that the soul is in most cases accessible through the body, take their measures and train their men accordingly.

'She'll do now,' said Brother Victor, in a whisper. 'It's internal bleeding, I fear, and a certain amount of injury to the brain. She has a husband, of course?'

'They all have, more's the pity.'

'Yes, there's a domesticity about these injuries that shows their origin.' He lowered his voice. 'It's a perfectly hopeless business, you understand. Twelve hours at the most.'

Badalia's right hand began to beat on the counterpane, palm down.

'I think you are wrong,' said the Church of England. 'She is going.'

'No, that's not the picking at the counterpane,' said the Church of Rome. 'She wants to say something; you know her better than I.'

The curate bent very low.

'Send for Miss Eva,' said Badalia, with a cough.

'In the morning. She will come in the morning,' said the curate, and Badalia was content. Only the Church of Rome, who knew something of the human heart, knitted his brows and said nothing. After all the law of his Order was plain. His duty was to watch till the dawn while the moon went down.

It was a little before her sinking that the Revd Eustace Hanna said, 'Hadn't we better send for Sister Eva? She seems to be going fast.'

Brother Victor made no answer, but as early as decency admitted there came one to the door of the house of the Little Sisters of the Red Diamond and demanded Sister Eva, that she might soothe the pain of Badalia Herodsfoot. That man, saying very little, led her to Gunnison Street, No. 17, and into the room where Badalia lay. Then he stood on the landing, and bit the flesh of his fingers in agony, because he was a priest trained to know, and knew how the hearts of men and women beat back at the rebound, so that Love is born out of horror, and passion declares itself when the soul is quivering with pain.

Badalia, wise to the last, husbanded her strength till the coming of Sister Eva. It is generally maintained by the Little Sisters of the Red Diamond that she died in delirium, but since one Sister at least took a half of her dying advice, this seems uncharitable.

She tried to turn feebly on the bed, and the poor broken human machinery protested according to its nature.

Sister Eva started forward, thinking that she heard the dread forerunner of the death-rattle. Badalia lay still conscious, and spoke with startling distinctness, the irrepressible irreverence of the street-hawker, the girl who had danced on the winkle-barrow twinkling; in her one available eye.

'Sounds jest like Mrs Jessel, don't it? Before she's 'ad 'er lunch an' 'as been talkin' all the mornin' to her classes.'

Neither Sister Eva nor the curate said anything. Brother Victor stood without the door, and the breath came harshly between his teeth, for he was in pain.

'Put a cloth over my 'ead,' said Badalia. 'I've got it good, an' I don't want Miss Eva to see. I ain't pretty this time.'

'Who was it?' said the curate.

'Man from outside. Never seed 'im no more'n Adam. Drunk, I s'pose. S'elp me Gawd, that's truth! Is Miss Eva 'ere? I can't see under the towel. I've got it good, Miss Eva. Excuse my not shakin' 'ands with you, but I'm not strong, an' it's fourpence for Mrs Imeny's beef-tea, an' wot you can give 'er for baby-linning. Allus 'avin' kids, these people. I 'adn't oughter talk, for *my* 'usband 'e never come a-nigh me these two years, or I'd a-bin as bad as the rest; but 'e never come a-nigh me . . . A man come and 'it me over the 'ead, an' 'e kicked me, Miss Eva; so it was just the same's if I had ha' had a 'usband, ain't it? The book's in the drawer, Mister 'Anna, an' it's all right, an' I never guv up a copper o' the trust money – not a copper. You look under the chist o' drawers – all wot isn't spent this week is there . . . An', Miss Eva, don't you wear that grey bonnick no more. I kep' you from the diptheery, an' – an' I didn't want to keep you so, but the curick said it 'ad to be done. I'd a sooner ha' took up with 'im than anyone, only Tom 'e come, an' then – you see, Miss Eva, Tom 'e never come a-nigh me for two years, nor I 'aven't seen 'im yet. S'elp me Gawd, I 'aven't. Do you 'ear? But you two go along, and make a match of it. I've wished otherways often, but o' course it was not for the likes o' me. If Tom 'ad come back, which 'e never did, I'd ha' been like the rest – sixpence for beef-tea for the baby, an' a shilling for layin' out the baby. You've seen it in the books, Mister 'Anna. That's what it is; an' o' course, you couldn't never 'ave nothing to do with me. But a woman she wishes as she looks, an' never you 'ave no doubt about 'im, Miss Eva. I've seen it in 'is face time an' agin – time an' agin . . . Make it a four pound ten funeral – with a pall.'

It was a seven pound fifteen shilling funeral, and all Gunnison Street turned out to do it honour. All but two; for Lascar Loo's mother saw that a Power had departed, and that her road lay clear to the custards. Therefore, when the carriages rattled off, the cat on the doorstep heard the wail of the dying prostitute who could not die –

'Oh, mother, mother, won't you even let me lick the spoon!'

# 8

# *The Ship that Found Herself*

We now, held in captivity,
Spring to our labour nor grieve!
See now, how it is blesseder,
Brothers, to give than receive!
Keep trust, wherefore ye were made
Paying the duty ye owe;
For a clean thrust and the sheer of the blade
Shall carry us where we should go.

*Song of the Engines*

IT WAS HER FIRST VOYAGE, and though she was but a cargo-steamer of twelve hundred tons, she was the very best of her kind, the outcome of forty years of experiments and improvements in framework and machinery; and her designers and owner thought as much of her as though she had been the *Lucania.* Anyone can make a floating hotel that will pay expenses, if he puts enough money into the saloon, and charges for private baths, suites of rooms, and such like; but in these days of competition and low freights every square inch of a cargo-boat must be built for cheapness, great hold-capacity, and a certain steady speed. This boat was, perhaps, two hundred and forty feet long and thirty-two feet wide, with arrangements that enabled her to carry cattle on her main and sheep on her upper deck if she wanted to; but her great glory was the amount of cargo that she could store away in her holds. Her owners – they were a very well known Scotch firm – came round with her from the north, where she had been launched and christened and fitted, to Liverpool, where she was to take cargo for New York; and the owner's daughter, Miss Frazier, went to and fro on the clean decks, admiring the new paint and the brass work, and the patent winches, and particularly the strong, straight bow, over which she had cracked a bottle of champagne when she named the steamer the *Dimbula*. It was a beautiful September afternoon, and the boat in all her newness – she was painted lead-colour with a red funnel – looked very fine indeed. Her house-flag was flying, and her whistle from time to time acknowledged the salutes of friendly boats, who saw that she was new to the High and Narrow Seas and wished to make her welcome.

'And now,' said Miss Frazier delightedly, to the captain, 'she's a real ship, isn't she? It seems only the other day father gave the order for her, and now – and now – isn't she a beauty!' The girl was proud of the firm, and talked as though she were the controlling partner.

'Oh, she's no so bad,' the skipper replied cautiously. 'But I'm sayin' that it takes more than christenin' to mak' a ship. In the nature o' things, Miss Frazier, if ye follow me, she's just irons and rivets and plates put into the form of a ship. She has to find herself yet.'

'I thought father said she was exceptionally well found.'

'So she is,' said the skipper, with a laugh. 'But it's this way wi' ships, Miss Frazier. She's all here, but the parrts of her have not learned to work together yet. They've had no chance.'

'The engines are working beautifully. I can hear them.'

'Yes, indeed. But there's more than engines to a ship. Every inch of her, ye'll understand, has to be livened up and made to work wi' its neighbour – sweetenin' her, we call it, technically.'

'And how will you do it?' the girl asked.

'We can no more than drive and steer her, and so forth; but if we have rough weather this trip – it's likely – she'll learn the rest by heart! For a ship, ye'll obsairve, Miss Frazier, is in no sense a reegid body closed at both ends. She's a highly complex structure o' various an' conflictin' strains, wi' tissues that must give an' tak' accordin' to her personal modulus of elasteecity.' Mr Buchanan, the chief engineer, was coming towards them. 'I'm sayin' to Miss Frazier, here, that our little *Dimbula* has to be sweetened yet, and nothin' but a gale will do it. How's all wi' your engines, Buck?'

'Well enough – true by plumb an' rule, o' course; but there's no spontaneeity yet.' He turned to the girl. 'Take my word, Miss Frazier, and maybe ye'll comprehend later; even after a pretty girl's christened a ship it does not follow that there's such a thing as a ship under the men that work her.'

'I was sayin' the very same, Mr Buchanan,' the skipper interrupted.

'That's more metaphysical than I can follow,' said Miss Frazier, laughing.

'Why so? Ye're good Scotch, an' – I knew your mother's father, he was fra' Dumfries – ye've a vested right in metapheesics, Miss Frazier, just as ye have in the *Dimbula,*' the engineer said.

'Eh, well, we must go down to the deep watters, an' earn Miss Frazier her deevidends. Will you not come to my cabin for tea?' said the skipper. 'We'll be in dock the night, and when you're goin' back to Glasgie ye can think of us loadin' her down an' drivin' her forth – all for your sake.'

In the next few days they stowed some two thousand tons' dead weight into the *Dimbula,* and took her out from Liverpool. As soon as she met the lift of the open water, she naturally began to talk. If you lay your ear to the side of the cabin the next time you are in a steamer, you will hear hundreds of little voices in every direction, thrilling and buzzing, and whispering and popping, and gurgling and sobbing and squeaking exactly like a telephone in a thunderstorm. Wooden ships shriek and growl and grunt, but iron vessels throb and quiver through all their hundreds of ribs and thousands of rivets. The *Dimbula* was very strongly built, and every piece of her had a letter or number, or both, to describe it; and every piece had been hammered, or forged, or rolled, or punched by man, and had lived in the roar and rattle of the ship-yard for months. Therefore, every piece had its own separate voice in exact proportion to the amount of trouble spent upon it. Cast-iron, as a rule, says very little; but mild steel plates and wrought-iron, and ribs and beams that have been much bent and welded and riveted, talk continuously. Their conversation, of course, is not half as wise as our human talk, because they are all, though they do not know it, bound down one to the other in a black darkness, where they cannot tell what is happening near them, nor what will overtake them next.

As soon as she had cleared the Irish coast a sullen, grey-headed old wave of the Atlantic climbed leisurely over her straight bows, and sat down on her steam-capstan used for hauling up the anchor. Now the capstan and the engine that drove it had been newly painted red and green; besides which, nobody likes being ducked.

'Don't you do that again,' the capstan sputtered through the teeth of his cogs. 'Hi! Where's the fellow gone?'

The wave had slouched overside with a plop and a chuckle; but 'Plenty more where he came from,' said a brother-wave, and went through and over the capstan, who was bolted firmly to an iron plate on the iron deck-beams below.

'Can't you keep still up there?' said the deck-beams. 'What's the matter with you? One minute you weigh twice as much as you ought to, and the next you don't!'

'It isn't my fault,' said the capstan. 'There's a green brute outside that comes and hits me on the head.'

'Tell that to the shipwrights. You've been in position for months and you've never wriggled like this before. If you aren't careful you'll strain *us.*'

'Talking of strain,' said a low, rasping, unpleasant voice, 'are any of you fellows – you deck-beams, we mean – aware that those exceedingly ugly knees of yours happen to be riveted into our structure – *ours?*

'Who might you be?' the deck-beams enquired.

'Oh, nobody in particular,' was the answer. 'We're only the port and starboard upper-deck stringers; and if you persist in heaving and hiking like this, we shall be reluctantly compelled to take steps.'

Now the stringers of the ship are long iron girders, so to speak, that run lengthways from stern to bow. They keep the iron frames (what are called ribs in a wooden ship) in place, and also help to hold the ends of the deck-beams, which go from side to side of the ship. Stringers always consider themselves most important, because they are so long.

'You will take steps – will you?' This was a long echoing rumble. It came from the frames – scores and scores of them, each one about eighteen inches distant from the next, and each riveted to the stringers in four places. 'We think you will have a certain amount of trouble in *that';* and thousands and thousands of the little rivets that held everything together whispered: 'You will. You will! Stop quivering and be quiet. Hold on, brethren! Hold on! Hot Punches! What's that?'

Rivets have no teeth, so they cannot chatter with fright; but they did their best as a fluttering jar swept along the ship from stern to bow, and she shook like a rat in a terrier's mouth.

An unusually severe pitch, for the sea was rising, had lifted the big throbbing screw nearly to the surface, and it was spinning round in a kind of soda-water – half sea and half air – going much faster than was proper, because there was no deep water for it to work in. As it sank again, the engines – and they were triple expansion, three cylinders in a row – snorted through all their three pistons. 'Was that a joke, you fellow outside? It's an uncommonly poor one. How are we to do our work if you fly off the handle that way?'

'I didn't fly off the handle,' said the screw, twirling huskily at the end of the screw-shaft. 'If I had, you'd have been scrap-iron by this time. The sea dropped away from under me, and I had nothing to catch on to. That's all.'

'That's all, d'you call it?' said the thrust-block, whose business it is to take the push of the screw; for if a screw had nothing to hold it back it would crawl right into the engine-room. (It is the holding back of the screwing action that gives the drive to a ship.) 'I know I do my work deep down and out of sight, but I warn you I expect justice. All I ask for is bare justice. Why can't you push steadily and evenly, instead of whizzing like a whirligig, and making me hot under all my collars.' The thrust-block had six collars, each faced with brass, and he did not wish to get them heated.

All the bearings that supported the fifty feet of screw-shaft as it ran to the stern whispered: 'Justice – give us justice.'

'I can only give you what I can get,' the screw answered. 'Look out! It's coming again!'

He rose with a roar as the *Dimbula* plunged, and 'whack – flack – whack – whack' went the engines, furiously, for they had little to check them.

'I'm the noblest outcome of human ingenuity – Mr Buchanan says so,' squealed the high-pressure cylinder. 'This is simply ridiculous!' The piston went up savagely, and choked, for half the steam behind it was mixed with dirty water. 'Help! Oiler! Fitter! Stoker! Help! I'm choking,' it gasped. 'Never in the history of maritime invention has such a calamity overtaken one so young and strong. And if I go, who's to drive the ship?'

'Hush! oh, hush!' whispered the Steam, who, of course, had been to sea many times before. He used to spend his leisure ashore in a cloud, or a gutter, or a flower-pot, or a thunderstorm, or anywhere else where water was needed. 'That's only a little priming, a little carrying-over, as they call it. It'll happen all night, on and off. I don't say it's nice, but it's the best we can do under the circumstances.'

'What difference can circumstances make? I'm here to do my work – on clean, dry steam. Blow circumstances!' the cylinder roared.

'The circumstances will attend to the blowing. I've worked on the North Atlantic run a good many times – it's going to be rough before morning.'

'It isn't distressingly calm now,' said the extra-strong frames – they were called web-frames – in the engine-room. 'There's an upward thrust that we don't understand, and there's a twist that is very bad for our brackets and diamond-plates, and there's a sort of west-northwesterly pull that follows the twist, which seriously annoys us. We mention this because we happened to cost a good deal of money, and we feel sure that the owner would not approve of our being treated in this frivolous way.'

'I'm afraid the matter is out of the owner's hands for the present,' said the Steam, slipping into the condenser. 'You're left to your own devices till the weather betters.'

'I wouldn't mind the weather,' said a flat bass voice below; 'it's this confounded cargo that's breaking my heart. I'm the garboard-strake, and I'm twice as thick as most of the others, and I ought to know something.'

The garboard-strake is the lowest plate in the bottom of a ship, and the *Dimbula's* garboard-strake was nearly three-quarters of an inch mild steel.

'The sea pushes me up in a way I should never have expected,' the strake grunted, 'and the cargo pushes me down, and, between the two, I don't know what I'm supposed to do.'

'When in doubt, hold on,' rumbled the Steam, making head in the boilers.

'Yes; but there's only dark, and cold, and hurry, down here; and how do I know whether the other plates are doing their duty? Those bulwark-plates up above, I've heard, ain't more than five-sixteenths of an inch thick – scandalous, I call it.'

'I agree with you,' said a huge web-frame by the main cargo-hatch. He was deeper and thicker than all the others, and curved half-way across the ship in the shape of half an arch, to support the deck where deck-beams would have been in the way of cargo coming up and down.

'I work entirely unsupported, and I observe that I am the sole strength of this vessel, so far as my vision extends. The responsibility, I assure you, is enormous. I believe the money-value of the cargo is over one hundred and fifty thousand pounds. Think of that!'

'And every pound of it is dependent on my personal exertions.' Here spoke a sea-valve that communicated directly with the water outside, and was seated not very far from the garboard-strake. 'I rejoice to think that I am a Prince-Hyde Valve, with best Pará rubber facings. Five patents cover me – I mention this without pride – five separate and several patents, each one finer than the other. At present I am screwed fast. Should I open, you would immediately be swamped. This is incontrovertible!'

Patent things always use the longest words they can. It is a trick that they pick up from their inventors.

'That's news,' said a big centrifugal bilge-pump. 'I had an idea that you were employed to clean decks and things with. At least, I've used you for that more than once. I forget the precise number, in thousands, of gallons which I am guaranteed to throw per hour; but I assure you, my complaining friends, that there is not the least danger. I alone am capable of clearing any water that may find its way here. By my Biggest Deliveries, we pitched then!'

The sea was getting up in a workmanlike style. It was a dead westerly gale, blown from under a ragged opening of green sky, narrowed on all sides by fat, grey clouds; and the wind bit like pincers as it fretted the spray into lacework on the flanks of the waves.

'I tell you what it is,' the foremast telephoned down its wire-stays. 'I'm up here, and I can take a dispassionate view of things. There's an organised conspiracy against us. I'm sure of it, because every single one of these waves is heading directly for our bows. The whole sea is concerned in it – and so's the wind. It's awful!'

'What's awful?' said a wave, drowning the capstan for the hundredth time.

'This organised conspiracy on your part,' the capstan gurgled, taking his cue from the mast.

'Organised bubbles and spindrift! There has been a depression in the Gulf of Mexico. Excuse me!' He leaped overside; but his friends took up the tale one after another.

'Which has advanced – ' That wave hove green water over the funnel.

'As far as Cape Hatteras – ' He drenched the bridge.

'And is now going out to sea – to sea – to sea!' The third went free in three surges, making a clean sweep of a boat, which turned bottom up and sank in the darkening troughs alongside, while the broken falls whipped the davits.

'That's all there is to it,' seethed the white water roaring through the scuppers. 'There's no animus in our proceedings. We're only meteorological corollaries.'

'Is it going to get any worse?' said the bow-anchor chained down to the deck, where he could only breathe once in five minutes.

'Not knowing, can't say. Wind may blow a bit by midnight. Thanks awfully. Goodbye.'

The wave that spoke so politely had travelled some distance aft, and found itself all mixed up on the deck amidships, which was a well-deck sunk between high bulwarks. One of the bulwark plates, which was hung on hinges to open outward, had swung out, and passed the bulk of the water back to the sea again with a clean smack.

'Evidently that's what I'm made for,' said the plate, closing again with a sputter of pride. 'Oh no, you don't, my friend!'

The top of a wave was trying to get in from the outside, but as the plate did not open in that direction, the defeated water spurted back.

'Not bad for five-sixteenths of an inch,' said the bulwark-plate. 'My work, I see, is laid down for the night;' and it began opening and shutting with the motion of the ship as it was designed to do.

'We are not what you might call idle,' groaned all the frames together, as the *Dimbula* climbed a big wave, lay on her side at the top, and shot into the next hollow, twisting in the descent. A huge swell pushed up exactly under her middle, and her bow and stern hung free with nothing to support them. Then one joking wave caught her up at the bow, and another at the stern, while the rest of the water slunk away from under her just to see how she would like it; so she was held up at her two ends only, and the weight of the cargo and the machinery fell on the groaning iron keels and bilge-stringers.

'Ease off! Ease off, there!' roared the garboard-strake. 'I want one-eighth of an inch fair play. D'you hear me, you rivets!'

'Ease off! Ease off!' cried the bilge-stringers. 'Don't hold us so tight to the frames!'

'Ease off!' grunted the deck-beams, as the *Dimbula* rolled fearfully.

'You've cramped our knees into the stringers, and we can't move. Ease off, you flat-headed little nuisances.'

Then two converging seas hit the bows, one on each side, and fell away in torrents of streaming thunder.

'Ease off!' shouted the forward collision-bulkhead. 'I want to crumple up, but I'm stiffened in every direction. Ease off, you dirty little forge-filings. Let me breathe!'

All the hundreds of plates that are riveted to the frames, and make the outside skin of every steamer, echoed the call, for each plate wanted to shift and creep a little, and each plate, according to its position, complained against the rivets.

'We can't help it! *We* can't help it!' they murmured in reply. 'We're put here to hold you, and we're going to do it; you never pull us twice in the same direction. If you'd say what you were going to do next, we'd try to meet your views.'

'As far as I could feel,' said the upper-deck planking, and that was four inches thick, 'every single iron near me was pushing or pulling in opposite directions. Now, what's the sense of that? My friends, let us all pull together.'

'Pull any way you please,' roared the funnel, 'so long as you don't try your experiments on *me*. I need seven wire ropes, all pulling in different directions, to hold me steady. Isn't that so?'

'We believe you, my boy!' whistled the funnel-stays through their clinched teeth, as they twanged in the wind from the top of the funnel to the deck.

'Nonsense! We must all pull together,' the decks repeated. 'Pull lengthways.'

'Very good,' said the stringers; 'then stop pushing sideways when you get wet. Be content to run gracefully fore and aft, and curve in at the ends as we do.'

'No – no curves at the end! A very slight workmanlike curve from side to side, with a good grip at each knee, and little pieces welded on,' said the deck-beams.

'Fiddle!' cried the iron pillars of the deep, dark hold. 'Who ever heard of curves? Stand up straight; be a perfectly round column, and carry tons of good solid weight – like that! There!' A big sea smashed on the deck above, and the pillars stiffened themselves to the load.

'Straight up and down is not bad,' said the frames, who ran that way in the sides of the ship, 'but you must also expand yourselves sideways. Expansion is the law of life, children. Open out! open out!'

'Come back!' said the deck-beams savagely, as the upward heave of the sea made the frames try to open. 'Come back to your bearings, you slack-jawed irons!'

'Rigidity! Rigidity! Rigidity!' thumped the engines. 'Absolute, unvarying rigidity – rigidity!'

'You see!' whined the rivets in chorus. 'No two of you will ever pull alike, and – and you blame it all on us. We only know how to go through a plate and bite down on both sides so that it can't, and mustn't, and shan't move.'

'I've got one-fraction of an inch play, at any rate,' said the garboard-strake, triumphantly. So he had, and all the bottom of the ship felt the easier for it.

'Then we're no good,' sobbed the bottom rivets. 'We were ordered – we were ordered – never to give; and we've given, and the sea will come in, and we'll all go to the bottom together! First we're blamed for everything unpleasant, and now we haven't the consolation of having done our work.'

'Don't say I told you,' whispered the Steam consolingly; 'but, between you and me and the last cloud I came from, it was bound to happen sooner or later. You *had* to give a fraction, and you've given without knowing it. Now, hold on, as before.'

'What's the use?' a few hundred rivets chattered. 'We've given – we've given; and the sooner we confess that we can't keep the ship together, and go off our little heads, the easier it will be. No rivet forged can stand this strain.'

'No one rivet was ever meant to. Share it among you,' the Steam answered.

'The others can have my share. I'm going to pull out,' said a rivet in one of the forward plates.

'If you go, others will follow,' hissed the Steam. 'There's nothing so contagious in a boat as rivets going.

Why, I knew a little chap like you – he was an eighth of an inch fatter, though – on a steamer – to be sure, she was only nine hundred tons, now I come to think of it – in exactly the same place as you are. He pulled out in a bit of a bobble of a sea, not half as bad as this, and he started all his friends on the same butt-strap, and the plates opened like a furnace door, and I had to climb into the nearest fog-bank, while the boat went down.'

'Now that's peculiarly disgraceful,' said the rivet. 'Fatter than me, was he, and in a steamer half our tonnage? Reedy little peg! I blush for the family, sir.' He settled himself more firmly than ever in his place, and the Steam chuckled.

'You see,' he went on, quite gravely, 'a rivet, and especially a rivet in your position, is really the one indispensable part of the ship.'

The Steam did not say that he had whispered the very same thing to every single piece of iron aboard. There is no sense in telling too much truth.

And all that while the little *Dimhula* pitched and chopped, and swung and slewed, and lay down as though she were going to die, and got up as though she had been stung, and threw her nose round and round in circles half a dozen times as she dipped; for the gale was at its worst. It was inky black, in spite of the tearing white froth on the waves, and, to top everything, the rain began to fall in sheets, so that you could not see your hand before your face. This did not make much difference to the ironwork below, but it troubled the foremast a good deal.

'Now it's all finished,' he said dismally. 'The conspiracy is too strong for us. There is nothing left but to – '

'*Hurraar! Brrrraaah! Brmrrp!*' roared the Steam through the foghorn, till the decks quivered. 'Don't be frightened, below. It's only me, just throwing out a few words, in case anyone happens to be rolling round tonight.'

'You don't mean to say there's anyone except *us* on the sea in such weather?' said the funnel in a husky snuffle.

'Scores of 'em,' said the Steam, clearing its throat; '*Rrrrrraaa! Brraaaaa! Prrrrp!* It's a trifle windy up here; and, Great Boilers! how it rains!'

'We're drowning,' said the scuppers. They had been doing nothing else all night, but this steady thrash of rain above them seemed to be the end of the world.

'That's all right. We'll be easier in an hour or two. First the wind and then the rain. Soon you may make sail again! *Grrraaaaaah! Drrrraaaa! Drrrp!* I have a notion that the sea is going down already. If it does you'll learn something about rolling. We've only pitched till now. By the way, aren't you chaps in the hold a little easier than you were?'

There was just as much groaning and straining as ever, but it was not so loud or squeaky in tone; and when the ship quivered she did not jar stiffly, like a poker hit on the floor, but gave with a supple little waggle, like a perfectly balanced golf-club.

'We have made a most amazing discovery,' said the stringers, one after another. 'A discovery that entirely changes the situation. We have found, for the first time in the history of shipbuilding, that the inward pull of the deck-beams and the outward thrust of the frames lock us, as it were, more closely in our places, and enables us to endure a strain which is entirely without parallel in the records of marine architecture.'

The Steam turned a laugh quickly into a roar up the fog-horn. 'What massive intellects you great stringers have,' he said softly, when he had finished.

'We also,' began the deck-beams, 'are discoverers and geniuses. We are of opinion that the support of the hold-pillars materially helps us. We find that we lock up on them when we are subjected to a heavy and singular weight of sea above.'

Here the *Dimbula* shot down a hollow, lying almost on her side – righting at the bottom with a wrench and a spasm.

'In these cases – are you aware of this, Steam? – the plating at the bows, and particularly at the stern – we would also mention the floors beneath us – help *us* to resist any tendency to spring.' The frames spoke, in the solemn, awed voice which people use when they have just come across something entirely new for the very first time.

'I'm only a poor puffy little flutterer,' said the Steam, 'but I have to stand a good deal of pressure in my business. It's all tremendously interesting. Tell us some more. You fellows are so strong.'

'Watch us and you'll see,' said the bow-plates, proudly. 'Ready, behind there! Here's the Father and Mother of Waves coming! Sit tight, rivets all!' A great sluicing comber thundered by, but through the scuffle and confusion the Steam could hear the low, quick cries of the ironwork as the various strains took them – cries like these: 'Easy, now – easy! *Now* push for all your strength! Hold out! Give a fraction! Hold up! Pull in! Shove crossways! Mind the strain at the ends! Grip, now! Bite tight! Let the water get away from under – and there she goes!'

The wave raced off into the darkness, shouting, 'Not bad, that, if it's your first run!' and the drenched and ducked ship throbbed to the beat of the engines inside her. All three cylinders were white with the salt spray that had come down through the engine-room hatch; there was white fur on the canvas-bound steam-pipes, and even the bright-work deep below was speckled and soiled; but the cylinders had learned to make the most of steam that was half water, and were pounding along cheerfully.

'How's the noblest outcome of human ingenuity hitting it?' said the Steam, as he whirled through the engine-room.

'Nothing for nothing in this world of woe,' the cylinders answered, as though they had been working for centuries, 'and precious little for seventy-five pounds' head. We've made two knots this last hour and a quarter! Rather humiliating for eight hundred horse-power, isn't it?'

'Well, it's better than drifting astern, at any rate. You seem rather less – how shall I put it? – stiff in the back than you were.'

'If you'd been hammered as we've been this night, you wouldn't be stiff- iff- iff, either. Theoreti – retri – retti – cally, of course, rigidity is the thing. Purrr – purr – practically, there has to be a little give and take. *We* found that out by working on our sides for five minutes at a stretch – cheh – chh. How's the weather?'

'Sea's going down fast,' said the Steam.

'Good business,' said the high-pressure cylinder. 'Whack her up, boys. They've given us five pounds more steam,' and he began humming the first bars of 'Said the young Obadiah to the old Obadiah', which, as you may have noticed, is a pet tune among engines not built for high speed. Racing-liners with twin-screws sing 'The Turkish Patrol' and the overture to the 'Bronze Horse', and 'Madame Angot', till something goes wrong, and then they render Gounod's 'Funeral March of a Marionette', with variations.

'You'll learn a song of your own some fine day,' said the Steam, as he flew up the fog-horn for one last bellow.

Next day the sky cleared and the sea dropped a little, and the *Dimbula* began to roll from side to side till every inch of iron in her was sick and giddy. But luckily they did not all feel ill at the same time: otherwise she would have opened out like a wet paper box.

The Steam whistled warnings as he went about his business: it is in this short, quick roll and tumble that follows a heavy sea that most of the accidents happen, for then everything thinks that the worst is over and goes off guard. So he orated and chattered till the beams and frames and floors and stringers and things had learned how to lock down and lock up on one another, and endure this new kind of strain.

They found ample time to practise, for they were sixteen days at sea, and it was foul weather till within a hundred miles of New York. The *Dimbula* picked up her pilot, and came in covered with salt and red rust. Her funnel was dirty grey from top to bottom; two boats had been carried away; three copper ventilators looked like hats after a fight with the police; the bridge had a dimple in the middle of it; the house that covered the steam steering-gear was split as with hatchets; mere was a bill for small repairs in the engine-room almost as long as the screw-shaft; the forward cargo-hatch fell into bucket-staves when they raised the iron cross-bars; and the steam-capstan had been badly wrenched on its bed. Altogether, as the skipper said, it was 'a pretty general average'.

'But she's soupled,' he said to Mr Buchanan. 'For all her dead weight she rode like a yacht. Ye mind that last blow off the Banks? I am proud of her, Buck.'

'It's vera good,' said the chief engineer, looking along the dishevelled decks. 'Now, a man judgin' superfeecially would say we were a wreck, but we know otherwise – by experience.'

Naturally everything in the *Dimbula* fairly stiffened with pride, and the foremast and the forward collision-bulkhead, who are pushing creatures, begged the Steam to warn the Port of New York of their arrival. 'Tell those big boats all about us,' they said. 'They seem to take us quite as a matter of course.'

It was a glorious, clear, dead calm morning, and in single file, with less than half a mile between each, their bands playing and their tugboats shouting and waving handkerchiefs, were the *Majestic,* the *Paris,* the *Touraine,* the *Servia,* the *Kaiser Wilhelm II,* and the *Werkendam,* all statelily going out to sea. As the *Dimbula* shifted her helm to give the great boats clear way, the Steam (who knows far too much to mind making an exhibition of himself now and then) shouted:

'Oyez! Oyez! Oyez! Princes, Dukes, and Barons of the High Seas! Know ye by these presents, we are the *Dimbula,* fifteen days nine hours from Liverpool, having crossed the Atlantic with three thousand ton of cargo for the first time in our career! We have not foundered. We are here. '*Eer! 'Eer*! We are not disabled. But we have had a time wholly unparalleled in the annals of ship-building! Our decks were swept! We pitched; we rolled! We thought we were going to die! *Hi! Hi!* But we didn't. We wish to give notice that we have come to New York all the way across the Atlantic, through the worst weather in the world; and we are the *Dimbula!* We are – arr – ha – ha – ha-r-r-r!'

The beautiful line of boats swept by as steadily as the procession of the Seasons. The *Dimbula* heard the *Majestic* say, 'Hmph!' and the *Paris* grunted, 'How!' and the *Touraine* said, 'Oui!' with a little coquettish flicker of steam; and the *Servia* said, 'Haw!' and the *Kaiser* and the *Werkendam,* said, 'Hoch!' Dutch-fashion – and that was absolutely all.

'I did my best,' said the Steam, gravely, 'but I don't think they were much impressed with us, somehow. Do you?'

'It's simply disgusting,' said the bow-plates. 'They might have seen what we've been through. There isn't a ship on the sea that has suffered as we have – is there, now?'

'Well, I wouldn't go so far as that,' said the Steam, 'because I've worked on some of those boats, and sent them through weather quite as bad as the fortnight that we've had, in six days; and some of them are a little over ten thousand tons, I believe. Now I've seen the *Majestic,* for instance, ducked from her bows to her funnel; and I've helped the *Arizona,* I think she was, to back off an iceberg she met with one dark night; and I had to run out of the *Paris's* engine-room, one day, because there was thirty foot of water in it. Of course, I don't deny – ' The Steam shut off suddenly, as a tug-boat, loaded with a political club and a brass band, that had been to see a New York senator off to

Europe, crossed their bows, going to Hoboken. There was a long silence that reached, without a break, from the cut-water to the propeller-blades of the *Dimbula.*

Then a new, big voice said slowly and thickly, as though the owner had just waked up: 'It's my conviction that I have made a fool of myself.'

The Steam knew what had happened at once; for when a ship finds herself all the talking of the separate pieces ceases and melts into one voice, which is the soul of the ship.

'Who are you?' he said, with a laugh.

'I am the *Dimbula,* of course. I've never been anything else except that-and a fool!'

The tug-boat, which was doing its very best to be run down, got away just in time, its band playing clashily and brassily a popular but impolite air:

> In the days of old Rameses – are you on?
> In the days of old Rameses – are you on?
> In the days of old Rameses,
> That story had paresis,
> Are you on – are you on – are you on?

'Well, I'm glad you've found yourself,' said the Steam. 'To tell the truth I was a little tired of talking to all those ribs and stringers. Here's Quarantine. After that we'll go to our wharf and clean up a little, and – next month we'll do it all over again.'

# 9

# *The Maltese Cat*

THEY HAD good reason to be proud, and better reason to be afraid, all twelve of them; for, though they had fought their way, game by game, up the teams entered for the polo tournament, they were meeting the Archangels that afternoon in the final match; and the Archangels' men were playing with half a dozen ponies apiece. As the game was divided into six quarters of eight minutes each, that meant a fresh pony after every halt. The Skidars' team, even supposing there were no accidents, could only supply one pony for every other change; and two to one is heavy odds. Again, as Shiraz, the grey Syrian, pointed out, they were meeting the pink and pick of the polo ponies of Upper India; ponies that had cost from a thousand rupees each, while they themselves were a cheap lot gathered, often from country carts, by their masters who belonged to a poor but honest native infantry regiment.

'Money means pace and weight,' said Shiraz, rubbing his black silk nose dolefully along his neat-fitting boot, 'and by the maxims of the game as I know it – '

'Ah, but we aren't playing the maxims,' said the Maltese Cat. 'We're playing the game, and we've the great advantage of knowing the game. Just think a stride, Shiraz. We've pulled up from bottom to second place in two weeks against all those fellows on the ground here; and that's because we play with our heads as well as with our feet'

'It makes me feel undersized and unhappy all the same,' said Kittiwynk, a mouse-coloured mare with a red browband and the cleanest pair of legs that ever an aged pony owned. 'They've twice our size, these others.'

Kittiwynk looked at the gathering and sighed. The hard, dusty Umballa polo-ground was lined with thousands of soldiers, black and white, not counting hundreds and hundreds of carriages, and drags, and dog-carts, and ladies with brilliant-coloured parasols, and officers in uniform and out of it, and crowds of natives behind them; and orderlies on camels who had halted to watch the game, instead of carrying letters up and down the station, and native horse-dealers running about on thin-eared Biluchi mares, looking for a chance to sell a few first-class polo ponies. Then there were the ponies of thirty teams that had entered for the Upper India Free-for-All Cup – nearly every pony of worth and dignity from Mhow to Peshawar, from Allahabad to Multan; prize ponies, Arabs, Syrian, Barb, country bred, Deccanee, Waziri, and Kabul ponies of every colour and shape and temper that you could imagine. Some of them were in mat-roofed stables close to the polo-ground, but most were under saddle while their masters, who had been defeated in the earlier games, trotted in and out and told each other exactly how the game should be played.

It was a glorious sight, and the come-and-go of the little quick hoofs, and the incessant salutations of ponies that had met before on other polo-grounds or racecourses, were enough to drive a four-footed thing wild.

But the Skidars' team were careful not to know their neighbours, though half the ponies on the ground were anxious to scrape acquaintance with the little fellows that had come from the North, and, so far, had swept the board.

'Let's see,' said a soft, golden-coloured Arab, who had been playing very badly the day before, to the Maltese Cat, 'didn't we meet in Abdul Rahman's stable in Bombay four seasons ago? I won the Paikpattan Cup next season, you may remember.'

'Not me,' said the Maltese Cat politely. 'I was at Malta then, pulling a vegetable cart. I don't race. I play the game.'

'O–oh!' said the Arab, cocking his tail and swaggering off.

'Keep yourselves to yourselves,' said the Maltese Cat to his companions. 'We don't want to rub noses with all those goose-rumped half-breeds of Upper India. When we've won this cup they'll give their shoes to know us.'

'*We* shan't win the cup,' said Shiraz. 'How do you feel?'

'Stale as last night's feed when a muskrat has run over it,' said Polaris, a rather heavy-shouldered grey, and the rest of the team agreed with him.

'The sooner you forget that the better,' said the Maltese Cat cheerfully. 'They've finished tiffin in the big tent. We shall be wanted now. If your saddles are not comfy, kick. If your bits aren't easy, rear, and let the *saises* know whether your boots are tight.'

Each pony had his *sais,* his groom, who lived and ate and slept with the pony, and had betted a great deal more than he could afford on the result of the game. There was no chance of anything going wrong, and, to make sure, each *sais* was shampooing the legs of his pony to the last minute. Behind the *saises* sat as many of the Skidars' regiment as had leave to attend the match – about half the native officers, and a hundred or two dark, black-bearded men with the regimental pipers nervously fingering the big beribboned bagpipes. The Skidars were what they call a Pioneer regiment; and the bagpipes made the national music of half the men. The native officers held bundles of polo-sticks, long cane-handled mallets, and as the grandstand filled after lunch they arranged themselves by ones and twos at different points round the ground, so that if a stick were broken the player would not have for to ride for a new one. An impatient British cavalry band struck up 'If you want to know the time, ask a p'leeceman!' and the two umpires in light dust-coats danced out on two little excited ponies. The four players of the Archangels' team followed, and the sight of their beautiful mounts made Shiraz groan again.

'Wait till we know,' said the Maltese Cat. 'Two of 'em are playing in blinkers, and that means they can't see to get out of the way of their own side, or they *may* shy at the umpires' ponies. They've *all* got white web reins that are sure to stretch or slip!'

'And,' said Kittiwynk, dancing to take the stiffness out of her, 'they carry their whips in their hands instead of on their wrists. Hah!'

'True enough. No man can manage his stick and his reins, and his whip that way,' said the Maltese Cat. 'I've fallen over every square yard of the Malta ground, and *I* ought to know.' He quivered his little flea-bitten withers just to show how satisfied he felt; but his heart was not so light. Ever since he had drifted into India on a troopship, taken, with an old rifle, as part payment for a racing debt, the Maltese Cat had played and preached polo to the Skidars' team on the Skidars' stony polo-ground. Now a polo-pony is like a poet. If he is born with a love for the game he can be made. The Maltese Cat knew that bamboos grew solely in order that polo-balls might be turned from their roots, that grain was given to ponies to keep them in hard condition, and that ponies were shod to prevent them slipping on a turn. But, besides all these things, he knew every trick and device of the finest game of the world, and for two seasons he had been teaching the others all he knew or guessed.

'Remember,' he said for the hundredth time as the riders came up, 'we *must* play together, and you *must* play with your heads. Whatever happens, follow the ball. Who goes out first?'

Kittiwynk, Shiraz, Polaris, and a short high little bay fellow with tremendous hocks and no withers worth speaking of (he was called Corks) were being girthed up, and the soldiers in the background stared with all their eyes.

'I want you men to keep quiet,' said Lutyens, the captain of the team, 'and especially *not* to blow your pipes.'

'Not if we win, Captain Sahib?' asked a piper.

'If we win, you can do what you please,' said Lutyens, with a smile, as he slipped the loop of his stick over his wrist, and wheeled to canter to his place. The Archangels' ponies were a little bit above themselves on account of the many-coloured crowd so close to the ground. Their riders were excellent players, but they were a team of crack players instead of a crack team; and that made all the difference in the world. They honestly meant to play together, but it is very hard for four men, each the best of the team he is picked from, to remember that in polo no brilliancy of hitting or riding makes up for playing alone. Their captain shouted his orders to them by name, and it is a curious thing that if you call his name aloud in public after an Englishman you make him hot and fretty. Lutyens said nothing to his men because it had all been said before. He pulled up Shiraz, for he was playing 'back', to guard the goal. Powell on Polaris was half-back, and Macnamara and Hughes on Corks and Kittiwynk were forwards. The tough bamboo-root ball was put into the middle of the ground one hundred and fifty yards from the ends, and Hughes crossed sticks, heads-up, with the captain of the Archangels, who saw fit to play forward, and that is a place from which you cannot easily control the team. The little click as the cane-shafts met was heard all over the ground, and then Hughes made some sort of quick wrist-stroke that just dribbled the ball a few yards. Kittiwynk knew that stroke of old, and followed as a cat follows a mouse. While the captain of the Archangels was wrenching his pony round Hughes struck with all his strength, and next instant Kittiwynk was away, Corks followed close behind her, their little feet pattering like raindrops on glass.

'Pull out to the left,' said Kittiwynk between her teeth, 'it's coming our way, Corks!'

The back and half-back of the Archangels were tearing down on her just as she was within reach of the ball. Hughes leaned forward with a loose rein, and cut it away to the left almost under Kittiwynk's feet, and it hopped and skipped off to Corks, who saw that, if he were not quick, it would run beyond the boundaries. That long bouncing drive gave the Archangels time to wheel and send three men across the ground to head off Corks. Kittiwynk stayed where she was, for she knew the game. Corks was on the ball half a fraction of a second before the others came up, and Macnamara, with a back-handed stroke, sent it back across the ground to Hughes, who saw the way clear to the

Archangels' goal, and smacked the ball in before anyone quite knew what had happened.

'That's luck,' said Corks, as they changed ends. 'A goal in three minutes for three hits and no riding to speak of.'

'Don't know,' said Polaris. 'We've made 'em angry too soon. Shouldn't wonder if they try to rush us off our feet next time.'

'Keep the ball hanging then,' said Shiraz. 'That wears out every pony that isn't used to it.'

Next time there was no easy galloping across the ground. All the Archangels closed up as one man, but there they stayed, for Corks, Kittiwynk, and Polaris were somewhere on the top of the ball, marking time among the rattling sticks, while Shiraz circled about outside, waiting for a chance.

'*We* can do this all day,' said Polaris, ramming his quarters into the side of another pony. 'Where do you think you're shoving to?'

'I'll – I'll be driven in an *ekka* if I know,' was the gasping reply, 'and I'd give a week's feed to get my blinkers off. I can't see anything.'

'The dust is rather bad. Whew! That was one for my off hock. Where's the ball, Corks?'

'Under my tail. At least a man's looking for it there. This is beautiful. They can't use their sticks, and it's driving 'em wild. Give old blinkers a push and he'll go over!'

'Here, don't touch me! I can't see. I'll – I'll back out, I think,' said the pony in blinkers, who knew that if you can't see all round your head you cannot prop yourself against a shock.

Corks was watching the ball where it lay in the dust close to his near fore with Macnamara's shortened stick tap-tapping it from time to time. Kittiwynk was edging her way out of the scrimmage, whisking her stump of a tail with nervous excitement

'Ho! They've got it,' she snorted. 'Let me out!' and she galloped like a rifle-bullet just behind a tall lanky pony of the Archangels, whose rider was swinging up his stick for a stroke.

'Not today, thank you,' said Hughes, as the blow slid off his raised stick, and Kittiwynk laid her shoulder to the tall pony's quarters, and shoved him aside just as Lutyens on Shiraz sent the ball where it had come from, and the tall pony went skating and slipping away to the left. Kittiwynk, seeing that Polaris had joined Corks in the chase for the ball up the ground, dropped into Polaris's place, and then time was called.

The Skidars' ponies wasted no time in kicking or fuming. They knew each minute's rest meant so much gain, and trotted off to the rails and their *saises,* who began to scrape and blanket and rub them at once.

'Whew!' said Corks, stiffening up to get all the tickle out of the big vulcanite scraper. 'If we were playing pony for pony we'd bend those Archangels double in half an hour. But they'll bring out fresh ones and fresh ones, and fresh ones after that – you see.'

'Who cares?' said Polaris. 'We've drawn first blood. Is my hock swelling?'

'Looks puffy,' said Corks. 'You must have had rather a swipe. Don't let it stiffen. You'll be wanted again in half an hour.'

'What's the game like?' said the Maltese Cat.

'Ground's like your shoe, except where they've put too much water on it,' said Kittiwynk. 'Then it's slippery. Don't play in the centre. There's a bog there. I don't know how their next four are going to behave, but we kept the ball hanging and made 'em lather for nothing. Who goes out? Two Arabs and a couple of countrybreds! That's bad. What a comfort it is to wash your mouth out!'

Kitty was talking with a neck of a leather-covered soda-water bottle between her teeth and trying to look over her withers at the same time. This gave her a very coquettish air.

'What's bad?' said Grey Dawn, giving to the girth and admiring his well-set shoulders.

'You Arabs can't gallop fast enough to keep yourselves warm – that's what Kitty means', said Polaris, limping to show that his hock needed attention. 'Are you playing "back", Grey Dawn?'

'Looks like it,' said Grey Dawn, as Lutyens swung himself up. Powell mounted the Rabbit, a plain bay countrybred much like Corks, but with mulish ears. Macnamara took Faiz Ullah, a handy short-backed little red Arab with a long tail, and Hughes mounted Benami, an old and sullen brown beast, who stood over in front more than a polo pony should.

'Benami looks like business,' said Shiraz. 'How's your temper, Ben?' The old campaigner hobbled off without answering, and the Maltese Cat looked at the new Archangel ponies prancing about on the ground. They were four beautiful blacks, and they saddled big enough and strong enough to eat the Skidars' team and gallop away with the meal inside them.

'Blinkers again,' said the Maltese Cat. 'Good enough!'

'They're chargers – cavalry chargers!' said Kittiwynk indignantly. '*They'll* never see thirteen three again.'

'They've all been fairly measured and they've all got their certificates,' said the Maltese Cat, 'or they wouldn't be here. We must take things as they come along, and keep our eyes on the ball.'

The game began, but this time the Skidars were penned to their own end of the ground, and the watching ponies did not approve of that.

'Faiz Ullah is shirking, as usual,' said Polaris, with a scornful grunt

'Faiz Ullah is eating whip,' said Corks. They could hear the leather-thonged polo quirt lacing the little fellow's well-rounded barrel. Then the Rabbit's shrill neigh came across the ground. 'I can't do all the work,' he cried.

'Play the game, don't talk,' the Maltese Cat whickered; and all the ponies wriggled with excitement, and the soldiers and the grooms gripped the railings and shouted. A black pony with blinkers had singled out old Benami, and was interfering with him in every possible way. They could see Benami shaking his head up and down and flapping his underlip.

'There'll be a fall in a minute,' said Polaris. 'Benami is getting stuffy.'

The game flickered up and down between goal-post and goal-post, and the black ponies were getting more confident as they felt they had the legs of the others. The ball was hit out of a little scrimmage, and Benami and the Rabbit followed it; Faiz Ullah only too glad to be quiet for an instant.

The blinkered black pony came up like a hawk, with two of his own side behind him, and Benami's eye glittered as he raced. The question was which pony should make way for the other; each rider was perfectly willing to risk a fall in a good cause. The black who had been driven nearly crazy by his blinkers trusted to his weight and his temper, but Benami knew how to apply his weight and how to keep his temper. They met, and there was a cloud of dust. The black was lying on his side with all the breath knocked out of his body. The Rabbit was a hundred yards up the ground with the ball, and Benami was sitting down. He had slid nearly ten yards, but he had had his revenge, and sat cracking his nostrils till the black pony rose.

'That's what you get for interfering. Do you want any more?' said Benami, and he plunged into the game. Nothing was done because Faiz Ullah would not gallop, though Macnamara beat him whenever he could spare a second. The fall of the black pony had impressed his companions tremendously, and so the Archangels could not profit by Faiz Ullah's bad behaviour.

But as the Maltese Cat said, when time was called and the four came back blowing and dripping, Faiz Ullah ought to have been kicked all round Umballa. If he did not behave better next time, the Maltese Cat promised to pull out his Arab tail by the root and eat it.

There was no time to talk, for the third four were ordered out.

The third quarter of a game is generally the hottest, for each side thinks that the others must be pumped; and most of the winning play in a game is made about that time.

Lutyens took over the Maltese Cat with a pat and a hug, for Lutyens valued him more than anything else in the world. Powell had Shikast, a little grey rat with no pedigree and no manners outside polo; Macnamara mounted Bamboo, the largest of the team, and Hughes took Who's Who, *alias* The Animal. He was supposed to have Australian blood in his veins, but he looked like a clothes horse, and you could whack him on the legs with an iron crow-bar without hurting him.

They went out to meet the very flower of the Archangels' team, and when Who's Who saw their elegantly booted legs and their beautiful satiny skins he grinned a grin through his light, well-worn bridle.

'My word!' said Who's Who. 'We must give 'em a little football. Those gentlemen need a rubbing down.'

'No biting,' said the Maltese Cat warningly, for once or twice in his career Who's Who had been known to forget himself in that way.

'Who said anything about biting? I'm not playing tiddlywinks. I'm playing the game.'

The Archangels came down like a wolf on the fold, for they were tired of football and they wanted polo. They got it more and more. Just after the game began, Lutyens hit a ball that was coming towards him rapidly, and it rose in the air, as a ball sometimes will, with the whirr of a frightened partridge. Shikast heard, but could not see it for the minute, though he looked everywhere and up into the air as the

Maltese Cat had taught him. When he saw it ahead and overhead, he went forward with Powell as fast as he could put foot to ground. It was then that Powell, a quiet and level-headed man as a rule, became inspired and played a stroke that sometimes comes off successfully on a quiet afternoon of long practice. He took his stick in both hands, and standing up in his stirrups, swiped at the ball in the air, Munipore fashion. There was one second of paralysed astonishment, and then all four sides of the ground went up in a yell of applause and delight as the ball flew true (you could see the amazed Archangels ducking in their saddles to get out of the line of flight, and looking at it with open mouths), and the regimental pipes of the Skidars squealed from the railings as long as the piper had breath.

Shikast heard the stroke; but he heard the head of the stick fly off at the same time. Nine hundred and ninety-nine ponies out of a thousand would have gone tearing on after the ball with a useless player pulling at their heads, but Powell knew him, and he knew Powell; and the instant he felt Powell's right leg shift a trifle on the saddle-flap he headed to the boundary, where a native officer was frantically waving a new stick. Before the shouts had ended Powell was armed again.

Once before in his life the Maltese Cat had heard that very same stroke played off his own back, and had profited by the confusion it made. This time he acted on experience, and leaving Bamboo to guard the goal in case of accidents, came through the others like a flash, head and tail low, Lutyens standing up to ease him – swept on and on before the other side knew what was the matter, and nearly pitched on his head between the Archangels' goalpost as Lutyens tipped the ball in after a straight scurry of a hundred and fifty yards. If there was one thing more than another upon which the Maltese Cat prided himself it was on this quick, streaking kind of run half across the ground. He did not believe in taking balls round the field unless you were clearly overmatched. After this they gave the Archangels five minutes' football, and an expensive fast pony hates football because it rumples his temper.

Who's Who showed himself even better than Polaris in this game. He did not permit any wriggling away, but bored joyfully into the scrimmage as if he had his nose in a feed-box, and were looking for something nice. Little Shikast jumped on the ball the minute it got clear, and every time an Archangel pony followed it he found Shikast standing over it asking what was the matter.

'If we can live through this quarter,' said the Maltese Cat, 'I shan't care. Don't take it out of yourselves. Let them do the lathering.'

So the ponies, as their riders explained afterwards, 'shut up'. The Archangels kept them tied fast in front of their goal, but it cost the Archangels' ponies all that was left of their tempers; and ponies began to kick, and men began to repeat compliments, and they chopped at the legs of Who's Who, and he set his teeth and stayed where he was, and the dust stood up like a tree over the scrimmage till that hot quarter ended.

They found the ponies very excited and confident when they went to their *saises,* and the Maltese Cat had to warn them that the worst of the game was coming.

'Now *we* are all going in for the second time,' said he, 'and *they* are trotting out fresh ponies. You'll think you can gallop, but you'll find you can't; and then you'll be sorry.'

'But two goals to nothing is a halter-long lead,' said Kittiwynk prancing.

'How long does it take to get a goal?' the Maltese Cat answered. 'For pity's sake, don't run away with the notion that the game is half-won just because we happen to be in luck now. They'll ride you into the grandstand if they can; you must *not* give 'em a chance. Follow the ball'

'Football, as usual?' said Polaris. 'My hock's half as big as a nose-bag.'

'Don't let them have a look at the ball if you can help it. Now leave me alone. I must get all the rest I can before the last quarter.'

He hung down his head and let all his muscles go slack; Shikast, Bamboo, and Who's Who copying his example.

'Better not watch the game,' he said. 'We aren't playing, and we shall only take it out of ourselves if we grow anxious. Look at the ground and pretend it's fly-time.'

They did their best, but it was hard advice to follow. The hoofs were drumming and the sticks were rattling all up and down the ground, and yells of applause from the English troops told that the Archangels were pressing the Skidars hard. The native soldiers behind the ponies groaned and grunted, and said things in undertones, and presently they heard a long-drawn shout and a clatter of hurrahs!

'One to the Archangels,' said Shikast, without raising his head. 'Time's nearly up. Oh, my sire and dam!'

'Faiz Ullah,' said the Maltese Cat, 'if you don't play to the last nail in your shoes this time, I'll kick you on the ground before all the other ponies.'

'I'll do my best when my time comes,' said the little Arab sturdily.

The *saises* looked at each other gravely as they rubbed their ponies' legs. This was the first time when long purses began to tell, and everybody knew it. Kittiwynk and the others came back with the sweat dripping over their hoofs and their tails telling sad stories.

'They're better than we are,' said Shiraz. 'I knew how it would be.'

'Shut your big head,' said the Maltese Cat; 'we've one goal to the good yet.'

'Yes, but it's two Arabs and two countrybreds to play now,' said Corks. 'Faiz Ullah, remember!' He spoke in a biting voice.

As Lutyens mounted Grey Dawn he looked at his men, and they did not look pretty. They were covered with dust and sweat in streaks. Their yellow boots were almost black, their wrists were red and lumpy, and their eyes seemed two inches deep in their heads, but the expression in the eyes was satisfactory.

'Did you take anything at tiffin?' said Lutyens, and the team shook their heads. They were too dry to talk.

'All right. The Archangels did. They are worse pumped than we are.'

'They've got the better ponies,' said Powell. 'I shan't be sorry when this business is over.'

That fifth quarter was a sad one in every way. Faiz Ullah played like a little red demon; and the Rabbit seemed to be everywhere at once, and Benami rode straight at anything and everything that came in his way, while the umpires on their ponies wheeled like gulls outside the shifting game. But the Archangels had the better mounts – they had kept their racers till late in the game – and never allowed the Skidars to play football. They hit the ball up and down the width of the ground till Benami and the rest were outpaced. Then they went forward, and time and again Lutyens and Grey Dawn were just, and only just, able to send the ball away with a long splitting backhander. Grey Dawn forgot that he was an Arab; and turned from grey to blue as he galloped. Indeed, he forgot too well, for he did not keep his eyes on the ground as an Arab should, but stuck out his nose and scuttled for the dear honour of the game. They had watered the ground once or twice between the quarters, and a careless waterman had emptied the last of his skinful all in one place near the Skidars' goal. It was close to the end of play, and for the tenth time Grey Dawn was bolting after a ball when his near hind foot slipped on the greasy mud and he rolled over and over, pitching Lutyens just clear of the goalpost; and the triumphant Archangels made their goal. Then time was called – two goals all; but Lutyens had to be helped up, and Grey Dawn rose with his near hind leg strained somewhere.

'What's the damage?' said Powell, his arm round Lutyens.

'Collar-bone, of course,' said Lutyens between his teeth. It was the third time he had broken it in two years, and it hurt him.

Powell and the others whistled. 'Game's up,' said Hughes.

'Hold on. We've five good minutes yet, and it isn't my right hand,' said Lutyens. 'We'll stick it out.'

'I say,' said the captain of the Archangels, trotting up. 'Are you hurt, Lutyens? We'll wait if you care to put in a substitute. I wish –I mean – the fact is, you fellows deserve this game if any team does. Wish we could give you a man or some of our ponies – or something.'

'You're awfully good, but we'll play it to a finish, I think.

The captain of the Archangels stared for a little. 'That's not half bad,' he said, and went back to his own side, while Lutyens borrowed a scarf from one of his native officers and made a sling of it. Then an Archangel galloped up with a big bath-sponge and advised Lutyens to put it under his arm-pit to ease his shoulder, and between them they tied up his left arm scientifically, and one of the native officers leaped forward with four long glasses that fizzed and bubbled.

The team looked at Lutyens piteously, and he nodded. It was the last quarter, and nothing would matter after that. They drank out the dark golden drink, and wiped their moustaches, and things looked more hopeful.'

The Maltese Cat had put his nose into the front of Lutyens' shirt, and was trying to say how sorry he was.

'He knows,' said Lutyens, proudly. 'The beggar knows. I've played him without a bridle before now – for fun.'

'It's no fun now,' said Powell. 'But we haven't a decent substitute.'

'No,' said Lutyens. 'It's the last quarter, and we've got to make our goal and win. I'll trust the Cat.'

'If you fall this time you'll suffer a little,' said Macnamara.

'I'll trust the Cat,' said Lutyens.

'You hear that?' said the Maltese Cat proudly to the others. 'It's worth while playing polo for ten years to have that said of you. Now then, my sons, come along. We'll kick up a little bit, just to show the Archangels *this* team haven't suffered.'

And, sure enough, as they went on to the ground the Maltese Cat, after satisfying himself that Lutyens was home in the saddle, kicked out three or four times, and Lutyens laughed. The reins were caught up anyhow in the tips of his strapped hand, and he never pretended to rely on them. He knew the Cat would answer to the least pressure of the leg, and by way of showing off – for his shoulder hurt him very much – he bent the little fellow in a close figure-of-eight in and out between the goalposts. There was a roar from the native officers and men, who dearly loved a piece of *dugabashi* (horse-trick work), as they called it, and the pipes very quietly and scornfully droned out the first bars of a common bazaar-tune called 'Freshly Fresh and Newly New', just as a warning to the other regiments that the Skidars were fit. All the natives laughed.

'And now,' said the Cat, as they took their place, 'remember that this is the last quarter, and follow the ball!'

'Don't need to be told,' said Who's Who.

'Let me go on. All those people on all four sides will begin to crowd in – just as they did at Malta. You'll hear people calling out, and moving forward and being pushed back, and that is going to make the Archangel ponies very unhappy. But if a ball is struck to the boundary, you go after it, and let the people get out of your way. I went over the pole of a four-in-hand once, and picked a game out of the dust by it. Back me up when I run, and follow the ball.'

There was a sort of an all-round sound of sympathy and wonder as the last quarter opened, and then there began exactly what the Maltese Cat had foreseen. People crowded in close to the boundaries, and the Archangels' ponies kept looking sideways at the narrowing space. If you know how a man feels to be cramped at tennis – not because he wants to run out of the court, but because he likes to know that he can at a pinch – you will guess how ponies must feel when they are playing in a box of human beings.

'I'll bend some of those men if I can get away,' said Who's Who, as he rocketed behind the ball; and Bamboo nodded without speaking. They were playing the last ounce in them, and the Maltese Cat had left the goal undefended to join them. Lutyens gave him every order that he could to bring him back, but this was the first time in his career that the little wise grey had ever played polo on his own responsibility, and he was going to make the most of it.

'What are you doing here?' said Hughes, as the Cat crossed in front of him and rode off an Archangel.

'The Cat's in charge – mind the goal!' shouted Lutyens, and bowing forward hit the ball full, and followed on, forcing the Archangels towards their own goal.

'No football,' said the Cat. 'Keep the ball by the boundaries and cramp 'em. Play open order and drive 'em to the boundaries.'

Across and across the ground in big diagonals flew the ball, and whenever it came to a flying rush and a stroke close to the boundaries the Archangel ponies moved stiffly. They did not care to go headlong at a wall of men and carriages, though if the ground had been open they could have turned on a sixpence.

'Wriggle her up the sides,' said the Cat. 'Keep her close to the crowd. They hate the carriages. Shikast, keep her up this side.'

Shikast with Powell lay left and right behind the uneasy scuffle of an open scrimmage, and every time the ball was hit away Shikast galloped on it at such an angle that Powell was forced to hit it towards the boundary; and when the crowd had been driven away from that side, Lutyens would send the ball over to the other, and Shikast would slide desperately after it till his friends came down to help. It was billiards, and no football, this time – billiards in a corner pocket; and the cues were not well chalked.

'If they get us out in the middle of the ground they'll walk away from us. Dribble her along the sides,' cried the Cat.

So they dribbled all along the boundary, where a pony could not come on their right-hand side; and the Archangels were furious, and the umpires had to neglect the game to shout at the people to get back, and several blundering mounted policemen tried to restore order, all close to the scrimmage, and the nerves of the Archangels' ponies stretched and broke like cobwebs.

Five or six times an Archangel hit the ball up into the middle of the ground, and each time the watchful Shikast gave Powell his chance to send it back, and after each return, when the dust had settled, men could see that the Skidars had gained a few yards.

Every now and again there were shouts of ' 'Side! Off side!' from the spectators; but the teams were too busy to care, and the umpires had all they could do to keep their maddened ponies clear of the scuffle.

At last Lutyens missed a short easy stroke, and the Skidars had to fly back helter-skelter to protect their own goal, Shikast leading. Powell stopped the ball with a backhander when it was not fifty yards from the goalposts, and Shikast spun round with a wrench that nearly hoisted Powell out of his saddle.

'Now's our last chance,' said the Cat, wheeling like a cockchafer on a pin. 'We've got to ride it out. Come along.'

Lutyens felt the little chap take a deep breath, and, as it were, crouch under his rider. The ball was hopping towards the right-hand boundary, an Archangel riding for it with both spurs and a whip; but neither spur nor whip would make his pony stretch himself as he neared the crowd. The Maltese Cat glided under his very nose, picking up his hind legs sharp, for there was not a foot to spare between his quarters and the other pony's bit. It was as neat an exhibition as fancy figure-skating. Lutyens hit with all the strength he had left, but the stick slipped a little in his hand, and the ball flew off to the left instead of keeping close to the boundary. Who's Who was far across the ground, thinking hard as he galloped. He repeated, stride for stride, the Cat's manoeuvres with another Archangel pony, nipping the ball away from under his bridle, and clearing his opponent by half a fraction of an inch, for Who's Who was clumsy behind. Then he drove away towards the right as the Maltese Cat came up from the left; and Bamboo held a middle course exactly between them. The three were making a sort of Government-broad-arrow-shaped attack; and there was only the Archangels' back to guard the goal; but immediately behind them were three Archangels racing all they knew, and mixed up with them was Powell, sending Shikast along on what he felt was their last hope. It takes a very good man to stand up to the rush of seven crazy ponies in the last quarters of a cup game, when men are riding with their necks for sale, and the ponies are delirious. The Archangels' back missed his stroke, and pulled aside just in time to let the rush go by. Bamboo and Who's Who shortened stride to give the Maltese Cat room, and Lutyens got the goal with a clean, smooth, smacking stroke that was heard all over the field. But there was no stopping the ponies. They poured through the goalposts in one mixed mob, winners and losers together, for the pace had been terrific. The Maltese Cat knew by experience what would happen, and, to save Lutyens, turned to the right with one last effort that strained a back-sinew beyond hope of repair. As he did so he heard the right-hand goal-post crack as a pony cannoned into it – crack, splinter, and fall like a mast. It had been sawed three parts through in case of accidents, but it upset the pony nevertheless, and he blundered into another, who blundered into the left-hand post, and then there was confusion and dust and wood. Bamboo was lying on the ground, seeing stars; an Archangel pony rolled beside him, breathless and angry; Shikast had sat down dog-fashion to avoid falling over the others, and was sliding along on his little bobtail in a cloud of dust; and Powell was sitting on the ground, hammering with his stick and trying to cheer. All the others were shouting at the top of what was left of their voices, and the men who had been split were shouting too. As soon as the people saw no one was hurt, ten thousand native and English shouted and clapped and yelled, and before anyone could stop them the pipers of the Skidars broke on to the ground, with all the native officers and men behind them, and marched up and down, playing a wild northern tune called 'Zakhme Bagãn', and through the insolent blaring of the pipes and the high-pitched native yells you could hear the Archangels' band hammering, 'For they are all jolly good fellows', and then reproachfully to the losing team, 'Ooh, Kafoozalum! Kafoozalum! Kafoozalum!'

Besides all these things and many more, there was a Commander-in-Chief, and an Inspector-General of Cavalry, and the principal veterinary officer in all India, standing on the top of a regimental coach, yelling like schoolboys; and brigadiers and colonels and commissioners, and hundreds of pretty ladies joined the chorus. But the Maltese Cat stood with his head down, wondering how many legs were left to him; and Lutyens watched the men and ponies pick themselves out of the wreck of the two goalposts, and he patted the Cat very tenderly.

'I say,' said the captain of the Archangels, spitting a pebble out of his mouth, 'will you take three thousand for that pony – as he stands?'

'No, thank you. I've an idea he's saved my life,' said Lutyens, getting off and lying down at full length. Both teams were on the ground too, waving their boots in the air, and coughing and drawing deep breaths, as the *saises* ran up to take away the ponies, and an officious water-carrier sprinkled the players with dirty water till they sat up.

'My Aunt!' said Powell, rubbing his back and looking at the stumps of the goalposts, 'that was a game!'

They played it over again, every stroke of it, that night at the big dinner, when the Free-for-All Cup was filled and passed down the table, and emptied and filled again, and everybody made most eloquent speeches. About two in the morning, when there might have been some singing, a wise little, plain little, grey little head looked in through the open door.

'Hurrah! Bring him in,' said the Archangels; and his *sais,* who was very happy indeed, patted the Maltese Cat on the flank, and he limped in to the blaze of light and the glittering uniforms, looking for Lutyens. He was used to messes, and men's bedrooms, and places where ponies are not usually encouraged, and in his youth had jumped on and off a mess-table for a bet. So he behaved himself very politely, and ate bread dipped in salt, and was petted all round the table, moving gingerly; and they drank his health, because he had done more to win the Cup than any man or horse on the ground.

That was glory and honour enough for the rest of his days, and the Maltese Cat did not complain much when his veterinary surgeon said that he would be no good for polo any more. When Lutyens married, his wife did not allow him to play, so he was forced to be an umpire; and his pony on these occasions was a flea-bitten grey with a neat polo-tail, lame all round, but desperately quick on his feet, and, as everybody knew, Past Pluperfect Prestissimo Player of the Game.

## KASPAR'S SONG IN 'VARDA'

*(from the Swedish of Stagnelius)*

Eyes aloft, over dangerous places,
The children follow where Psyche flies,
And, in the sweat of their upturned faces,
Slash with a net at the empty skies.

So it goes they fall amid brambles,
And sting their toes on the nettle-tops,
Till after a thousand scratches and scrambles
They wipe their brows, and the hunting stops.

Then to quiet them comes their father
And stills the riot of pain and grief,
Saying, 'Little ones, go and gather
Out of my garden a cabbage leaf.

'You will find on it whorls and clots of
Dull grey eggs that, properly fed,
Turn, by way of the worm, to lots of
Radiant Psyches raised from the dead.'

'Heaven is beautiful, Earth is ugly,'
The three-dimensioned preacher saith,
So we must not look where the snail and the slug lie
For Psyche's birth . . . And that is our death!

# 10
# *'Wireless'*

'It's a funny thing, this Marconi business, isn't it?' said Mr Shaynor, coughing heavily. 'Nothing seems to make any difference, by what they tell me – storms, hills, or anything; but if that's true we shall know before morning.'

'Of course it's true,' I answered, stepping behind the counter. 'Where's old Mr Cashell?'

'He's had to go to bed on account of his influenza. He said you'd very likely drop in.'

'Where's his nephew?'

'Inside, getting the things ready. He told me that the last time they experimented they put the pole on the roof of one of the big hotels here, and the batteries electrified all the water-supply, and' – he giggled – 'the ladies got shocks when they took their baths.'

'I never heard of that'

'The hotel wouldn't exactly advertise it, would it? Just now, by what Mr Cashell tells me, they're trying to signal from here to Poole, and they're using stronger batteries than ever. But, you see, he being the guvnor's nephew and all that (and it will be in the papers too), it doesn't matter how they electrify things in this house. Are you going to watch?'

'Very much. I've never seen this game. Aren't you going to bed?'

'We don't close till ten on Saturdays. There's a good deal of influenza in town, too, and there'll be a dozen prescriptions coming in before morning. I generally sleep in the chair here. It's warmer than jumping out of bed every time. Bitter cold, isn't it?'

'Freezing hard. I'm sorry your cough's worse.'

'Thank you. I don't mind cold so much. It's this wind that fair cuts me to pieces.' He coughed again hard and hackingly, as an old lady came in for ammoniated quinine. 'We've just run out of it in bottles, madam,' said Mr Shaynor, returning to the professional tone, 'but if you will wait two minutes, I'll make it up for you, madam.'

I had used the shop for some time, and my acquaintance with the proprietor had ripened into friendship. It was Mr Cashell who revealed to me the purpose and power of Apothecaries' Hall what time a fellow-chemist had made an error in a prescription of mine, had lied to cover his sloth, and when error and lie were brought home to him had written vain letters.

'A disgrace to our profession,' said the thin, mild-eyed man, hotly, after studying the evidence. 'You couldn't do a better service to the profession than report him to Apothecaries' Hall.'

I did so, not knowing what djinns I should evoke; and the result was such an apology as one might make who had spent a night on the rack. I conceived great respect for Apothecaries' Hall, and esteem for Mr Cashell, a zealous craftsman who magnified his calling. Until Mr Shaynor came down from the North his assistants had by no means agreed with Mr Cashell. 'They forget,' said he, 'that, first and foremost, the compounder is a medicine-man. On him depends the physician's reputation. He holds it literally in the hollow of his hand, sir.'

Mr Shaynor's manners had not, perhaps, the polish of the grocery and Italian warehouse next door, but he knew and loved his dispensary work in every detail. For relaxation he seemed to go no farther afield than the romance of drugs – their discovery, preparation, packing, and export – but it led him to the ends of the earth, and on this subject, and the Pharmaceutical Formulary, and Nicholas Culpepper, most confident of physicians, we met.

Little by little I grew to know something of his beginnings and his hopes – of his mother, who had been a schoolteacher in one of the northern counties, and of his red-headed father, a small job-master at Kirby Moors, who died when he was a child; of the examinations he had passed and of their exceeding and increasing difficulty; of his dreams of a shop in London; of his hate for the price-cutting Cooperative stores; and, most interesting, of his mental attitude towards customers.

'There's a way you get into,' he told me, 'of serving them carefully, and I hope, politely, without stopping your own thinking. I've been reading Christie's *New Commercial Plants* all this autumn, and that needs keeping your mind on it, I can tell you. So long as it isn't a prescription, of course, I can carry as much as half a page of Christie in my head, and at the same time I could sell out all that window twice over, and not a penny wrong at the end. As to prescriptions, I think I could make up the general run of 'em in my sleep, almost.'

For reasons of my own, I was deeply interested in Marconi experiments at their outset in England; and it was of a piece with Mr Cashell's unvarying thoughtfulness that, when his nephew the electrician appropriated the house for a long-range installation, he should, as I have said, invite me to see the result.

The old lady went away with her medicine, and Mr Shaynor and I stamped on the tiled floor behind the counter to keep ourselves warm. The shop, by the light of the many electrics, looked like a Paris-diamond mine, for Mr Cashell believed in all the ritual of his craft. Three superb glass jars – red, green, and blue – of the sort that led Rosamund to parting with her shoes – blazed in the broad plate-glass windows, and there was a confused smell of orris, Kodak films, vulcanite, tooth-powder, sachets, and almond-cream in the air. Mr Shaynor fed the dispensary stove, and we sucked cayenne-pepper jujubes and menthol lozenges. The brutal east wind had cleared the streets, and the few passers-by were muffled to their puckered eyes, in the Italian warehouse next door some gay feathered birds and game, hung upon hooks, sagged to the wind across the left edge of our window-frame.

'They ought to take these poultry in – all knocked about like that,' said Mr Shaynor. 'Doesn't it make you feel fair perishing? See that old hare! The wind's nearly blowing the fur off him.'

I saw the belly-fur of the dead beast blown apart in ridges and streaks as the wind caught it, showing bluish skin underneath. 'Bitter cold,' said Mr Shaynor, shuddering. 'Fancy going out on a night like this! Oh, here's young Mr Cashell.'

The door of the inner office behind the dispensary opened, and an energetic, spade-bearded man stepped forth, rubbing his hands.

'I want a bit of tin-foil, Shaynor,' he said. 'Good-evening. My uncle told me you might be coming.' This to me, as I began the first of a hundred questions.

'I've everything in order,' he replied. 'We're only waiting until Poole calls us up. Excuse me a minute. You can come in whenever you like – but I'd better be with the instruments. Give me that tin-foil. Thanks.'

While we were talking, a girl – evidently no customer – had come into the shop, and the face and bearing of Mr Shaynor changed. She leaned confidently across the counter.

'But I can't,' I heard him whisper uneasily – the flush on his cheek was dull red, and his eyes shone like a drugged moth's. 'I can't. I tell you I'm alone in the place.'

'No, you aren't. Who's *that?* Let him look after it for half an hour. A brisk walk will do you good. Ah, come now, John.'

'But he isn't – '

'I don't care. I want you to; we'll only go round by St Agnes. If you don't – '

He crossed to where I stood in the shadow of the dispensary counter, and began some sort of broken apology about a lady-friend.

'Yes,' she interrupted. 'You take the shop for half an hour – to oblige *me,* won't you?'

She had a singularly rich and promising voice that well matched her outline.

'All right,' I said. 'I'll do it – but you'd better wrap yourself up, Mr Shaynor.'

'Oh, a brisk walk ought to help me. We're only going round by the church.' I heard him cough grievously as they went out together.

I refilled the stove, and, after reckless expenditure of Mr Cashell's coal, drove some warmth into the shop. I explored many of the glass-knobbed drawers that lined the walls, tasted some disconcerting drugs, and, by the aid of a few cardamoms, ground ginger, chloric-ether, and dilute alcohol, manufactured a new and wildish drink, of which I bore a glassful to young Mr Cashell, busy in the back office. He laughed shortly when I told him that Mr Shaynor had stepped out – but a frail coil of wire held all his attention, and he had no word for me bewildered among the batteries and rods. The noise of the sea on the beach began to make itself heard as the traffic in the street ceased. Then briefly, but very lucidly, he gave me the names and uses of the mechanism that crowded the tables and the floor.

'When do you expect to get the message from Poole?' I demanded, sipping my liquor out of a graduated glass.

'About midnight, if everything is in order. We've got our installation-pole fixed to the roof of the house. I shouldn't advise you to turn on a tap or anything tonight. We've connected up with the plumbing, and all the water will be electrified.' He repeated to me the history of the agitated ladies at the hotel at the time of the first installation.

'But what *is* it?' I asked. 'Electricity is out of my beat altogether.'

'Ah, if you knew *that* you'd know something nobody knows. It's just It – what we call Electricity, but the magic – the manifestations – the Hertzian waves – are all revealed by *this*. The coherer, we call it.'

He picked up a glass tube not much thicker than a thermometer, in which, almost touching, were two tiny silver plugs, and between them an infinitesimal pinch of metallic dust. 'That's all,' he said, proudly, as though himself responsible for the wonder. 'That is the thing that will reveal to us the Powers whatever the Powers may be – at work – through space – a long distance away.'

Just then Mr Shaynor returned alone and stood coughing his heart out on the mat.

'Serves you right for being such a fool,' said young Mr Cashell, as annoyed as myself at the interruption. 'Never mind – we've all the night before us to see wonders.'

Shaynor clutched the counter, his handkerchief to his lips. When he brought it away I saw two bright red stains.

'I – I've got a bit of a rasped throat from smoking cigarettes,' he panted. 'I think I'll try a cubeb.'

'Better take some of this. I've been compounding while you've been away.' I handed him the brew.

' 'Twon't make me drunk, will it? I'm almost a teetotaller. My word! That's grateful and comforting.'

He set down the empty glass to cough afresh.

'Brr! But it was cold out there! I shouldn't care to be lying in my grave a night like this. Don't *you* ever have a sore throat from smoking?' He pocketed the handkerchief after a furtive peep.

'Oh, yes, sometimes,' I replied, wondering, while I spoke, into what agonies of terror I should fall if ever I saw those bright-red danger-signals under my nose. Young Mr Cashell among the batteries coughed slightly to show that he was quite ready to continue his scientific explanations, but I was thinking still of the girl with the rich voice and the significantly cut mouth, at whose command I had taken charge of the shop. It flashed across me that she distantly resembled the seductive shape on a gold-framed toilet-water advertisement whose charms were unholily heightened by the glare from the red bottle in the window. Turning to make sure, I saw Mr Shaynor's eyes bent in the same direction, and by instinct recognised that the flamboyant thing was to him a shrine. 'What do you take for your – cough?' I asked.

'Well, I'm the wrong side of the counter to believe much in patent medicines. But there are asthma cigarettes and there are pastilles. To tell you the truth, if you don't object to the smell, which is very like incense, I believe, though I'm not a Roman Catholic, Blaudett's Cathedral Pastilles relieve me as much as anything.'

'Let's try.' I had never raided a chemist's shop before, so I was thorough. We unearthed the pastilles – brown, gummy cones of benzoin – and set them alight under the toilet-water advertisement, where they fumed in thin blue spirals.

'Of course,' said Mr Shaynor, to my question, 'what one uses in the shop for one's self comes out of one's pocket. Why, stocktaking in our business is nearly the same as with jewellers – and I can't say more than that. But one gets them' – he pointed to the pastille-box – 'at trade-prices.' Evidently the censing of the gay, seven-tinted wench with the teeth was an established ritual which cost something.

'And when do we shut up shop?'

'We stay like this all night. The guv – old Mr Cashell – doesn't believe in locks and shutters as compared with electric light. Besides, it brings trade. I'll just sit here in the chair by the stove and write a letter, if you don't mind. Electricity isn't my prescription.'

The energetic young Mr Cashell snorted within, and Shaynor settled himself up in his chair over which he had thrown a staring red, black, and yellow Austrian jute blanket, rather like a table-cover. I cast about, amid patent-medicine pamphlets, for something to read, but finding little, returned to the manufacture of the new drink. The Italian warehouse took down its game and went to bed. Across the street blank shutters flung back the gaslight in cold smears; the dried pavement seemed to rough up in goose-flesh under the scouring of the savage wind, and we could hear, long ere he passed, the policeman flapping his arms to keep himself warm. Within, the flavours of cardamoms and chloric-ether disputed those of the pastilles and a score of drugs and perfume and soap scents. Our electric lights, set low down in the windows before the tun-bellied Rosamund jars, flung inward three monstrous daubs of red, blue, and green, that broke into kaleidoscopic lights on the facetted knobs of the drug-drawers, the cut-glass scent flagons, and the bulbs of the sparklet bottles. They flushed the white-tiled floor in gorgeous patches; splashed along the nickel-silver counter-rails, and turned the polished mahogany counter-panels to the likeness of intricate grained marbles – slabs of porphyry and malachite. Mr Shaynor unlocked a drawer, and ere he began to write, took out a meagre bundle of letters. From my place by the stove, I could see the scalloped edges of the paper with a flaring monogram in the corner and could even smell the reek of chypre. At each page he turned toward the toilet-water lady of the advertisement and devoured her with over-luminous eyes. He had drawn the Austrian blanket over his shoulders, and among those warring lights he looked more than ever the incarnation of a drugged moth – a tiger-moth as I thought.

He put his letter into an envelope, stamped it with stiff mechanical movements, and dropped it in the drawer. Then I became aware of the silence of a great city asleep – the silence that underlaid the even voice of the breakers along the sea-front – a thick, tingling quiet of warm life stilled down for its appointed time, and unconsciously I moved about the glittering shop as one moves in a sick-room. Young Mr Cashell was adjusting some wire that crackled from time to time with the tense, knuckle-stretching sound of the electric spark. Upstairs, where a door shut and opened swiftly, I could hear his uncle coughing abed.

'Here,' I said, when the drink was properly warmed, 'take some of this, Mr Shaynor.'

He jerked in his chair with a start and a wrench, and held out his hand for the glass. The mixture, of a rich port-wine colour, frothed at the top.

'It looks,' he said, suddenly, 'it looks – those bubbles – like a string of pearls winking at you – rather like the pearls round that young lady's neck.' He turned again to the advertisement where the female in the dove-coloured corset had seen fit to put on all her pearls before she cleaned her teeth.

'Not bad, is it?' I said.

'Eh?'

He rolled his eyes heavily full on me, and, as I stared, I beheld all meaning and consciousness die out of the swiftly dilating pupils. His figure lost its stark rigidity, softened into the chair, and, chin on chest, hands dropped before him, he rested open-eyed, absolutely still.

'I'm afraid I've rather cooked Shaynor's goose,' I said, bearing the fresh drink to young Mr Cashell. 'Perhaps it was the chloric-ether.'

'Oh, he's all right.' The spade-bearded man glanced at him pityingly. 'Consumptives go off in those sort of doses very often. It's exhaustion . . . I don't wonder. I dare say the liquor will do him good. It's grand stuff,' he finished his share appreciatively. 'Well, as I was saying – before he interrupted – about this little coherer. The pinch of dust, you see, is nickel-filings. The Hertzian waves, you see, come out of space from the station that despatches 'em, and all these little particles are attracted together – cohere, we call it – for just so long as the current passes through them. Now, it's important to remember that the current is an induced current. There are a good many kinds of induction – '

'Yes, but what *is* induction?'

'That's rather hard to explain untechnically. But the long and the short of it is that when a current of electricity passes through a wire there's a lot of magnetism present round that wire; and if you put another wire parallel to, and within what we call its magnetic field – why then, the second wire will also become charged with electricity.'

'On its own account?'

'On its own account.'

'Then let's see if I've got it correctly. Miles off, at Poole, or wherever it is – '

'It will be anywhere in ten years.'

'You've got a charged wire – '

'Charged with Hertzian waves which vibrate, say, two hundred and thirty million times a second.' Mr Cashell snaked his forefinger rapidly through the air.

'All right – a charged wire at Poole, giving out these waves into space. Then this wire of yours sticking out into space – on the roof of the house – in some mysterious way gets charged with those waves from Poole – '

'Or anywhere – it only happens to be Poole tonight.'

'And those waves set the coherer at work, just like an ordinary telegraph-office ticker?'

'No! That's where so many people make the mistake. The Hertzian waves wouldn't be strong enough to work a great heavy Morse instrument like ours. They can only just make that dust cohere, and while it coheres (a little while for a dot and a longer while for a dash) the current from this battery – the home battery' – he laid his hand on the thing – 'can get through to the Morse printing-machine to record the dot or dash. Let me make it clearer. Do you know anything about steam?'

'Very little. But go on.'

'Well, the coherer is like a steam-valve. Any child can open a valve and start a steamer's engines, because a turn of the hand lets in the main steam, doesn't it? Now, this home battery here ready to print is the main steam. The coherer is the valve, always ready to be turned on. The Hertzian wave is the child's hand that turns it.'

'I see. That's marvellous.'

'Marvellous, isn't it? And, remember, we're only at the beginning. There's nothing we shan't be able to do in ten years. I want to live – my God, how I want to live, and see it develop!' He looked through the door at Shaynor breathing lightly in his chair. 'Poor beast! And he wants to keep company with Fanny Brand.'

'Fanny *who?"* I said, for the name struck an obscurely familiar chord in my brain – something connected with a stained handkerchief, and the word 'arterial'.

'Fanny Brand – the girl you kept shop for.' He laughed. 'That's all I know about her, and for the life of me I can't see what Shaynor sees in her, or she in him.'

'*Can't* you see what he sees in her?' I insisted.

'Oh, yes, if *that's* what you mean. She's a great, big, fat lump of a girl, and so on. I suppose that's why he's so crazy after her. She isn't his sort. Well, it doesn't matter. My uncle says he's bound to die before the year's out. Your drink's given him a good sleep, at any rate.' Young Mr Cashell could not catch Mr Shaynor's face, which was half turned to the advertisement.

I stoked the stove anew, for the room was growing cold, and lighted another pastille. Mr Shaynor in his chair, never moving, looked through and over me with eyes as wide and lustreless as those of a dead hare.

'Poole's late,' said young Mr Cashell, when I stepped back. 'I'll just send them a call.'

He pressed a key in the semi-darkness, and with a rending crackle there leaped between two brass knobs a spark, streams of sparks, and sparks again.

'Grand, isn't it? *That's* the Power – our unknown Power – kicking and fighting to be let loose,' said young Mr Cashell. 'There she goes – kick – kick – kick into space. I never get over the strangeness of it when I work a sending-machine – waves going into space, you know. T. R. is our call. Poole ought to answer with L. L. L.'

We waited two, three, five minutes. In that silence, of which the boom of the tide was an orderly part, I caught the clear '*kiss – kiss – kiss*' of the halliards on the roof, as they were blown against the installation-pole.

'Poole is not ready. I'll stay here and call you when he is.'

I returned to the shop, and set down my glass on a marble slab with a careless clink. As I did so, Shaynor rose to his feet, his eyes fixed once more on the advertisement, where the young woman bathed in the light from the red jar simpered pinkly over her pearls. His lips moved without cessation. I stepped nearer to listen. 'And threw – and threw – and threw,' he repeated, his face all sharp with some inexplicable agony.

I moved forward astonished. But it was then he found words – delivered roundly and clearly. These –

> And threw warm gules on Madeleine's young breast.

The trouble passed off his countenance, and he returned lightly to his place, rubbing his hands.

It had never occurred to me, though we had many times discussed reading and prize-competitions as a diversion, that Mr Shaynor ever read Keats, or could quote him at all appositely. There was, after all, a certain stained-glass effect of light on the high bosom of the highly-polished picture which might, by stretch of fancy, suggest, as a vile chromo recalls some incomparable canvas, the line he had spoken. Night, my drink, and solitude were evidently turning Mr Shaynor into a poet. He sat down again and wrote swiftly on his villainous note-paper, his lips quivering.

I shut the door into the inner office and moved up behind him. He made no sign that he saw or heard. I looked over his shoulder, and read, amid half-formed words, sentences, and wild scratches –

– Very cold it was. Very cold
The hare – the hare – the hare –
The birds –

He raised his head sharply, and frowned toward the blank shutters of the poulterer's shop where they jutted out against our window. Then one clear line came –

The hare, in spite of fur, was very cold.

The head, moving machine-like, turned right to the advertisement where the Blaudett's Cathedral Pastille reeked abominably. He grunted, and went on –

Incense in a censer –
Before her darling picture framed in gold –
Maiden's picture – angel's portrait –

'Hsh!' said Mr Cashell guardedly from the inner office, as though in the presence of spirits. 'There's something coming through from somewhere; but it isn't Poole.' I heard the crackle of sparks as he depressed the keys of the transmitter. In my own brain, too, something crackled, or it might have been the hair on my head. Then I heard my own voice, in a harsh whisper: 'Mr Cashell, there is something coming through here, too. Leave me alone till I tell you.'

'But I thought you'd come to see this wonderful thing – sir,' indignantly at the end.

'Leave me alone till I tell you. Be quiet.'

I watched –I waited. Under the blue-veined hand – the dry hand of the consumptive – came away clear, without erasure –

> And my weak spirit fails
> To think how the dead must freeze –

he shivered as he wrote –

> Beneath the churchyard mould.

Then he stopped, laid the pen down, and leaned back.

For an instant, that was half an eternity, the shop spun before me in a rainbow-tinted whirl, in and through which my own soul most dispassionately considered my own soul as that fought with an over-mastering fear. Then I smelt the strong smell of cigarettes from Mr Shaynor's clothing, and heard, as though it had been the rending of trumpets, the rattle of his breathing. I was still in my place of observation, much as one would watch a rifle-shot at the butts, half-bent, hands on my knees, and head within a few inches of the black, red, and yellow blanket of his shoulder. I was whispering encouragement, evidently to my other self, sounding sentences, such as men pronounce in dreams.

'If he has read Keats, it proves nothing. If he hasn't – like causes *must* beget like effects. There is no escape from this law. *You* ought to be grateful that you know 'St Agnes' Eve' without the book; because, given the circumstances, such as Fanny Brand, who is the key of the enigma, and approximately represents the latitude and longitude of Fanny Brawne; allowing also for the bright red colour of the arterial blood upon the handkerchief, which was just what you were puzzling over in the shop just now; and counting the effect of the professional environment, here almost perfectly duplicated – the result is logical and inevitable. As inevitable as induction.'

Still, the other half of my soul refused to be comforted. It was cowering in some minute and inadequate corner – at an immense distance.

Hereafter, I found myself one person again, my hands still gripping my knees, and my eyes glued on the page before Mr Shaynor. As dreamers accept and explain the upheaval of landscapes and the resurrection of the dead, with excerpts from the evening hymn or the multiplication-table, so I had accepted the facts, whatever they might be, that I should witness, and had devised a theory, sane and plausible to my mind, that explained them all. Nay, I was even in advance of my facts, walking hurriedly before them, assured that they would fit my theory. And all that I now recall of that epoch-making theory are the lofty words: 'If he has read Keats it's the chloric-ether. If he hasn't, it's the identical bacillus, or Hertzian wave of tuberculosis, *plus* Fanny Brand and the professional status which, in conjunction with the mainstream of subconscious thought common to all mankind, has thrown up temporarily an induced Keats.'

Mr Shaynor returned to his work, erasing and rewriting as before with swiftness. Two or three blank pages he tossed aside. Then he wrote, muttering –

The little smoke of a candle that goes out.

'No,' he muttered. 'Little smoke – little smoke – little smoke. What else?' He thrust his chin forward toward the advertisement, where-under the last of the Blaudett's Cathedral Pastilles fumed in its holder. 'Ah!' Then with relief –

The little smoke that dies in moonlight cold.

Evidently he was snared by the rhymes of his first verse, for he wrote and rewrote 'gold – cold – mould' many times. Again he sought inspiration from the advertisement, and set down, without erasure, the line I had overheard –

And threw warm gules on Madeleine's young breast.

As I remembered the original it is 'fair' – a trite word – instead of 'young', and I found myself nodding approval, though I admitted that the attempt to reproduce 'its little smoke in pallid moonlight died' was a failure.

Followed without a break ten or fifteen lines of bald prose – the naked soul's confession of its physical yearning for its beloved – unclean as we count uncleanliness; unwholesome, but human exceedingly; the raw material, so it seemed to me in that hour and in that place, whence Keats wove the twenty-sixth, seventh, and eighth stanzas of his poem. Shame I had none in overseeing this revelation; and my fear had gone with the smoke of the pastille.

'That's it,' I murmured. 'That's how it's blocked out. Go on! Ink it in, man. Ink it in!'

Mr Shaynor returned to broken verse wherein 'loveliness' was made to rhyme with a desire to look upon 'her empty dress'. He picked up a fold of the gay, soft blanket, spread it over one hand, caressed it with infinite tenderness, thought, muttered, traced some snatches which I could not decipher, shut his eyes drowsily, shook his head, and dropped the stuff. Here I found myself at fault, for I could not then see (as I do now) in what manner a red, black, and yellow Austrian blanket coloured his dreams.

In a few minutes he laid aside his pen, and, chin on hand, considered the shop with thoughtful and intelligent eyes. He threw down the blanket, rose, passed along a line of drug-drawers, and read the names on the labels aloud. Returning, he took from his desk Christie's *New Commercial Plants* and the old Culpepper that I had given him, opened and laid them side by side with a clerky air, all trace of passion gone from his face, read first in one and then in the other, and paused with pen behind his ear.

'What wonder of Heaven's coming now?' I thought.

'Manna – manna – manna,' he said at last, under wrinkled brows. 'That's what I wanted. Good! Now then! Now then! Good! Good! Oh, by God, that's good!' His voice rose and he spoke rightly and fully without a falter –

> Candied apple, quince and plum and gourd,
> And jellies smoother than the creamy curd,
> And lucent syrups tinct with cinnamon,
> Manna and dates in Argosy transferred
> From Fez; and spiced dainties, every one
> From silken Samarkand to cedared Lebanon.

He repeated it once more, using 'blander' for 'smoother' in the second line; then wrote it down without erasure, but this time (my set eyes missed no stroke of any word) he substituted 'soother' for his atrocious second thought, so that it came away under his hand as it is written in the book – as it is written in the book

A wind went shouting down the street, and on the heels of the wind followed a spurt and rattle of rain.

After a smiling pause – and good right had he to smile – he began anew, always tossing the last sheet over his shoulder –

> The sharp rain falling on the window-pane,
> Rattling sleet – the wind-blown sleet.

Then prose: 'It is very cold of mornings when the wind brings rain and sleet with it. I heard the sleet on the window-pane outside, and thought of you, my darling. I am always thinking of you. I wish we could both run away like two lovers into the storm and get that little cottage by the sea which we are always thinking about, my own dear darling. We could sit and watch the sea beneath our windows. It would be a fairyland all of our own – a fairy sea – a fairy sea . . .'

He stopped, raised his head, and listened. The steady drone of the Channel along the seafront that had borne us company so long leaped up a note to the sudden fuller surge that signals the change from ebb to flood. It beat in like the change of step throughout an army – this renewed pulse of the sea – and filled our ears till they, accepting it, marked it no longer.

A fairyland for you and me
Across the foam – beyond . . .
A magic foam, a perilous sea.

He grunted again with effort and bit his underlip. My throat dried, but I dared not gulp to moisten it lest I should break the spell that was drawing him nearer and nearer to the high-water mark but two of the sons of Adam have reached. Remember that in all the millions permitted there are no more than five – five little lines – of which one can say: 'These are the pure Magic. These are the clear Vision. The rest is only poetry.' And Mr Shaynor was playing hot and cold with two of them!

I vowed no unconscious thought of mine should influence the blindfold soul, and pinned myself desperately to the other three, repeating and re-repeating –

A savage spot as holy and enchanted
As e'er beneath a waning moon was haunted
By woman wailing for her demon lover.

But though I believed my brain thus occupied, my every sense hung upon the writing under the dry, bony hand, all brown-fingered with chemicals and cigarette-smoke.

Our windows fronting on the dangerous foam,

(he wrote, after long, irresolute snatches), and then –

Our open casements facing desolate seas
Forlorn – forlorn –

Here again his face grew peaked and anxious with that sense of loss I had first seen when the Power snatched him. But this time the agony was tenfold keener. As I watched it mounted like mercury in the tube. It lighted his face from within till I thought the visibly scourged soul must leap forth naked between his jaws, unable to endure. A drop of sweat trickled from my forehead down my nose and splashed on the back of my hand.

> Our windows facing on the desolate seas
> And pearly foam of magic fairyland –

'Not yet – not yet,' he muttered, 'wait a minute. *Please* wait a minute. I shall get it then –

> Our magic windows fronting on the sea,
> The dangerous foam of desolate seas . . .
> For aye.

*Ouh*, my God!'

From head to heel he shook – shook from the marrow of his bones outwards – then leaped to his feet with raised arms, and slid the chair screeching across the tiled floor where it struck the drawers behind and fell with a jar. Mechanically, I stooped to recover it.

As I rose, Mr Shaynor was stretching and yawning at leisure.

'I've had a bit of a doze,' he said. 'How did I come to knock the chair over? You look rather – '

'The chair startled me,' I answered. 'It was so sudden in this quiet.'

Young Mr Cashell behind his shut door was offendedly silent.

'I suppose I must have been dreaming,' said Mr Shaynor.

'I suppose you must,' I said. 'Talking of dreams – I – I noticed you writing – before – '

He flushed consciously.

'I meant to ask you if you've ever read anything written by a man called Keats.'

'Oh! I haven't much time to read poetry, and I can't say that I remember the name exactly. Is he a popular writer?'

'Middling. I thought you might know him because he's the only poet who was ever a druggist. And he's rather what's called the lover's poet.'

'Indeed. I must dip into him. What did he write about?'

'A lot of things. Here's a sample that may interest you.'

Then and there, carefully, I repeated the verse he had twice spoken and once written not ten minutes ago.

'Ah! Anybody could see he was a druggist from that line about the tinctures and syrups. It's a fine tribute to our profession.'

'I don't know,' said young Mr Cashell, with icy politeness, opening the door one half-inch, 'if you still happen to be interested in our trifling experiments. But, should such be the case – '

I drew him aside, whispering, 'Shaynor seemed going off into some sort of fit when I spoke to you just now. I thought, even at the risk of being rude, it wouldn't do to take you off your instruments just as the call was coming through. Don't you see?'

'Granted – granted as soon as asked,' he said, unbending. 'I *did* think it a shade odd at the time. So that was why he knocked the chair down?'

'I hope I haven't missed anything,' I said.

'I'm afraid I can't say that, but you're just in time for the end of a rather curious performance. You can come in too, Mr Shaynor. Listen, while I read it off.'

The Morse instrument was ticking furiously. Mr Cashell interpreted: ' "*K.K.V. Can make nothing of your signals.*" ' A pause.' "*M.M.V. M.M.V. Signals unintelligible. Purpose anchor Sandown Bay. Examine instruments tomorrow.*" Do you know what that means? It's a couple of men-o'-war working Marconi signals off the Isle of Wight. They are trying to talk to each other. Neither can read the other's messages, but all their messages are being taken in by our receiver here. They've been going on for ever so long. I wish you could have heard it.'

'How wonderful!' I said. 'Do you mean we're overhearing Portsmouth ships trying to talk to each other – that we're eavesdropping across half South England?'

'Just that. Their transmitters are all right, but their receivers are out of order, so they only get a dot here and a dash there. Nothing clear.'

'Why is that?'

'God knows – and Science will know tomorrow. Perhaps the induction is faulty; perhaps the receivers aren't tuned to receive just the number of vibrations per second that the transmitter sends. Only a word here and there. Just enough to tantalise.'

Again the Morse sprang to life.

'That's one of 'em complaining now. Listen: "*Disheartening – most disheartening.*" It's quite pathetic. Have you ever seen a spiritualistic seance? It reminds me of that sometimes – odds and ends of messages coming out of nowhere – a word here and there – no good at all.'

'But mediums are all impostors,' said Mr Shaynor, in the doorway, lighting an asthma-cigarette. 'They only do it for the money they can make. I've seen 'em.'

'Here's Poole, at last – clear as a bell. L.L.L. *Now* we shan't be long.' Mr Cashell rattled the keys merrily. 'Anything you'd like to tell 'em?'

'No, I don't think so,' I said. 'I'll go home and get to bed. I'm feeling a little tired.'

Neither the harps nor the crowns amused, nor the
cherubs' dove-winged races –
Holding hands forlornly the Children wandered beneath
the Dome;
Plucking the radiant robes of the passers-by, and with
pitiful faces
Begging what Princes and Powers refused: 'Ah, please
will you let us go home?'

Over the jewelled floor, nigh weeping, ran to them Mary
the Mother,
Kneeled and caressed and made promise with kisses,
and drew them along to the gateway –
Yea, the all-iron unbribeable Door which Peter must
guard and none other,
Straightway She took the Keys from his keeping, and
opened and freed them straightway.

Then to Her Son, Who had seen and smiled, She said:
'On the night that I bore Thee,
What didst Thou care for a love beyond mine or a
heaven that was not my arm?
Didst Thou push from the nipple, O Child, to hear the
angels adore Thee?
When we two lay in the breath of the kine?' And He
said: 'Thou hast done no harm.'

So through the Void the Children ran homeward merrily
hand in hand,
Looking neither to left nor right where the breathless
Heavens stood still;
And the Guards of the Void re-sheathed their swords,
for they heard the Command:
'Shall I that have suffered the Children to come to me
hold them against their will?'

# 11

# *'They'*

One view called me to another; one hilltop to its fellow, half across the county, and since I could answer at no more trouble than the snapping forward of a lever, I let the county flow under my wheels. The orchid-studded flats of the East gave way to the thyme, ilex, and grey grass of the Downs; these again to the rich cornland and fig trees of the lower coast, where you carry the beat of the tide on your left hand for fifteen level miles; and when at last I turned inland through a huddle of rounded hills and woods I had run myself clean out of my known marks. Beyond that precise hamlet which stands godmother to the capital of the United States, I found hidden villages where bees, the only things awake, boomed in eighty-foot lindens that overhung grey Norman churches; miraculous brooks diving under stone bridges built for heavier traffic than would ever vex them again; tithe-barns larger than their churches, and an old smithy that cried out aloud how it had once been a hall of the Knights of the Temple. Gypsies I found on a common where the gorse, bracken, and heath fought it out together up a mile of Roman road; and a little farther on I disturbed a red fox rolling dog-fashion in the naked sunlight.

As the wooded hills closed about me I stood up in the car to take the bearings of that great Down whose ringed head is a landmark for fifty miles across the low countries.

I judged that the lie of the country would bring me across some westward-running road that went to his feet, but I did not allow for the confusing veils of the woods. A quick turn plunged me first into a green cutting brim-full of liquid sunshine, next into a gloomy tunnel where last year's dead leaves whispered and scuffled about my tyres. The strong hazel stuff meeting overhead had not been cut for a couple of generations at least, nor had any axe helped the moss-cankered oak and beech to spring above them. Here the road changed frankly into a carpeted ride on whose brown velvet spent primrose-clumps showed like jade, and a few sickly, white-stalked bluebells nodded together. As the slope favoured I shut off the power and slid over the whirled leaves, expecting every moment to meet a keeper; but I only heard a jay, far off, arguing against the silence under the twilight of the trees.

Still the track descended. I was on the point of reversing and working my way back on the second speed ere I ended in some swamp, when I saw sunshine through the tangle ahead and lifted the brake.

It was down again at once. As the light beat across my face my fore-wheels took the turf of a great still lawn from which sprang horsemen ten feet high with levelled lances, monstrous peacocks, and sleek round-headed maids of honour – blue, black, and glistening – all of clipped yew. Across the lawn – the marshalled woods besieged it on three sides – stood an ancient house of lichened and weather-worn stone, with mullioned windows and roofs of rose-red tile. It was flanked by semi-circular walls, also rose-red, that closed the lawn on the fourth side, and at their feet a box hedge grew man-high. There were doves on the roof about the slim brick chimneys, and I caught a glimpse of an octagonal dove-house behind the screening wall.

Here, then, I stayed; a horseman's green spear laid at my breast; held by the exceeding beauty of that jewel in that setting.

'If I am not packed off for a trespasser, or if this knight does not ride a wallop at me,' thought I, 'Shakespeare and Queen Elizabeth at least must come out of that half-open garden door and ask me to tea.'

A child appeared at an upper window, and I thought the little thing waved a friendly hand. But it was to call a companion, for presently another bright head showed. Then I heard a laugh among the yew-peacocks, and turning to make sure (till then I had been watching the house only) I saw the silver of a fountain behind a hedge thrown up against the sun. The doves on the roof cooed to the cooing water; but between the two notes I caught the utterly happy chuckle of a child absorbed in some light mischief.

The garden door – heavy oak sunk deep in the thickness of the wall – opened further: a woman in a big garden hat set her foot slowly on the time-hollowed stone step and as slowly walked across the turf. I was forming some apology when she lifted up her head and I saw that she was blind.

'I heard you,' she said. 'Isn't that a motor car?'

'I'm afraid I've made a mistake in my road. I should have turned off up above –I never dreamed . . .' I began.

'But I'm very glad. Fancy a motor car coming into the garden! It will be such a treat – '

She turned and made as though looking about her. 'You – you haven't seen anyone, have you – perhaps?'

'No one to speak to, but the children seemed interested at a distance.'

'Which?'

'I saw a couple up at the window just now, and I think I heard a little chap in the grounds.'

'Oh, lucky you!' she cried, and her face brightened. 'I hear them, of course, but that's all. You've seen them and heard them?'

'Yes,' I answered. 'And if I know anything of children, one of them's having a beautiful time by the fountain yonder. Escaped, I should imagine.'

'You're fond of children?'

I gave her one or two reasons why I did not altogether hate them.

'Of course, of course,' she said. 'Then you understand. Then you won't think it foolish if I ask you to take your car through the gardens, once or twice – quite slowly. I'm sure they'd like to see it. They see so little, poor things. One tries to make their life pleasant, but – ' she threw out her hands towards the woods. 'We're so out of the world here.'

'That will be splendid,' I said. 'But I can't cut up your grass.'

She faced to the right. 'Wait a minute,' she said. 'We're at the South gate, aren't we? Behind those peacocks there's a flagged path. We call it the Peacocks' Walk. You can't see it from here, they tell me, but if you squeeze along by the edge of the wood you can turn at the first peacock and get on to the flags.'

It was sacrilege to wake that dreaming house-front with the clatter of machinery, but I swung the car to clear the turf, brushed along the edge of the wood and turned in on the broad stone path where the fountain-basin lay like one star-sapphire.

'May I come too?' she cried. 'No, please don't help me. They'll like it better if they see me.'

She felt her way lightly to the front of the car, and with one foot on the step she called: 'Children, oh, children! Look and see what's going to happen!'

The voice would have drawn lost souls from the Pit, for the yearning that underlay its sweetness, and I was not surprised to hear an answering shout behind the yews. It must have been the child by the fountain, but he fled at our approach, leaving a little toy boat in the water. I saw the glint of his blue blouse among the still horsemen.

Very disposedly we paraded the length of the walk and at her request backed again. This time the child had got the better of his panic, but stood far off and doubting.

'The little fellow's watching us,' I said. 'I wonder if he'd like a ride.'

'They're very shy still. Very shy. But, oh, lucky you to be able to see them! Let's listen.'

I stopped the machine at once, and the humid stillness, heavy with the scent of box, cloaked us deep. Shears I could hear where some gardener was clipping; a mumble of bees and broken voices that might have been the doves.

'Oh, unkind!' she said weariedly.

'Perhaps they're only shy of the motor. The little maid at the window looks tremendously interested.'

'Yes?' She raised her head. 'It was wrong of me to say that. They are really fond of me. It's the only thing that makes life worth living – when they're fond of you, isn't it? I daren't think what the place would be without them. By the way, is it beautiful?'

'I think it is the most beautiful place I have ever seen.'

'So they all tell me. I can feel it, of course, but that isn't quite the same thing.'

'Then have you never – ?' I began, but stopped abashed.

'Not since I can remember. It happened when I was only a few months old, they tell me. And yet I must remember something, else how could I dream about colours. I see light in my dreams, and colours, but I never see *them.* I only hear them just as I do when I'm awake.'

'It's difficult to see faces in dreams. Some people can, but most of us haven't the gift,' I went on, looking up at the window where the child stood all but hidden.

'I've heard that too,' she said. 'And they tell me that one never sees a dead person's face in a dream. Is that true?'

'I believe it is – now I come to think of it.'

'But how is it with yourself – yourself?' The blind eyes turned towards me.

'I have never seen the faces of my dead in any dream,' I answered.

'Then it must be as bad as being blind.'

The sun had dipped behind the woods and the long shades were possessing the insolent horsemen one by one. I saw the light the from off the top of a glossy-leaved lance and all the brave hard green turn to soft black. The house, accepting another day at end, as it had accepted an hundred thousand gone, seemed to settle deeper into its rest among the shadows.

'Have you ever wanted to?' she said after the silence

'Very much sometimes,' I replied. The child had left the window as the shadows closed upon it.

'Ah! So've I, but I don't suppose it's allowed . . . Where d'you live?'

'Quite the other side of the county – sixty miles and more, and I must be going back. I've come without my big lamp.'

'But it's not dark yet I can feel it.'

'I'm afraid it will be by the time I get home. Could you lend me someone to set me on my road at first? I've utterly lost myself.'

'I'll send Madden with you to the crossroads. We are so out of the world, I don't wonder you were lost! I'll guide you round to the front of the house; but you will go slowly, won't you, till you're out of the grounds? It isn't foolish, do you think?'

'I promise you I'll go like this,' I said, and let the car start herself down the flagged path.

We skirted the left wing of the house, whose elaborately cast lead guttering alone was worth a day's journey; passed under a great rose-grown gate in the red wall, and so round to the high front of the house which in beauty and stateliness as much excelled the back as that all others I had seen.

'Is it so very beautiful?' she said wistfully when she heard my raptures. 'And you like the lead-figures too?

There's the old azalea garden behind. They say that this place must have been made for children. Will you help me out, please? I should like to come with you as far as the crossroads, but I mustn't leave them. Is that you, Madden? I want you to show this gentleman the way to the crossroads. He has lost his way but – he has seen them.'

A butler appeared noiselessly at the miracle of old oak that must be called the front door, and slipped aside to put on his hat. She stood looking at me with open blue eyes in which no sight lay, and I saw for the first time that she was beautiful.

'Remember,' she said quietly, 'if you are fond of them you will come again,' and disappeared within the house.

The butler in the car said nothing till we were nearly at the lodge gates, where catching a glimpse of a blue blouse in a shrubbery I swerved amply lest the devil that leads little boys to play should drag me into child-murder.

'Excuse me,' he asked of a sudden, 'but why did you do that, sir?'

'The child yonder.'

'Our young gentleman in blue?'

'Of course.'

'He runs about a good deal. Did you see him by the fountain, sir?'

'Oh, yes, several times. Do we turn here?'

'Yes, sir. And did you 'appen to see them upstairs too?'

'At the upper window? Yes.'

'Was that before the mistress come out to speak to you, sir?'

'A little before that. Why d'you want to know?'

He paused a little. 'Only to make sure that – that they had seen the car, sir, because with children running about, though I'm sure you're driving particularly careful, there might be an accident. That was all, sir. Here are the crossroads. You can't miss your way from now on. Thank you, sir, but that isn't *our* custom, not with – '

'I beg your pardon,' I said, and thrust away the British silver.

'Oh, it's quite right with the rest of 'em as a rule. Goodbye, sir.'

He retired into the armour-plated conning tower of his caste and walked away. Evidently a butler solicitous for the honour of his house, and interested, probably through a maid, in the nursery.

Once beyond the signposts at the crossroads I looked back, but the crumpled hills interlaced so jealously that I could not see where the house had lain. When I asked its name at a cottage along the road, the fat woman who sold sweetmeats there gave me to understand that people with motor cars had small right to live – much less to 'go about talking like carriage folk'. They were not a pleasant-mannered community.

When I retraced my route on the map that evening I was little wiser. Hawkin's Old Farm appeared to be the Survey title of the place, and the old County Gazetteer, generally so ample, did not allude to it. The big house of those parts was Hodnington Hall, Georgian with early Victorian embellishments, as an atrocious steel engraving attested. I carried my difficulty to a neighbour – a deep-rooted tree of that soil – and he gave me a name of a family which conveyed no meaning.

A month or so later – I went again, or it may have been that my car took the road of her own volition. She over-ran the fruitless Downs, threaded every turn of the maze of lanes below the hills, drew through the high-walled woods, impenetrable in their full leaf, came out at the crossroads where the butler had left me, and a little farther on developed an internal trouble which forced me to turn her in on a grass way-waste that cut into a summer-silent hazel wood. So far as I could make sure by the sun and a six-inch Ordnance map, this should be the road flank of that wood which I had first explored from the heights above. I made a mighty serious business of my repairs and a glittering shop of my repair kit, spanners, pump, and the like, which I spread out orderly upon a rug. It was a trap to catch all childhood, for on such a day, I argued, the children would not be far off. When I paused in my work I listened, but the wood was so full of the noises of summer (though the birds had mated) that I could not at first distinguish these from the tread of small cautious feet stealing across the dead leaves. I rang my bell in an alluring manner, but the feet fled, and I repented, for to a child a sudden noise is very real terror. I must have been at work half an hour when I heard in the wood the voice of the blind woman crying: 'Children, oh, children! Where are you?' and the stillness made slow to close on the perfection of that cry. She came towards me, half feeling her way between the tree boles, and though a child it seemed clung to her skirt, it swerved into the leafage like a rabbit as she drew nearer.

'Is that you?' she said, 'from the other side of the county?'

'Yes, it's me from the other side of the county.'

'Then why didn't you come through the upper woods? They were there just now.'

'They were here a few minutes ago. I expect they knew my car had broken down, and came to see the fun.'

'Nothing serious, I hope? How do cars break down?'

'In fifty different ways. Only mine has chosen the fifty-first.'

She laughed merrily at the tiny joke, cooed with delicious laughter, and pushed her hat back.

'Let me hear,' she said.

'Wait a moment,' I cried, 'and I'll get you a cushion.'

She set her foot on the rug all covered with spare parts, and stooped above it eagerly. 'What delightful things!' The hands through which she saw glanced in the chequered sunlight. 'A box here – another box! Why, you've arranged them like playing shop!'

'I confess now that I put it out to attract them. I don't need half those things really.'

'How nice of you! I heard your bell in the upper wood. You say they were here before that?'

'I'm sure of it. Why are they so shy? That little fellow in blue who was with you just now ought to have got over his fright. He's been watching me like a Red Indian.'

'It must have been your bell,' she said. 'I heard one of them go past me in trouble when I was coming down. They're shy – so shy even with me.' She turned her face over her shoulder and cried again: 'Children, oh, children! Look and see!'

'They must have gone off together on their own affairs,' I suggested, for there was a murmur behind us of lowered voices broken by the sudden squeaking giggles of childhood. I returned to my tinkerings and she leaned forward, her chin on her hand, listening interestedly.

'How many are they?' I said at last. The work was finished, but I saw no reason to go.

Her forehead puckered a little in thought. 'I don't quite know,' she said simply. 'Sometimes more – sometimes less. They come and stay with me because I love them, you see.'

'That must be very jolly,' I said, replacing a drawer, and as I spoke I heard the inanity of my answer.

'You – you aren't laughing at me,' she cried. 'I – I haven't any of my own. I never married. People laugh at me sometimes about them because – because – '

'Because they're savages,' I returned. 'It's nothing to fret for. That sort laugh at everything that isn't in their own fat lives.'

'I don't know. How should I? I only don't like being laughed at about *them.* It hurts; and when one can't see . . . I don't want to seem silly,' her chin quivered like a child's as she spoke, 'but we blindies have only one skin, I think. Everything outside hits straight at our souls. It's different with you. You've such good defences in your eyes – looking out – before anyone can really pain you in your soul. People forget that with us.'

I was silent reviewing that inexhaustible matter – the more than inherited (since it is also carefully taught) brutality of the Christian peoples, beside which the mere heathendom of the West Coast nigger is clean and restrained. It led me a long distance into myself.

'Don't do that!' she said of a sudden, putting her hands before her eyes.

'What?'

She made a gesture with her hand.

'That! It's – it's all purple and black. Don't! That colour hurts.'

'But, how in the world do you know about colours?' I exclaimed, for here was a revelation indeed.

'Colours as colours?' she asked.

'No. *Those* Colours which you saw just now.'

'You know as well as I do,' she laughed, 'else you wouldn't have asked that question. They aren't in the world at all. They're in *you* – when you went so angry.'

'D'you mean a dull purplish patch, like port wine mixed with ink?' I said.

'I've never seen ink or port wine, but the colours aren't mixed. They are separate – all separate.'

'Do you mean black streaks and jags across the purple?'

She nodded. 'Yes – if they are like this,' and zigzagged her finger again, 'but it's more red than purple – that bad colour.'

'And what are the colours at the top of the – whatever you see?'

Slowly she leaned forward and traced on the rug the figure of the Egg itself.

'I see them so,' she said, pointing with a grass stem, 'white, green, yellow, red, purple, and when people are angry or bad, black across the red – as you were just now.'

'Who told you anything about it – in the beginning?' I demanded.

'About the Colours? No one. I used to ask what colours were when I was little – in table-covers and curtains and carpets, you see – because some colours hurt me and some made me happy. People told me; and when I got older that was how I saw people.' Again she traced the outline of the Egg which it is given to very few of us to see.

'All by yourself?' I repeated.

'All by myself. There wasn't anyone else. I only found out afterwards that other people did not see the Colours.'

She leaned against the tree-bole plaiting and unplaiting chance-plucked grass stems. The children in the wood had drawn nearer. I could see them with the tail of my eye frolicking like squirrels.

'Now I am sure you will never laugh at me,' she went on after a long silence. 'Nor at *them.*'

'Goodness! No!' I cried, jolted out of my train of thought. 'A man who laughs at a child – unless the child is laughing too – is a heathen!'

'I didn't mean that, of course. You'd never laugh *at* children, but I thought – I used to think – that perhaps you might laugh about *them.* So now I beg your pardon . . . What are you going to laugh at?'

I had made no sound, but she knew.

'At the notion of your begging my pardon. If you had done your duty as a pillar of the State and a landed proprietress you ought to have summoned me for trespass when I barged through your woods the other day. It was disgraceful of me – inexcusable.'

She looked at me, her head against the tree trunk – long and steadfastly – this woman who could see the naked soul.

'How curious,' she half whispered. 'How very curious.'

'Why, what have I done?'

'You don't understand . . . and yet you understood about the Colours. Don't you understand?'

She spoke with a passion that nothing had justified, and I faced her bewilderedly as she rose. The children had gathered themselves in a roundel behind a bramble bush. One sleek head bent over something smaller, and the set of the little shoulders told me that fingers were on lips. They, too, had some child's tremendous secret. I alone was hopelessly astray there in the broad sunlight.

'No,' I said, and shook my head as though the dead eyes could note. 'Whatever it is, I don't understand yet. Perhaps I shall later – if you'll let me come again.'

'You will come again,' she answered. 'You will surely come again and walk in the wood.'

'Perhaps the children will know me well enough by that time to let me play with them – as a favour. You know what children are like.'

'It isn't a matter of favour but of right,' she replied, and while I wondered what she meant, a dishevelled woman plunged round the bend of the road, loose-haired, purple, almost lowing with agony as she ran. It was my rude, fat friend of the sweetmeat shop. The blind woman heard and stepped forward. 'What is it, Mrs Madehurst?' she asked.

The woman flung her apron over her head and literally grovelled in the dust, crying that her grandchild was sick to death, that the local doctor was away fishing, that Jenny the mother was at her wits' end, and so forth, with repetitions and bellowings.

'Where's the next nearest doctor?' I asked between paroxysms.

'Madden will tell you. Go round to the house and take him with you. I'll attend to this. Be quick!' She half supported the fat woman into the shade. In two minutes I was blowing all the horns of Jericho under the front of the House Beautiful, and Madden, in the pantry, rose to the crisis like a butler and a man.

A quarter of an hour at illegal speeds caught us a doctor five miles away. Within the half-hour we had decanted him, much interested in motors, at the door of the sweetmeat shop, and drew up the road to await the verdict.

'Useful things cars,' said Madden, all man and no butler. 'If I'd had one when mine took sick she wouldn't have died.'

'How was it?' I asked.

'Croup. Mrs Madden was away. No one knew what to do. I drove eight miles in a tax cart for the doctor. She was choked when we came back. This car 'd ha' saved her. She'd have been close on ten now.'

'I'm sorry,' I said. 'I thought you were rather fond of children from what you told me going to the crossroads the other day.'

'Have you seen 'em again, sir – this mornin'?'

'Yes, but they're well broke to cars. I couldn't get any of them within twenty yards of it.'

He looked at me carefully as a scout considers a stranger – not as a menial should lift his eyes to his divinely appointed superior.

'I wonder why,' he said just above the breath that he drew.

We waited on. A light wind from the sea wandered up and down the long lines of the woods, and the wayside grasses, whitened already with summer dust, rose and bowed in sallow waves. A woman, wiping the suds off her arms, came out of the cottage next the sweetmeat shop.

'I've be'n listenin' in de backyard,' she said cheerily. 'He says Arthur's unaccountable bad. Did ye hear him shruck just now? Unaccountable bad. I reckon 'twill come Jenny's turn to walk in de wood nex' week along, Mr Madden.'

'Excuse me, sir, but your lap-robe is slipping,' said Madden deferentially. The woman started, dropped a curtsey, and hurried away.

'What does she mean by "walking in the wood"?' I asked.

'It must be some saying they use hereabouts. I'm from Norfolk myself,' said Madden. 'They're an independent lot in this county. She took you for a chauffeur, sir.'

I saw the doctor come out of the cottage followed by a draggle-tailed wench who clung to his arm as though he could make treaty for her with Death. 'Dat sort,' she wailed – 'dey're just as much to us dat has 'em as if dey was lawful born. Just as much – just as much! An' God he'd be just as pleased if you saved 'un, doctor. Don't take it from me. Miss Florence will tell ye de very same. Don't leave 'im, doctor!'

'I know, I know,' said the man; 'but he'll be quiet for a while now. We'll get the nurse and the medicine as fast as we can.' He signalled me to come forward with the car, and I strove not to be privy to what followed; but I saw the girl's face, blotched and frozen with grief, and I felt the hand without a ring clutching at my knees when we moved away.

The doctor was a man of some humour, for I remember he claimed my car under the Oath of Aesculapius, and used it and me without mercy. First we convoyed Mrs Madehurst and the blind woman to wait by the sick bed till the nurse should come. Next we invaded a neat county town for prescriptions (the doctor said the trouble was cerebro-spinal meningitis), and when the County Institute, banked and flanked with scared market cattle, reported itself out of nurses for the moment we literally flung ourselves loose upon the county. We conferred with the owners of great houses – magnates at the ends of overarching avenues whose big-boned womenfolk strode away from their tea-tables to listen to the imperious doctor. At last a white-haired lady sitting under a cedar of Lebanon and surrounded by a court of magnificent Borzois – all hostile to motors – gave the doctor, who received them as from a princess, written orders which we bore many miles at top speed, through a park, to a French nunnery, where we took over in exchange a pallid-faced and trembling Sister. She knelt at the bottom of the tonneau telling her beads without pause till, by short cuts of the doctor's invention, we had her to the sweetmeat shop once more. It was a long afternoon crowded with mad episodes that rose and dissolved like the dust of our wheels; cross-sections of remote and incomprehensible lives through which we raced at right angles; and I went home in the dusk, wearied out, to dream of the clashing horns of cattle; round-eyed nuns walking in a garden of graves; pleasant tea-parties beneath shaded trees; the carbolic-scented, grey-painted corridors of the County Institute; the steps of shy children in the wood, and the hands that clung to my knees as the motor began to move.

I had intended to return in a day or two, but it pleased Fate to hold me from that side of the county, on many pretexts, till the elder and the wild rose had fruited. There came at last a brilliant day, swept clear from the south-west, that brought the hills within hand's reach – a day of unstable airs and high filmy clouds. Through no merit of my own I was free, and set the car for the third time on that known road. As I reached the crest of the Downs I felt the soft air change, saw it glaze under the sun; and, looking down at the sea, in that instant beheld the blue of the Channel turn through polished silver and dulled steel to dingy pewter. A laden collier hugging the coast steered outward for deeper water, and, across copper-coloured haze, I saw sails rise one by one on the anchored fishing-fleet. In a deep dene behind me an eddy of sudden wind drummed through sheltered oaks, and spun aloft the first dry sample of autumn leaves. When I reached the beach road the sea-fog fumed over the brickfields, and the tide was telling all the groins of the gale beyond Ushant. In less than an hour summer England vanished in chill grey. We were again the shut island of the North, all the ships of the world bellowing at our perilous gates; and between their outcries ran the piping of bewildered gulls. My cap dripped moisture, the folds of the rug held it in pools or sluiced it away in runnels, and the salt-rime stuck to my lips.

Inland the smell of autumn loaded the thickened fog among the trees, and the drip became a continuous shower. Yet the late flowers – mallow of the wayside, scabious of the field, and dahlia of the garden – showed gay in the mist, and beyond the sea's breath there was little sign of decay in the leaf. Yet in the villages the house doors were all open, and bare-legged, bare-headed children sat at ease on the damp doorsteps to shout 'pip-pip' at the stranger.

I made bold to call at the sweetmeat shop, where Mrs Madehurst met me with a fat woman's hospitable tears. Jenny's child, she said, had died two days after the nun had come. It was, she felt, best out of the way, even though insurance offices, for reasons which she did not pretend to follow, would not willingly insure such stray lives. 'Not but what Jenny didn't tend to Arthur as though he'd come all proper at de end of de first year – like Jenny herself.' Thanks to Miss Florence, the child had been buried with a pomp which, in Mrs Madehurst's opinion, more than covered the small irregularity of its birth. She described the coffin, within and without, the glass hearse, and the evergreen lining of the grave.

'But how's the mother?' I asked.

'Jenny? Oh, she'll get over it. I've felt dat way with one or two o' my own. She'll get over. She's walkin' in de wood now.'

'In this weather?'

Mrs Madehurst looked at me with narrowed eyes across the counter.

'I dunno but it opens de 'eart like. Yes it opens de 'eart. Dat's where losin' and bearin' comes so alike in de long run, we do say.'

Now the wisdom of the old wives is greater than that of all the Fathers, and this last oracle sent me thinking so extendedly as I went up the road, that I nearly ran over a woman and a child at the wooded corner by the lodge gates of the House Beautiful.

'Awful weather!' I cried, as I slowed dead for the turn.

'Not so bad,' she answered placidly out of the fog. 'Mine's used to 'un. You'll find yours indoors, I reckon.'

Indoors, Madden received me with professional courtesy, and kind enquiries for the health of the motor, which he would put under cover.

I waited in a still, nut-brown hall, pleasant with late flowers and warmed with a delicious wood fire – a place of good influence and great peace. (Men and women may sometimes, after great effort, achieve a creditable lie; but the house, which is their temple, cannot say anything save the truth of those who have lived in it.) A child's cart and a doll lay on the black-and-white floor, where a rug had been kicked back. I felt that the children had only just hurried away – to hide themselves, most like – in the many turns of the great adzed staircase that climbed statelily out of the hall, or to crouch at gaze behind the lions and roses of the carven gallery above. Then I heard her voice above me, singing as the blind sing – from the soul:

'In the pleasant orchard-closes . . .'

And all my early summer came back at the call.

'In the pleasant orchard-closes,
God bless all our gains say we –
But may God bless all our losses,
Better suits with our degree.'

She dropped the marring fifth line, and repeated –

'Better suits with our degree!'

I saw her lean over the gallery, her linked hands white as pearl against the oak.

'Is that you – from the other side of the county?' she called.

'Yes, me – from the other side of the county,' I answered, laughing.

'What a long time before you had to come here again.' She ran down the stairs, one hand lightly touching the broad rail. 'It's two months and four days. Summer's gone!'

'I meant to come before, but Fate prevented.'

'I knew it. Please do something to that fire. They won't let me play with it, but I can feel it's behaving badly. Hit it!'

I looked on either side of the deep fireplace, and found but a half-charred hedge-stake with which I punched a black log into flame.

'It never goes out, day or night,' she said, as though explaining. 'In case anyone comes in with cold toes, you see.'

'It's even lovelier inside than it was out,' I murmured. The red light poured itself along the age-polished dusky panels till the Tudor roses and lions of the gallery took colour and motion. An old eagle-topped convex mirror gathered the picture into its mysterious heart, distorting afresh the distorted shadows, and curving the gallery lines into the curves of a ship. The day was shutting down in half a gale as the fog turned to stringy scud. Through the uncurtained mullions of the broad window I could see valiant horsemen of the lawn rear and recover against the wind that taunted them with legions of dead leaves.

'Yes, it must be beautiful,' she said. 'Would you like to go over it? There's still light enough upstairs.'

I followed her up the unflinching, wagon-wide staircase to the gallery whence opened the thin fluted Elizabethan doors.

'Feel how they put the latch low down for the sake of the children.' She swung a light door inward.

'By the way, where are they?' I asked. 'I haven't even heard them today.'

She did not answer at once. Then, 'I can only hear them,' she replied softly. 'This is one of their rooms – everything ready, you see.'

She pointed into a heavily-timbered room. There were little low gate tables and children's chairs. A doll's house, its hooked front half open, faced a great dappled rocking-horse, from whose padded saddle it was but a child's scramble to the broad window-seat overlooking the lawn. A toy gun lay in a corner beside a gilt wooden cannon.

'Surely they've only just gone,' I whispered. In the failing light a door creaked cautiously. I heard the rustle of a frock and the patter of feet – quick feet through a room beyond.

'I heard that,' she cried triumphantly. 'Did you? Children, oh, children! Where are you?'

The voice filled the walls that held it lovingly to the last perfect note, but there came no answering shout such as I had heard in the garden. We hurried on from room to oak-floored room; up a step here, down three steps there; among a maze of passages; always mocked by our quarry. One might as well have tried to work an unstopped warren with a single ferret. There were bolt-holes innumerable – recesses in walls, embrasures of deep-slit windows now darkened, whence they could start up behind us; and abandoned fireplaces, six feet deep in the masonry, as well as the tangle of communicating doors. Above all, they had the twilight for their helper in our game. I had caught one or two joyous chuckles of evasion, and once or twice had seen the silhouette of a child's frock against some darkening window at the end of a passage; but we returned empty-handed to the gallery, just as a middle-aged woman was setting a lamp in its niche.

'No, I haven't seen her either this evening, Miss Florence,' I heard her say, 'but that Turpin he says he wants to see you about his shed.'

'Oh, Mr Turpin must want to see me very badly. Tell him to come to the hall, Mrs Madden.'

I looked down into the hall whose only light was the dulled fire, and deep in the shadow I saw them at last. They must have slipped down while we were in the passages, and now thought themselves perfectly hidden behind an old gilt leather screen. By child's law, my fruitless chase was as good as an introduction, but since I had taken so much trouble I resolved to force them to come forward later by the simple trick, which children detest, of pretending not to notice them. They lay close, in a little huddle, no more than shadows except when a quick flame betrayed an outline.

'And now we'll have some tea,' she said. 'I believe I ought to have offered it you at first, but one doesn't arrive at manners somehow when one lives alone and is considered – h'm – peculiar.' Then with very pretty scorn, 'Would you like a lamp to see to eat by?'

'The firelight's much pleasanter, I think.' We descended into that delicious gloom and Madden brought tea.

I took my chair in the direction of the screen ready to surprise or be surprised as the game should go, and at her permission, since a hearth is always sacred, bent forward to play with the fire.

'Where do you get these beautiful short faggots from?' I asked idly. 'Why, they are tallies!'

'Of course,' she said. 'As I can't read or write I'm driven back on the early English tally for my accounts. Give me one and I'll tell you what it meant.'

I passed her an unburned hazel-tally, about a foot long, and she ran her thumb down the nicks.

'This is the milk record for the home farm for the month of April last year, in gallons,' said she. 'I don't know what I should have done without tallies. An old forester of mine taught me the system. It's out of date now for every one else; but my tenants respect it. One of them's coming now to see me. Oh, it doesn't matter. He has no business here out of office hours. He's a greedy, ignorant man – very greedy or – he wouldn't come here after dark.'

'Have you much land then?'

'Only a couple of hundred acres in hand, thank goodness. The other six hundred are nearly all let to folk who knew my folk before me, but this Turpin is quite a new man – and a highway robber.'

'But are you sure I shan't be – ?'

'Certainly not. You have the right. He hasn't any children.'

'Ah, the children!' I said, and slid my low chair back till it nearly touched the screen that hid them. 'I wonder whether they'll come out for me.'

There was a murmur of voices – Madden's and a deeper note – at the low, dark side door, and a ginger-headed, canvas-gaitered giant of the unmistakable tenant-farmer type stumbled or was pushed in.

'Come to the fire, Mr Turpin,' she said.

'If – if you please, miss, I'll – I'll be quite as well by the door.' He clung to the latch as he spoke like a frightened child. Of a sudden I realised that he was in the grip of some almost overpowering fear.

'Well?'

'About that new shed for the young stock – that was all. These first autumn storms settin' in. . . . but I'll come again, miss.' His teeth did not chatter much more than the door latch.

'I think not,' she answered levelly. 'The new shed – m'm. What did my agent write you on the 15th?'

'I – fancied p'raps that if I came to see you – ma – man-to-man like, miss. But – '

His eyes rolled into every corner of the room wide with horror. He half opened the door through which he had entered, but I noticed it shut again – from without and firmly.

'He wrote what I told him,' she went on. 'You are overstocked already. Dunnett's Farm never carried more than fifty bullocks – even in Mr Wright's time. And *he* used cake. You've sixty-seven and you don't cake. You've broken the lease in that respect. You're dragging the heart out of the farm.'

'I'm – I'm getting some minerals – superphosphates – next week. I've as good as ordered a truck-load already. I'll go down to the station tomorrow about 'em. Then I can come and see you man to man like, miss, in the daylight. . . That gentleman's not going away, is he?' He almost shrieked.

I had only slid the chair a little farther back, reaching behind me to tap on the leather of the screen, but he jumped like a rat.

'No. Please attend to me, Mr Turpin.' She turned in her chair and faced him with his back to the door. It was an old and sordid little piece of scheming that she forced from him – his plea for the new cowshed at his landlady's expense, that he might with the covered manure pay his next year's rent out of the valuation after, as she made clear, he had bled the enriched pastures to the bone. I could not but admire the intensity of his greed, when I saw him out-facing for its sake whatever terror it was that ran wet on his forehead.

I ceased to tap the leather – was, indeed, calculating the cost of the shed – when I felt my relaxed hand taken and turned softly between the soft hands of a child. So at last I had triumphed. In a moment I would turn and acquaint myself with those quick-footed wanderers . . .

The little brushing kiss fell in the centre of my palm – as a gift on which the fingers were, once, expected to close: as the all-faithful half-reproachful signal of a waiting child not used to neglect even when grown-ups were busiest – a fragment of the mute code devised very long ago.

Then I knew. And it was as though I had known from the first day when I looked across the lawn at the high window.

I heard the door shut. The woman turned to me in silence, and I felt that she knew.

What time passed after this I cannot say. I was roused by the fall of a log, and mechanically rose to put it back. Then I returned to my place in the chair very close to the screen.

'Now you understand,' she whispered, across the packed shadows.

'Yes, I understand – now. Thank you.'

'I – I only hear them.' She bowed her head in her hands. 'I have no right, you know – no other right. I have neither borne nor lost – neither borne nor lost!'

'Be very glad then,' said I, for my soul was torn open within me.

'Forgive me!'

She was still, and I went back to my sorrow and my joy.

'It was because I loved them so,' she said at last, brokenly. '*That* was why it was, even from the first – even before I knew that they – they were all I should ever have. And I loved them so!'

She stretched out her arms to the shadows and the shadows within the shadow.

'They came because I loved them – because I needed them. I – I must have made them come. Was that wrong, think you?'

'No-no.'

'I – I grant you that the toys and – and all that sort of thing were nonsense, but – but I used to so hate empty rooms myself when I was little.' She pointed to the gallery. 'And the passages all empty . . . And how could I ever bear the garden door shut? Suppose – '

'Don't! For pity's sake, don't!' I cried. The twilight had brought a cold rain with gusty squalls that plucked at the leaded windows.

'And the same thing with keeping the fire in all night. *I* don't think it so foolish – do you?'

I looked at the broad brick hearth, saw, through tears I believe, that there was no unpassable iron on or near it, and bowed my head.

'I did all that and lots of other things – just to make believe. Then they came. I heard them, but I didn't know that they were not mine by right till Mrs Madden told me – '

'The butler's wife? What?'

'One of them – I heard – she saw. And knew. Hers! *Not* for me. I didn't know at first. Perhaps I was jealous. Afterwards, I began to understand that it was only because I loved them not because . . . Oh, you *must* bear or lose,' she said piteously. 'There is no other way – and yet they love me. They must! Don't they?'

There was no sound in the room except the lapping voices of the fire, but we two listened intently, and she at least took comfort from what she heard. She recovered herself and half rose. I sat still in my chair by the screen.

'Don't think me a wretch to whine about myself like this, but – but I'm all in the dark, you know, and you can see.'

In truth I could see, and my vision confirmed me in my resolve, though that was like the very parting of spirit and flesh. Yet a little longer I would stay since it was the last time.

'You think it is wrong, then?' she cried sharply, though I had said nothing.

'Not for you. A thousand times no. For you it is right. . . I am grateful to you beyond words. For me it would be wrong. For me only. . .'

'Why?' she said, but passed her hand before her face as she had done at our second meeting in the wood. 'Oh, I see,' she went on simply as a child. 'For you it would be wrong.' Then with a little indrawn laugh, 'And, d'you remember, I called you lucky – once – at first. You who must never come here again!'

She left me to sit a little longer by the screen, and I heard the sound of her feet die out along the gallery above.

## FROM LYDEN'S *Irenius*

ACT III – SCENE II

GOW. – Had it been your Prince instead of a groom caught in this noose there's not an astrologer of the city –

PRINCE – Sacked! Sacked! We were a city yesterday.

GOW. – So be it, but I was not governor. Not an astrologer, but would ha' sworn he'd foreseen it at the last versary of Venus, when Vulcan caught her with Mars in the house of stinking Capricorn. But since 'tis Jack of the Straw that hangs, the forgetful stars had it not on their tablets.

PRINCE – Another life! Were there any left to die? How did the poor fool come by it?

GOW. – *Simpliciter* thus. She that damned him to death knew not that she did it, or would have died ere she had done it. For she loved him. He that hangs him does so in obedience to the Duke, and asks no more than 'Where is the rope?' The Duke, very exactly he hath told us, works God's will, in which holy employ he's not to be questioned. We have then left upon his finger, only Jack whose soul now plucks the left sleeve of Destiny in Hell to overtake why she clapped him up like a fly on a sunny wall. Whuff! Soh!

PRINCE –Your cloak, Ferdinand. I'll sleep now.

FERDINAND – Sleep, then . . . He too, loved his life?

GOW. – He was born of woman . . . but at the end threw life from him, like your Prince, for a little sleep . . . 'Have I any look of a King?' said he, clanking his chain – 'to be so baited on all sides by Fortune, that I must e'en die now to live with myself one day longer.' I left him railing at Fortune and woman's love.

FERDINAND – Ah, woman's love!

*(Aside)* Who knows not Fortune, glutted on easy thrones,
Stealing from feasts as rare to coneycatch,
Privily in the hedgerows for a clown
With that same cruel-lustful hand and eye,
Those nails and wedges, that one hammer and lead,
And the very gerb of long-stored lightnings loosed
Yesterday 'gainst some King.

# 12
# *Mrs Bathurst*

THE DAY that I chose to visit HMS *Peridot* in Simon's Bay was the day that the Admiral had chosen to send her up the coast. She was just steaming out to sea as my train came in, and since the rest of the Fleet were either coaling or busy at the rifle-ranges a thousand feet up the hill, I found myself stranded, lunchless, on the sea-front with no hope of return to Cape Town before 5 p.m. At this crisis I had the luck to come across my friend Inspector Hooper, Cape Government Railways, in command of an engine and a brake-van chalked for repair.

'If you get something to eat,' he said, 'I'll run you down to Glengariff siding till the goods comes along. It's cooler there than here, you see.'

I got food and drink from the Greeks who sell all things at a price, and the engine trotted us a couple of miles up the line to a bay of drifted sand and a plank-platform half buried in sand not a hundred yards from the edge of the surf. Moulded dunes, whiter than any snow, rolled far inland up a brown and purple valley of splintered rocks and dry scrub. A crowd of Malays hauled at a net beside two blue and green boats on the beach; a picnic party danced and shouted barefoot where a tiny river trickled across the flat, and a circle of dry hills, whose feet were set in sands of silver, locked us in against a seven-coloured sea. At either horn of the bay the railway line cut just above high-water mark, ran round a shoulder of piled rocks, and disappeared.

'You see there's always a breeze here,' said Hooper, opening the door as the engine left us in the siding on the sand, and the strong south-easter buffeting under Elsie's Peak dusted sand into our tickey* beer. Presently he sat down to a file full of spiked documents. He had returned from a long trip up-country, where he had been reporting on damaged rolling-stock, as far away as Rhodesia. The weight of the bland wind on my eyelids; the song of it under the car roof, and high up among the rocks; the drift of fine grains chasing each other musically ashore; the tramp of the surf; the voices of the picnickers; the rustle of Hooper's file, and the presence of the assured sun, joined with the beer to cast me into magical slumber. The hills of False Bay were just dissolving into those of fairyland when I heard footsteps on the sand outside, and the clink of our couplings.

'Stop that!' snapped Hooper, without raising his head from his work. 'It's those dirty little Malay boys, you see: they're always playing with the trucks . . .'

'Don't be hard on 'em. The railway's a general refuge in Africa,' I replied.

' 'Tis – up-country at any rate. That reminds me,' he felt in his waistcoat-pocket, 'I've got a curiosity for you from Wankies – beyond Buluwayo. It's more of a souvenir perhaps than – '

'The old hotel's inhabited,' cried a voice. 'White men, from the language. Marines to the front! Come on, Pritch. Here's your Belmont. Wha-i-i!'

The last word dragged like a rope as Mr Pyecroft ran round to the open door, and stood looking up into my face.

* Old South African threepenny bit.

Behind him an enormous Sergeant of Marines trailed a stalk of dried seaweed, and dusted the sand nervously from his fingers.

'What are you doing here?' I asked. 'I thought the *Hierophant* was down the coast?'

'We came in last Tuesday – from Tristan de Cunha – for overhaul, and we shall be in dockyard 'ands for two months, with boiler-seatings.'

'Come and sit down.' Hooper put away the file.

'This is Mr Hooper of the Railway,' I exclaimed, as Pyecroft turned to haul up the black-moustached sergeant.

'This is Sergeant Pritchard, of the *Agaric,* an old shipmate,' said he. 'We were strollin' on the beach.' The monster blushed and nodded. He filled up one side of the van when he sat down.

'And this is my friend, Mr Pyecroft,' I added to Hooper, already busy with the extra beer which my prophetic soul had bought from the Greeks.

'*Moi aussi'* quoth Pyecroft, and drew out beneath his coat a labelled quart bottle.

'Why, it's Bass!' cried Hooper.

'It was Pritchard,' said Pyecroft. 'They can't resist him.'

'That's not so,' said Pritchard mildly.

'Not *verbatim,* per'aps, but the look in the eye came to the same thing.'

'Where was it?' I demanded.

'Just on beyond here – at Kalk Bay. She was slappin' a rug in a back verandah. Pritch 'adn't more than brought his batteries to bear, before she stepped indoors an' sent it flyin' over the wall.'

Pyecroft patted the warm bottle.

'It was all a mistake,' said Pritchard. 'I shouldn't wonder if she mistook me for Maclean. We're about of a size.'

I had heard householders of Muizenburg, St James's, and Kalk Bay complain of the difficulty of keeping beer or good servants at the seaside, and I began to see the reason. None the less, it was excellent Bass, and I too drank to the health of that large-minded maid.

'It's the uniform that fetches 'em, an' they fetch it,' said Pyecroft. 'My simple navy blue is respectable, but not fascinatin'. Now Pritch in 'is Number One rig is always "purr Mary, on the terrace" – *ex officio* as you might say.'

'She took me for Maclean, I tell you,' Pritchard insisted. 'Why – why – to listen to him you wouldn't think that only yesterday – '

'Pritch,' said Pyecroft, 'be warned in time. If we begin tellin' what we know about each other we'll be turned out of the pub. Not to mention aggravated desertion on several occasions – '

'Never anything more than absence without leaf – I defy you to prove it,' said the Sergeant hotly. 'An' if it comes to that, how about Vancouver in '87?'

'How about it? Who pulled bow in the gig going ashore? Who told Boy Niven . . . ?'

'Surely you were court-martialled for that?' I said. The story of Boy Niven who lured seven or eight able-bodied seamen and marines into the woods of British Columbia used to be a legend of the Fleet.

'Yes, we were court-martialled to rights,' said Pritchard, 'but we should have been tried for murder if Boy Niven 'adn't been unusually tough. He told us he had an uncle 'oo'd give us land to farm. 'E said he was born at the back o' Vancouver Island, and *all* the time the beggar was a balmy Barnardo Orphan!'

'*But* we believed him,' said Pyecroft. 'I did – you did – Paterson did – an' 'oo was the Marine that married the cocoanut-woman afterwards – him with the mouth?'

'Oh, Jones, Spit-Kid Jones. I 'aven't thought of 'im in years,' said Pritchard. 'Yes, Spit-Kid believed it, an' George Anstey and Moon. We were very young an' very curious.'

'*But* lovin' an' trustful to a degree,' said Pyecroft.

'Remember when 'e told us to walk in single file for fear o' bears? Remember, Pye, when 'e 'opped about in that bog full o' ferns an' sniffed an' said 'e could smell the smoke of 'is uncle's farm? An' *all* the time it was a dirty little outlyin' uninhabited island. We walked round it in a day, an' come back to our boat lyin' on the beach. A whole day Boy Niven kept us walkin' in circles lookin' for 'is uncle's farm! He said his uncle was compelled by the law of the land to give us a farm!'

'Don't get hot, Pritch. We believed,' said Pyecroft.

'He'd been readin' books. He only did it to get a run ashore an' have himself talked of. A day an' a night – eight of us – followin' Boy Niven round an uninhabited island in the Vancouver archipelago! Then the picket came for us an' a nice pack o' idiots we looked!'

'What did you get for it?' Hooper asked.

'Heavy thunder with continuous lightning for two hours. Thereafter sleet-squalls, a confused sea, and cold, unfriendly weather till conclusion o' cruise,' said Pyecroft. 'It was only what we expected, but what we felt – an' I assure you, Mr Hooper, even a sailor-man has a heart to break – was bein' told that we able seamen an' promisin' marines 'ad misled Boy Niven. Yes, we poor back-to-the-landers was supposed to 'ave misled him! He rounded on us, o' course, an' got off easy.'

'Excep' for what we gave him in the steerin'-flat when we came out o' cells. 'Eard anything of 'im lately, Pye?'

'Signal Boatswain in the Channel Fleet, I believe – Mr L. L. Niven is.'

'An' Anstey died o' fever in Benin,' Pritchard mused. 'What come to Moon? Spit-Kid we know about'

'Moon – Moon! Now where did I last. . . ? Oh yes, when I was in the *Palladium.* I met Quigley at Buncrana Station. He told me Moon 'ad run when the *Astrild* sloop was cruising among the South Seas three years back. He always showed signs o' bein' a Mormonastic beggar. Yes, he slipped off quietly an' they 'adn't time to chase 'im round the islands even if the navigatin' officer 'ad been equal to the job.'

'Wasn't he?' said Hooper.

'Not so. Accordin' to Quigley the *Astrild* spent half her commission rompin' up the beach like a she-turtle, an' the other half hatching turtles' eggs on the top o' numerous reefs. When she was docked at Sydney her copper looked like Aunt Maria's washing on the line – an' her 'mid-ship frames was sprung. The commander swore the dockyard 'ad done it haulin' the pore thing on to the slips. They *do* do strange things at sea, Mr Hooper.'

'Ah! I'm not a taxpayer,' said Hooper, and opened a fresh bottle. The Sergeant seemed to be one who had a difficulty in dropping subjects.

'How it all comes back, don't it?' he said. 'Why, Moon must 'ave 'ad sixteen years' service before he ran.'

'It takes 'em at all ages. Look at – you know,' said Pyecroft.

'Who?' I asked.

'A service man within eighteen months of his pension is the party you're thinkin' of,' said Pritchard. 'A warrant 'oo's name begins with a V, isn't it?'

'But, in a way o' puttin' it, we can't say that he actually did desert,' Pyecroft suggested.

'Oh no,' said Pritchard. 'It was only permanent absence up-country without leaf. That was all.'

'Up-country?' said Hooper. 'Did they circulate his description?'

'What for?' said Pritchard, most impolitely.

'Because deserters are like columns in the war. They don't move away from the line, you see. I've known a chap caught at Salisbury that way tryin' to get to Nyassa. They tell me, but o' course I don't know, that they don't ask questions on the Nyassa Lake Flotilla up there. I've heard of a P. & O. quartermaster in full command of an armed launch there.'

'Do you think Click 'ud ha' gone up that way?' Pritchard asked.

'There's no saying. He was sent up to Bloemfontein to take over some Navy ammunition left in the fort. We know he took it over and saw it into the trucks. Then there was no more Click – then or thereafter. Four months ago it transpired, and thus the *casus belli* stands at present,' said Pyecroft.

'What were his marks?' said Hooper again.

'Does the Railway get a reward for returnin' 'em, then?' said Pritchard.

'If I did d'you suppose I'd talk about it?' Hooper retorted angrily.

'You seemed so very interested,' said Pritchard with equal crispness.

'Why was he called Click?' I asked, to tide over an uneasy little break in the conversation. The two men were staring at each other very fixedly.

'Because of an ammunition hoist carryin' away,' said Pyecroft. 'And it carried away four of 'is teeth – on the lower port side, wasn't it, Pritch? The substitutes which he bought weren't screwed home, in a manner o' sayin'. When he talked fast they used to lift a little on the bed-plate. 'Ence, "Click". They called 'im a superior man, which is what we'd call a long, black-'aired, genteelly speakin', 'alf-bred beggar on the lower deck.'

'Four false teeth in the lower left jaw,' said Hooper, his hand in his waistcoat-pocket. 'What tattoo marks?'

'Look here,' began Pritchard, half rising. 'I'm sure we're very grateful to you as a gentleman for your 'orspitality, but per'aps we may 'ave made an error in – '

I looked at Pyecroft for aid – Hooper was crimsoning rapidly.

'If the fat marine now occupying the fo'c's'le will kindly bring 'is *status quo* to an anchor yet once more, we may be able to talk like gentlemen – not to say friends,' said Pyecroft. 'He regards you, Mr Hooper, as a emissary of the Law.'

'I only wish to observe that when a gentleman exhibits such a peculiar, or I should rather say, such a *bloomin'* curiosity in identification marks as our friend here – '

'Mr Pritchard,' I interposed, 'I'll take all the responsibility for Mr Hooper.'

'An' *you'll* apologise all round,' said Pyecroft. 'You're a rude little man, Pritch.'

'But how was I – ' he began, wavering.

'I don't know an' I don't care. Apologise!'

The giant looked round bewildered and took our little hands into his vast grip, one by one.

'I was wrong,' he said meekly as a sheep. 'My suspicions was unfounded. Mr Hooper, I apologise.'

'You did quite right to look out for your own end o' the line,' said Hooper. 'I'd ha' done the same with a gentleman I didn't know, you see. If you don't mind I'd like to hear a little more o' your Mr Vickery. It's safe with me, you see.'

'Why did Vickery run?' I began, but Pyecroft's smile made me turn my question to 'Who was she?'

'She kep' a little hotel at Hauraki – near Auckland,' said Pyecroft.

'By Gawd!' roared Pritchard, slapping his hand on his leg. 'Not Mrs Bathurst!'

Pyecroft nodded slowly, and the Sergeant called all the powers of darkness to witness his bewilderment.

'So far as I could get at it, Mrs B. was the lady in question.'

'But Click was married,' cried Pritchard.

'An' 'ad a fifteen-year-old daughter. 'E's shown me her photograph. Settin' that aside, so to say, 'ave you ever found these little things make much difference? Because I haven't.'

'Good Lord Alive an' Watchin'! . . . Mrs Bathurst. . .' Then with another roar: 'You can say what you please, Pye, but you don't make me believe it was any of 'er fault. She wasn't *that!*'

'If I was going to say what I please, I'd begin by callin' you a silly ox an' work up to the higher pressures at leisure. I'm trying to say solely what transpired. M'rover, for once you're right. It wasn't her fault.'

'You couldn't 'aven't made me believe it if it 'ad been,' was the answer.

Such faith in a Sergeant of Marines interested me greatly. 'Never mind about that,' I cried. 'Tell me what she was like.'

'She was a widow,' said Pyecroft. 'Left so very young and never re-spliced. She kep' a little hotel for warrants and non-coms close to Auckland, an' she always wore black silk, and 'er neck – '

'You ask what she was like,' Pritchard broke in. 'Let me give you an instance. I was at Auckland first in '97, at the end o' the *Marroquin's* commission, an' as I'd been promoted I went up with the others. She used to look after us all, an' she never lost by it – not a penny! "Pay me now," she'd say, "or settle later. I know you won't let me suffer. Send the money from home if you like." Why, gentlemen all, I tell you I've seen that lady take her own gold watch an' chain off her neck in the bar an' pass it to a bosun 'oo'd come ashore without 'is ticker an' 'ad to catch the last boat.

"I don't know your name," she said, "but when you've done with it, you'll find plenty that know me on the front. Send it back by one o' them." And it was worth thirty pounds if it was worth 'arf a crown. The little gold watch, Pye, with the blue monogram at the back. But, as I was sayin', in those days she kep' a beer that agreed with me – Slits it was called. One way an' another I must 'ave punished a good few bottles of it while we was in the bay – comin' ashore every night or so. Chaffin' across the bar like, once when we were alone, "Mrs B.," I said, "when next I call I want you to remember that this is my particular – just as you're my particular." (She'd let you go *that* far!) "Just as you're my particular," I said. "Oh, thank you, Sergeant Pritchard," she says, an' put 'er hand up to the curl be'ind 'er ear. Remember that way she had, Pye?'

'I think so,' said the sailor.

'Yes, "Thank you, Sergeant Pritchard," she says. "The least I can do is to mark it for you in case you change your mind. There's no great demand for it in the Fleet," she says, "but to make sure I'll put it at the back o' the shelf," an' she snipped off a piece of her hair ribbon with that old dolphin cigar-cutter on the bar – remember it, Pye? – an' she tied a bow round what was left – just four bottles. That was '97 – no, '96. In '98 I was in the *Resiliant* – China station – full commission. In Nineteen One, mark you, I was in the *Carthusian,* back in Auckland Bay again. Of course I went up to Mrs B.'s with the rest of us to see how things were goin'. They were the same as ever. (Remember the big tree on the pavement by the side-bar, Pye?) I never said anythin' in special (there was too many of us talkin' to her), but she saw me at once.'

'That wasn't difficult?' I ventured.

'Ah, but wait. I was comin' up to the bar, when, "Ada," she says to her niece, "get me Sergeant Pritchard's particular," and, gentlemen all, I tell you before I could shake 'ands with the lady, there were those four bottles o' Slits, with 'er 'air ribbon in a bow round each o' their necks, set down in front o' me, an' as she drew the cork she looked at me under her eyebrows in that blindish way she had o' lookin', an', "Sergeant Pritchard," she says, "I do 'ope you 'aven't changed your mind about your particulars." That's the kind o' woman she was – after five years!'

'I don't *see* her yet somehow,' said Hooper, but with sympathy.

'She – she never scrupled to feed a lame duck or set 'er foot on a scorpion at any time of 'er life,' Pritchard added valiantly.

'That don't help me either. My mother's like that for one.'

The giant heaved inside his uniform and rolled his eyes at the car-roof. Said Pyecroft suddenly –

'How many women have you been intimate with all over the world, Pritch?'

Pritchard blushed plum colour to the short hairs of his seventeen-inch neck.

' 'Undreds,' said Pyecroft. 'So've I. How many of 'em can you remember in your own mind, settin' aside the first – an' per'aps the last – *and one more?'*

'Few, wonderful few, now I tax myself,' said Sergeant Pritchard relievedly.

'An' how many times might you 'ave been at Auckland?'

'One – two,' he began – 'why, I can't make it more than three times in ten years. But I can remember every time that I ever saw Mrs B.'

'So can I – an' I've only been to Auckland twice – how she stood an' what she was sayin' an' what she looked like. That's the secret. Tisn't beauty, so to speak, nor good talk necessarily. It's just It. Some women'll stay in a man's memory if they once walk down a street, but most of 'em you can live with a month on end, an' next commission you'd be put to it to certify whether they talked in their sleep or not, as one might say.'

'Ah!' said Hooper. 'That's more the idea. I've known just two women of that nature.'

'An' it was no fault o' theirs?' asked Pritchard.

'None whatever. I know *that.*'

'An' if a man gets struck with that kind o' woman, Mr Hooper?' Pritchard went on.

'He goes crazy – or just saves himself,' was the slow answer.

'You've hit it,' said the Sergeant. 'You've seen an' known somethin' in the course o' your life, Mr Hooper. I'm lookin' at you!' He set down his bottle.

'And how often had Vickery seen her?' I asked.

'That's the dark an' bloody mystery,' Pyecroft answered. 'I'd never come across him till I come out in the *Hierophant* just now, an' there wasn't anyone in the ship who knew much about him. You see, he was what you call a superior man. 'E spoke to me once or twice about Auckland and Mrs B. on the voyage out. I called that to mind subsequently. There must 'ave been a good deal between 'em, to my way o' thinkin'. Mind you, I'm only giving you my *résumé* of it all, because all I know is second-'and so to speak, or rather I should say more than second-'and.'

'How?' said Hooper peremptorily. 'You must have seen it or heard it.'

'Ye-es,' said Pyecroft. 'I used to think seein' and hearin' was the only regulation aids to ascertainin' facts, but as we get older we get more accommodatin'. The cylinders work easier, I suppose . . . Were you in Cape Town last December when Phyllis's Circus came?'

'No – up-country,' said Hooper, a little nettled at the change of venue.

'I ask because they had a new turn of a scientific nature called "Home and Friends for a Tickey".'

'Oh, you mean the cinematograph – the pictures of prize-fights and steamers. I've seen 'em up-country.'

'Biograph or cinematograph was what I was alludin' to. London Bridge with the omnibuses – a troopship goin' to the war – marines on parade at Portsmouth, an' the Plymouth Express arrivin' at Paddin'ton.'

'Seen 'em all. Seen 'em all,' said Hooper impatiently.

'We *Hierophants* came in just before Christmas week an' leaf was easy.'

'I think a man gets fed up with Cape Town quicker than anywhere else on the station. Why, even Durban's more like Nature. We was there for Christmas,' Pritchard put in.

'Not bein' a devotee of Indian *peeris,* as our doctor said to the Pusser, I can't exactly say. Phyllis's was good enough after musketry practice at Mozambique. I couldn't get off the first two or three nights on account of what you might call an imbroglio with our Torpedo Lieutenant in the submerged flat, where some pride of the West country had sugared up a gyroscope; but I remember Vickery went ashore with our Carpenter Rigdon – old Crocus we called him. As a general rule Crocus never left 'is ship unless an' until he was 'oisted out with a winch, but *when 'e* went 'e would return noddin' like a lily gemmed with dew. We smothered him down below that night, but the things 'e said about Vickery as a fittin' playmate for a Warrant Officer of 'is cubic capacity, before we got him quiet, was what I should call pointed.'

'I've been with Crocus – in the *Redoubtable,'* said the Sergeant. 'He's a character if there is one.'

'Next night I went into Cape Town with Dawson and Pratt; but just at the door of the Circus I came across Vickery. "Oh!" he says, "you're the man I'm looking for. Come and sit next me. This way to the shillin' places!" I went astern at once, protestin' because tickey seats better suited my so-called finances. "Come on," says Vickery, "I'm payin'." Naturally I abandoned Pratt and Dawson in anticipation o' drinks to match the seats. "No," he says, when this was 'inted – "not now. Not now. As many as you please afterwards, but I want you sober for the occasion." I caught 'is face under a lamp just then, an' the appearance of it quite cured me of my thirsts. Don't mistake. It didn't frighten me. It made me anxious. I can't tell you what it was like, but that was the effect which it 'ad on me. If you want to know, it reminded me of those things in bottles in those herbalistic shops at Plymouth – preserved in spirits of wine. White an' crumply things – previous to birth as you might say.'

'You 'ave a beastial mind, Pye,' said the Sergeant, relighting his pipe.

'Perhaps. We were in the front row, an' "Home an' Friends" came on early. Vickery touched me on the knee when the number went up. "If you see anything that strikes you," he says, "drop me a hint;" then he went on clicking. We saw London Bridge an' so forth an' so on, an' it was most interestin'. I'd never seen it before. You 'eard a little dynamo like buzzin', but the pictures were the real thing – alive an' movin'.'

'I've seen 'em,' said Hooper. 'Of course they are taken from the very thing itself- you see.'

'Then the Western Mail came in to Paddin'ton on the big magic lantern sheet. First we saw the platform empty an' the porters standin' by. Then the engine come in, head on, an' the women in the front row jumped: she headed so straight. Then the doors opened and the passengers came out and the porters got the luggage – just like life. Only – only when anyone came down too far towards us that was watchin', they walked right out o' the picture, so to speak. I was 'ighly interested, I can tell you. So were all of us. I watched an old man with a rug 'oo'd dropped a book an' was tryin' to pick it up, when quite slowly, from be'ind two porters – carryin' a little reticule an' lookin' from side to side – comes out Mrs Bathurst. There was no mistakin' the walk in a hundred thousand. She come forward – right forward – she looked out straight at us with that blindish look which Pritch alluded to. She walked on and on till she melted out of the picture – like – like a shadow jumpin' over a candle, an' as she went I 'eard Dawson in the tickey seats be'ind sing out: "Christ! there's Mrs B.!" '

Hooper swallowed, and leaned forward intently.

'Vickery touched me on the knee again. He was clickin' his four false teeth with his jaw down like an enteric at the last kick. "Are you sure?" says he. "Sure," I says, "didn't you 'ear Dawson give tongue? Why, it's the woman herself." "I was sure before," he says, "but I brought you to make sure. Will you come again with me tomorrow?"

' "Willingly," I says, "it's like meetin' old friends."

' "Yes," he says, openin' his watch, "very like. It will be four-and-twenty hours less four minutes before I see her again Come and have a drink," he says. "It may amuse you, but it's no sort of earthly use to me." He went out shaking his head an' stumblin' over people's feet as if he was drunk already. I anticipated a swift drink an' a speedy return, because I wanted to see the performin' elephants. Instead o' which Vickery began to navigate the town at the rate o' knots, lookin' in at a bar every three minutes approximate Greenwich time. I'm not a drinkin' man, though there are those present' – he cocked his unforgettable eye at me – 'who may have seen me more or less imbued with the fragrant spirit. None the less when I drink I like to do it at anchor an' not at an average speed of eighteen knots on the measured mile. There's a tank as you might say at the back o' that big hotel up the hill – what do they call it?'

'The Molteno Reservoir,' I said, and Hooper nodded.

'That was his limit o' drift. We walked there an' we come down through the Gardens – there was a South-Easter blowin' – an' we finished up by the Docks. Then we bore up the road to Salt River, and wherever there was a pub Vickery put in sweatin'. He didn't look at what he drunk – he didn't look at the change. He walked an' he drunk an' he perspired in rivers. I understood why old Crocus 'ad come back in the condition 'e did, because Vickery an' I 'ad two an' a half hours o' this gypsy manoeuvre, an' when we got back to the station there wasn't a dry atom on or in me.'

'Did he say anything?' Pritchard asked.

'The sum total of 'is conversation from 7.45 p.m. till 11.15 p.m. was "Let's have another." Thus the mornin' an' the evenin' were the first day, as Scripture says . . . To abbreviate a lengthy narrative, I went into Cape Town for five consecutive nights with Master Vickery, and in that time I must 'ave logged about fifty knots over the ground an' taken in two gallon o' all the worst spirits south the Equator. The evolution never varied. Two shilling seats for us two; five minutes o' the pictures, an' perhaps forty-five seconds o' Mrs B. walking down towards us with that blindish look in her eyes an' the reticule in her hand. Then out walk – and drink till train time.'

'What did you think?' said Hooper, his hand fingering his waistcoat-pocket.

'Several things,' said Pyecroft. 'To tell you the truth, I aren't quite done thinkin' about it yet. Mad? The man was a dumb lunatic – must 'ave been for months – years p'raps. I know somethin' o' maniacs, as every man in the Service must, I've been shipmates with a mad skipper – an' a lunatic Number One, but never both together I thank 'Eaven. I could give you the names o' three captains now 'oo ought to be in an asylum, but you don't find me interferin' with the mentally afflicted till they begin to lay about 'em with rammers an' winch-handles. Only once I crept up a little into the wind towards Master Vickery. "I wonder what she's doin' in England," I says. "Don't it seem to you she's lookin' for somebody?" That was in the Gardens again, with the South-Easter blowin' as we were makin' our desperate round. "She's lookin' for me," he says, stoppin' dead under a lamp an' clickin'. When he wasn't drinkin', in which case all 'is teeth clicked on the glass, 'e was clickin' 'is four false teeth like a Marconi ticker. "Yes! lookin' for me," he said, an' he went on very softly an' as you might say affectionately. "*But,*" he went on, "in future, Mr Pyecroft, I should take it kindly of you if you'd confine your remarks to the drinks set before you. Otherwise," he says, "with the best will in the world towards you, I may find myself guilty of murder! Do you understand?" he says. "Perfectly," I says, "but would it at all soothe you to know that in such a case the chances o' your being killed are precisely equivalent to the chances o' me being outed." "Why, no," he says, "I'm almost afraid that 'ud be a temptation." Then I said – we was right under the lamp by that arch at the end o' the Gardens where the trams come round – "Assumin' murder was done – or attempted murder – I put it to you that you would still be left so badly crippled, as one might say, that your subsequent capture by the police – to 'oom you would 'ave to explain – would be largely inevitable." "That's better," 'e says, passin' 'is hands over his forehead. "That's much better, because," he says, "do you know, as I am now, Pye, I'm not so sure if I could explain anything much." Those were the only particular words I had with 'im in our walks as I remember.'

'What walks!' said Hooper. 'Oh my soul, what walks!'

'They were chronic,' said Pyecroft gravely, 'but I didn't anticipate any danger till the Circus left. Then I anticipated that, bein' deprived of 'is stimulant, he might react on me, so to say, with a hatchet. Consequently, after the final performance an' the ensuin' wet walk, I kep' myself aloof from my superior officer on board in the execution of 'is duty, as you might put it. Consequently, I was interested when the sentry informs me while I was passin' on my lawful occasions that Click had asked to see the captain. As a general rule warrant officers don't dissipate much of the owner's time, but Click put in an hour and more be'ind that door. My duties kep' me within eyeshot of it. Vickery came out first, an' 'e actually nodded at me an' smiled. This knocked me out o' the boat, because, havin' seen 'is face for five consecutive nights, I didn't anticipate any change there more than a condenser in hell, so to speak. The owner emerged later. His face didn't read off at all, so I fell back on his cox, 'oo'd been eight years with him and knew him better than boat signals. Lamson – that was the cox's name – crossed 'is bows once or twice at low speeds an' dropped down to me visibly concerned. "He's shipped 'is court-martial face," says Lamson. "Someone's goin' to be 'ung. I've never seen that look but once before when they chucked the gun-sights overboard in the *Fantastic.*" Throwin' gun-sights overboard, Mr Hooper, is the equivalent for mutiny in these degenerate days. It's done to attract the notice of the authorities an' the *Western Mornin' News* – generally by a stoker. Naturally, word went round the lower deck an' we had a private over'aul of our little consciences. But, barrin' a shirt which a second-class stoker said 'ad walked into 'is bag from the marines' flat by itself, nothin' vital transpired. The owner went about flyin' the signal for "attend public execution," so to say, but there was no corpse at the yard-arm. 'E lunched on the beach an' 'e returned with 'is regulation harbour-routine face about 3 p.m. Thus Lamson lost prestige for raising false alarms. The only person 'oo might 'ave connected the epicycloidal gears correctly was one Pyecroft, when he was told that Mr Vickery would go up-country that same evening to take over certain naval ammunition left after the war in Bloemfontein Fort. No details was ordered to accompany Master Vickery. He was told off first person singular – as a unit – by himself.'

The marine whistled penetratingly.

'That's what I thought,' said Pyecroft. 'I went ashore with him in the cutter an' 'e asked me to walk through the station. He was clickin' audibly, but otherwise seemed happy-ish.

' "You might like to know," he says, stoppin' just opposite the Admiral's front gate, "that Phyllis's Circus will be performin' at Worcester tomorrow night. So I shall see 'er yet once again. You've been very patient with me," he says.

' "Look here, Vickery," I said, "this thing's come to be just as much as I can stand. Consume your own smoke. I don't want to know any more."

' "You!" he said. "What have you got to complain of? – you've only 'ad to watch. I'm *it,"* he says, "but that's neither here nor there," he says. "I've one thing to say before shakin' 'ands. Remember," 'e says – we were just by the Admiral's garden-gate then – "remember, that I am *not* a murderer, because my lawful wife died in childbed six weeks after I came out. That much at least I am clear of," 'e says.'

' "Then what have you done that signifies?" I said. "What's the rest of it?"

' "The rest," 'e says, "is silence," an' he shook 'ands and went clickin' into Simonstown station.'

'Did he stop to see Mrs Bathurst at Worcester?' I asked.

'It's not known. He reported at Bloemfontein, saw the ammunition into the trucks, and then 'e disappeared. Went out – deserted, if you care to put it so – within eighteen months of his pension, an' if what 'e said about 'is wife was true he was a free man as 'e then stood. How do you read it off?'

'Poor devil!' said Hooper. 'To see her that way every night! I wonder what it was.'

'I've made my 'ead ache in that direction many a long night.'

'But I'll swear Mrs B. 'ad no 'and in it,' said the Sergeant, unshaken.

'No. Whatever the wrong or deceit was, he did it, I'm sure o' that. I 'ad to look at 'is face for five consecutive nights. I'm not so fond o' navigatin' about Cape Town with a South-Easter blowin' these days. I can hear those teeth click, so to say.'

'Ah, those teeth,' said Hooper, and his hand went to his waistcoat-pocket once more. 'Permanent things false teeth are. You read about 'em in all the murder trials.'

'What d'you suppose the captain knew – or did?' I asked.

'I've never turned my searchlight that way,' Pyecroft answered unblushingly.

We all reflected together, and drummed on empty beer bottles as the picnic-party, sunburned, wet, and sandy, passed our door singing 'The Honeysuckle and the Bee'.

'Pretty girl under that kapje,' said Pyecroft.

'They never circulated his description?' said Pritchard.

'I was askin' you before these gentlemen came,' said Hooper to me, 'whether you knew Wankies – on the way to the Zambesi – beyond Buluwayo?'

'Would he pass there – tryin' to get to that Lake what's 'is name?' said Pritchard.

Hooper shook his head and went on: 'There's a curious bit o' line there, you see. It runs through solid teak forest – a sort o' mahogany really – seventy-two miles without a curve. I've had a train derailed there twenty-three times in forty miles. I was up there a month ago relievin' a sick inspector, you see. He told me to look out for a couple of tramps in the teak.'

'Two?' Pyecroft said. 'I don't envy that other man if-'

'We get heaps of tramps up there since the war. The inspector told me I'd find 'em at M'Bindwe siding waiting to go North. He'd given 'em some grub and quinine, you see. I went up on a construction train. I looked out for 'em. I saw them miles ahead along the straight, waiting in the teak. One of 'em was standin' up by the dead-end of the siding an' the other was squattin' down lookin' up at 'im, you see.'

'What did you do for 'em?' said Pritchard.

'There wasn't much I could do, except bury 'em. There'd been a bit of a thunderstorm in the teak, you see, and they were both stone dead and as black as charcoal. That's what they really were, you see – charcoal. They fell to bits when we tried to shift 'em. The man who was standin' up had the false teeth. I saw 'em shinin' against the black Fell to bits he did too, like his mate squatting down an' watchin' him, both of 'em all wet in the rain. Both burned to charcoal, you see. And – that's what made me ask about marks just now – the false-toother was tattooed on the arms and chest – a crown and foul anchor with M. V. above.'

'I've seen that,' said Pyecroft quickly. 'It was so.'

'But if he was all charcoal-like?' said Pritchard, shuddering.

'You know how writing shows up white on a burned letter? Well, it was like that, you see. We buried 'em in the teak and I kept. . . But he was a friend of you two gentlemen, you see.'

Mr Hooper brought his hand away from his waistcoat-pocket – empty.

Pritchard covered his face with his hands for a moment, like a child shutting out an ugliness.

'And to think of her at Hauraki!' he murmured – 'with 'er 'air-ribbon on my beer. "Ada," she said to her niece . . . Oh, my Gawd! . . .'

'On a summer afternoon, when the honeysuckle blooms,
    And all Nature seems at rest,
Underneath the bower, 'mid the perfume of the flower,
    Sat a maiden with the one she loves the best – '

sang the picnic-party waiting for their train at Glengariff.

'Well, I don't know how you feel about it,' said Pyecroft, 'but 'avin' seen 'is face for five consecutive nights on end, I'm inclined to finish what's left of the beer an' thank Gawd he's dead!'

By – they are by with mirth and tears,
Wit or the works of Desire –
Cushioned about on the kindly years
Between the wall and the fire.

The grapes are pressed, the corn is shocked –
Standeth no more to glean;
For the Gates of Love and Learning locked
When they went out between.

All lore our Lady Venus bares
Signalled it was or told
By the dear lips long given to theirs
And longer to the mould.

All Profit, all Device, all Truth
Written it was or said
By the mighty men of their mighty youth,
Which is mighty being dead.

The film that floats before their eyes
The Temple's Veil they call;
And the dust that on the Shewbread lies
Is holy over all.

Warn them of seas that slip our yoke
Of slow conspiring stars –
The ancient Front of Things unbroke
But heavy with new wars?

By – they are by with mirth and tears,
Wit or the waste of Desire –
Cushioned about on the kindly years
Between the wall and the fire.

# 13

# *Below the Mill Dam*

'Book – Book – Domesday Book!' They were letting in the water for the evening stint at Robert's Mill, and the wooden Wheel where lived the Spirit of the Mill settled to its nine-hundred-year-old song: 'Here Azor, a freeman, held one rod, but it never paid geld. *Nun-nun-nunquam geldavit.* Here Reinbert has one villein and four cottars with one plough – and wood for six hogs and two fisheries of sixpence and a mill of ten shillings – *unum molinum* – one mill. Reinbert's mill – Robert's Mill. Then and afterwards and now – *tunc et post et modo* – Robert's Mill. Book – Book – Domesday Book!'

'I confess,' said the Black Rat on the crossbeam, luxuriously trimming his whiskers – 'I confess I am not above appreciating my position and all it means.' He was a genuine old English black rat, a breed which, report says, is rapidly diminishing before the incursions of the brown variety.

'Appreciation is the surest sign of inadequacy,' said the Grey Cat, coiled up on a piece of sacking.

'But I know what you mean,' she added. 'To sit by right at the heart of things – eh?'

'Yes,' said the Black Rat, as the old mill shook and the heavy stones thuttered on the grist. 'To possess – er – all this environment as an integral part of one's daily life must insensibly of course . . . You see?'

'I feel,' said the Grey Cat. 'Indeed, if *we* are not saturated with the spirit of the Mill, who should be?'

'Book – Book – Domesday Book!' The Wheel, set to his work, was running off the tenure of the whole rape, for he knew Domesday Book backwards and forwards: '*In Ferle tenuit Abbatia de Wiltuna unam hidam et unam virgam et dimidiam. Nunquam geldavit.* And Agemond, a freeman, has half a hide and one rod. I remember Agemond well. Charmin' fellow – friend of mine. He married a Norman girl in the days when we rather looked down on the Normans as upstarts. An' Agemond's dead? So he is. Eh, dearie me! dearie me! I remember the wolves howling outside his door in the big frost of Ten Fifty-Nine . . . *Essewelde hundredum nunquam geldum reddidit.* Book! Book! Domesday Book!'

'After all,' the Grey Cat continued, 'atmosphere is life. It is the influences under which we live that count in the long run. Now, outside' – she cocked one ear towards the half-opened door – 'there is an absurd convention that rats and cats are, I won't go so far as to say natural enemies, but opposed forces. Some such ruling may be crudely effective – I don't for a minute presume to set up my standards as final – among the ditches; but from the larger point of view that one gains by living at the heart of things, it seems for a rule of life a little overstrained. Why, because some of your associates have, shall I say, liberal views on the ultimate destination of a sack of – er – middlings don't they call them – '

'Something of that sort,' said the Black Rat, a most sharp and sweet-toothed judge of everything ground in the mill for the last three years.

'Thanks – middlings be it. *Why,* as I was saying, must I disarrange my fur and my digestion to chase you round the dusty arena whenever we happen to meet?'

'As little reason,' said the Black Rat, 'as there is for me, who, I trust, am a person of ordinarily decent instincts, to wait till you have gone on a round of calls, and then to assassinate your very charming children.'

'Exactly! It has its humorous side though.' The Grey Cat yawned. 'The miller seems afflicted by it. He shouted large and vague threats to my address, last night at tea, that he wasn't going to keep cats who "caught no mice". Those were his words. I remember the grammar sticking in my throat like a herring-bone.'

'And what did you do?'

'What does one do when a barbarian utters? One ceases to utter and removes. I removed – towards his pantry. It was a *riposte* he might appreciate.'

'Really those people grow absolutely insufferable,' said the Black Rat. 'There is a local ruffian who answers to the name of Mangles – a builder – who has taken possession of the outhouses on the far side of the Wheel for the last fortnight. He has constructed cubical horrors in red brick where those deliriously picturesque pigsties used to stand. Have you noticed?'

'There has been much misdirected activity of late among the humans. They jabber inordinately. I haven't yet been able to arrive at their reason for existence.' The Cat yawned.

'A couple of them came in here last week with wires, and fixed them all about the walls. Wires protected by some abominable composition, ending in iron brackets with glass bulbs. Utterly useless for any purpose and artistically absolutely hideous. What do they mean?'

'Aaah! I have known *four*-and-twenty leaders of revolt in Faenza,' said the Cat, who kept good company with the boarders spending a summer at the Mill Farm. 'It means nothing except that humans occasionally bring their dogs with them. I object to dogs in all forms.'

'Shouldn't object to dogs,' said the Wheel sleepily . . . 'The Abbot of Wilton kept the best pack in the county. He enclosed all the Harryngton Woods to Sturt Common. Aluric, a freeman, was dispossessed of his holding. They tried the case at Lewes, but he got no change out of William de Warrenne on the bench. William de Warrenne fined Aluric eight and fourpence for treason, and the Abbot of Wilton excommunicated him for blasphemy. Aluric was no sportsman. Then the Abbot's brother married . . . I've forgotten her name, but she was a charmin' little woman. The Lady Philippa was her daughter. That was after the barony was conferred. She rode devilish straight to hounds. They were a bit throatier than we breed now, but a good pack: one of the best. The Abbot kept 'em in splendid shape. Now, who was the woman the Abbot kept? Book – Book! I shall have to go right back to Domesday and work up the centuries: *Modo per omnia reddit burgum tunc – tunc – tunc!* Was it *burgum* or *hundredum?* I shall remember in a minute. There's no hurry.' He paused as he turned over silvered with showering drops.

'This won't do,' said the Waters in the sluice. 'Keep moving.'

The Wheel swung forward; the Waters roared on the buckets and dropped down to the darkness below.

'Noisier than usual,' said the Black Rat. 'It must have been raining up the valley.'

'Floods maybe,' said the Wheel dreamily. 'It isn't the proper season, but they can come without warning. I shall never forget the big one – when the Miller went to sleep and forgot to open the hatches. More than two hundred years ago it was, but I recall it distinctly. Most unsettling.'

'We lifted that wheel off his bearings,' cried the Waters. 'We said, "Take away that bauble!" And in the morning he was five miles down the valley – hung up in a tree.'

'Vulgar!' said the Cat. 'But I am sure he never lost his dignity.'

'We don't know. He looked like the Ace of Diamonds when we had finished with him. . . Move on there! Keep on moving. Over! Get over!'

'And why on this day more than any other,' said the Wheel statelily. 'I am not aware that my department requires the stimulus of external pressure to keep it up to its duties. I trust I have the elementary instincts of a gentleman.'

'Maybe,' the Waters answered together, leaping down on the buckets. 'We only know that you are very stiff on your bearings. Over, get over!'

The Wheel creaked and groaned. There was certainly greater pressure upon him than he had ever felt, and his revolutions had increased from six and three-quarters to eight and a third per minute. But the uproar between the narrow, weed-hung walls annoyed the Grey Cat.

'Isn't it almost time,' she said plaintively, 'that the person who is paid to understand these things shuts off those vehement drippings with that screw-thing on the top of that box-thing.'

'They'll be shut off at eight o'clock as usual,' said the Rat; 'then we can go to dinner.'

'But we shan't be shut off till ever so late,' said the Waters gaily. 'We shall keep it up all night.'

'The ineradicable offensiveness of youth is partially compensated for by its eternal hopefulness,' said the Cat. 'Our dam is not, I am glad to say, designed to furnish water for more than four hours at a time. Reserve is Life.'

'Thank goodness!' said the Black Rat. 'Then they can return to their native ditches.'

'Ditches!' cried the Waters; 'Raven's Gill Brook is no ditch. It is almost navigable, and *we* come from there away.' They slid over solid and compact till the Wheel thudded under their weight.

'Raven's Gill Brook,' said the Rat. 'I never heard of Raven's Gill.'

'We are the waters of Harpenden Brook – down from under Callton Rise. Phew! how the race stinks compared with the heather country.' Another five foot of water flung itself against the Wheel, broke, roared, gurgled, and was gone.

'Indeed,' said the Grey Cat, 'I am sorry to tell you that Raven's Gill Brook is cut off from this valley by an absolutely impassable range of mountains, and Callton Rise is more than nine miles away. It belongs to another system entirely.'

'Ah yes,' said the Rat, grinning, 'but we forget that, for the young, water always runs uphill.'

'Oh, hopeless! hopeless! hopeless!' cried the Waters, descending open-palmed upon the Wheel. 'There is nothing between here and Raven's Gill Brook that a hundred yards of channelling and a few square feet of concrete could not remove; and hasn't removed!'

'And Harpenden Brook is north of Raven's Gill and runs into Raven's Gill at the foot of Callton Rise, where the big ilex trees are, and *we* come from there!' These were the glassy, clear waters of the high chalk.

'And Batten's Ponds, that are fed by springs, have been led through Trott's Wood, taking the spare water from the old Witches' Spring under Churt Haw, and we – we – we are their combined waters!' Those were the Waters from the upland bogs and moors – a porter-coloured, dusky, and foam-flecked flood.

'It's all very interesting,' purred the Cat to the sliding waters, 'and I have no doubt that Trott's Woods and Bott's Woods are tremendously important places; but if you could manage to do your work – whose value I don't in the least dispute – a little more soberly, I, for one, should be grateful.'

'Book – book – book – book – book – Domesday Book!' The urged Wheel was fairly clattering now: 'In Burgelstaltone a monk holds of Earl Godwin one hide and a half with eight villeins. There is a church – and a monk . . . I remember that monk. Blessed if he could rattle his rosary off any quicker than I am doing now . . . and wood for seven hogs. I must be running twelve to the minute . . . almost as fast as Steam. Damnable invention, Steam! . . . Surely it's time we went to dinner or prayers – or something. Can't keep up this pressure, day in and day out, and not feel it I don't mind for myself, of course. *Noblesse oblige,* you know. I'm only thinking of the Upper and the

Nether Millstones. They came out of the common rock. They can't be expected to – '

'Don't worry on our account, please,' said the Millstones huskily. 'So long as you supply the power we'll supply the weight and the bite.'

'Isn't it a trifle blasphemous, though, to work you in this way?' grunted the Wheel. 'I seem to remember something about the Mills of God grinding "slowly". *Slowly* was the word!'

'But we are not the Mills of God. We're only the Upper and the Nether Millstones. We have received no instructions to be anything else. We are actuated by power transmitted through you.'

'Ah, but let us be merciful as we are strong. Think of all the beautiful little plants that grow on my woodwork. There are five varieties of rare moss within less than one square yard – and all these delicate jewels of nature are being grievously knocked about by this excessive rush of the water.'

'Umph!' growled the Millstones. 'What with your religious scruples and your taste for botany we'd hardly know you for the Wheel that put the carter's son under last autumn. You never worried about *him*!

'He ought to have known better.'

'So ought your jewels of nature. Tell 'em to grow where it's safe.'

'How a purely mercantile life debases and brutalises!' said the Cat to the Rat.

'They were such beautiful little plants too,' said the Rat tenderly. 'Maiden's-tongue and hart's-hair fern trellising all over the wall just as they do on the sides of churches in the Downs. Think what a joy the sight of them must be to our sturdy peasants pulling hay!'

'Golly!' said the Millstones. 'There's nothing like coming to the heart of things for information,' and they returned to the song that all English water-mills have sung from time beyond telling:

'There was a jovial miller once
Lived on the River Dee,
And this the burden of his song
For ever used to be . . .'

Then, as fresh grist poured in and dulled the note:

'I care for nobody – no, not I,
And nobody cares for me.'

'Even these stones have absorbed something of our atmosphere,' said the Grey Cat. 'Nine-tenths of the trouble in this world comes from lack of detachment.'

'One of your people died from forgetting that, didn't she?' said the Rat.

'One only. The example has sufficed us for generations.'

'Ah! but what happened to Don't Care?' the Waters demanded.

'Brutal riding to death of the casual analogy is another mark of provincialism!' The Grey Cat raised her tufted chin. 'I am going to sleep. With my social obligations I must snatch rest when I can; but, as our old friend here says,

*Noblesse oblige* . . . Pity me! Three functions tonight in the village, and a barn-dance across the valley!'

'There's no chance, I suppose, of your looking in on the loft about two. Some of our young people are going to amuse themselves with a new sacque-dance – best white flour only,' said the Black Rat.

'I believe I am officially supposed not to countenance that sort of thing, but youth is youth . . . By the way, the humans set my milk-bowl in the loft these days; I hope your youngsters respect it.'

'My dear lady,' said the Black Rat, bowing, 'you grieve me. You hurt me inexpressibly. After all these years, too!'

'A general crush is so mixed – highways and hedges – all that sort of thing – and no one can answer for one's best friends. *I* never try. So long as mine are amusin' and in full voice, and can hold their own at a tile-party, I'm as catholic as these mixed waters in the dam here!'

'We aren't mixed. We *have* mixed. We are one now,' said the Waters sulkily.

'Still uttering?' said the Cat. 'Never mind, here's the Miller coming to shut you off. Ye-es, I have known – *four* – or five is it? – and twenty leaders of revolt in Faenza . . . A little more babble in the dam, a little more noise in the sluice, a little extra splashing on the wheel, and then – '

'They will find that nothing has occurred,' said the Black Rat. 'The old things persist and survive and are recognised – our old friend here first of all. By the way,' he turned toward the Wheel, 'I believe we have to congratulate you on your latest honour.'

'Profoundly well deserved – even if he had never – as he has – laboured strenuously through a long life for the amelioration of millkind,' said the Cat, who belonged to many tile and outhouse committees. 'Doubly deserved, I may say, for the silent and dignified rebuke his existence offers to the clattering, fidgety-footed demands of – er – some people. What form did the honour take?'

'It was,' said the Wheel bashfully, 'a machine-moulded pinion.'

'Pinions! Oh, how heavenly!' the Black Rat sighed. 'I never see a bat without wishing for wings.'

'Not exactly that sort of pinion,' said the Wheel, 'but a really ornate circle of toothed iron wheels. Absurd, of course, but gratifying. Mr Mangles and an associate herald invested me with it personally – on my left rim – the side that you can't see from the mill. I hadn't meant to say anything about it – or the new steel straps round my axles – bright red, you know – to be worn on all occasions – but, without false modesty, I assure you that the recognition cheered me not a little.'

'How intensely gratifying!' said the Black Rat. 'I must really steal an hour between lights someday and see what they are doing on your left side.'

'By the way, have you any light on this recent activity of Mr Mangles?' the Grey Cat asked. 'He seems to be building small houses on the far side of the tail-race. Believe me, I don't ask from any vulgar curiosity.'

'It affects our Order,' said the Black Rat simply but firmly.

'Thank you,' said the Wheel. 'Let me see if I can tabulate it properly. Nothing like system in accounts of all kinds. Book! Book! Book! On the side of the Wheel towards the hundred of Burgelstaltone, where till now was a stye of three hogs, Mangles, a freeman, with four villeins and two carts of two thousand bricks, has a new small house of five yards and a half, and one roof of iron and a floor of cement. Then, now, and afterwards beer in large tankards. And Felden, a stranger, with three villeins and one very great cart, deposits on it one engine of iron and brass and a small iron mill of four feet, and a broad strap of leather. And Mangles, the builder, with two villeins, constructs the floor for the same, and a floor of new brick with wires for the small mill. There are there also chalices filled with iron and water, in number fifty-seven. The whole is valued at one hundred and seventy-four pounds . . . I'm sorry I can't make myself clearer, but you can see for yourself.'

'Amazingly lucid,' said the Cat. She was the more to be admired because the language of Domesday Book is not, perhaps, the clearest medium wherein to describe a small but complete electric-light installation, deriving its power from a water-wheel by means of cogs and gearing.

'See for yourself – by all means, see for yourself,' said the Waters, spluttering and choking with mirth.

'Upon my word,' said the Black Rat furiously, 'I may be at fault, but I wholly fail to perceive where these offensive eavesdroppers – er – come in. We were discussing a matter that solely affected our Order.'

Suddenly they heard, as they had heard many times before, the Miller shutting off the water. To the rattle and rumble of the labouring stones succeeded thick silence, punctuated with little drops from the stayed wheel. Then some water-bird in the dam fluttered her wings as she slid to her nest, and the plop of a water-rat sounded like the fall of a log in the water.

'It is all over – it always is all over at just this time. Listen, the Miller is going to bed – as usual. Nothing has occurred,' said the Cat.

Something creaked in the house where the pigstyes had stood, as metal engaged on metal with a clink and a burr.

'Shall I turn her on?' cried the Miller.

'Ay,' said the voice from the dynamo-house.

'A human in Mangles' new house!' the Rat squeaked.

'What of it?' said the Grey Cat. 'Even supposing Mr Mangles' cat's-meat-coloured hovel ululated with humans, can't you see for yourself – that – ?'

There was a solid crash of released waters leaping upon the wheel more furiously than ever, a grinding of cogs, a hum like the hum of a hornet, and then the unvisited darkness of the old mill was scattered by intolerable white light. It threw up every cobweb, every burl and knot in the beams and the floor; till the shadows behind the flakes of rough plaster on the wall lay clear-cut as shadows of mountains on the photographed moon.

'See! See! See!' hissed the Waters in full flood. 'Yes, see for yourselves. Nothing has occurred. Can't you see?'

The Rat, amazed, had fallen from his foothold and lay half-stunned on the floor. The Cat, following her instinct, leaped nigh to the ceiling, and with flattened ears and bared teeth backed in a corner ready to fight whatever terror might be loosed on her. But nothing happened. Through the long aching minutes nothing whatever happened, and her wire-brush tail returned slowly to its proper shape.

'Whatever it is,' she said at last, 'it's overdone. They can never keep it up, you know.'

'Much you know,' said the Waters. 'Over you go, old man. You can take the full head of us now. Those new steel axle-straps of yours can stand anything. Come along, Raven's Gill, Harpenden, Callton Rise, Batten's Ponds, Witches' Spring, all together! Let's show these gentlemen how to work!'

'But – but – I thought it was a decoration. Why – why – why – it only means more work for *me!*

'Exactly. You're to supply about sixty eight-candle lights when required. But they won't be all in use at once – '

'Ah! I thought as much,' said the Cat. 'The reaction is bound to come.'

*'And,'* said the Waters, 'you will do the ordinary work of the mill as well.'

'Impossible!' the old Wheel quivered as it drove. 'Aluric never did it – nor Azor, nor Reinbert. Not even William de Warrenne or the Papal Legate. There's no precedent for it. I tell you there's no precedent for working a wheel like this.'

'Wait a while! We're making one as fast as we can. Aluric and Co. are dead. So's the Papal Legate. You've no notion how dead they are, but we're here – the Waters of Five Separate Systems. We're just as interesting as Domesday Book. Would you like to hear about the land-tenure in Trott's Wood? It's squat-right, chiefly.' The mocking Waters leaped one over the other, chuckling and chattering profanely.

'In that hundred Jenkins, a tinker, with one dog – *unus canis* – holds, by the Grace of God and a habit he has of working hard, *unam hidam* – a large potato patch. Charmin' fellow, Jenkins. Friend of ours. Now, who the dooce did Jenkins keep? . . . In the hundred of Callton is one charcoal-burner *irreligiosissimus homo* – a bit of a rip – but a thorough sportsman. *Ibi est ecclesia. Non multum.* Not much of a church, *quia* because, *episcopus* the Vicar irritated the Nonconformists *tunc et post et modo* – then and afterwards and now – until they built a cut-stone Congregational chapel with red brick facings that did not return itself – *defendebat se* – at four thousand pounds.'

'Charcoal-burners, vicars, schismatics, and red brick facings,' groaned the Wheel. 'But this is sheer blasphemy. What waters have they let in upon me?'

'Floods from the gutters. Faugh, this light is positively sickening!' said the Cat, rearranging her fur.

'We come down from the clouds or up from the springs, exactly like all other waters everywhere. Is that what's surprising you?' sang the Waters.

'Of course not. I know my work if you don't. What I complain of is your lack of reverence and repose. You've no instinct of deference towards your betters – your heartless parody of the Sacred volume (the Wheel meant Domesday Book) proves it.'

'Our betters?' said the Waters most solemnly. 'What is there in all this dammed race that hasn't come down from the clouds, or – '

'Spare me that talk please,' the Wheel persisted. 'You'd *never* understand. It's the tone – your tone that we object to.'

'Yes. It's your tone,' said the Black Rat, picking himself up limb by limb.

'If you thought a trifle more about the work you're supposed to do, and a trifle less about your precious feelings, you'd render a little more duty in return for the power vested in you – we mean wasted on you,' the Waters replied.

'I have been some hundreds of years laboriously acquiring the knowledge which you see fit to challenge so light-heartedly,' the Wheel jarred.

'Challenge him! Challenge him!' clamoured the little waves riddling down through the tail-race. 'As well now as later. Take him up!'

The main mass of the Waters plunging on the Wheel shocked that well-bolted structure almost into the box-lids by saying: 'Very good. Tell us what you suppose yourself to be doing at the present moment.'

'Waiving the offensive form of your question, I answer, purely as a matter of courtesy, that I am engaged in the trituration of farinaceous substances whose ultimate destination it would be a breach of the trust reposed in me to reveal.'

'Fiddle!' said the Waters. 'We knew it all along! The first direct question shows his ignorance of his own Job. Listen, old thing. Thanks to us, you are now actuating a machine of whose construction you know nothing, that that machine may, over wires of whose ramifications you are, by your very position, profoundly ignorant, deliver a power which you can never realise, to localities beyond the extreme limits of your mental horizon, with the object of producing phenomena which in your wildest dreams (if you ever dream) you could never çomprehend. Is that clear, or would you like it all in words of four syllables?'

'Your assumptions are deliciously sweeping, but may I point out that a decent and – the dear old Abbot of Wilton would have put it in his resonant monkish Latin much better than I can – a scholarly reserve does not necessarily connote blank vacuity of mind on all subjects.'

'Ah, the dear old Abbot of Wilton,' said the Rat sympathetically, as one nursed in that bosom. 'Charmin' fellow – thorough scholar and gentleman. Such a pity!'

'Oh, Sacred Fountains!' – the Waters were fairly boiling. 'He goes out of his way to expose his ignorance by triple bucketfuls. He creaks to high Heaven that he is hopelessly behind the common order of things! He invites the streams of Five Watersheds to witness his su-su-supernal incompetence, and then he talks as though there were untold reserves of knowledge behind him that he is too modest to bring forward. For a bland, circular, absolutely sincere impostor, you're a miracle, O Wheel!'

'I do not pretend to be anything more than an integral portion of an accepted and not altogether mushroom institution.'

'Quite so,' said the Waters. 'Then go round – hard – '

'To what end?' asked the Wheel.

'Till a big box of tanks in your house begins to fizz and fume – gassing is the proper word.'

'It would be,' said the Cat, sniffing.

'That will show that your accumulators are full. When the accumulators are exhausted, and the lights burn badly, you will find us whacking you round and round again.'

'The end of life as decreed by Mangles and his creatures is to go whacking round and round for ever,' said the Cat.

'In order,' the Rat said, 'that you may throw raw and unnecessary illumination upon all the unloveliness in the world. Unloveliness which we shall – er – have always with us. At the same time you will riotously neglect the so-called little but vital graces that make up Life.'

'Yes, Life,' said the Cat, 'with its dim delicious half-tones and veiled indeterminate distances. Its surprisals, escapes, encounters, and dizzying leaps – its full-throated choruses in honour of the morning star, and its melting reveries beneath the sun-warmed wall.'

'Oh, you can go on the tiles, Pussalina, just the same as usual,' said the laughing Waters. *We* shan't interfere with you.'

'On the tiles, forsooth!' hissed the Cat.

'Well, that's what it amounts to,' persisted the Waters. 'We see a good deal of the minor graces of life on our way down to our job.'

'And – but I fear I speak to deaf ears – do they never impress you?' said the Wheel.

'Enormously,' said the Waters. 'We have already learned six refined synonyms for loafing.'

'But (here again I feel as though preaching in the wilderness) it never occurs to you that there may exist some small difference between the wholly animal – ah – rumination of bovine minds and the discerning, well-apportioned leisure of the finer type of intellect?'

'Oh, yes. The bovine mind goes to sleep under a hedge and makes no bones about it when it's shouted at. We've seen *that* – in haying-time – all along the meadows. The finer type is wide awake enough to fudge up excuses for shirking, and mean enough to get stuffy when its excuses aren't accepted. Turn over!'

'But, my good people, no gentleman gets stuffy as you call it. A certain proper pride, to put it no higher, forbids – '

'Nothing that he wants to do if he really wants to do it. Get along! What are you giving us? D'you suppose we've scoured half heaven in the clouds, and half earth in the mists, to be taken in at this time of the day by a bone-idle, old hand-quern of your type?'

'It is not for me to bandy personalities with you. I can only say that I simply decline to accept the situation.'

'Decline away. It doesn't make any odds. They'll probably put in a turbine if you decline too much.'

'What's a turbine?' said the Wheel quickly.

'A little thing you don't see, that performs surprising revolutions. But you won't decline. You'll hang on to your two nice red-strapped axles and your new machine-moulded pinions like – a – like a leech on a lily stem! There's centuries of work in your old bones if you'd only apply yourself to it; and, mechanically, an overshot wheel with this head of water is about as efficient as a turbine.'

'So in future I am to be considered mechanically? I have been painted by at least five Royal Academicians.'

'Oh, you can be painted by five hundred when you aren't at work, of course. But while you are at work you'll work. You won't half-stop and think and talk about rare plants and dicky-birds and farinaceous fiduciary interests. You'll continue to revolve, and this new head of water will see that you do so continue.'

'It is a matter on which it would be exceedingly ill-advised to form a hasty or a premature conclusion. I will give it my most careful consideration,' said the Wheel.

'Please do,' said the Waters gravely. 'Hullo! Here's the Miller again.'

The Cat coiled herself in a picturesque attitude on the softest corner of a sack, and the Rat without haste, yet certainly without rest, slipped behind the sacking as though an appointment had just occurred to him.

In the doorway, with the young Engineer, stood the Miller grinning amazedly.

'Well – well – well! 'tis true-ly won'erful. An' what a power o' dirt! It come over me now looking at these lights, that I've never rightly seen my own mill before. She needs a lot bein' done to her.'

'Ah! I suppose one must make oneself moderately agreeable to the baser sort. They have their uses. This thing controls the dairy.' The Cat, pincing on her toes, came forward and rubbed her head against the Miller's knee.'

'Ay, you pretty puss,' he said,.stooping. 'You're as big a cheat as the rest of 'em that catch no mice about me. A won'erful smooth-skinned, rough-tongued cheat you be. I've more than half a mind – '

'She does her work well,' said the Engineer, pointing to where the Rat's beady eyes showed behind the sacking. 'Cats and Rats livin' together – see?'

'Too much they do – too long they've done. I'm sick and tired of it. Go and take a swim and larn to find your own vittles honest when you come out, Pussy.'

'My word!' said the Waters, as a sprawling Cat landed all unannounced in the centre of the tail-race. 'Is that you, Mewsalina? You seem to have been quarrelling with your best friend. Get over to the left. It's shallowest there. Up on that alder-root with all four paws. Good-night!'

'You'll never get any they rats,' said the Miller, as the young Engineer struck wrathfully with his stick at the sacking. 'They're not the common sort. They're the old black English sort.'

'Are they, by Jove? I must catch one to stuff, someday.'

* * * * *

Six months later, in the chill of a January afternoon, they were letting in the Waters as usual.

'Come along! It's both gears this evening,' said the Wheel, kicking joyously in the first rush of the icy stream. 'There's a heavy load of grist just in from Lamber's Wood. Eleven miles it came in an hour and a half in our new motor-lorry, and the Miller's rigged five new five-candle lights in his cow-stables. I'm feeding 'em tonight. There's a cow due to calve. Oh, while I think of it, what's the news from Callton Rise?'

'The waters are finding their level as usual – but why do you ask?' said the deep outpouring Waters.

'Because Mangles and Felden and the Miller are talking of increasing the plant here and running a sawmill by electricity. I was wondering whether we – '

'I beg your pardon,' said the Waters, chuckling. '*What* did you say?'

'Whether *we,* of course, had power enough for the job. It will be a biggish contract. There's all Harpenden Brook to be considered and Batten's Ponds as well, and Witches' Fountain, and the Churt's Hawd system.'

'We've power enough for anything in the world,' said the Waters. 'The only question is whether you could stand the strain if we came down on you full head.'

'Of course I can,' said the Wheel. 'Mangles is going to turn me into a set of turbines – beauties.'

'Oh – er – I suppose it's the frost that has made us a little thick-headed, but to whom are we talking?' asked the amazed Waters.

'To me – the Spirit of the Mill, of course.'

'Not to the old Wheel, then?'

'I happen to be living in the old Wheel just at present. When the turbines are installed I shall go and live in them. What earthly difference does it make?'

'Absolutely none,' said the Waters, 'in the earth or in the waters under the earth. But we thought turbines didn't appeal to you.'

'Not like turbines? Me? My dear fellows, turbines are good for fifteen hundred revolutions a minute – and with our power we can drive 'em at full speed. Why there's nothing we couldn't grind or saw or illuminate or heat with a set of turbines! That's to say if all the Five Watersheds are agreeable.'

'Oh, we've been agreeable for ever so long.'

'Then why didn't you tell me?'

'Don't know. Suppose it slipped our memory.' The Waters were holding themselves in for fear of bursting with mirth.

'How careless of you! You should keep abreast of the age, my dear fellows. We might have settled it long ago, if you'd only spoken. Yes, four good turbines and a neat brick penstock – eh? This old Wheel's absurdly out of date.'

'Well,' said the Cat, who after a little proud seclusion had returned to her place impenitent as ever. 'Praised be Pasht and the Old Gods, that whatever may have happened I, at least, have preserved the Spirit of the Mill!'

She looked round as if expecting her faithful ally, the Black Rat; but that very week the Engineer had caught and stuffed him, and had put him in a glass case; he being a genuine old English black rat. That breed, the report says, is rapidly diminishing before the incursions of the brown variety.

**THE END**